Th

Maurice Gee is the author of both adult ~~~~~~~~~~~~~~~~~~~~ e
lives in Wellington with his wife, and has a grown-up family of two
daughters and a son. He has won the James Tait Black Memorial
Prize in Britain and numerous awards and prizes in New Zealand. He
is the author of the award-winning trilogy *Plumb*.

The Burning Boy

MAURICE GEE

faber and faber
LONDON · BOSTON

First published in 1990
by Faber and Faber Limited
3 Queen Square London WC1N 3AU
This paperback edition first published in 1992

Photoset by Parker Typesetting Service Leicester
Printed in England by Clays Ltd, St Ives plc

© Maurice Gee, 1990

Maurice Gee is hereby identified
as author of this work in
accordance with Section 77 of
the Copyright, Designs and
Patents Act 1988.

A CIP record for this book
is available from the British Library

ISBN 0-571-16419-6

2 4 6 8 10 9 7 5 3 1

Acknowledgement

Thanks are due to the Pegasus Press and Mrs J. Baxter
for permission to quote from
'Prize-giving Speech' by James K. Baxter.

Author's note

Saxton, in my novel, is the misshapen twin of a real town, and Saxton College for Girls of a real school. The people, though, staff and pupils, parents, lovers, enemies, friends, all the citizens of the town, are imaginary and have no existence outside these pages. I would like to thank the New Zealand Literary Fund for its Scholarship and Letters, 1987, and the Victoria University of Wellington for its Writing Fellowship, 1989. Without these awards I would not have been able to complete this novel.

Contents

ONE

Spring Rain

1

The boy with the burn scars on his face waited for his sister at the gates. Rain beat on his parka and made a shallow puddle round his feet. He held his fingers stiff and seemed to count the drops of water leaking from the tips.

His name was Duncan Round. He was fifteen.

The woman watching from her office window was Norma Sangster, principal of Saxton College for Girls. She peered through the oak leaves at his face. 'Poor boy,' she thought, and 'lucky to be alive', but wanted responses more orderly than that. She could tolerate contradictions and enjoy paradox but did not like emotions pulling her in two directions at once. She did not like, especially, 'better if he had died'.

The town was Saxton and the season spring; the rain a sharp unseasonable storm. It came from the south-east, slanting down the hills and crossing the plain, one of a family of squalls falling from the same iron cloud.

When it stopped Duncan Round turned back his hood. He combed his fingers through his hair and looked at the girls in the windows of the typing room. He moved his eyes along as though trying to sort out which one he would have.

And why should scars disqualify? Norma thought. She supposed he must live more in his mind than other boys. Though he stood there unconcerned, there might be rich fulfilments taking place in his half-bald, puckered cranium. Or monstrous orgiastic goings-on; although a fearsome sadness was more likely, for was he not a prisoner locked away for the rest of his life?

She did not like that thought. Far too easy; too evasive. She tried to see Duncan Round with a measuring eye. The burning had created a landscape that someone with an interest in textures might admire. Like papier mâché tinted with lemon and rose-pink. The ridges looked sharp enough to cut your fingers on. Good boy, she thought, admiring his acceptance of all this. Better to think of strength and will than screams of pain inside that damaged skull –

3

too horrible – or shouts of rage; though rage she would have given her acceptance, qualified.

He was keeping the girls quiet at least. She could almost feel the *frisson* there. No doubt some would be disgusted too, that was understandable, they needed time to learn compassion. And a few would make disgusting jokes. Norma felt that Duncan would understand; then was annoyed at the way he worked on her. She left the window and wrote '*Stella Round*' on her desk pad. She would tell the girl her brother should wait somewhere else, it would be kinder – though kinder to whom was hard to say. The girls in the typing room might benefit from waking up. And she herself needed no protection, although it was the fourth or fifth time this thundery spring she had been disturbed by Duncan Round. Kinder to the boy then? She could not even be sure of that. He was, in a way, impossible to see, although he stood there so sharply defined.

He had turned his back on the school and was guiding raindrops on Stella's car windscreen into streams and making them run to the bottom. Methodical, with his childish finger at work. Perhaps his brain was damaged – she must ask Josie. Before the accident he had caught no one's attention, the ordinary one among the Rounds, the Round who was not brilliant, she had heard; oppressed, no doubt, and stunted in his growth, by those clever sisters and charismatic dad and arty mum, a weed in that garden of scented shrubs. Appalling people, in some ways, the Rounds, working so hard at their cleverness and straining at spontaneity. One saw the sinews stand in their throats as their talk and laughter rang out. Duncan had never made a place with them. She wondered that Tom Round had done so little to bring him forward. A prize-winning son would have set him off just as winning daughters set him off and made him shine. Perhaps though, being early on the scene, Tom had understood there wasn't any hope and had let the boy take his own way; which ended with that flash of fire in the double garage.

Ended? Had he ended? Duncan Round at the point where he could go no further? What evidence was there for that? He refused to go back to school but that marked only one sort of termination. There were teachers who had no sense of life after school, who seemed to feel that lives were three years long, or four, or five, and five years measured success; but for Norma world and future were

4

the prize. She would not think of end for that boy there – insufficient evidence – he was simply at a point on his way. It was, though, quite plainly an altered way, there was evidence for that.

She sat down and her chair squeaked, and her desk, as she pressed her hands on it, made the little sound, half groan, half purr, she had come to think of as conjunctive. Desks became extensions of oneself and took on functions. Hers connected her with staff and girls, with corporate being, separate cells. These she was empowered to order and control and invest with spirit if she could – a possessive act? Conjunctive act? Each had truth of a sort; and that would indicate a conflict in her. She was pleased by it for she often seemed ordinary to herself. In fact, at times her ordinariness appalled her and was a shameful secret she must keep. She became impostor, deceiver, always on the point of being found out, and quantities of work were the only cure. She must then, before being wholly restored, recognize its high quality. She was renowned for being a worker – and put down too as a frustrated widow using up her sexual energy there.

That judgement troubled her from time to time, although she could refute it with evidence – husband, lovers, troop of men friends wanting (some of them aiming) to be more. She put her uneasiness by as psycho-reductive, a female burden she would not take on. Men weren't asked to carry extra weight. Yet the pressures and frustrations of her role must affect her differently, she knew.

There was pressure on her now. She had the brief to finish for the new gymnasium and it was hard, in summing up, not to show her dissatisfaction that the school was getting a gym before a new library building. The library would be put off for years now – always a harder thing to show mental than physical needs. She did not deny it was one of her jobs to keep nine hundred girls bouncing fit, and the gym would be a good one, she'd see to that; but the pinched little double-room of books on the second floor was a deformity in her school. Talk of extending herself! It was a sore she could not help scratching. 'The ghetto', someone had called it, and indeed it was as much as one could do not to simply throw books in and lock the door.

Norma set her mind and pen to work. She wrote a paragraph and chopped out words. Compression was one of her skills, which she used in speech – when she remembered – as well as in writing.

Some people took it for severity, for a gauntness in her mind, but it was more a matter of aesthetics. And, in a curious way, it was a means of giving herself weight, of increasing her mass while reducing her size. She had come to think it healthy, callisthenics for the mind and for language both, with the rewards of better lifting, better moving and incidental to it, flashes of beauty. She did not expect those in her brief but one never knew. Neatness and sharpness had a way of flaring out.

Desirée Norma, born 1941. In the euphoria of her birth 'Desirée' seemed a good idea to her parents. Later it troubled them. A name like that might open ways a good girl should not follow. So they dropped it and Desirée was Norma, Norma Schwass. She grew up on a dairy farm in a valley south of Saxton. Every two or three years there was a flood and Norma remembers walking in her gumboots in mud inches thick on the sitting-room carpet and sweeping grey water out of the kitchen with a yard-broom. One year the family had to climb on to the roof. They were rescued by two soldiers in a dinghy. She never wanted to be a farmer after that, or marry one, and was glad to be away at boarding school from eleven to seventeen – at Saxton College for Girls, where she's principal now.

Her degree is in biology and maths. After university she went to teachers' training college and she has a secret about that (she'd tell it to her friends if they asked). When the office lady came round with the oath of allegiance for the students to sign Norma refused. She was not the only one, there were two Jews. Up in the principal's office they swore on the Old Testament; but Norma still said no. She could not, she said, allow the state *carte blanche*, but must retain her right to make her own mind up on certain things. She became more aggressive than she'd meant to because she was not being fully honest. Fifty-one per cent, she told herself in later life. Forty-nine was her desire to get out of teaching while she could. She needed the whole wide world, not just classrooms, but had no way of paying back the bursary that had kept her at university for three years. So she planned to be thrown out because of her beliefs.

Go away and think it over, the principal said. We can't have you without the oath. Look, it doesn't mean much, sign it, eh? I'll be in touch again in a day or two.

He never was in touch, not over that. Norma learned how some problems are solved simply by being put out of the way. She wonders if he forged her signature. But playing the incident back, as she does now and then, she's able to think of herself as a rebel – though she sniffs and says, Not much of one. It helps her when she's enforcing rules she doesn't believe in. There's a lot of that at Saxton College for Girls.

Sangster, the man she married, was a physical education teacher at a neighbouring school. Norma had decided to get her country service out of the way and had gone to a town south of Auckland. One day she took a busload of children fifteen miles through the gorge to the next town to play rugby and hockey against the school there. She disliked Sangster at first because of his good looks. She did not believe a man so handsome could have a full share of honesty, even though he muddied himself refereeing the rugby match and sweat dripped from the end of his nose. He had a pompous way of speaking and used bigger words than he needed. 'That's what I'd call an heroic encounter,' he said of the match. She never admired him much, she knew he had an ordinary mind and trivial interests, although he was good at pretending and easily picked up the right thing to say; but she was passionate about having him. When he died in a blizzard on the Copland Pass four years after they were married she thought she would die too, she felt weight robbed from her and saw her body float away lighter than air. It was not grief so much as loss of being; and was a condition she recovered from. She felt herself taking on weight almost as soon as the body was down from the mountain. She found she had little sense of Sangster's personality, and her sense of his person, depending on gratifications and excitements, quickly became a memory. How did one grieve for someone who had not been properly there? At times she accused herself of being deficient in feeling, but soon was able to put that aside. Her four-year infatuation with Donald Sangster – his perfection of torso, biceps, skull shape, tooth and tongue – devalued her and she wished for a dead husband with crooked teeth and a stringy neck and lop ears and a mind. Why had she not married for love? The things she might have done if she had loved. But she was not troubled frequently. She never felt freer in her life than in the year after Sangster's death, even though she cried a good deal of the time.

There are those who say Norma has come so far – principal of a big girls' school in her middle forties – because she's a widow. If it hadn't been for that blizzard she'd have had a family and that would have been the end of her. She owes it all to Sangster, they seem to say. Norma doesn't argue with nonsense of that sort. Why bother? After failing to escape from teaching she made up her mind to get to the top. Ambition made her lively, made her free. She worked hard and loved her distant goal. Sangster was an indulgence and in those times when she could not do without him she told herself he wouldn't keep her, no fear of that, she'd keep him. She saw no reason why two children – no more than two – could not be integrated into her career. Integrated was the term she used. Later on, when she found it evasive, she realized her marriage would have failed fairly soon, and if there'd been children they would have gone with her husband. She does not like that knowledge and is glad it never had to be put to the test. Stronger than her sense of her ordinariness is her sense of her worth. She knows that she can do most things she sets her mind to.

Her career goes well, but not simply because she is determined that it shall. She's intelligent, decisive, has a sense of when to move and when draw back, and gravity and lightness at proper times, and social ease, cultured interests, good voice and looks and taste. (Voice between the Oxford and the Auckland, words delivered not in the shape of an egg but a mussel-shell shape.) She moves her body slowly, she's big and buttery. It's an easy way of shifting, nothing languid. She's deceptive and makes you look again and see that she's not heavy but sure. Yet with this she gives the impression of being untried. She's on the point of finding something out. Norma is not finished, rounded off. She has warmth and diffidence and shyness in her nature and finds herself bewildered by contradictory feelings. She has a quick instinctive sense of good and evil (it fades away most often in happiness or uneasiness). She trembles before a nameless horror, but cannot tell whether it exists 'out there' or in her mind. People take intimations of her complexity from half-spoken words and silences, and from the way she laughs or does not laugh, but they can't hold on and come away believing she has abilities not shown them yet. This, perhaps, is why she was appointed to her job though several better-qualified women applied for it too.

She meets selfishness and generosity daily, sees violence more

8

frequently than tenderness, for the reason that it's easier to see, and does not take these things as evidence of battles in our nature of any deep spiritual import, or as defeats or victories, although she'll place them, often for illustration or argument, in a moral sphere. 'Spiritual' is a term she tries not to use and the concept one she cannot hold. It gets away from her and she has come to think 'spirit' is not a useful word and chooses 'mind', 'energy', 'life', 'courage', 'vital force' – but finds she has to bring them out in clusters. It makes her impatient. Language, which should be sharp, is too often blunt.

'Soul' she does not say, except when she comes on it in morning prayers, part of her job. She does not believe in God, or disbelieve, regards him as a case that can't be proven, but thinks it useful for young people to have him as a reference point. He's a metaphor for the thing – that word-cluster, spirit if you must – lying beyond the spatial-temporal world; an attempt at an explanation. It's good for young minds to go out there, whether by tracking down or leap of faith. Norma puts her uneasiness by. She offers a dry word or two about her role in guidance. Small evasions, small dishonesties, are part of the shifting ground on which we stand; but stand we do, Norma says, and we defy the larger harmful things.

She's sometimes able to say what those things are. But 'good' and 'evil' are not available. The parsons have pinched them, one of her men friends said; about the only useful thing he gave her. Excellent, she'll say, instead of good. Horrible, dreadful, she'll say, feeling ill. Once she had to run to the lavatory and be sick while reading a book about Gestapo atrocities. None of this seems extraordinary to her.

There's behaviour, she's inclined to believe, beyond conscience. There's a disposition in us towards love or wickedness. Norma sees Original Sin as a great explanation and wishes it would do for her, but of course it won't, because it leaves out too much she's convinced of, leaves out knowledge of all sorts. 'Ha!' she says to that, caught in a trap. She has given up thinking about it. Just now and then she's lifted up by an example of love, or wants, as she puts it, to resign from the human race. She does not understand how ready she is with these responses or how deeply they affect her behaviour.

Her friends describe her as mature and sensible. Some say wise and sensitive. They all agree that even when she's quiet you know she's there.

The brilliant interval came to an end, colour went out, and Norma reached the window in time to see hail strike. It rattled on the window panes and bounced like tiny balls in the street. School was due to finish in seven minutes and she considered having the bell delayed. Some of the pieces of ice looked big and sharp enough to cut the flesh. Then she thought of strawberries and apples and tried to see where the storm was coming from. There looked to be fine weather at the port, and the other way the sun was lighting the top of Stovepipe Hill. With any luck the hail was in a band and would miss her brother's berry farm and John Toft's apple orchard. A storm had wiped out Clive's crop three seasons ago and she pictured him standing in his vine rows, letting today's hail cut his face. Clive could not help making big gestures, usually of despair and rage. She had better telephone him as soon as the storm was over. And telephone John Toft. She saw him watching from his back porch, smiling enigmatically and stroking his chin.

Duncan Round had taken an unusual posture too. He had pulled up his hood and squatted so the skirt of his parka touched the pavement and was safe and dry inside a shell with hailstones shooting off in arcs as though a force in him repelled them. High over his back a green field on Stovepipe sank into a cloud-hole and was gone. Hail came in harder strokes, with a fierce downward thrust. Norma shivered – but smiled at the tame end of it all, the little coy curved domestic bounce on path and lawn. The storm drew itself in and moved away. Saxton increased in size; it came out, enamelled, in the sun. The bell for the end of school rang at that moment. Norma found it all appropriate. There was a balance in all this.

The girls walked out hesitating, giving little cries at a world so fresh. They scooped up hail and tried it on their tongues. They looked at the receding storm, pointing as though at an aeroplane, and turned to see the huge bright sky on the other side. Norma watched them possessively.

Duncan Round took a handful of hailstones from the angle of

the car windscreen and seemed to weigh them in his palm. He too tried their coldness on his tongue. Belinda, his young sister, crossed the road with her school pack low on her back in the style that was fashionable, and turned his hand over, spilling the hail. She took out her handkerchief and wiped his fingers dry. Norma found it touching, even though Duncan did not need this sort of care. Belinda was the nicest of the Rounds by a long way, and no less clever than her sisters. One somehow expected kindness to reduce cleverness but in this case it was not so. Mind you, the girl did not waste kindness on her friends but treated them in the Round way. They shouted to her across the street but she took no notice. She gave Duncan a piece of chewing-gum.

Now the ten-speed bikes came down, cutting neat parabolas among the turning cars. Norma put her window up and watched for near-misses. She admired the skill and energy of the girls and wished they showed it more in class. There was Hayley Birtles, with hissing tyres, making Stella Round step back – that took some doing – and throwing a word at her, ugly no doubt, as she went by. And there was the shoplifting gang, subdued now that they had been caught, riding in a bunch for solidarity. Would they break up and go straight home as they had been ordered or was it all a waste of time? Spray rose from their tyres and wet the legs of the footpath mums.

This spinning-off of bits, this disintegrating of school at the end of the day, was sometimes painful to Norma but filled her with relief at other times. Today she felt elated and regretful – that the world outside was beautiful and her girls should live in it, and that all this imperfection, all this unmade, unmakeable, stuff should be loosed on it.

Stella Round crossed the road and got into her car. She opened the rear door for Duncan, then said something sharp to him and handed him the key. He took his wet parka off and put it in the boot. He seemed too thinly clad standing there, in white T-shirt (with words on it?) and washed-out jeans and sneakers without socks. His face and arm and finger-backs were baby-naked. The burning had almost glazed him, Norma thought. She hoped it had been too shocking for pain. Pain must have come later, in hospital; and was there even now perhaps? She did not know much about the pathology of burns, but surely nerve endings were affected.

11

Stella, discomposed – one almost never saw that – leaned out her door and called him in. The words on his T-shirt made Norma laugh. How marvellously inappropriate: *Hump your ass off*. (Tom Round's little joke, no doubt. He had recently visited 'the US of A'.) Duncan had probably pulled it on without reading it; or perhaps – was he capable of malice? – had meant to embarrass his sister. He did not hurry into the car but gave girls walking by a chance to read.

Stella leaned back. She grabbed his ruined arm and hauled him in, and the Rounds drove away.

The road was warming up and starting to steam. Teachers hurried out along with the girls: Sandra Duff, in her Indian cottons and silver bells, looking too fierce and concentrated for such filmy wear (what indiscretion had she committed? There was a new one every day); Helen Streeter in leather suit and leather hair, untouched, or seeming untouched, by her day relating over crayons and clay to a hundred girls; David Dobson, like a bearded tramp, with whisky flask shaped to the curve of his buttock (no secret from the girls, though he hunched in dark places to drink from it); and Lex Clearwater, in his red utility with the rust-eaten panels, looking like Heathcliff escaping to the moors. He had started as a heart-throb but now he was a joke.

The teachers were no more finished than the girls. They were lumpy with their imperfections; a paradox Norma wrestled with. She did not leave her own imperfections out, and sometimes found herself wanting to teach only simple verifiable facts – that the two angles of the hypotenuse, so on, so on. There seemed to be not much else she could justify. Do this and this, not that, or else you'll hurt someone, and you'll be unhappy yourself. She looked at her half-happy and damaged staff, and was appalled by the certainties they uttered and felt she must not let them dump their rubbish on the girls; and yet she uttered certainties, dogma, herself. And was half-happy, damaged, too. Yet she must present a perfect shape.

Two equal sides of Norma broke apart. Hard work, not argument, would make her whole.

She telephoned Clive. Daphne, his wife, said he was out in the boysenberries. The storm had gone by on the other side of the inlet. Come and see us soon, Daphne said. Norma telephoned

John Toft and let the phone ring for a minute or two. John never ran to answer it but walked in from the yard at his normal pace and shrugged and turned away if it stopped. Today he did not come, was almost certainly too far down the orchard to hear.

She hung up and went back to her brief.

On Saturday morning Norma went to a softball match. She understood the rules of the game but found the rituals difficult to grasp. Some of the gestures were a form of praise – that slapping of palm on palm as the batter ran back after scoring, quite attractive. Much else about the game she could not like: the shouting and gum-chewing and the apishness in stance and the mock-American speech. These girls were broken from the mould that had fixed her and made it impossible that she should ever squat with thighs so wide and work her jaws and shrill those exhortations to hit, run, throw, slide, win – but were they as free as they liked to think? Were they not simply fixed in a new mould? She decided, though, that the new reality (like the old) shaped only externals. The things that had always mattered were the same. There was no change in the verities. So smile, applaud, she told herself, and look as though you're pleased, and keep your old-fashioned judgements out of the way.

The girl who had just scored was drinking greedily at the water fountain. Norma touched her shoulder. 'That was a whopping hit, Hayley.'

'Yeah, Mrs Sangster. I thought I bust the ball.'

'We're ahead now, aren't we?'

'Yeah. Three-one.' She wiped her mouth.

'Are we going to win?'

'Easy. We made a coupla' errors, that's how they got their run. They can't hit our pitching, that's for sure.'

'Who's our pitcher?'

'Me.'

'Oh well, congratulations.' She had to work for ease in these exchanges and felt the tiny failures in tone she was guilty of must be huge to the girls and a subject for contempt or mirth.

'Bit of gum, Mrs Sangster?' Hayley fished the packet from her sock and offered it with a stick poking out like a tongue. She watched Norma with an alertness that might be friendly or insolent. All that animal health in Hayley Birtles, that full sack of vigour, but was her measure of happiness large enough? And her measure of intelligence? Norma wanted *access* to her girls. She imagined a place like a subterranean lake, with a roof bending over in the dark and gleaming like bone. They had no proper access themselves, and her job . . .

'Want one, eh?'

'Not just now, thank you. It amazes me you girls don't choke on it.' She'd made that protest to the phys. ed. teacher when told players must chew because it was traditional in the game. Everywhere else in the school chewing was banned – along with half a hundred other things. Those thin strips of leather for example, tied around ankle or wrist. Hayley was wearing half a dozen of them. Were they gang badge or decoration? Whichever it was, the ban had turned them into cause.

'You're not supposed to wear those, Hayley. I think you know.'

'Trouble is you can't untie the knots, Mrs Sangster. You gotta wait till they wear out.'

The sincerity was bogus, insolent too, and Norma felt a tiredness in her mind, the sort of thing only a flash of anger would clear. It did not come. Synapses out of order, she supposed; though a simpler reason might be that she was uncertain. She did not want to lead Hayley Birtles here or there, but help her find a path for herself – and leave trivialities out of it.

The school team innings came to an end with an easy catch and Hayley said, 'Gotta go, eh, Mrs Sang,' and turned her back and loped away, ending discussion; and that, Norma thought, put things in a proper perspective, and put her back where she belonged, tiny figure on the horizon, with expression too minute to be seen. She climbed the zig-zag path above the playing area – diamond, was it called? – putting herself physically out of the way. Mrs Sang! She hadn't heard that one before, but it was just tongue laziness, or perhaps the wad of gum got in the way. As for leather bracelets, time for that next week. She hoped they would be worn out by then.

Hayley threw a trial pitch and the opposition batter stepped up. It was a game, really, with very little flow, just stop and start, and all tightly bound in rules and space – diamond, box, mound, home plate – but Norma found the geometry of it mildly interesting, and there was interest in the physics too. Bat striking ball must generate considerable dynamic force. She wondered if anyone had measured it. Not that bat was striking ball at the moment. Hayley Birtles saw to that. The tunnel from her hand to the strike zone must be a thing she could visualize, and the skill required to hurl the ball along it, underarm, without having it bend or climb outside, must come from long practice as much as natural ability. What a pity she could not turn that effort into mental pursuits and use that visualizing, kinetic skill to achieve something more valuable. Yet value for the girl so plainly lay here. What a marvellous combination she displayed of concentration and vitality. Zip went the ball, flat and true, with a little dip at the end that took it underneath the swinging bat, and smack, lovely sound, into the catcher's mitt. 'She's all yours, Hayley. She's got nothing.' Insulting the opposition was part of the game, though it seemed out of place on school playing fields. Out of place only to Norma Sangster. The truth was 'school' and 'playing fields' had no meaning for the girls. They had been swallowed into the past and new things given value in their place. It seemed a loss; and yet, Norma repeated, the verities aren't in danger, they have to be approached in other ways and looked at in a different light, that's all.

Hayley struck the batter out. The poor girl's no beauty, Norma thought; then cancelled the judgement. Hayley didn't conform to her snobbish notion of what was pleasing; but managed to please in other ways, with knotty calves, slab-muscled thighs, square torso, big strong hands. Her face had an American prettiness, that roundness and plumpness, that no-shape, one saw on their beauty queens. Norma liked jaw and cheekbone to declare themselves. She preferred roundness in to roundness out. 'Hollow of cheek as though it drank the wind . . .' and that applied to the male as well as the female face. Hayley Birtles had the well-fed look that seemed so far removed from history. That's not to say she doesn't suffer, Norma said. It struck her too that the girl might have a natural place in events that she must hold on to consciously or surrender. She had a sudden dizziness, suffered a loss of reference points, that made her think she floated in some universe minutely displaced from the one she saw, or lived a beat outside present time, and would never come back to synchrony. Hayley Birtles seemed a giantess, whirling her arm, and the ball spun like a planet, and

Norma felt her own tininess, almost non-being; until the bat, slow as a swinging boom, made dent in the arc of the ball and bent it, egg-shaped, out of course. Then she snapped back, heard it whirring like a quail, and began to move out of its line. A man standing down the slope from her made two steps and raised his arm and picked the ball out of the air in front of her face. With a flick of his wrist and forearm he sent it back to Hayley on the mound. It was so quickly done, the ball was in her glove before Norma realized she would not be hit.

'Thank you,' she said to the man. 'I think that would have got me fair and square.'

'No sweat,' he answered, and she saw from his face sliding away that he was made uneasy by her too-articulated speech. It made her angry. She sometimes saw her work as an attempt to unite the valuable things in the primitive and the civilized states, and it was hard, but the thing she was contracted for. It was too much to meet the same challenge outside work.

'You're Mr Birtles, aren't you? Hayley is just about a one-girl team.'

He climbed up to join her on the path, a man of about her height, slightly built, with an evasiveness about him that made her want to take him by the shoulders and face him front. It was impossible to see him as dynamic softball coach, yet that was how the sports page in the newspaper portrayed him, and he had whipped his team – Deepsea Fisheries, was it? – to the local women's title three years in a row.

'Oh, lovely one. That was another strike out, wasn't it?'

'Yeah,' he said. 'Inside ball.'

'She's really very good.'

'She's got a lot to learn yet. Like all kids she wants to chuck 'em fast. I've got to teach her how to pitch slow.'

Norma hunted for the term. 'The bean ball?'

'No, lady. That's the one that clonks you on the head.'

'Oh.' She wondered if he knew who she was. She wasn't used to parents calling her 'lady'. But he had warmed up, there was a grin on his face; and he explained about pitching, making a cup of his hand and half-swings with his arm to show the work put on the ball. Again Norma found the physics intriguing.

'There's quite a lot of science in it.'

17

'Sure thing. It's not a game for meatheads, I'll tell you that. See what Hayley's doing now. She's going to make this one curve away. This is a batter who swings late. The ball will be gone before she gets there.'

'Ah.'

'Nice pitch, Hayley.'

His accent was English Midlands, she could not be more exact than that. It had a solid, nicely smoothed-off vowel. His love of an un-English game was a little surprising, but perhaps he was one of those who put their Englishness off on arriving here. It was often class snobbery they rejected. She wondered about Mr Birtles. Anger and prickliness and comic hatred were not on show. He seemed rather private. His rattle of talk might conceal unhappiness.

For a moment she could not remember the name of the boy who had died – burned in that accident with Duncan Round. Then she had it, Wayne. All the Birtles children were named after movie stars. She must not, of course, mention him, and should not, for her own sake, think of him, in his wrap of fire; but there was a question she should ask, even though it was difficult. She had a legitimate interest. When he had been quiet a moment, intent on the game, she asked in a voice both bright and neutral, 'How is Shelley getting on, Mr Birtles?'

'Shelley?'

'I was sorry to hear about her spot of bother.'

'Shelley's . . .' He shrugged, which seemed to mean he could not say.

'I hope she won't let it set her back. A lot of young people get into trouble and come out the other side unscathed. I suppose it's really a matter of treating it as a learning experience.' She saw Mr Birtles blink at that, and she did not like it herself.

'She needed a bloody good hiding, Shelley did,' Birtles said.

'Oh surely not. A fine is a kind of hiding anyway. We were all so proud of Shelley, her running I mean. I do hope she's going to keep it up.'

Mr Birtles said nothing. Did that mean the answer was no? An image of Shelley Birtles appeared in Norma's mind: pony-tailed fifteen-year-old breaking the tape, with arms flung wide and breasts flattened under her blue school singlet and brown knee fore-flung, shining like an egg; and she grieved that it was in the

18

past and would never come back – the physical moment done, achievement done with, beauty gone, and the girl immersed in ugliness.

'Is she still in Saxton?'

'Gotta be. The judge says she's gotta report.'

'Well, if there's any way the school can help . . .' Which was a stupid thing to say. Once they were gone they never came back. The good thing was the girl's name was on the honours board as record holder and Norma hoped it would help her, even though it was a slender and receding thing.

The next question, one she could not ask, was whether Hayley would go the same way and wind up in court. It seemed possible, even likely, for the older sister had surely been less tough and sly than Hayley. Less intelligent too; although Hayley's was intelligence not put to use, unless in a pricking at weak spots and a managing of events. She had little doubt the girl was sexually active – one could tell – but that did not bother her as long as it did not lead to promiscuity. She had been fairly busy herself at sixteen, with a certain boy, though virgin until nineteen in body if not in mind; and sixteen then was roughly fourteen now. A time came for some girls when sex couldn't be put off unless by some dark prohibition or false ideal that set them on an equally dangerous course. She was ready to argue that prohibitive morality and free sex led to defeat or viciousness about equally. Defeat and viciousness she feared; and Hayley was a candidate for both. Sport, however, saved a good many girls.

She hoped Hayley would keep on with it, and Shelley come back.

Duncan Round scraped lichen from the headstone to see how long the woman had been dead.

'Ninety-eight years and a hundred and twenty-two days.'

He would have liked to know the hours as well but held his hand vertical and calculated the angle of the stone instead. 'Twelve degrees.' It had some way to go before it fell, although that depended on how much support was at the base. The woman in the coffin, if any of the coffin was left, would be dry bones, or damp perhaps, depending on the water-table here. Her flesh would be changed into earth. Hair would be left, and bits of whatever she had been buried in. It seemed a waste of clothes to bury them. Then he remembered 'shroud' for putting bodies in, and wondered if they used them in 1888, and exactly what they were. It sounded like a sheet, but maybe it was black. How many times would it wrap round, and were a person's arms held by his sides or made into a cross on his chest? The cross was a Christian sign so it was probably that, but they might also choose it because it took less room and the coffin could be built narrower. Fat people must have fat coffins, and thin people thin or they would move, and babies must be buried in boxes half a metre long. How many pall-bearers would a baby need? One on each side would be enough, or a man could carry the coffin like a suitcase by his side. Babies who were born dead were stuck in cardboard boxes and put out with the rubbish at the hospital. Born dead? A contradiction. Born lucky, born liar, born victim, stillborn. Each phrase made a tick like a clock as he thought of it and he smiled with pleasure at the increase in himself.

Ants came out of a hole between the headstone and the slab and went along a rusty iron bar and over the root of a tree, past some empty beer cans and a Kentucky Fried Chicken box. The scent trail must be strong to keep them in such an orderly line. He had read a book on ants and knew they used visual markers too. Would it confuse them if he moved the box? It would be like moving a skyscraper. But Duncan felt uneasy at that. Likenesses, supposing, made a tiny hot place in his mind and he had learned not to let one thing remind him too much of another. The colonel who had found the recipe had no real eyes to see the ants go by. He was not a giant looking down. Duncan made a shiver at the thought and felt a stronger burning in his head, and set himself the job of counting ants, using a worm-hole to fix his eye. When they came by too many to count he started again, refusing to cheat, and he was there a long time before he reached a hundred. Then he tore the lid off the chicken box and laid it on the trail. The ants did a lot of scurrying but found their way again. Duncan turned the lid a quarter round, making the scent lead at right angles. The confusion lasted only a moment. Ants weren't dumb. They found their line and went on as though nothing had happened.

If they had no memory, nothing had happened of course. And if they could not think or feel it was not even right to say now was the only time they had. They did not have that much. There wasn't *now*. A huge gap between himself and ants opened up. He did not know how to look at it, and wondered if he did, and found out all the things there were to know, whether the space inside his head would fill, and if the black wall would reappear. Filling up the space was his occupation and finding the wall the end of it. He did not know when he would arrive or what he would do when he got there. The wall made him elated and afraid and was a thing he probably shouldn't have seen. He kept it secret, and kept the space he filled up secret too. People were worried about his mind. He spent his time away from other people. Even when he was with them he had learned to be away.

The Round children are Miranda, Stella, Duncan and Belinda. Tom Round chose the girls' names and Josie, his wife, their mother, who defines herself in neither of these ways ('Bugger it, I'm me first, Josie Duncan, those other things come after that'), chose the boy's. They had agreed on it. If the numbers favour Tom that's simply luck. She accuses him of choosing trendy names and sometimes sings 'anda, ella, inda' to annoy him. 'Shut up, Josie Dunnycan,' he replies. He still finds the girls' names poetic, though they're shortened now to Mandy, Stell and Bel.

He's happy to let the boy be Josie's boy and now and then calls him Duncan Duncan. Having a son doesn't interest him.

Tom Round is an architect. A couple of his friends who don't like him much refer to him as Home Beautiful. Some of his houses have won awards, and articles on them and him appear in magazines. Living in Saxton, being 'unspoiled', is part of his image and he won't leave, although he's been described too as 'a national treasure' and 'totally unprovincial in his attitudes'. 'I don't have to hunt up work, work comes to me,' Tom says. 'I'll make this town the architectural capital of the country.' Saxton is proud of him. It won't be long before the PR office starts running a tour of Tom Round houses.

He's a good-looking man; tough good looks – wide face, Mongolian cheekbones, with a corbel of hard flesh propping them up, nose a little flattened, making him look as if he boxed in his youth (which he did: 'won a few, lost a few,' he says modestly), blue eyes, a burning look suggesting impatience, energy. His redness sits well with his pale-blond hair, which he has styled in a unisex shop. 'Lots of older men do that now,' Josie says.

'He thinks he's the centre of the universe.' Once at a party friends found her alone in an empty room. 'I can't remember loving him,' she wept, blocking tears with her hands and pushing them up her cheeks towards her eyes. She's not a woman who needs to play second fiddle to a man. At thirty-three, when Belinda started school, she took a weaving course at the polytech and soon was turning out saleable work. At forty she opened a shop with a potting friend and a silversmith friend. They called it Three Wise Women, and now there are nine and the shop, Wimmins Werk, is twice as big and on the main street. *North and South* ran an article on them and Josie, in the photo, looked smart and hard and happy and beautiful. She confessed that 'profitwise' she and her partners were doing well. 'We don't need any males round here. If there's a moral it's got to be that.' Tom Round has not been in *North and South*.

He says he's proud of her. 'It's a useful trade, making rugs. Some of her stuff doesn't look too bad in my houses. But let's keep it in perspective, all this shuttle-banging isn't art.' One of his jokes is that Josie has the new female disease, 'Urcarrhea'. 'It's worse than the trots. It's bloody incurable. But at least it stops her fixating on the boy.'

22

That is how he thinks of Duncan – the boy. He withdraws from going further than that. He talks about 'my girls' and is pleased with them in a way that's close to being sentimental – Mandy at medical school, Stella getting ready for the law, and Bel who's 'just a kid yet, but the smartest of the lot, and man has she got a spatial sense, you should see some of her designs'. Duncan is without qualities and has been so, in Tom's eyes, from the moment of his birth. Tom Round did not want a son but girls, another one, he wanted no models of himself but creatures to point up his uniqueness, and Duncan would be no good for that. His maleness – fact not quality – made Tom feel anger and revulsion. He wouldn't put it in those terms at all. He'd call his feelings disappointment and not examine the matter further than that. 'Josie got her hooks in and turned him into Mummy's boy. Now, the poor little sod, bloody burns. Jesus, I can't bear to look at him.' His eyes fill with tears. Tom has come to believe he loved Duncan once.

Josie though is filled with love and pity, now and then. It pours into her and she pours it out, and when she's empty, when she's cold and free, goes back to her other life feeling great. She mustn't be blamed for it. She believes she has done Duncan good and tells herself she must survive 'as a functioning person', survive in the world and in her 'self', if she's to keep on helping him. She doesn't pretend she's staying whole only for Duncan. She cannot, in fact, feel any hope for him and finds herself thinking of him as her son who died, and this burned creature, for whom she has these floods of feeling, someone new; and someone not quite human, who's had part of his humanness burned away. She asks herself if he's her responsibility, and quickly answers yes, and loves him uncontrollably for a moment, and then is resentful of the job he's given her. She despises Tom for pitying him, for she sees how this feeling is swallowed up in pity for himself.

Duncan has known from early in his life that his mother loves him too much, and not properly or all the time, and his father doesn't love him at all. Love is a thing he has little use for and he doesn't prefer one parent to the other. Tom and Josie both seem foolish to him. He had a word he used on their approach: beware. He liked that sort of word for a year or two and has kept it in use, with an exclamation he makes silently when he's been in his

23

parents' company a while: Ho hum! 'Ho hum' relieves him from 'beware'. It's safe to go away at that point for they don't need him any more.

'Nobody needs me,' he once cried happily. 'I do, Duncan,' Belinda said. He had not known she was behind his door, lifting things with a Lego crane. 'You're a kid,' he said, 'you don't count.' But he was pleased with her because he did not have to take her seriously, and because she was there to grin at when he needed. He could see she was pretty and knew she was clever because everyone said so all the time, but this did not make him like her less. His older sisters were clever and pretty too but unlike them, Belinda wasn't 'up herself'. That was a phrase he liked especially and he chanted in his head, up yourself, up yourself, when Mandy and Stella were displaying. The mechanics of it, explained by Wayne Birtles, delighted him.

Duncan was not the dull boy people thought him. They formed that opinion because he would not learn things that did not interest him, and his method of refusal was to lock himself away inside his head. He was interested in the fitting of one thing with another, in the force one exerted on another, in joints and locks and levers, knots and gears, sockets, spines, bearings, in what pressed down or raised up or bored in. A thing as simple as a mattress-spring delighted him. The off-set teeth on saws made him grin and a screw going into timber was a marvel. He slept once with a carpenter's bit on his bedside table and dreamed of crushed wood turning in a groove. None of this was any help at school. He did not even do well at woodwork. The perfect motions, forces, in his head would not make their way into his hands. He botched things up, he cut himself and dropped tools on his feet. There were teachers who enjoyed the thickheadedness of this son of a famous father. 'Has no interest in anything,' one of them wrote on a report; but Duncan had been interested all year in the pressure of the man's belly on his belt. He wondered if there were some way of measuring it and working out when the leather would snap.

No one saw that Duncan Round was a happy boy.

That was all a couple of years ago. Things are different now. His happiness still rests on the private workings of his mind, but not on discovery any longer, and the weight and pull and pressure of things. He remembers that time, can call up every moment of his life, but rarely bothers – leaves it there, a tiny piece of him shaded in. The rest lies spread in front, a plain of light; and Duncan's job is to occupy it, every inch, fill it up with seconds, hours, days, with smells and sights and movements, fill the huge emptiness he saw in the burning moment; and so he must stay alert and see, must work at it, for some things fill better than others. He grows tired of the job, yet is not unhappy. It's a task he can manage, and at the end of it some huge revolution will occur, some moving of thing through thing, atom through atom. His life will turn over on itself and he'll understand what it's all about. Until then he's not curious.

Not long ago he came on a book by an artist who made large, intricate drawings by filling up his paper with tiny dots of a mapping pen. There were centipedes on a rotten log, with leaves as a frame. There was beach and sea, there were trees with twisted roots, pebbles, ferns, lichen, ants, sand. There were waterfalls with each bit of spray marked by a dot. He looked at the book and did not find the drawings beautiful or ugly or anything, but added them to what he possessed; then came on the artist's description of an experiment he'd made to count the number of dots in a picture. There were eight or nine thousand in one square inch (which took twelve or thirteen minutes to fill) and two and a half million to a normal sized picture. 'Hey,' Duncan said, 'that's what I do,' and he looked back over his days like pictures, but instead of being in a book they were edge to edge and each one was a dot in a larger picture. At times he was frightened by what he had to do and it helped him to know there was a man who worked at the same sort of thing.

Duncan read the books that lay about. He read Mandy's university texts and Stella's seventh-form texts and the books his mother brought home on arts and crafts and monasteries and mythology and travel and diet and feminine consciousness and female hygiene. He sometimes looked up words, though understanding and information were not what he was after. He did not want knowledge but accumulated sentences, filled moments. He would sooner watch a fly on a window-pane than read a book. He once spent half an hour watching a fly, then let it out, and spent another useful time retracing its route on the pane with his fingertip. He does not do this sort of thing on a plan, just watches, sees, does, where he happens to be, using what he finds, but takes more pleasure in some things than in others. Birds please him, small birds especially, and often he will close his eyes and create exactly the arrival, feeding, departure of a tribe of wax-eyes in a plum tree, or the bathing of sparrows in the dust. These are not things he imagines but remembers. Remembering is his relaxation.

'What are you thinking about?' his mother asks.

'Nothing.'

'You can't think about nothing.'

'OK. Birds.'

She buys him books on birds. He reads them with no interest. At the library, on those afternoons when Stella drops him off on her way back to school, he reads whatever is lying on the table. Sometimes he wanders off and walks in the town. He plays the machines in the game parlours now and then, but would just as soon walk by the river watching water running on the stones.

Duncan makes some people jumpy. Others try to talk to him and he answers yes or no. There are those who think he should be in an institution, and kept out of children's sight with his burns. Others say he's bound to do something violent one day because the pain has probably warped his mind. He's not interested in what people think of him. He watches when they move in useful ways and will follow a postman up a street or stand by a hole in the footpath watching P and T men solder wires. He's getting to be a well-known figure in the town.

There has been plastic surgery and more is planned when the time is right. He does not mind but Josie is against it. She can't believe anything can improve him. 'Cutting and pasting' is her name for it and 'tinkering' describes the psychological treatment Duncan has. Tinkering is a defensive term. She simply wants to forget what the psychologist has said: one day Duncan will have to scream. 'Then perhaps we can move ahead.'

Duncan feigns indifference with this man. He plays at being three-quarters dead. He pretends that feeling and consciousness are burned out, while knowing that the truth is different: feeling is gone, most of it, but consciousness is the huge bright land up

26

ahead. He sees it stretching off into the haze.

Duncan has enough to keep him busy.

The accident happened on a summer afternoon when Duncan had just turned fourteen. He and his friend Wayne Birtles had ridden to the beach on their ten-speeds and eaten fried chicken for lunch and spent the rest of their money on the hydroslide. They were making the most of their holidays. On Monday it was form four – teachers who speak with forked tongue, seniors who were up themselves, Wayne said. He was a sharp-tongued boy, given to mimicry and extravagant statement and Duncan found the tension between what Wayne liked and what he liked of great interest. It was the first time he'd understood that other people's ideas and behaviour might affect his own by sympathetic leverage. (Compulsive leverage was the sort he was used to.) He was grateful for Wayne's company although he knew he had it by default as Wayne's better friends were away on holiday.

They rode back from the beach and stopped at the Birtles's house. No one was home so they shared a can of beer from the washhouse then rode to the Round house for a swim in the pool. They went by the river road and down by the footbridge saw the gang of street kids who had come to Saxton at Christmas and been in the newspaper ever since sniffing glue from plastic bags.

'Killing off their brain cells,' Duncan said. He imagined huge panels like the control board in a generator house and red lights winking out one by one.

'Who told you that?' Being on the bag gave you a buzz, Wayne said. You didn't give a stuff about anything.

'Have you done it?'

Wayne had: sniffed paint and petrol and glue and fingernail polish. Lots of things could turn you on he said.

The Round house was two kilometres up the river, on a hillside overlooking the golf course, with the city council's pine plantation coming down the slope and the state forest going into the distance, hill after hill. (It's a Tom Round house and a show place – one of those that's won a prize and been in magazines. It looks like a series of white pill-boxes dropping down the hillside, or, if you half close your eyes, a waterfall in the pines. It has pantiles on its slopes of roof and solar heating panels, and inside are slate-covered concrete floors to store the heat. They warm up in the sun and radiate in the night and even in midwinter the house is toasty warm, Josie tells the interviewer.)

Duncan and Wayne rode up and left their bikes leaning on the brick garden wall. 'It's like the town shithouse,' Wayne complained.

They climbed the wall and dropped into a rock garden and stepped down among prickly plants. The swimming-pool was shaped like an egg and its blue tiles made it look icy cold. Striped canvas chairs stood on the lawn with cane tables beside them and folded sun umbrellas on the grass. The house was through a glass room filled with plants. Wayne could not work out if it was meant to be inside or out.

'Hey Mandy, put your togs on,' Duncan said.

Wayne saw a naked girl lying on a towel by a flower-bed. She was tanned an even brown down her front and she shone with oil. The hair between her legs was sticking up as though she'd dried it hard with a towel and her flattened breasts fell one each way. She had a straw hat over her face and did not bother to lift it as she said, 'Get lost, Dunc.'

'Wayne and me want to have a swim.'

'Wayne and I, for Christ's sake,' the girl said. She lifted her hat and looked at Wayne and rolled on to her stomach, flicking an edge of her towel over her buttocks. 'Don't let him piss in the pool.'

Wayne heard himself grunt. He felt sick. The world seemed to tilt on an angle and bits of it lose their joining place with other bits. Then it all came back with a clang. He wanted to run at the girl and come down with his knees on her spine.

'Fuckin' bitch.'

'Come on.' Duncan plucked at him. He led him to the garage. 'You don't want to let Mandy upset you.'

'I should piss in the bloody pool.' He was sweating from his ride and wanted a swim, but he had to get even first. He had another trouble too: with her naked there he'd get horny and she'd see. His togs were the sort that wouldn't hide it. (Wayne had that problem at the beach now and then but there he could go in the water till it stopped.)

'Come on. Get changed.'

28

'In a minute.' He looked around the garage. It was big enough to hold the Birtles's house, with golf-clubs and skis and canoes on the walls and only one car home, a Honda City.

'Whose car is that?'

'Anyone's, I guess. Mandy's using it tonight.'

Wayne Birtles smiled. He found a nail on the work-bench and pressed it in the valve on the Honda's rear wheel, letting it down. Duncan did not interfere. Mandy had asked for it. He liked it even better when Wayne let down the spare tyre too. He could see Mandy changing the tyre – she'd do it herself, didn't believe in asking men for help – and lowering the jack and finding the spare flat as well. He admired Wayne for thinking of that, there was something really evil about it. Then Wayne did a thing he did not like. He saw the keys in the car's ignition and took them out and opened the petrol cap. 'Drain her tank.'

Duncan wanted to change sides. He didn't think Mandy deserved to be stuck on the road; and Wayne was treating him too with contempt. 'Lay off,' he said.

'Chicken. Where's a siphon?'

Wayne found some plastic tube coiled on the wall and siphoned petrol into a can. When it was full he looked for another, then changed his plan. 'Grab a couple of tins, I'll show you how to sniff.'

Duncan did as he was told. The silent rush of the coloured fluid in the plastic and Wayne's casual folding of the tube to block the flow had set up a pressure and motion in his head and he wanted more. He fetched two Jellimeat tins his mother kept for potting native trees and Wayne let petrol flow into them, stopping it an inch from the top. He pulled the siphon out and closed the cap.

'Bring them over here out of the sun.'

They squatted in a corner and started to sniff. The fumes attacked Duncan in his head, lightening and squeezing at once. He felt himself float and roll and sink, all in one motion, and waited for the quick soaring flight that somehow was promised beyond this. Wayne stood up. He walked away without seeming to turn. Duncan heard the car door open at the end of a tunnel. His mind was stretched out and folded back. He felt he could reach Wayne with his arm and bend it round him like a garden hose. Wayne slid up beside him and shrank to half his height. He had Josie's cigarettes and lighter and he flicked a cigarette half out and pulled it with his mouth. The 'J' in Josie picked Duncan up and turned him in a slow loop and slid him down its tail. Wayne's thumb rose and bent and Duncan felt the working of its joint and the oily roll of bone on bone. 'Better not,' he said. The words came out long and thick and changed into a python, which turned and looked at him with small bright eyes.

'Eeeee,' Duncan said.

The snake swallowed Wayne, then made an easy loop and swallowed him . . .

Mandy heard the clap and felt air lift the brim of her hat. She was on her knees when he came out. Fire stood on top of his head and made a yellow rippling down his side. He walked cork-screwing on the lawn, escaping it. She does not remember how she crossed the space from her to him but feels sometimes the softness of his arm and the hardness of the bones inside as she runs him at the pool. He stumbles like a child dragged by its mother and swings in a quarter circle as she heaves him in. Then Mandy jumps in the pool herself and holds him afloat and knows enough to keep him there cooling his burns and enough to keep his air passages open. Saves his life. Loves him, then and after; but will not look at it, and gives no sign.

Wayne Birtles burns on the garage floor, lying on his elbow, with one leg under him and one out straight. 'You mustn't imagine pain,' they tell his parents. 'He really wouldn't be conscious any more, after the first shock.' They believe it, and Josie Round too rules out pain. She can't believe in pain without some quickness and it comforts her to think of him in semi-conscious wonder at his death.

Josie was in her studio half a level higher than the garage next door. She was sitting on a rug by the window, seeming to stare along the edge of the forest, but had her eyes closed and was meditating. (Mail-order meditation, some of her friends say. She does not dispute it – instructions and her mantra came by mail – but it does her good and she sees no need for 'the real thing' they try to get her started on. It's dangerously close to a religion she feels.) She was just getting on to her plateau when she heard the *Whoomp* from the garage, heard the door rattle, and felt a pressure on her ear-drums. She climbed to her knees and heard Mandy yelling at the pool; knew from the sound she made that their lives were changed. She ran to the door and into the garage and saw the boy lying on his blanket of fire.

She thought it was Duncan and called his name, then saw a face looking calmly out. No expression. Saw a face completely in repose. She ran down the stairs and half-way to him, then back to her studio where a pile of new rugs ticketed for the shop lay by the door. She ran back with armfuls several times and threw them over Wayne until she could see him no more, then brought a hose and ran water on the smoking pile as hard as she could and all around at the burning petrol on the floor until it went out. She left the hose running and tried to shift rugs and find his face but uncovered parts wrongly coloured, wrongly made.

Tom drove up and ran first to the pool, then to the garage. He pulled the rugs off Wayne and looked at him and saw there was nothing he could do, but took the hose and played water on his head and chest. Josie went into the house and dialled 111 and got ambulance and fire engine and police. But Wayne was burned all over and could not live.

It was a thing of circumstances, of this which followed that, inside and outside the head, but do the connections have the force of law? If, one is impelled to say. If the day had been cooler and the boys not wanted another swim. If Wayne had not seen street kids sniffing glue. Would that have been enough to alter things? If Mandy had not been so irritated by Duncan's grammar that she said something cruel to his friend. If she had been wearing her togs. And Josie not forgotten her cigarettes. So on, so on. They reached a certain point. Then came a quantum leap. All other possibilities collapsed. Wayne is dead, and Duncan scarred, it can't be changed.

The Rounds learned a new language, of full-thickness burns and hypovolemic shock and the rule of nines. Josie found the phrase 'gross physical insult' very helpful and claimed there was psychological insult as well, for all of them. Nobody blamed 'the other side', not openly. The Round and the Birtles parents met and both pairs edged away as soon as they could. Neither wanted any connection. 'There's no call for anything ongoing,' Josie said.

The police worked out how it had happened. Tom Round was

upset about the scorching on the garage floor. Duncan had nothing to say. Months later, when he was able to talk, he told Belinda he had seen it happen before it happened. He had seen Wayne lift the lighter to his cigarette but did not have time to stop him even though it happened rather slowly.

'You should have teleported yourself away,' Belinda said.

Although the plastic surgery allowed him only one side of his mouth, Duncan smiled.

Norma paused by the tennis-courts, where Stella and Belinda were
playing a match. The difference in their styles made her smile.
Belinda joggled in her puppy fat. She grunted as she hit, snapped
her teeth, argued that the ball was in or out, and called her winning
score with a grin. She flicked her hair away and blew it noisily from
in front of her mouth. She scratched her ribs and hooked her finger
in the crotch of her shorts to loosen them. Stella moved with an
easy flow, like glycerine, and hit the ball with a 'pokking' sound,
but seemed to let style get in her way and was often late or soft in
her returns. She lobbed a good deal and never came to the net,
where Belinda loved to crouch and jump for the ball sailing over her
head. Belinda had pulled her sweat band off and thrown it by the
net. Stella's hair was tied with a green silk scarf and she patted her
damp upper lip with a handkerchief.

It's more than just their ages, Norma thought, they seem to come
out of separate times. Yet, strangely, Belinda was the old-fashioned
one. Self-esteem was not in short supply with the Rounds, but hers
seemed natural, while Stella's was an artefact and always on display. Norma knew that she was in a poor trade in Stella's eyes. The
law, where Stella went, was for 'top minds' and being a schoolteacher a job for second-raters. Tom had fixed the hierarchy –
architecture, law, medicine, mathematics and physics, scientific
research – and Stella put the argument in an essay much read and
commented on in the staffroom. Norma had not been able to laugh.
The steely hardness of that crafted thing, Stella Round, made her
want to cover her vulnerable parts.

Well, Norma smiled, at least she can't play tennis very well. She
laughed at Belinda's glee in whacking Stella's half-lob away.
Belinda would win her share of contests with her sister, and win in
pleasing people as well – although she did not seem to care about it;
gave her headmistress no second glance.

Norma went on, thinking of the Rounds: of Josie, her
untrustworthy friend; and Tom who made it plain he would be

her lover. But Tom would simply have her – have, exactly – then betray. She had seen it in his self-regarding eye as he smooth-talked her. In his heavy redness and the hungry swelling of his throat. Being wanted in that way was most unpleasant. Unpleasant, too, the mind in his desire. But Norma had sufficient of her own self-esteem to know it wasn't just his daughters' teacher he was after. He said she had a Mona Lisa smile. 'You'll never know what's amusing me,' she had replied. She had a taste for light remarks carrying heavy loads.

As for Josie – well, she was not a Round; she was Josie Duncan. She had the Round quickness and cleverness though. She saw connections in their hard sharp way. Where she fell short was in self-love. Josie must try for improvement and that caused her untrustworthiness. Other people took on a simplified shape; were silhouettes magnetized on a board, with Josie in the centre, full-faced coloured Josie smiling there. Friends dropped off at intervals. She could never work out why. But Norma stayed on, for it was like a stammer Josie had and not dandruff or dirty nails. She liked her less only on occasions. Josie had good feeling at least. Norma doubted Tom had that at all. She saw at times another face under his smiling face – a muzzle structure somehow lupine.

'I can cope with his women,' Josie said. 'What I can't tolerate is the way he treats me as part of himself. God, the self-referral. Whatever I do is to the greater glory of Tom Round.'

'What you need is a marriage sabbatical. Six months away.'

'What I need is Tom crawling. Then I'll go.'

Rounds can dominate your life, Norma thought. You can't afford to let them get a grip. Even the girls made one look back and study them – an awful fascination. They were crocodiles and birds of paradise. They were like dentists, they drilled at you.

She watched Stella and Belinda win a point each, then went on and turned among the graves, letting the Rounds go with the fading 'pok pok' of their game. The cheering of girls came from the softball ground and she heard the name Hayley cried like an incantation. Then a squealing, a ululation, rose like a wave and fell away. It meant, from its duration, home run; and Norma was pleased. Hayley needed all the triumphs she could get. 'Round' might colour, enfeather one, but 'Birtles', it had come to seem, marked with a shadow . . .

A movement in the graves startled her. A head looked over the top of a broken column and withdrew, leaving a ghostly image that seemed improper. Some furtive thing was there; some bit of villainy was going on among the graves. Norma thought of girls – her girls – and walked across to investigate. The smart teacher looked the other way out of school but she had never been able to do that. Parents might bristle and pupils and their boyfriends laugh at her, it did not matter. Once, along the river, she had taken a razor-blade from a girl who was trying to work up nerve to cut her wrists. (That girl was doing well at university now – not that that was the end of it, there was no end, Norma said.)

By the time she reached the grave she had recognized the shape and knew it was the Round boy she would find. He had his back to her and was hunkered in the way of Indian beggars, watching black ants on a chicken bone. His sisters must have brought him for the ride and he had wandered off among the graves – as good a place to be as watching tennis, although it seemed to show a lack of care on their part. She watched him for a moment, knowing he must hear her panting from her climb.

'Do you like ants, Duncan?'

He lowered his head and made an angry sound. 'You made me lose count.'

'You were counting ants?'

Still without looking at her – 'I count all sorts of things.'

His healthy skin joined neatly with his burned skin and his hair was boyish on his undamaged side. Norma wanted to touch him. She moved across to a grave and rested her hip on the iron railing.

'Did you come into town with your sisters?'

He made a forward jerk of his head.

'It's nice and quiet up here. Do you like old graves?'

'They're all right.'

'Why do you count ants?'

'To see how many I can get.'

'And how many is that? Do you have a record?'

'Two hundred and eighty-three. They move too fast.'

'Two hundred and eighty-three is very good.'

He shot her a look of contempt. 'Tom,' he said, 'I think it's time for a few plain words. Josie is my friend but apart from that, attraction isn't there and it's a prerequisite wouldn't you say? I won't come into your house again unless you keep your hands to yourself. Norma.'

He turned his head as he spoke her name and looked at her with eyes aslant. There was no malice in him. He was simply showing her what he could do; and she kept the smile that, in spite of shock, his mispronunciation of 'prerequisite' had caused. She should have used the plain words she had promised.

'Where did you find it?'

'In his car.'

'Well, I hope you burned it.' She went cold at the word.

Duncan grinned. His mouth moved freely on its undamaged side. 'I just left it there.'

'There's nothing between me and your father.'

'Wouldn't worry me if there was.'

She felt the chill of life among the Rounds. The boy was double victim, and yet gave the impression of being untouched.

'Do you remember everything you read?'

'If I want to.'

'I wrote that letter back in April. May?'

'26 April you put on it.'

He was ready to go back to his ants but she would not let him. She was at the edge of some extraordinary place and refused to have her entry closed. His scarring had stopped affecting her, even that pulling-tight of skin that misaligned one eye and the building up of his nose that brutalized him.

'Tell me something else you've read.'

'Like what?'

'Well, if you remember things . . . is that what you do?'

'I can remember.'

'Something nice. Something interesting.' But 'nice' and 'interesting' made no part of it; she saw a closing up in his look. 'Hard then,' she said quickly, 'hard to remember.'

'Nothing's hard.'

'All right, you choose. I promise I won't tell.'

He picked up the chicken bone and forced its smaller knuckle into the ground six inches away. The ants milled and scurried; then found it and swarmed to the top.

'There's no stopping ants,' Norma said.

No reply.

'If you like you can come around and read books at my place. Or play my records. Do you like music?'

'Not much.'

'Can you remember it the way you do letters?'

He gave a tiny smile at her joke and she felt her heart lift at the sign.

'It's all just the same after the first time,' he said.

'You don't need to hear it again?' She wanted to ask about beauty, and how it made him feel, but was afraid.

'Tell me a page out of a book then, Duncan. Please.' She thought he was not going to respond. Then, still squatting, with his eyes closed, he began: 'The retina is a thin sheet of interconnected nerve cells, including the light-sensitive rod and cone cells which convert light into electrical impulses – the language of the nervous system. It was not always obvious that the retina is the first stage of visual sensation. The Greeks thought . . .' He carried on for several minutes, without inflection or hesitation. The memory feat was remarkable, but Norma found herself grieving for what was lost. 'That's very good. Do you know what it means?'

He looked at her as though he was insulted. 'Doesn't matter what it means.'

'Do you like it? Are you interested in the eye?'

'What for?'

'Why did you read about it then?'

'There was lots of words. It was lying there.'

'And you remember the whole book, cover to cover?'

He nodded with that butting of his head. 'That's easy.'

'How long ago?'

'Last year. When I came out of hospital.'

'Do you look up words you don't know in the dictionary?'

'No.'

'And looking at ants is more or less the same? What do they do? Inside your head?'

She'd frightened him and he would not answer.

'Duncan, are there things you read and like? Things that you like more than other things?'

'Yes.' She barely heard him.

'Read me one. Say it from the book. I won't tell. Is that what frightens you, someone finding out what you can do?'

37

He nodded.

'Look at me, Duncan. You can trust me.'

He liked the look of her well enough. She was old but her skin hadn't wrinkled yet, and that was why his father wanted her. 'Here comes La bloody Gioconda' – which was a famous painting, Belinda said. Sneering showed Tom Round couldn't have what he wanted. Good old Mrs Sangster, Duncan thought now and then.

Her eyes were putting on a look he was supposed to trust, kind of soft and twinkly. He did not trust her eyes. They must get lots of practice looking like that with girls at school and she could probably change them when she wanted. He knew she could be tough because of what she'd written to his father. But he liked her mouth and was not sure its softness was a lie. It was like a girl's mouth, pink and clean and not with bits of flaky skin and greasy bits of lipstick. It smiled in a way he did not think could be put on. A rush of feeling started in his chest, almost making him cry. (He could not cry with one eye because the tear ducts were taken out.)

He turned his head away from her.

> 'Came a bird from Lapland flying,
> From the north-east came an eagle,
> Not the largest of the eagles,
> Nor was he among the smallest,
> With one wing he swept the water,
> To the sky was swung the other;
> On the sea his tail he rested,
> On the cliffs his beak he rattled.'

He enjoyed the brightness about those words, the little space around them, like a coloured coat.

'Where did you find that?' Mrs Sangster said.

'In a book.'

'And it's something you like? Do you like birds?'

'I like watching them.'

'And not just to store them in your head?'

It puzzled him that she was so pleased. People got angry or embarrassed around him, and tears came into some women's eyes, which was OK, it really had nothing to do with him. Mrs Sangster, though, was pleased because of what he had done. He did not know why she should feel like that but supposed it was because of poetry. She asked him if liking things made them easy to learn. He hadn't thought about it, but told her there wasn't any difference he could see, the difference was they kept on coming back and had a kind of coloured space around them; and they hurt.

'Hurt?'

'Not too bad.' He was alarmed. He pinched a bit of skin on his wrist. 'About like that. It makes all the colours come out.' She moved her head, very quick, and seemed to be sniffing, and he remembered dogs around a rat-hole and knew she was excited and wanted to get something out of him. But still her mouth smiled and he trusted her.

'Walk with me a little way,' she said.

'Where to?'

'My house. It's just through the cemetery. Would you like a drink? Or a biscuit?'

He went at her side through the graves. The older ones were deep in the trees, with names on the headstones he could not read. He wanted to scrape them to find out but she kept on putting her hand on his back and giving him a little push along. He liked her long round fingers on the numb place where his scars began. He had, in his mind, a map of his back, made from feeling it not from seeing, and could draw it on paper if someone asked. He was pleased he had dead places on his skin, and an armpit that did not sweat, and an eye that could not cry. The parts of him that itched were getting smaller. Sometimes he squeezed them in his head and made them shrink. He turned them cold and stopped them altogether, but could not keep it up for long and was bad-tempered when he stopped.

'That's my great-grandmother's grave,' Mrs Sangster said. 'She died when she was only twenty-two. Giving birth.'

'What year?'

'Eighteen-sixty something.' She rubbed the headstone, making moss and lichen powder off. 'Eighteen-sixty-nine.'

'One hundred and seventeen years. That's fourteen hundred and four months.'

'Oh, so you do arithmetic too.'

'I can work the days out if you like.' Her amusement made him happy. 'I don't use paper for anything.' He grinned. 'Except . . .'

39

Mrs Sangster twisted her mouth and gave a snort. 'That's understood. I'm pleased you make connections.' He did not know what she meant. 'Writing-paper and toilet-paper.'

'It was a joke.' He felt in danger. 'I just fill things up. I put in dots. That's nothing much.'

They came out of the trees and looked down towards the tennis-courts, where Stella and Belinda ran and hit. 'That's my sisters.'

'Yes, I know. I wonder who's winning.'

'Stell will win. She just hits them soft and Belinda gets mad and starts bashing.' He was pleased to have this to talk about. 'Last time Stella won six–four, six–three. The time before it was six–four, six–love. Belinda hit one ball over the road into the school. She was trying to hit Stella but she missed.'

Mrs Sangster laughed. 'Do you play tennis?'

'I'm no good at sport. I chucked my bat away at softball once and hit the umpire fair on the head.' He looked at the girls playing softball on the bottom field. 'That's Hayley Birtles pitching. She was Wayne's sister. Wayne was the one that got burned with me.'

Mrs Sangster drew in her breath. She waited a while before she spoke. 'Do you mind talking about that?'

'I don't mind. No one ever asks me. Belinda used to ask me but she stopped. I think they think I'll get upset or something.'

'Do you miss Wayne?'

'He was never one of my best friends. He was bloody silly lighting that cigarette.'

'And the petrol just exploded?'

'Yeah. How dumb can you get?'

'Do you remember much after it happened? Straight after?'

'Not much. Mandy chucked me in the pool. Mum lost all her new rugs trying to put Wayne out.'

A bump moved in her throat where the skin was loose. It surprised him that a headmistress should be like anyone else, with tubes and spit, and a flake of dry snot in her nose, moving up and down as she breathed. He wondered if he should tell her about it. He guessed the question she was getting ready to ask.

'Did it hurt very much?'

'Didn't hurt at all. It only hurt in hospital.'

'They gave you things for that, of course.'

'Still hurt. These grafts hurt.' He touched his right hand with his left.

'Can you use that hand all right?'

'I can pick things up. They reckon I'm lucky.'

'And your eye?'

'I can see things.' He grinned, enjoying her interest. 'Can't cry though. Lucky I'm not a girl.'

Mrs Sangster seemed to feel a tickling in her nose. She took out her handkerchief and blew.

'Some girls don't cry a lot. And some boys do. You can do it without tears, you know.'

'Yeah?' He did not know what she meant and was disappointed she didn't ask more questions about him. They went through an iron gate with spearheads on top and crossed a bit of park thick with clover and went through a back gate into her garden. New plants were growing in straight rows – lettuce were the only ones he knew – and she stopped to pull a weed out. One of her knees went click and she said, 'Ouch!

'My apology for a garden,' she said, straightening up. 'I don't get enough time for it. Do you grow things?'

'Me? No.'

'Josie does, doesn't she?'

'Herbs and stuff.'

'And Tom? Your father?'

'He only grows green peppers. For the salad. He's trying to grow bananas too, in a kind of sun-trap, but they only grow about five centimetres long. He hit one bunch with a hammer once.'

Mrs Sangster laughed. 'I think Tom would like to speak the word. Come and have a drink. You must be thirsty.'

They crossed a lawn where clothes were drying on a line. She felt a pair of knickers with her hand, then on her cheek. They had lace on the edge and see-through cloth. His mother had some pairs the same and he knew old women wore sexy things, though he wondered what for. 'They're pants for taking off,' Belinda said. Who would want to take them off women as old as that? (except his father). When she picked up a cat on the back porch and rubbed her face on it the way its fur sloped, that was more the sort of thing she should do. It was a skinny cat with blue eyes and a ratty tail and it stretched its legs and put out its claws, which got caught in her

41

dress. 'Little devil,' she said, dropping it by her feet. 'Do you have a cat?'

'Mum's got one. It dribbles on her pillow. It's pretty old.'

'And Belinda's got a dog, hasn't she? What sort is that?'

'A kind of dachshund corgi cross. Its stomach rubs on the ground when it walks. She reckons she's going to take it to the vet and get it put down.'

'I'm sure she's just saying that.'

'You don't know Bel. She says ' – he put on her voice – '"You can't argue with necessity."'

Mrs Sangster laughed. 'Poor dog.'

'It has to get its anal glands squeezed all the time.'

'Well, one doesn't keep pets unless one can cope with their little ways. Come in, Duncan. Go in there, in the sitting room. What would you like to drink?'

'What have you got?'

'Tea. Coffee. Fruit juice. Ginger ale.'

'I'll have ginger ale.'

He felt he was on a picnic.

Norma poured a glass of ginger ale and, to be companionable, a glass of apple juice topped up with soda. She found it interesting that Duncan, after his suspicious start, had relaxed so much. Josie complained that he gave only one word answers or a shrug, and asked no questions, made no observations. (He was, she said, like a robot or an android – then blushed and shivered, remembering, Norma guessed, that plastic-seeming skin that stretched over so much of him.) But here he was chattering and grinning and making jokes. There was more to it than just her skill in drawing young people out. He seemed to recognize that he was safe – and Norma understood she had taken on a job. Really she had meant just to be kind but kindness had a way of trapping one. She was pleased he liked her though – and found her amusing. He had his share of masculine contempt.

Ginger ale slopped on to her fingers. Why did one top things up for males, as though they had a right to extra shares? She tipped a half inch off his glass, wiped her hand on the sink-cloth, and went into the sitting room, where he was standing, hands on hips, looking about.

'Nice room.'

'Thank you.'

'Lots of books.'

'If you see any that you'd like to borrow . . .'

'Got plenty at home.'

'Do you read novels?'

'Read anything. Bel's the only one who's got any stories. *Sweet Valley High.*' He grinned – and again she felt a lurch of fear and pain at the surgical work round his mouth. '"Roger Barrett has always had a hopeless crush on glamorous, wealthy Lila Fowler. The only attention Lila ever pays him, though, is to make fun of him in front of her friends. But why shouldn't she, he thinks. After all, he's clumsy and shy and works secretly as a janitor after school."'

'I'm surprised at Belinda.'

'"Elizabeth Wakefield is stunned when Nicholas Morrow asks her for a date. A newcomer to Sweet Valley, Nicholas is fabulously wealthy and extremely handsome –"'

'Yes, I get the picture. You read those to fill your head up, do you?'

'Good as anything else. "Has Elizabeth found a new love?" "Can Roger melt Lila's icy heart?"'

'I'm glad it amuses you.'

'Stell reckons Belinda's rotting her brain.'

'What do you think?'

'Me? It's words, that's all. Hey, you've got some incense. Mum uses this stuff.'

'Do you like the smell?' She gave up waiting for him to take his drink and put it on the coffee-table. 'We can have some if you like.'

'Aladdin's Dream. Mum's got Perfumed Garden. And Bam Bam Bhole. That's from India.'

Chatter, she thought, he's like a three-year-old just learned to speak. 'Shall we have some Lemon-grass? That's not too strong for morning.'

'Sure. Mum likes Frankincense best. Because of the name. There's Frankincense, Honeysuckle, Wistaria, Freesia, Jasmine . . .'

'You really do remember things, don't you?' She put a stick of incense in the holder and picked up the matches. The rattle of the box made her throw a look at him. She tried to hurry taking out the match.

'It was Mum's lighter Wayne used. Can I light it?' He came to her side and took the match. 'Fire doesn't scare me if that's what you think.' He lit the incense, watched the smoke rise, cut the plume in half with his finger. Sniffed deeply. 'Good, eh?'

'Do you remember smells the same as words?'

'Yes. Musk is what I like. And Patchouli.'

'Can you actually smell them, as you name them?'

'Never tried.' He closed his eyes a moment; opened them with a startled look. 'Yeah, I can.'

'Let's see, then. Magnolia.'

'I can get that.'

'Carnation.'

He blinked his eyes, nodded. 'Yes.'

'Frangipani.'

'Yes.'

'You really are a most remarkable boy. You actually smell them?'

'Kind of.' He withdrew. She guessed it was her word 'remarkable' that closed him up.

'Have your drink, Duncan. Before it loses its fizz. Ah, lovely incense. It would be nice to call up smells.'

'Onions,' he said. 'Fowl manure.'

She laughed. 'Duncan, I don't want to pry. But can I ask some questions? You can stop me when you want.'

'What sort of questions?'

'Easy ones. I won't tell anyone. That's a promise.'

He drank again, emptied half his glass. 'Fire away.' It was one of his father's expressions and made her smile. The uncertainty under his assurance reminded her of the care she must take.

'Well, you say when the accident happened it didn't hurt.'

'Didn't. I didn't feel a thing.'

'But there was shock –'

'Hypovolemic shock is what it's called. I had that. And capillary leak. I had everything.' He smiled at her. 'I read a book Mum had at home. That's how I know the words.'

'Ah, so you do use what you find?'

'Some of it. "When lay people first meet a person who is very disfigured, it is not uncommon for them to express the opinion that such people should not have been resuscitated."'

*

44

Norma does not know how to take this. She thinks she has grasped Duncan, then he eludes her. She thinks him childish – regressed in some things almost to a state of infancy – then finds him middle-aged and wise; hears him chatter, then finds him remote. She's certain of this and that going on in his head, but halted by the mystery of what goes on in some parallel or deeper or concentric place. She grasps him and is amused and sad; then cannot grasp and finds herself hollowed out with fright.

But Norma is not a person who gives up. She asks him how he feels about the way people react to his appearance, and he replies it does not bother him. She knows it's true. Asks him questions one would judge more safe – whether he intends going back to school? – and is surprised to find she has made him angry. Trying to find the reason, she goes on – with his ability to remember things there's really nothing he shouldn't be able to do scholastically. If school does not appeal to him, what about private lessons? It's a dreadful pity to waste such a gift – (gift of the fire, she thinks, appalled at herself).

They sit quiet a while, sipping their drinks. He says, 'I don't want to learn things. I'm not going back to school.'

'Let's leave that aside for a while.' Asks him, with great care, what he remembers about the accident. The actual seconds after it, she means.

There's nothing he remembers. He didn't see Wayne any more. He doesn't remember standing up, or getting outside, or Mandy throwing him in the pool. But he's evasive and she turns him back, placing a finger on his wrist. 'Did nothing, nothing happen in your mind?'

There was, he admits, a kind of flash. He watches her finger, which expands into a hand resting on his arm. He feels a firm softness, and a palm-shaped warmth and cold; cannot tell which comes from him and which from her.

And then he was flying, he begins; you know on television when you're kind of in a plane going close to the ground, and the ground is going back under you, and you go over hills and go up rivers and over plains, and everything's zipping underneath, and it goes on forever, valleys and hills and mountain ranges . . .

That's why he likes the eagle, she thinks; and understands the landscape is his brain and he has seen the length and breadth of it; and now he tries to fill it up.

'And what was there,' she says, 'at the end?'

He hesitates, then shakes his head. 'There wasn't any end. I guess I kind of blacked out when Mandy threw me in the pool.'

The length and breadth. All the places dark and unexplored, all the places locked up we can never use. Duncan has been there. She starts to take her hand from his arm, then puts it back and holds on to him.

'Duncan! Duncan!' The cry is like the pecking of a bird. She comes back with a righting of herself, is back at the place she started from – but has turned over, travelled impossibly. She shivers, lets him go, stands up in the room, goes to the window. Belinda strides on the clover slope.

'Belinda. In here. He's here with me.'

The girl looked at her, did not smile, but turned after a moment and yelled into the graveyard, 'Stell, he's in Mrs Sangster's place.'

Stella's voice came clearly, 'Bugger him.'

'Can you tell him we're waiting, Mrs Sangster?' Belinda said.

Animal heat seemed to radiate from the girl; probably her anger, Norma thought. All very honest and direct, and quite appealing; it made her smile. The other one, coming from the trees, was not so nice – had something of Tom Round's foxy wolfishness. 'How did he get in there?' she asked Belinda.

'I invited him,' Norma cried.

'I hope he hasn't been a wretched nuisance, Mrs Sangster.'

'Not a bit. Why should he? I met him in the cemetery and asked him for a glass of ginger ale. Why don't you join us? You must be hot after tennis.'

'I don't want to go in there,' Belinda whispered.

'Sound travels very clearly on the hillside, Belinda. Go round by the hedge, you'll find a gate.'

She turned back to Duncan, not knowing what to expect, and saw him at her bookshelves, reading along the titles. 'You don't mind them coming?'

'It's OK with me.'

She went to the kitchen and poured two glasses of ginger ale. 'Come in, girls.'

They left their rackets in the porch and came in smelling of sweat and rubber shoes and deodorant and exuding a hot sulkiness, on

Belinda's part, and social competence on Stella's.

'This is very kind of you, Mrs Sangster.'

'Who won?'

'I did. Belinda's getting better though. I think she'll beat me before long. Don't get worked up, Bel, it's only a game.'

'There should be a rule against lobbing,' Belinda said.

'It's a most effective shot.'

'Well I think it's cheating.'

'Bring your drinks in here,' Norma said. She went ahead of them into the sitting-room and saw Duncan lighting a stick of incense.

'Who told you you could do that, Duncan?' Stella said from the door.

'It's all right,' Norma said. 'What sort, Duncan?'

'Sandalwood.' He went back to the bookshelves.

'Sit down, girls. I hope you like incense. And ginger ale.'

'It's beautiful and cold,' Stella said. She sat down and crossed her legs and looked round the room. 'I think it's marvellous how you manage. Running a big school, with all that must entail, and having a house and garden and books and music' – she looked at the record player. 'You really must have a very busy life, Mrs Sangster. Very full.'

She's patronizing me, Norma thought, and was fascinated by the girl's performance. 'All that must entail' – she had brought it out beautifully, with only the smallest suggestion of carelessness. And 'Very full' – the tiniest bit of cool surprise. She's going to be a very formidable lady, and horribly unpleasant to know.

'Would you like me to put a record on?'

'Oh, I don't think we've got time for that, we're expected home. Did you really not find him any bother?'

'None at all. He's good company. We've had a very interesting chat.'

Duncan was still reading titles. Belinda had gone to his side and was reading them too. She offered her half-drunk glass of ginger ale without looking at him and he took it and sipped and kept it in his hand.

'I can pour you some more,' Norma said.

Neither made a reply.

'For heaven's sake answer when you're spoken to,' Stella said.

'They're all right, leave them. Have you heard from Mandy? How's she getting on?'

'Brilliantly of course, you know Mandy. I just hope she doesn't end up pushing pills. What she'd like to do is specialize in gynaecology and get it out of the hands of men.'

'She's got plenty of years before she needs to think of specializing. Is she having some fun?'

'Oh yes, of course. Having affairs, learning life.'

'I hope she doesn't overdo it.'

'That's the danger, I suppose. Life just blows up in your face.'

The reference was to Duncan, although Stella's eyes made no move. Norma revised her judgement – the girl was ignorant in many ways, and egotistical to an unbearable degree, yet was no fool, and was not the finished thing she strove to be. Like all the rest of them, nine hundred girls, was simply at a point on her way, had not 'ended up' – that hideous phrase – but could move in any one of a number of ways. Norma felt tender and generous towards her. She said lightly, 'Nothing's final. Not when you're young. Are you working hard, Stella? You take time off for tennis, I'm pleased to see.'

'I jog in the forest every morning,' Stella said.

'A billy-goat charged her,' Belinda said. 'She had to climb a tree and Mr Clearwater had to get her down.'

Stella was pink and angry; a quick girl in her feelings. Norma stifled her laugh. 'Was it one of his? How many goats has he got now?'

'He didn't get me down,' Stella said. 'He simply came and took the goat away. And I carried on running.'

'Good on you.'

'You nearly wet your pants,' Belinda said.

'You weren't there. You don't know.'

'A billy-goat can be pretty fierce,' Norma said. 'Had it broken out?'

'His fences are almost non-existent. In some places they're only bits of rusty wire-netting. If you're going to farm goats you should do it properly.'

'I don't think Lex is really into farming, it's a hobby. Anyway, you got out of it all right.'

'She'll dream about billy-goats,' Belinda said.

48

'He's got twenty-seven goats,' Duncan said. 'I've heard him talking to them.'

'Indeed,' Norma said. She was anxious to get off the subject of Lex Clearwater.

'What does he say? "Oh darling goats – "'

'No Belinda, not in front of me. How far do you jog, Stella? Does Josie jog?'

'She tried it once and nearly died. She thought she should be as good as me right from the start. Mum doesn't believe in intermediate stages.'

'Her exercise is sitting with her legs crossed meditating,' Belinda said.

'And what is yours, Belinda? Apart from tennis? I don't think you're in any of the school teams.'

'I don't go in for sport. Dad says it's overdone anyway.'

'In the school? *Mens sana in corpore sano*. Have you heard of that?'

'A healthy mind in a healthy body,' Stella said; and went pink for being obvious.

'It's all the stuff about winning I don't like,' Belinda said. 'And doing it for the honour and glory of the school.'

'Oh surely we don't say that.'

'Some of them do. Mrs Muir does.' She moved impatiently. 'I can smell my sweat, I need a swim.'

'Isn't it too cold?'

'Dad's rigged up a solar panel.'

'It takes the chill off,' Stella said. 'I think we should go, Mrs Sangster. It's been very nice.'

'It's been nice for me too. I don't see enough of girls outside school. Duncan, do you see anything you'd like to borrow?'

He turned from the books and shook his head. A bank of hair slid down and seemed to hiss on the slick skin above his ear – that melted ear without curl or lobe. Seeing his face suddenly was a shock. She smiled at him. 'Remember what I said, you can come whenever you like. And borrow anything. You girls as well.' Stella did not like being lumped in. Belinda, too, would not come again. No success with them, but Norma did not mean to let Duncan go. 'Here,' she pulled a book from the shelf, 'take this. It might help with some of those big words.'

His hand closed unwillingly on it. He had retreated. She would not let him. 'Stella, when you play tennis again you bring Duncan. And Duncan, you come here. I'll expect you.'

'Sure,' he said.

Belinda looked at the book. '*A Dictionary of Mathematics and Physics*?' she said, surprised.

'Meanings are important. Stella, bring him.'

'If you're sure he won't be a pest.'

'I'll ride my bike. I'll come by myself,' Duncan said.

'You fall off your bike.'

'Well, I'll walk.'

'We'll bring you, Dunc. So shut up, Stell,' Belinda said.

'It's settled then.' Norma felt herself relax as though a great danger had been passed. She smiled at Duncan, touched his arm. 'I've enjoyed talking to you. Tell Josie where you've been. Give her my love.'

'How about Dad?'

'Oh, leave him out.'

The girls were looking suspicious. She played the schoolteacher and shooed them out. They picked up their rackets in the porch and walked down the garden path with Duncan between them into the park.

'Goodbye,' Norma called. She went back to the sitting-room and watched them cross the clover slope to the graveyard; saw him like a prisoner between guards. She had seen a man marched into the bush in that way once. A documentary, on TV? Unnecessary person, taken off to be clubbed to death. The close-up showed his Adam's apple bouncing in his throat.

Oh no, Duncan, no, Norma cried. I'm not going to let that happen to you.

5

I'm inclined to get rid of the man I've called Clive Schwass; and Daphne, his wife. It's established that he owns a berry farm. Norma has pictured him out in his vines letting hailstones strike him on the face. I can't see much more than a sour expression. He's Norma's older brother, a man well-off in money and property but with a meanness in his nature that leads him to negative judgements on most things, including himself. He works hard, getting a sour pleasure from the monotony of his life. He thinks that Norma holds herself superior to him – and Norma, in fact, believes he has mental talents he's never used, or had them once, but it's too late now. His habit of denigration angers her. More than once she's snatched up her coat and bag and slammed out of his house; but knows that this behaviour satisfies him. Daphne is the one who patches things up.

Their children have grown up and gone. Francine is a secretary and Deborah a nurse. The boy, Mark, did not want to work with his father. He's in Australia driving an earth-moving machine. In the photograph he sent home last Christmas he stands only half the height of the giant wheel. Daphne worries about him getting killed or meeting a girl and marrying and not coming back to Saxton. Clive won't believe his story that he's saving lots of money. He's heard about the brothels in Australian work-towns and thinks his son will come home broke one day, with a disease.

Norma is fond of Mark. Don't stop at Australia, she writes, the whole world's there in front of you, keep on going. You shouldn't live too close to your father, she really means.

It would be easy to show Clive Schwass's coloration. But I don't need him yet and may not need him at all. He can wait on his berry farm.

Clive would be satisfied, in his way, with this offhand treatment.

There are parents too, that man and woman who farmed the flood-prone property in the valley. Age and illness and suburbia change configurations in these two. There's more open feeling in them

51

now, though no clear grasp of what is going on. Mrs Schwass, once so sharp and ungenerous, has turned into a happy old woman. She slides lightly over the difficulties of her life. After forty years of mud and milking and hosing-out there's nothing, not even ill-health, that can trouble her. She loves her warm rooms and thick-pile carpets and concrete paths. Mr Schwass, buttoned-up so long, now lets go. Mostly he's exactly where he is. His memories, when they come, are inside out and back to front.

They live in a townhouse. Expensive place in a cul-de-sac. There are nine white stucco units with red tile roofs, each set a little skewed from the next for privacy. Tom Round designed them. They suggest toy town only to those who don't understand space-saving architecture. Mr and Mrs Schwass are happy there. Their tiny back-yard is sunny and private. (Clive drives ten miles in to mow the lawn.) Mrs Schwass can walk down a right-of-way and sit under trees in a park. (Mr Schwass does not go out.) The kitchen is beautiful, with every device, and Norma would love to have it in her house. All the same she worries about her parents in the unit. Tom Round took advantage of the rising ground to give the owners a glimpse of the sea. Stairs lead half a storey up from the entrance hall to the living-room and kitchen and bedroom. Norma worries her parents will fall down. She wants to see them in more sensible place. But Mrs Schwass loves her view of the mudflats and the sea and passing yachts that slide along the edge of the soccer fields and will not move.

'The carpet's very soft, dear,' she says.

Norma called to see them after meeting Duncan Round. 'I can only stay a minute, Mum.' She was on her way to visit her orchardist friend. ('That I-surrender Eyetie' Mr Schwass calls him. His own name has never seemed foreign to him. 'No Dad, he's not Italian,' Norma says, but has given up explaining further than that.)

She had a good close look at both of them. There were whisker patches on her father's chin, so he, not the district nurse, had done the shaving. (Sometimes he gets fed up and stops half-way and goes about with a silver left cheek and jaw.) She kissed him and he said to his wife, 'Who's this pretty girl?' For a moment she thought he did not know her – always a shock – then saw he was recognizing people today and had paid her a compliment. It was a sign of

52

how well he felt that he wasn't in his dressing-gown and slippers but had dressed himself – slacks and shirt and cardigan and slip-on shoes. No socks. He always got impatient at the end. 'Stable door, Dad,' she said, but he was protesting about the change (which seemed only yesterday to him) from buttons to zips and made an angry push at her when she came too close. She wouldn't dream of trying to do up his fly, and saw no reason why it should be done, he never went out.

'What's the new district nurse like?'

Her parents answered together: 'A lovely girl', 'A stupid damned woman', which made Norma laugh.

'She holds me too damn tight. I've got bruises on my arm.'

'She had to hold you, Ken, because you tried to hit her.'

'I won't have a damned woman drying my bumhole.'

Norma went to the kitchen and put the kettle on. 'Has he been hitting you?' she asked her mother.

'Just a little punch now and then. It's nothing personal, dear. He gets so angry about things – chairs and tables and knives and forks, they won't do what he wants. He tore up last night's paper because he couldn't fold it properly. Never mind, there's never any nice news.'

'Where has he hit you?' She was worried her father would punch her on the chest.

'Nowhere that hurts.' But Norma saw her limping and guessed he had hit her legs with his walking-stick. He whacked her the way he'd whack a cow in the yard. There was no way to prevent it short of putting him in a home. Her father walked slowly and her mother was good at staying out of range – a quick mover in spite of her spindly legs and beetle hump. She saw her bruises as love trophies anyway. Norma knew the danger but could not work out the rights and wrongs of it.

She made tea and her mother put peanut brownies on a plate. Mrs Schwass made peanut brownies every morning. Creaming the butter and sugar, adding the flour and cocoa and peanuts; then putting neat dobs on the oven tray; and taking the hot cakes out, cooling them on a wire rack, stacking them neatly in a tin lined with greaseproof paper – she would not give this up for anything. Norma and Clive and the district nurses carried cakes away in paper bags. She left them out for the milkman and the postman and the paper-boy. Her husband did not eat them, nor did she, but she put out a plate with every cup of tea, and enjoyed looking at them, they made her feel she was in command of things. She made macaroni cheese as well but only on the days when meals-on-wheels didn't deliver. The meals-on-wheels lady got a bag of peanut brownies too. Norma ate the ones she took home, they were very tasty.

Today she carried away half a dozen for her friend. 'Mum, don't you let him bully you,' she said in the entrance hall.

'It's really all he can do for himself,' Mrs Schwass replied.

'Does the district nurse look at you too?'

'Oh yes, she's very thorough. Ken likes her or he wouldn't try to hit her. He likes pretty girls. I have to keep my eye on him.'

Norma could not say more than 'Good' to that. Then noticed there was no bulb in the hall light-socket.

'He forgot where the switch was to turn it off. So he got the kitchen stool and took the bulb out. He was careful' – seeing Norma look shocked ' – he used the tea-towel so he wouldn't burn his hand.'

'Good God, Mum – ' But it was no use, her mother would not be frightened by anything. And did it matter, Norma thought, if her father electrocuted himself or fell off the kitchen stool and broke his neck? Any time now the final thing could happen. She saw them innocent as two babies on a motorway. Death and danger rushed by everywhere but somehow they made it acceptable.

Norma put her cookies on the car seat and drove away to visit her 'Eyetie' friend.

South through Darwood, past the meat-works, round two sides of Schwass's berry farm. The road ran straight through pea fields, then followed the curving south shore of the inlet. She saw plover in the fields and black-backed gulls and herons on the mudflats. Tar-seal gave way to metal. She drove up a valley in low hills, leaving dust as fluffy as whipped egg-white behind her. John Toft's orchard lay at the head of the valley. Beyond it the road stopped at a padlocked gate and a clay forestry track went into pines. The forest was ready for milling and a consortium of Australian and New Zealand companies was buying the farms and orchards in the valley to build a timber mill and a chipboard plant. The residents were holding on – some only for a better price. Norma hoped that when John had to go he would buy a smaller place close to town.

His orchard was cut in two by the road. A creek ran through the lower half, where Red Delicious and Gala apples grew. John had planted a row of fig trees too but had never harvested a saleable crop. To a Norwegian, he said, the fig was as magical as snow and ice to a tropical islander. When he had grown a perfect fig he would be ready to surrender.

'You grow perfect mushrooms,' Norma replied. 'Give me mushrooms any day.' In autumn she picked buckets of them from the paddock beyond the fig row where John ran a score or so of sheep, and put those she could not use in the school staffroom for anyone to take. It was the most popular thing she did.

John did not like the taste of corruption in mushrooms.

Ready to surrender? Curious phrase. It troubled her. First, she did not like to think of anything beating him. Second, he was already beaten in some way and approached that event or place or time with a language of endings, light for other people, for her, but with another meaning for himself – kept in view a failure he had known. She could not imagine it, but supposed, on no evidence, it had to do with a woman. And could not imagine a cruelty or carelessness in him that might force self-banishment – for wasn't it a kind of banishment? Wasn't that what he hinted at? – 'From one tiny country to another, eh? From pole to pole, Norma, how I travel' – with a Nordic dying fall.

John Toft worried her, obsessed her. She felt very tender towards John – a feeling she would not classify except to consider what it was not. It was not maternal. Not sexual. She did not want to mother or sleep with John. She did not want to be his daughter either, although their ages fitted them for that. She wondered if they were simply achieving friendship. Would that account for her tenderness? It certainly wouldn't explain obsession. Wouldn't she, in *friendship*, simply accept, not engage in searching out his wound? For he had some wound – or perhaps some weighty thing inside that leaned him off true centre. She longed for simplicity with John; and sometimes seemed to achieve it, to be as whole and simple as – well, bird in the air; but then was nudged out of true herself. Nudged by what? What shift in him? Where did he move to with that step? And what was the need? Tell me, John.

55

She never spoke her questions aloud. How far they were from knowing each other, Norma would think as she drove home. But going there, up that metalled road, creek in the gully, apple trees – bare, in leaf, in blossom, in fruit – possessing the hill, she was confident of finding ease. She never felt freer from care or closer to joy. His house and sheds were on the upper side of the road, among the Gravensteins and Golden Delicious. As she urged her car up the little knoll into his yard she felt a painful lifting of her heart.

He came from one of the sheds, with lifted oily hand, Redskin salute. His Habsburg smile – that Habsburg mouth one came across in Scandinavians – marked his strangeness, put it before her once again. A smile that was misleading, for it had the figuration of bitterness yet was his free and open sign of welcome. He was a big old man with knobbly joints that looked arthritic and outsize hands, work-flattened finger pads, and feet in sandals he had cobbled himself; untanned leather as hard as wood – made, Norma complained, to torture feet. He had blue, faded eyes and silver lashes and wore half-glasses down on the knob of his nose and a blue towelling hat stained with grease pushed back on his head in a young man's way.

'More of the little brownies. What a baker she is.'

She left them on the car seat and climbed the hill with him to the back of the orchard; a walk that was ritual, giving her a view of his land and marking her acceptance in his place – so it seemed to her; but when she put it to him that way once he only smiled and said she had a heightened view of affairs, and drama and ceremony were not a necessary thing in life. She had shrugged and kept silent, but quarrelled with him in her head; and made the walk still, whatever the weather, alone or in his company, it did not matter which.

'How much did you lose in the storm?'

'I wish you had been here, Norma. It was the sort of thing you would have admired.' He smiled at her. 'It was very orderly but full of nature.'

She liked that very much and laughed aloud. The simplicities of his speech delighted her. He told her the storm had come up from the south, advancing like a wave, grey and black and heavy at the top and looking as if it might turn over and drown the valley. But its margin, he said, was drawn to the accuracy of a metre or two, and the world was divided in half – half in the sun, it sparkled, John said, and half in the cold and wet and dark. The hailstones cut his orchard in two. It was as clean as scything. He stood beside his house and one, two, three raindrops fell in the dust, and a handful of hail on his roof, and that was all. The storm followed the line of the creek. Here was sun, there was ice coming out of the sky like knives. Puffs of cold struck him on the face but the sun kept on shining, warming him. 'Two worlds, Norma. It was most symbolical.'

She ignored that. 'What about your Galas and Delicious?'

'All gone. Some will be for juicing, that is all.'

'You've still got your Coxes and Golden Delicious.'

'Everything that grows on the top side of the road. The Sturmers and the Gravensteins and the Granny Smiths. My neighbours say a miracle, I must thank God. I say an interesting phenomenon of nature.'

They went down to the house and drank tea and ate peanut brownies, talked and played some records, and John cooked a meal of meatballs in sauce and potatoes with anchovies, baked in a casserole. They ate and washed up and sat and talked again like a couple very used to each other, and when it was dark enough John carried his telescope into the yard – the refractor, not the big reflecting 'scope he used for searching deep into space – and for half an hour they looked at the nebula in Orion's sword, and the double star in the pointer to the Cross, and Mars and Saturn. The rings made her cry out and John said, 'Norma, you are good for me.' He laid his hand on the curve of her shoulder, she felt his flat abrasive finger pads, and did not know what sort of touch it was, it did not seem important to classify.

'I sometimes think it's forbidden to see. We look at our peril,' she said.

'That is just a game you play with feelings. Do not waste your time with games to play.'

He was not telling her she must not feel. He left his hand touching her.

Lars-Johan Toft. Forenames Swedish and surname Norwegian. It is not a good or likely mix, names or blood. There's no love lost. The fitting together defies convention and history. John has explained it to Norma, who, like most of us, had no idea.

'Norwegians do not like Swedes or Swedes Norwegians, they think we are the real turnip-heads. And nobody likes the Danes, and the Danes do not like anyone. It is a prickly time we have up there.' He told her the reasons: who had ruled whom, the tyranny of language over language – an old story, imperialism and nationalism and the winning of home rule. She was surprised to hear it had gone on in that old way; would have supposed reason to have had more influence, up in the cold.

'You say "we" when you say Norwegian but you're really half and half.'

'In my left brain I am Norwegian. The right brain is my Swedish side and would like to rule . . .'

'But you feel Norwegian, in your bones?'

He evaded her. 'Man of the north, marooned in the south.'

His father was an engineer from Bergen working on Swedish railway construction. He met a girl, one of the dark Swedes from Södra Lappland, and married her. 'Dark' does not refer to complexion. There is a melancholy in the north, a part of the nature of people there. Perhaps it comes from generations of living with long winters and the cold sun. They have a springtime gaiety too. John Toft remembers his mother's gaiety. It flashed out in her dark and then was gone. He cannot recall any time it lasted more than an hour or two. The lasting thing was her unlovingness. She was a beautiful woman but he remembers her with narrowed shoulders and her elbows clamped in at her sides. He has his bitter Habsburg smile from her.

'There is a kind of jolly Norwegian,' John went on. 'He likes to drink a lot and have a good time and make jokes.' That was his dad. John gets his big flat hands and knobbly nose from his dad.

When he was a small boy the family left Stockholm for Bergen. Stockholm is summer swimming in Lake Mälaren, baking on the glaciated rocks while steamers throb by to Drottningholm. And holidays, winter and summer, on an island in the skerries standing only a metre out of the sea; skating on the ice in the channel; reeling in big-jawed *gädda* hooked by his father, while evening yachts sail by to Saltsjöbaden.

'We had a little house there with two rooms and two beds and a *gädda* that could have swallowed your arm stuffed on the wall. Oil lamps, and a pump for water in the yard. Outside the door, I remember' – his face lights up – 'a wind-gauge with a woman pumping water, a Dalarna woman in a peasant skirt, and the harder the wind blew the harder she pumped, while her husband stood hands on hips and laughed.' And a sauna house and a smoke-box for smoking fish. 'We had to row to the big island for wood. Or drag it home by sled on the ice. Our own trees were ten birch trees and four pines. They have their roots in hollows in the rock, shallow like a saucer, and when they blow over you must stand them up again and tie them so they take a new hold. I wonder if my trees are growing still.'

Norma has been to Stockholm during a breathless European holiday. She spent her time – two days – in the Old Town and in Skansen and does not remember a lake with steamers, finds it hard to picture John's low island with ten trees. She was in Bergen too, one afternoon, catching a ferry to Newcastle, but remembers Bergen better, for it reminded her of Wellington. Oslo was like that too, a provincial city, outside time. Many things about Norway reminded her of New Zealand.

John agrees. But won't admit that is why he chose New Zealand to settle in. In Bergen he and his mother lived in a little house by the harbour while his father went away north to work – Tromsø, Narvik, Bodø, Mo. He made the language-shift, an easy thing, but was Swedish in behaviour from loyalty to his mother, who could not change, who became more closed-in and darkened in her thoughts. She had no friends and spoke to no one but her son for weeks on end. One day she wrote a note saying goodbye, said she loved him (the first time), and left while he was away at school – went back home to Sweden, to Storuman where she was born, and never left that town again. (It lies only a few miles over the border from Mo, where his father worked, but John thinks his parents never met again.)

'She closed the door quietly and left. That is how I see her. No bang crash like Nora Helmer, eh? She was not getting out of her cage but going back home to lock herself in. I think she must have been happy again, in her way. And I could be Norwegian after that. It was marvellous, to find it out.'

He boarded with an aunt, roamed the town and fishing quays

and market with his cousins – if there is a name that can make him draw his breath in sharp it is Bergen – and sailed in steamers on the road north to holiday with his father in Narvik, where the ore trains from Sweden's iron mountain at Kiruna dump their load. He hiked and skiied on the rock plateau and fished in the rivers with his father, and went north on steamer runs to Tromsø and Hammarfest, and west to Solvaer in the Lofotens. The whole arctic coast was his ground. He will maintain no place in the world is so cold and beautiful – ice and stone, the natural conjunction – and hears the glaciers grinding on bedrock. Hand on stone, warm hand, cold stone, that too was a happy pairing. He was natural to that landscape, he believed.

Then after Bergen, Oslo and the university, where he studied to become a marine biologist. It was either that or he would be an explorer. Nansen and Amundsen were his heroes, and Sven Hedin in warmer latitudes. 'You have heard of Sven Hedin? No. The British do not like him. He was pro-German in both wars, like many Swedes. The last of the great explorers though. I dreamed of deserts of sand and ice, interchangeably.' Until that day in April 1940 when an Oslo student could dream no more – the German fleet at the Drøbak Narrows, German troops in Carl Johans Gade, marching three abreast in iron hats.

Lars-Johan Toft did not know what to do. He was a simple boy and scatter-brained – 'Yes, Norma, these are words I use to pin myself out flat, so you can see. I am simple still, and scatter-brained.' Revulsion mounted in him as foreign soldiers marched into his street. He knew no politics but knew that some unnatural thing had happened, felt unclean; but made a sensible decision. He took his skis, his pack with clothes and food, and travelled through the forest of Nordmarka into the countryside to see if it was war or occupation. War he would join. Occupation he would escape from to Sweden, if he could, and see what fighting could be done from there.

He found a train going north. He found units of the Norwegian army, who would not take an untrained student. He made for Bergen, turned north when he found Germans there, and reached the coast at Namsos with the idea of picking up a boat and getting to Narvik to find his father. He was in time to see the British land and the Germans strike from the air, and was lucky to get out of the smashed town. Now he took his second choice and made the run for Sweden. Hunger and the mountains turned him back. He joined two young men like himself – 'country boys, they did not like my city ways' – looking for an army to fight in. Others, better organized, pointed them at the coast; and there they found a fishing boat that could pack them in, and out they went into a sea with waves like Telemark mountains, and came to Scotland in three days, sick and bruised and hungry.

'So, in that way, I found the war.'

He did not have what the British call 'a good war'. He tells it to Norma sketchily. She does not press him, taking his word for it that it was a boring time: long cold days, and waiting, always waiting, for action that never seemed to come. He was one of the first to join the Norwegian Independent Company, Company Linge, but, half-Swede, was not among those returned on missions to Norway. He missed the first Lofotens raid but was on the second in December 1941, and the joy of returning to his stone mountains and icy fiords overwhelmed him. Connections like the knitting of wounded flesh – Lars-Johan Toft and that cold land, the two were flesh and bone. We are here, he said, and will not go away. Everybody, British and Norwegian agreed. It was hoped to establish a naval base on the islands. But German bombers raided and the occupation lasted only one day. The islanders spat on the troops as they withdrew.

A small event in a small corner of the war. He marched with his fellow soldiers to the loading place and heard the cries of fear and rage and knew what would happen to these people when the Germans came back; kept his head down, hid his face, climbed the plank into the boat. What was taken from him? He would never come back to these islands where he had meant to spend the rest of his life. He took his step into exile and could no longer have a home.

That, John says, is to dress it up. I am a tiny thing in all that war, I do not count – and this he arrives at with no pity for himself; 'no groans and weeps'. Others had to kill. Others died.

'So you sailed back to Scotland? What happened then?'

'Oh, training to blow up and shoot guns straight.'

'Did you ever fight?'

'I chased along behind when the Germans ran away. Up in Finnmark. Nothing to tell.'

61

'Did you go back to Norway after the war?'

'For short times, now and then. I came here. Roundabout ways.'

He'll say no more than that.

Norma understands how painful that retreat from the Lofotens must have been but still thinks he's hiding a woman somewhere.

She drove home at close to midnight. The lights were out in her brother's house. In Darwood two cars were locked together and men and women argued in the street. She drove slowly over shattered glass and went into Saxton by the port, where police were bundling young men into a Black Maria. One of the girls in the shadows was Shelley Birtles – was that Shelley? – with a beer flagon under her arm. Let me take you home, you silly girl, Norma thought. She stopped along the road, but Shelley had vanished into the dark, and fighting broke out between two men. Norma drove on and drew up at her parents' house. She let herself in and looked at them. Her father shouted in his dreams – 'Give the buggers a taste of cold steel' – but her mother slept with a smile on her face. Norma closed the bedroom door softly. Her father charged night noises, broke vase and mirror and door panel with his stick. She slipped out of the house. 'Neighbourhood Support Area', a sign at the mouth of the cul-de-sac said; but no one had spotted her. She could get away with all the cash and jewellery in the street and not a question would be asked. Principal of Saxton College for Girls, what a cover for crime!

She drove past the school and cemetery and into her garage. The cat came from its bed of sacks to welcome her. 'Hallo, little devil,' she said, and picked it up and rubbed her cheek on it. 'Haven't I got some funny friends?'

A black skinny dog and a fat yellow one faced her on her walk to the door. 'So that's why you're nervous,' she said to the cat. She bent as though to pick up a stone and the dogs ran off into the park through the gate Belinda had left open. Norma closed it. She shone her torch to see if her vegetables were fouled – or, as Tom Round would have it, shat upon. Those Rounds are so damned careless, she thought, they just don't care about anyone else. Anyone not a Round was a square. She couldn't be cross with Belinda though. And with Duncan normal judgements shouldn't apply.

John said, 'Ah, this binomial habit of yours! I love these tales you tell, they are like science. Damaged girl and crippled woman, eh? And rudimentary man. And now you bring me burned boy.'

He said, 'Doesn't modern physics teach that matter and spirit are the same?'

'But he's got all this stuff stored in his brain and he doesn't know meanings. He doesn't even know what most words mean.'

'Perhaps he just transfers the world into his head. Out there becomes in here. Then perhaps he will be citizen. Denizen, eh?'

'No,' she said, 'it's not like that. I wish it were. What scares me, John – feeling seems to hurt him. It hurts him in his head.'

'Better then if he does not feel. It seems to me you should not interfere with this boy.'

She did not like his word. Always the accusation of interference when it was help she offered, first aid for the psyche, a band-aid for feelings that were bruised. She knew when to step back and insist that people help themselves. It was careless of John not to understand. She saw that he was in retreat again; that she had made Duncan Round alive. John withdrew from a person too dressed-up and too bare.

'I'm not going to let him get away,' she told the cat. 'If that's interfering, well too bad.'

She lay in bed watching the eastern sky – high thin cloud catching light from somewhere – and fist-shaped trees in the cemetery. She felt the weight and contour of her school, and the town and port further off. Night-time: everything was softened and eased, illusory connections became real. Shelley Birtles in the dark with brawling friends, and her brain muddled with alcohol. By now, almost certainly, it was sex on a mattress or a car seat. That, as edges softened in her brain, seemed less dreadful than enviable.

Once there had been a man who hailed her at each meeting: 'The lovely Norma, she who sleeps alone.' To which she had replied, 'I'm quite happy, thank you.' Until someone said, 'Only quite?' Quite, almost, relatively. She recognized them as her words; on which, in the end, her feelings snagged and a counter-motion set in, unravelling her involvements until there was nothing left. She was airy, insubstantial, with qualifying habits and complicating of easy things. Yet she was contented. She did not find it hard to sleep alone; but missed that focused tenderness and close demand and hungry interest she had known – how many times? Counted on her fingers, one, two, three, four, five; and pictured them. Men as various as the solar planets – yet, like them, cooked up in the same batch.

Norma snickered softly. She enjoyed getting them, her homunculi. She slept with her men under her pillow, laid out neatly in a row . . .

But someone not of that band came looming at her window. She sprang out of sleep with a cry. And listened to her house creak, listened to the beating of her heart. A wind had come up, making curtains stir and trees moan and lifting clouds across the sky. She coughed to signal she was back in her normal state. Night fears troubled her now and then but she put them off in this way: moved noisily in her bed, flicked on the bedside lamp to see the time. Burglars, rapists, would have to smash windows to get in. As for ghosts, she had several times walked among the headstones at night, sat on graves enjoying a night breeze, to demonstrate she had a rational mind; or, at least, held that there was there and here here. The dead made no intrusion in our lives, none of the grave-lifting sort at least. That looming at the window was black cloud; skitter of bony feet a squall of rain on her iron roof.

She lay awake thinking of John Toft's storm – the march of icy rain down the valley, the division of his world into light and dark. Things often made themselves neat for John, but for that very reason were unnatural. Gulfs lay hidden in what he saw; huge deeps beneath a surface; monstrous distances to a source. She had a sudden frightening sense of him as a graveyard creature, and heard herself whisper, 'Don't let him get me.' But later in the night she dreamed of standing by his side in his orchard with one hand locked in his and her feet in leather sandals he had made.

Her other arm was holding tight on the burning shoulders of Duncan Round.

6

Lex Clearwater gave up farming goats when his wife left him. After that he kept them as his friends.

He sits in a bracken nest on the hill above his house and watches golfers on the course half a mile away. Sunlight flashes off their steel clubs. Years ago he played that game but now he has little sense of what they are up to. Many things have receded in this way, the life of others takes place beyond his notice even when he passes close to it, and when circumstances force him to look he often fails to understand what he sees.

He has a bird's-eye view of his house; gutters, downpipes, back-step, sills, porch-railing. Once he would have laid on adjectives but now sees brown of rust and warp of wood and green of mould and is not provoked into description. His ute stands on the lawn, surrounded by patches of grass killed by oil. Cars run on the road, out of sight, coming down from the Baptist camp. The valley narrows in the east and turns into a gorge. Hills planted with pines reach up to the sky. Down valley, past the golf course, a window in the Round house flashes as a woman opens it. The river bisects the course and golfers pull their trundlers over the bridge where child-ren have built a rock dam and made a pool fifty metres long. Hikers turn up a gully, heading for the saddle that will bring them to the walkway and the sea. And here on his hill Lex Clearwater warms his face in the sun and is contented. A doe looks into his bracken nest. 'Gidday,' he says and puts out his hand to touch her nose. She backs off and turns away. 'Suit yourself.' Whatever the goats do is all right with him.

In mid-afternoon he goes down to the house and eats some bread and Marmite and makes himself a cup of instant coffee. He turns on the radio and hears a voice say, 'Last week's Heylen poll must have been a shock to them', and turns it off. He has forgotten Heylen polls and governments; and forgets electricity bills and rates demands and vehicle licensing until officials knock on his door.

Forgets to buy food until he finds the refrigerator empty, and has not bought new trousers and shirts for several years. People are worried about Lex. His parents, who live in Auckland, are worried. He does not write to them any more and his ex-wife tells them Lex has gone bananas. Norma Sangster is worried, and the school board wants to know if he's competent to teach young girls now he's not married any more. Competent is a word that's usefully vague. Soon they'll want to be more precise. But they need not worry. Lex is giving notice. Sandra Duff is the only one who knows. Sandra is worried too, she's frightened for him – wants to pull him back from the place he's in and set him on a safer path. She does not love him – won't love any man – but is fond of him and visits him for friendship and for sex now and then. She sees the goats as a symptom of something in his mind gone badly wrong. They're entertaining creatures but she'd like to bring a gun and shoot them all. 'Then maybe Lex can face himself and see what he wants to do.'

Sandra is way off the mark.

She arrives late on Sunday afternoon and finds him in the lean-to off the shed making yokes from plastic water-pipe. He snips off lengths and wires them into triangles. They won't last as long as wooden ones but don't rub the skin raw on the goats' necks. He would like to do without yokes altogether but that would mean doing without fences and he's had a warning from Forestry that animals in the forest will be shot. I'll shoot anyone who shoots my goats, Lex tells himself. But patches the holes in his boundary fence and puts in timber stoppers where the goats burrow under.

Sandra parks her car beside the ute and crosses the lawn to the shed, carrying a cask of dry white wine and a smoked chicken. She'll get nothing eatable or drinkable from Lex. In her bag, slung over her shoulder, are two letters from his box at the valley mouth and thirty English folders she's marked for him. She helps him out of friendship, not because she goes to bed with him. Bed is lots of fun and the feelings nicely uncomplicated. There's easy agreement in bed (or on the lawn, where they sometimes spread a blanket although she feels under the eye of goats), and nothing of wife or little woman in Sandra's sexual behaviour. She hopes that when Lex is finished with teaching he'll sell his land – ten hectares of steep hillside in bracken and scrub, eroding where the goats make shelters and tracks – and get a job he can handle and come back into discourse with human beings. She'll find him pretty boring then, she knows – he's thick already – but better boring than lunatic, better for him. Their sex thing will peter out, but *c'est la vie*, one has to keep on moving or the brain starts to die. So Sandra tries to do her best for Lex.

He turns and slips a yoke over her head. 'Suits you,' he grins.

Sandra puts down the wine and chicken and takes the yoke off and flings it into the long grass by the drive. 'Bugger you, Lex, I'm not one of your herd.'

'Joke,' he says, and retrieves the yoke. 'What have you got? Château Cardboard, eh? And a chicken? Feeding me up.'

'I just want a bit more than bread and Marmite. And Nescafé with bloody tadpoles in it.'

Lex grins again, though Sandra reminds him of his wife. Sometimes he's not sure which one is speaking.

'Want to come and help me put them on?' He threads the yokes on his arm.

'No, I don't.'

She watches him climb the fence and go sure-footed up the sliding shale above the house. The goats browse at the top of the hill, underneath a beetling row of pines. She looks at the trees and curls her lip. Sandra is an enemy of pines and she scowls harder as she looks up and down the valley and sees that foreign tree ranked on the hills. The goats are foreign too, land-killers too, but she has to admit they look at home. Their white and black and tan backs move in the bracken. And Lex is at home, he fits in. She hasn't seen it so clearly before and she grows confused and feels she does not know him at all. She goes into the house, finds a glass, pours wine, and puts the cask and chicken in the fridge – where there's nothing except a bottle of milk and a slice of luncheon sausage curling on a plate. The message from Lex's wife, written with felt-tipped pen on the door: 'Close the fridge door please. *Please!*' has its usual effect of making her cross. No woman should have to plead like that. The one on the lavatory cistern: 'Lift the seat before you pee!' pleases her more. It has a tone she approves of. But she knows it's invisible to Lex. Invisible wife, invisible message.

She takes her glass of wine outside and sits in the sun, watching him catch goats and strip the old yokes off and put new ones on. He pats and strokes them, sits in the bracken with one like a friend, holds another, picking something off, and Sandra guesses that he's catching lice. 'Jesus,' she says, and goes inside and refills her glass. People say his nanny-goats fill in for his wife and she wonders for a moment if it's true. (It isn't true, it hasn't crossed his mind and never will, but we shouldn't blame Sandra for thinking it. There's a relationship he has with goats.)

He comes leaping down the hill, skidding in the shale, raising dust. The bottom fence leans as he runs into it and he lies on it a moment before struggling off and pulling it upright. Sandra, hot with sun and flushed with wine, wants him *now*. But when he touches her she recoils. 'God, you stink. Go and have a shower.' He smells of sweat and goats. Goats is too much.

'Sure,' he says, and turns away, stripping off his singlet. 'Inside or out here?'

'Inside.' There are goat eyes watching from the bracken. She puts a clean sheet on his bed. The sheets only get changed when Sandra visits. He comes in with wet hair, smelling of soap – Sunlight, but a better smell than goat – and stops in the middle of the room because he knows she likes to look at him. Lex is a man with a big square chest and heavy shoulders and muscular arms. He narrows at the hips and has what Sandra calls a mingy bum but his legs are in proportion with chest and shoulders and the 'big beast' aspect of him excites her every time. She makes him stand up hard by looking at him, then they fuck on the wooden bed, whose head-board leans away from the wall more each weekend and threatens to close on them like the cover of a book. Fuck is a word Sandra insists on, she's contemptuous of make love and of slang and scientific terms. Fuck and cunt and cock are honest and exact, they neither dress up nor debase. (Lex finds this old-fashioned. He thinks of Sandra as a sixties girl, and rather sad.) They fuck three times, into the evening. His virility delights her and she's not too disappointed that he does very little with hands or mouth. With her hands and mouth she touches and caresses him all over, has her usual Sunday obsession with Lex, but is not clinging when it's over. Other women can't have him but that's a matter of hygiene more than possessiveness.

She showers in his grotty bathroom – mould on the ceiling, damp balls of dust by the skirting-boards – and cuts the chicken up and they sit eating and drinking at the kitchen table. Sandra takes out the English folders and explains her marking. 'That's a dumb essay subject. "A Moving Experience". Only three of them wrote about moving house.'

'Do you want me to look at any?'

'You're a lazy bugger, Lex. You should look at the lot.'

'Choose a couple, eh. Any good ones?'

'From that bunch of meatheads? Hold on, what do you think of this?' She takes a sheet of paper from a folder and reads in her sharp-edged voice:

'A Moving Experience. Me and Mum and Dad and my sister went to Aussie last year to see my aunty. One day we went to the Melbourne zoo. We were walking along for a while and then we came to the gorilla cage. A big gorilla was sitting up the back. He was so big I sort of couldn't breathe watching him. He sat and looked at us and we looked at him. He didn't blink his eyes and his eyes were so little. He looked as if he hated us. There was a kind of concrete wall down the side of his cage. A wooden door was stuck in it and then there was a knocking at the door like someone was trying to get in. He came down and put his head by the door and listened. Then he bent down and put his mouth at the bottom of the door and kind of sniffed and stuck his finger under. We went along a bit and looked in the next cage and there was the female – "f-e-e" – gorilla. She was bending down at the bottom of the door and she had her finger stuck in too touching his. We watched for a long time. Tears were running down Dad's face and me and my sister were crying too, it was so sad. That is my moving experience.'

Sandra looks at Lex. 'Hard to imagine with that one, eh?'

'Hayley Birtles?'

'It's the dumb ones who surprise you.' Sandra turns away. She does not want Lex to see her sympathy with the girl. She feels a hotness in her eyes and is afraid she will cry. She has a sense of something lost from her life and cannot find what it is.

Lex too is disturbed. Hayley Birtles is not a person, she's part of that sisterhood he calls the Blobs. He faces them four times a week and then forgets them and he does not like her coming forward to present herself. He shivers at her singleness. Once – when he was a schoolteacher long ago – he had loved it, the crashing of a new person into the foreground would keep him satisfied all year; keep him fizzing with her, and working to keep her single in ways so cunning and delicate he felt circuits open and new banks of neurons light up in his brain. They surprised themselves, these girls, with what they found, and were so ready to run, get out of there, where it was set up on display, back to their gum-chewing foul-mouthed sisterhood. He knew the relief of that retreat from the naked place they found themselves in, and worked hard to hold them; yet they got away, were so elusive; and fierce, rough, determined in escaping. He lost more than he kept; and now that he has given up being a teacher Lex does not want to try again.

'What did you give her?'

'Six out of ten. The grammar's not bad but it's full of spelling mistakes.'

'Give her seven.' The extra mark absolves him. He fills his glass at the winecask and wonders if Sandra will come back to bed before she goes. Knowing there's no obstacle, he puts it off a while, and finds himself thinking of the gorilla; sees black unblinking eyes fixed on him, and sees the huge beast pad four-footed down to the door in the wall and listen there. He makes a grunt of sympathy – sees Hayley Birtles's face wet with tears. 'Good girl,' he whispers, and stands by her side watching the gorilla in the cage.

Lex Clearwater was a suburban boy but asphalt streets and close-packed houses made little part of his growing up. Auckland was a ferry ride away. The beach was at his back door and he was by turns paddler of a canoe, P-class yachtie, surfboard rider, and crewman on an eighteen footer in world championship races. He hung out on a trapeze with the sharp waves grazing his back and watched the Sydney fliers up ahead. Learned to be not good enough – no hard lesson, it suited his abstracting, evaluating mind. Already, at nineteen, he was able to put things in an order of importance and not grieve over losses that seemed to knock great holes in other people.

For a while he thought his mind was very sharp, but came to see, at the university, that he lacked powers of analysis and argument. There were places where he simply could not get his mind to go, ideas receded from him down paths that remained dark and words

70

would not overlap their objects with the exactness he desired. The universe is a single atom and every atom is a universe – he loved to consider that sort of thing, but excitement never grew into understanding or simple thought into a chain. He gave up intellectual ambition and kept the disappointment from souring him by finding value in openness to experience, in feelings that broadened and enlightened. He thought for a while that he might lead and people follow and was not impatient to discover where. But this ambition broke on the otherness of his friends. They were, he discovered, impenetrable, and he came to see that his desire to love might fling him in an opposite direction, into hatred and contempt. He overreached himself and might suffer damage; might divorce himself from usefulness. He was a modest young man; but all the same was soured by coming to his limits a second time.

Teaching gave him boundaries and a discipline. He became narrow and exact, but seemed at times to glimpse a large adventurous self by finding forty pairs of eyes focused on him. It shocked him then to find he was not liked. 'Bilgewater', spoken with contempt, struck him like a blow in the face. He had always been sure of being popular. He shifted schools, working his way south, worked at finding a self he could be happy with; and managed some steps on that way by being noisy, being rough and rude – drinking too much, saying what he thought (even when he had not thought at all), and bending rules to suit himself. He won some popularity with his pupils and did not mind his nickname any more. Disapproval from parents and fellow teachers were winnings too.

Marriage seemed to settle him down. Rosalind was her name. She worked at the cosmetics counter in a department store, and was flawless, beautifully smooth, fantastically coloured; and patient and good-natured as well. 'She's apples,' Ros would say, meaning everything was all right (even when she had to change direction to make it so).

To please Lex, Ros became a tramper. They spent part of their honeymoon walking the Routeburn Track. They pitched their tent by the river on the flats and in that dark square metre were naked and ecstatic and warm and dreamless all through the night. Lex left Ros sleeping – unmade up she was so cold and pale – and crept out in the dawn to wash in the river. The icy water found out all his bones. He stood thigh-deep and soaped himself, then went in deeper, belly, chest and head, in a shocking plunge. Pain thinned him to a shiver, reduced his brain to a cold, smooth stone, and he had never been so complete in himself. Shrunken, wrapped in his towel, he squatted on the pebbles under the bank and looked at the cumulus of bush all around, the falls slanting down in leaps and runs, the grassy plain in the north branch, ending in a dead moraine, and Mt Somnus white and bare at the head of the valley. A mosquito hum of pleasure and arrival came from his throat. Ros came creeping down in his shirt and he washed her, quick and noisy, then rubbed her candy-pink with his rough towel, and they ran back to their tent to be warm. Happy time. Why, later on, should he remember Somnus rather than her, and hold the image of mountain rather than of naked girl in the river – and think of words like 'still', 'remote', 'absolutely simple' instead of others he might have found to bring back memories of love and sex?

Lex was a man who had started in half a dozen ways but not found it in his power to follow one. By the time Rosalind came along he had shed too much of himself to make a husband, he was very small and thin, and stillness, remoteness, simplicity beckoned him. None of this was clear at the time. For several years his life took on an ordinary appearance.

The Clearwaters came to Saxton, where Lex taught at the boys' school for a while, then shifted to the girls', arriving at the same time as Norma Sangster. They lived in town and Ros kept on working. She was nine years younger than Lex and there was no hurry to have babies. They sailed a small boat and went tramping and had friends who were mostly hers. Lex enjoyed saying outrageous things, attacking religion, the royal family, the National party, the Labour party – anything the people he found himself with believed in. He wasn't very good in argument but had a talent for extravagant statement and came to be looked on as a character. Ros learned to talk a little bit and be less obliging.

One day they went walking in the hills behind the town. Their destination was an old copper mine but after only half an hour they heard a sound that Ros took for a child crying. They stood and listened.

'It's some sort of bird,' Lex said. He walked back down the track and two steps down a bank and pushed a hole in the wall of scrub. He found an eye on him; was penetrated, shot through by it. He fell back half a step and put down his hand to keep his balance.

'What is it?' Ros said at his shoulder.

'A goat. Hold on.' He slid into the hollow and looked more closely. The animal jerked its legs frantically. 'Someone's tied the poor little bugger up. There's twine round his legs.'

'Isn't that cruel. Bring it up here, Lex.'

He made a sling of his arms and carried the goat on to the track. Its legs were tied in pairs, left with left and right with right.

'It would have died there,' Ros cried.

'They're probably coming back for it. What'll we do?'

'Untie it first.'

They unpicked the knots and freed the goat and Ros sat by the track holding it on her breast. 'It's just a baby. It's hardly weaned. Feel its heart.'

He put his hand on the white patch on the goat's shoulder and felt its heart whacking under its ribs; then stood off and watched it and felt his own heart beating hard. It was not the animal's fear or babiness that moved him but its yellow hard unblinking eye and coffin-shaped pupil, black as soot.

'What are we going to do with you?' Ros crooned.

'There's no wild goats up here. I reckon it's a tame one someone's pinched.' He pulled some leaves from a bush and offered them but the goat would not eat. 'It'll pee on you in a minute.'

'Can we take it home, Lex?'

'Put it down and see what it does.'

The goat was kicking with its hind legs. Ros put it on the track and it went to the corner in a dozen bounds and was gone.

'Why couldn't we have kept it?'

Lex ran to the corner. The goat was standing on the track twenty yards ahead. It set off when it saw him, veering from one hedge of scrub to the other.

'It's tame all right. It doesn't want to go into the bush.'

'It'll starve out here.'

'No it won't, there's plenty to eat. But if I can catch it you can have it.'

They followed the goat up into the hills, out of scrub into beech forest. Sometimes it got so far ahead they would not see it for several bends of the track, but then its black coat with the patch of white shone in sunlight sliding through the canopy, and Lex said,

'We'll get him. He's bound to tire.' Ros tried bleating to lure it but the goat kept on trotting and pausing on the track. At last a tramper coming down forced it into the bush. They saw it scampering down to a gully where a sound of running water could be heard.

'Now we've lost him.'

'No fear we haven't. You follow him down. Try and keep him in sight. I'll circle back from up ahead.'

Then for several hours they hunted the goat. It went ahead, always just in sight, as though it meant to lead them to a goal. Now and then it bleated in fright. 'Cry you little bugger, you're not getting away.'

'Lex, it's terrified. Let it go.'

'No fear.' His knees were bleeding from a fall on stones. A twig had jabbed the corner of his mouth and torn it open. He felt no elation in the chase but felt a cord that tied him to the goat and was only frightened it would break. 'You don't need to come, you wait here.' He left Ros and ran up the creek. The goat was too exhausted to climb. He trapped it at last by a waterfall; lunged at it and caught its hind leg, and lay half submerged in a pool, dragging it down, feeling it kick. He stood up waist deep; gathered it close, held it hard, until it stopped fighting. 'It's all right. I've got you. We're mates now, OK?'

That is how Lex Clearwater found goats. He took the animal – a female – home and tethered it in the backyard, where Ros treated it as a pet. Lex seemed to take little notice of it. He walked by and said, 'Howdy, pal,' and now and then fed it a handful of grass. No one knew he looked in its eyes and tried to know its perpetual now, which he saw as a kind of life in life, and death from everything outside the range of its senses. He knew that humans could not have that and stay human, and did not want it for himself except in flashes; was scared of it; and tried to like the goat (named Debbie by Ros) instead of know it; and ended up entranced by its mystery, obsessed with it. He spent his time openly with it then, and would not call it Debbie but mate or pal. (None of his goats has a name.) Ros said, 'He's gone bonkers over that goat.' She was pregnant and impatient with him now.

Against her will he bought a piece of land up the valley. He fenced it with hurricane wire and bought half a dozen feral goats.

The house appalled Ros. He spent some money doing it up but she warned him, 'I won't live here.'

'Come on love, there's money in goats. In a couple of years I'll knock it down and build a mansion for you.' He tried to amuse her with goat myth and goat lore. 'There's a goat in Valhalla that's got pure mead running from its udders. If I can breed a few like that one, eh?' When he nursed a sick goat in the house he told her that in medieval times people believed a billy-goat's breath would fill the house and keep plague germs out. Ros slammed the bedroom door and turned the key.

When the baby was two years old she left him. Ros was a grown-up person now, her softness and her silliness were gone and her bitterness had pauses in which she saw she must get herself and her baby away or not survive. One windy spring day the child was toddling round the edge of the lawn. The goat that had been Debbie was tethered on her rope. She did not like running with the herd and Lex gave in to her and kept her by the house. A gust of wind flipped a cardboard box across the lawn and the goat was spooked. She ran in a half-circle at the stretch of her rope, which caught the child Andrew on his chest and dragged him screaming through a patch of gorse. It was enough for Ros. She calmed and cuddled the child through the night, and packed her things and left in a taxi the next day. She went north to live and brings her child up in Auckland now – has a good job, lives without a permanent man, says she's all right thank you, getting by; doesn't say 'She's apples' any more. The divorce was fairly quick. Now and then she sends Lex a letter meant to hurt him, with photos of Andrew by himself. She sends him nasty clippings about goats. (One arrives with Sandra today. Lex does not pick his mail up any more.)

Lex gave up the idea of making money from goats. He had milked the does now and then but not sold the milk; had made a bit of cheese and given it away to people who mostly threw it out. After Ros left him he stopped pretending and let the goats run where they wanted inside the fence and breed how they would. He gave up drenching and treating for lice and the death-rate in the herd was high; but Lex looked on that as natural, he grieved and did not worry. He gave up reading books on goat husbandry, turned away from the word goat on any page. There was no understanding goats, or any animals, in that way. The goat as

75

production unit, the goat as symbol of this and that – he turned away. 'Even when we're just looking we colonize animals,' he said to a class. 'We can't see them as themselves, as goats, or fish, or birds, but have to give them meanings useful to us. Even the Maoris did it. Look at, say, the saddleback. Those brown feathers on his back, that's not a natural mark, oh no, that's scorch marks from the god Maui after his battle with the sun. Why can't we leave animals alone?'

'I don't know what you're on about, sir,' a girl complained.

No one knew what Lex was on about. He was not exactly sure himself and he stopped explaining to other people. He drew away from people and spent all his free time with his goats. He felt that somewhere in him was a goat consciousness and he must strip away layers of then and there and why and how and live with goats in their perpetual now and look out from that pupil and that eye. At times he realized he wasn't any longer right in the head; agreed with Ros that he was bananas, and with Sandra he was round the twist. It did not worry him. Few things worried Lex any more. He wanted just to go where he was going and had a longing for that unknown place.

Before Lex can take her back to bed Sandra remembers his mail. There's a rates bill and a letter and she flips them across the table. Lex pushes them aside. He knows Ros's handwriting and doesn't open her letters any more.

'Who's it from?'

'Only Ros.'

'Only? That was your wife.' Sandra is pleased and angry in equal parts. 'Aren't you going to see what she says?'

Lex shrugs. The letter contains something meant to hurt him, he knows that; but he doesn't stop Sandra from tearing it open. She unfolds a page from a newspaper. Lex looks away.

'Ha,' Sandra says after a moment. '"Those land-army tarts who handle my parts." How gross.'

He has to look. The photograph fills a quarter of the page: a man holds a doe up and open by its hind legs while a woman in overalls inserts a funnel. '. . . in Heather's right hand is the duck-billed speculum which has a light attached. She holds the pistolette containing semen in her left hand.'

76

'Enough to put you off sex,' Sandra says. 'Hey, come on, it's only science, the economy would collapse without frozen semen.'

But Lex heaves the table back and lurches outside. He jumps off the porch and runs bent over into the dark. She follows him and hears him being sick behind her car.

'Lex. You're a funny bugger, Lex.' She tries to put her arm round his shoulder but he knocks her away, sends her reeling, and runs between the shed and the house. Sandra hears the fence squeal as he climbs. She hears the crunch and slide of shale as he goes up the hill, and gets her torch from the car and tries to find him. But Lex has gone too far for the beam, and she calls out, 'Lex, are you all right?'

He reaches the bracken and takes hold. It's magical: at the prickly touch his rage subsides. He hears goats moving in the brittle growth and sees one dimly, greyish white.

'Well stuff you, Lex,' Sandra yells. Her torch beam slides weakly over the hill and then goes out. He sees her walk into the house and come back with her bag and drive down to the road. The glow of her car-lights moves under the hill. Soon she's in sight again by the golf course. A stretch of river gleams as she passes and part of a hillside lights up.

Lex groans. He feels he's letting out his life and feels a hollow where it used to be. Nothing comes to fill it and he falls into the bracken as though knocked flat by a swinging door. There are worlds, he thinks, and I'm in one and not the other. Where Ros and Sandra live, and everyone else. He can step back. He knows he can, though it will mean leaning against a force. And there he'll lose his stillness, and zap about like one of those mad balls in a slot machine, with bells ringing, lights flashing, springs propelling him. He wants no motion. He wants a cold stone-stillness. He wants no comprehension of his own subtleties; but hard, he wants, cold, he wants, complete, a self that's co-extensive with what his senses find. He wants to be his own single point, always now.

Lex burrows in the bracken, breasts it, swims it. He hears goats running off but knows they'll come back. He finds a shelter high on the hill where does have scraped a hollow under a bank for their kidding and he squats there smelling them and feeling their warmth in the ground. He's aware, after a time he cannot measure, of something moving in the dark and holds out his hand until the arm aches; until, at last, he feels a touch on his fingertips. He sees a goat marked on the sky and sees the gleam of horns and yellow eyes.

The goat comes into the shelter and lies down. Soon another comes and settles on his other side. He puts his hands on their silky flanks and rests his back against the bank and stays with them far into the night.

7

There's no resting place in the school year. Norma knows that each day will brim over with work, misfortune, happy accident.

She writes a letter to a publisher asking her to be guest speaker at the prize-giving. A judge and an athlete (both women) have turned her down. If the publisher says no, she has only an actress to fall back on and actresses are likely to say not only unpredictable but outrageous things. She'd like to have the actress but will be relieved if the publisher accepts.

'. . . with your vast experience, both here and overseas, in a profession acknowledged to be among the most fascinating . . .' Old ghosts and bags of wind, she thinks, gourds of the Judas tree – not knowing where the words are from any longer. They come back every year when she writes this letter; and trouble her sometimes as she stands on the stage and looks at the garden of faces . . . Norma gives a shiver. She puts the words aside. The publisher has a reputation for outspokenness, perhaps she'll be as outrageous as the actress. As long as she makes the girls laugh. Norma is tempted to write, 'Please tell some jokes.' She walks about the school at times longing to hear jokes. One of the good things about Sandra Duff is that she makes her girls laugh. And fascinates them in some way. There are times when Norma goes into Sandra's room and hears the hiss and hum of a mental life. Other teachers simply get laughed at. Lex Clearwater, David Dobson, Helen Streeter, Phyllis Muir.

Norma buzzes for her secretary and gives her the letter to type. 'Oh Jane, I think Miss Duff has a free period. If she's in the staffroom would you tell her I'd like to see her. No, on second thoughts I'll go myself.' She needs to get out into her school. It stretches, she can feel it, sprawled on the hill; limbs that are her own limbs, corridors her knowledge and her will, and love and pity – love and pity? Yes! – flow along. Single-voiced, nine-hundred-voiced . . . But she decides to stop that line of thought. Shakes herself, rubber-steps along. The only way to function is through practicalities. She looks into the staffroom and sees Sandra reading a magazine at a window table. 'The *Woman's Weekly*. That's not like you, Sandra.'

'There's an article on Tom Round. What a wanker.'

'Tom's very good at self promotion. Mind if I sit down?'

'Help yourself.' Sandra pushes out a chair, tinkling her Indian bells. Norma is aware Sandra does not like her, so she makes herself bright and simple and direct.

'I've had another letter from Mr Stanley.'

'Yeah?' Sandra's face wears an anticipatory grin – a trifle cruel.

'A poem called . . .' She looks although she knows, '"Electric Love". That's in a bulletin, isn't it?'

'Used to be. I copied it out. I've been using it with third forms for years. What's he say?'

'You'd better see.' She gives Sandra the letter. 'I don't take it seriously, by the way.'

Sandra reads, grinning, snapping her teeth. 'What a loony.'

'A loony with six daughters going through the school one by one.'

'"It is very plain that the words 'filament of being' refer to a certain organ of the body, and so to claim that love lights up that filament . . ." He's a bloody nutter.'

Norma wishes Sandra would not swear. 'But he has a point, don't you think? Poetry's supposed to be suggestive.'

'Yeah, I guess. Where'd he get a copy?'

'Oh, he does his homework, our Mr Stanley.' She takes the letter. 'I'll have to write to him. Is there anything you'd like me to say?'

'Tell him to jump off a cliff.'

'Something a bit more constructive than that.'

'I'm not going to stop using that poem if that's what you think.'

'I don't want you to, Sandra. As far as I can see it's a very good poem for girls of that age. It's intelligent and witty and – sentimental.' She blushes lightly at Sandra's contempt. 'But it doesn't hurt to know how other people feel about it.'

'Wanker Stanley doesn't get a vote.'

'I'm afraid he does. This time though, he's in a minority. I'm only telling you, Sandra, so you'll know what's going on if you hear about it. He's sent copies of this letter to the board.'

'Another bunch of Soapy Sams.'

Norma kept her temper. 'They're fairly reasonable people. Well, I've taken enough of your time. I'll let you get back to your Tom Round.'

'What you should do,' Sandra said, 'is back me up. Write to him and tell him we're educating people here, not locking them in little rooms and trying to pretend there's nothing outside. These girls have got bodies, they're not made of bloody scented soap. There's hormones rushing round in there. They menstruate. And they've got ideas in their heads, I mean *ideas*. They're ready to get outside and live and we lock them up with a set of rules. Shit, what's the use of talking to people like you? You let bloody Stanley in your school. And you've got Muir clucking round measuring the length of skirts and snipping off leather bracelets. What's the use?' She threw herself back in her chair with a rattle of bells.

Norma stood up. 'Well, I hope that makes you feel better.'

'For Christ's sake, I mean it.'

'I know you do. We've had this argument before. I agree with some of what you say. If it's any consolation I'll be telling Mr Stanley that he's wrong. But in my own words, if you don't mind.'

'All palsy-walsy.'

'He's no pal of mine. In fact he's a silly little man. But none of us are free from silliness.'

'Meaning me?'

'None of us.'

'God, you've got a face for everything. Who are you, Mrs Sangster? I'm not too sure there's anyone at home.'

Norma blinked. 'My word, you do go at things. Haven't you heard of moderation?'

'I've heard of copping out if that's what you mean.'

I mean, Norma thought, a middle way, but could not say it. The language she must use was soft and wet, rather like a jellyfish, no bones. She knew the realities of her position – compromise was in there, certainly – but found no way of stating them. Nobody at home. It made her tremble. John Toft had said something similar. 'You see this side and that, it is a condition. How can you have a job where decisions are made? You should be paralysed, Norma. Frozen like a statue, eh?' He made a pose. 'Not able to throw the discus far away or put it down.'

It's true, but only half, Norma thought; and seemed, with that, to illustrate their judgement. She shrugged it off, bristled at their cheek. 'Well,' she said, standing up – and knowing that in spite of her uncertainty and anger she managed to look unconcerned – 'I'm sorry we seem to be at cross purposes. I'd like you to be happy here, Sandra. But you have to fit in with us not us with you.'

'Is that a threat? And what do you mean "us" anyway? You and Muir and the governors? I'm in this school because of the girls.'

'Come and talk to me when you cool down. We can't go on like this I'm afraid.'

Norma left the staffroom. She heard a jingle of bells and hard little steps in the corridor, then a wheeze from the lavatory door. She wondered if Sandra had gone to have a cry. That would be a good thing. Something in her needed weeping out. Aggression and anger on that scale were a sickness; and one of her own questions would have to be what damage it might do to the girls. On the other hand there was life and bite in Sandra Duff . . .

Norma gave a short laugh. 'You see this side and that.' John knew what he was talking about.

She went into Phyllis Muir's office.

'Ah,' Phyllis said, 'I was coming to see you. Lex Clearwater hasn't turned up.'

'Have you rung him?'

'There's no reply.'

'I hope he isn't sick.'

'Do you? Well . . . I've got his classes covered. But I'll need to know what's happening tomorrow.'

'Keep on phoning.'

'And if there's no reply? I can't afford the time to be traipsing up there.'

'I'll go, Phyllis. Let me know at lunchtime. I need to have a talk with Lex.' But she counted Phyllis Muir a more serious problem and wanted her out of the school as badly as Phyllis wanted Lex. 'You must behave as if you feel His hand upon your back,' Phyllis told the girls, 'urging you along.' She went about the corridors with a forward lean and darting steps and elbows jutting sharply out behind. She changed direction like a huntaway. 'You! Girl! You with the red hair. Is that a T-shirt under your blouse?' She terrified new girls, but as they went up the school they learned to see her as a joke. There was a case, Norma thought, for having a man as

82

deputy principal in a girls' school – and a woman in a boys'.

'Anyone in the sickroom?'

'One girl with cramps and one with a migraine. A lack of intestinal fortitude in both cases.'

'Has Mrs Parr seen them?'

'Of course. Cramps and migraine are part of her holy writ.'

Norma sighed. 'Anything else?'

'Hayley Birtles. I caught her with leather bangles on her wrist and she refused to let me cut them off.' Phyllis dived her hand into her pocket and brought out a pair of nail scissors, which she snipped several times in the air. 'Said her father gave them to her, one for every home run she hits and he'd be "mad" if she took them off. I can't have girls defying me like that, in front of the others.'

'What did you do?'

'I've stood her down from the softball team for the rest of the year. I'd like you to back me up on that.'

Norma closed her eyes, steadied herself. 'No,' she said.

'What?'

'No, I said. I won't back you up.'

'Why not?'

'It sounds to me as if you set a confrontation up. And then, it seems, you over-reacted.'

'The girl defied me. In front of her friends.'

'Knowing Hayley Birtles, you shouldn't have done it in front of her friends.'

'I don't take kindly to that. I've been managing girls for thirty-five years.'

Norma would have liked to say, And doing it badly. She held the comment back. 'I think this girl is on a knife-edge, Phyllis. Her sister's in trouble, as you know. So I'm not going to take away the only thing she's good at.'

'You'll undermine my authority.'

'Oh no. I'll get those leathers off, you leave it to me. But Phyllis, please, try not to be so rigid in these things. A little give and take . . .' and Norma could not prevent a smile – this side and that, no doubt about it. And yet it seemed that she could make decisions.

Back in her office, she sent for Hayley Birtles. The girl came in boldly, mutinous, but, for all her weight of thigh and arm, with a bounce and lightness Norma found appealing. Scuffed shoes,

83

fingernails inked in different colours, and skirt, surely, an inch or two shorter than regulation. The leathers on her arm had a martial appearance.

'Sit down, Hayley.'

She plumped into the chair and met Norma's eye, no sliding away. Norma took a tissue from a packet in her drawer and walked round the desk. 'Gum in here.' For a moment Hayley seemed to consider defiance – touch and go. Then she took her gum out and dropped it in the tissue. Norma put it in the waste–paper basket.

'Well Hayley,' she sat in the other chair instead of going back behind her desk, 'you had a bit of trouble with Mrs Muir.'

Hayley shrugged.

'Tell me about it.' Get them talking, don't let them go dumb – Norma's rule.

Hayley made a jab with her shoulder as though warming up to pitch a ball. 'It was just the way she shouted. "You there! You! Come here!"' She had Phyllis Muir's bark and head-jut exactly. The secretary opened the door and looked in.

'It's all right, Jane. You think she was rude to you, Hayley?'

'I'm not a dog, Mrs Sangster. I didn't come here to get shouted at.'

'You know we do have rules though?'

'Yeah, well, some of us can't work out what they're for.'

'I sometimes can't work it out myself. But there they are, and changing them would be like trying to shift Mount Everest. The one about uniforms and ear-rings and so forth isn't going to change Hayley, not in your day and probably not in mine, though I'm working at it. If I say you can wear those leathers – and they don't seem harmful to me, in fact I like them – but if I say you can wear them I'll be in trouble. I'm principal, Hayley, but there are things I can do and things I can't.' I'm talking too much, get her to talk. 'Does your father really give you those or did you make that up?'

'I made it up. He knows I wear them though. He says tell you lot up here to mind your own business.'

'Does he?'

'He reckons people tell people what to do just to get a buzz.'

'That's not exactly true.'

'I reckon Mrs Muir gets a buzz.'

'Well, I do agree she shouldn't shout.'

'And these are for home runs anyway. But not from Dad. I put them on myself.'

'They'll be up to your elbow before the season's over.'

'Yeah.' Hayley grinned.

'Are they really so hard to untie?'

'I can do it. Takes a bit of time.'

'Well, why don't we reach a compromise?'

'What?'

'I give a bit, you give a bit. Nobody wins and nobody loses.'

'Sure. OK.' She sounded uncertain.

'I won't cheat you, Hayley. But how about this. We'll treat those leather bangles as a softball thing – '

'Am I still in the team?'

'Yes, of course. You can wear them when you play but you'll have to take them off in school time.'

Hayley frowned. 'Wear them in school matches? Midweek matches?'

'Yes, that's all right. But it's not a start for other decorations. You're not a ninny, you know how a little thing can lead to something bigger, and so on. In fact you and your mates are expert at it.' Hayley grinned. 'So, we play fair. You and I don't want to bang our heads.'

'Yeah, all right.'

'An agreement?'

'Sure. A deal. Do I have to say I'm sorry to Mrs Muir?'

Norma almost said yes. It would make things less difficult. But surely Phyllis should apologize too. Her shouting was assault and battery. 'I'll handle that. You just take those leathers off now. And when you go stop in the lavatory and clean that stuff off your fingernails.'

'It's just felt-tip. Comes off easy.'

'Good. The leathers first.'

Hayley unpicked the knots. Several were too tight for one hand and Norma helped.

'Hey Mrs Sangster, why doesn't Mrs Muir have her wart cut off?'

'It's not a wart, it's a mole.'

'Well, whatever. They do it with a little thing like a teaspoon, sort of scoop it out. Doesn't hurt.'

'I don't think it's something we can very well suggest. I really don't think it bothers her.'

'I bet it does. My aunty had a wart cut off and it was bigger than that. On a worse part of her face too. I reckon it would make her less bad tempered.'

Norma picked at the knots in silence. She could not work out whether Hayley was being malicious or compassionate and though the problem, the subject too, intrigued her, decided to get away from it. 'I was talking to your father on Saturday. He says he's got to teach you to pitch slow.'

'Yeah, the drop ball. I can do it. But it kinda seems like, I dunno, running scared.'

'It's taking a bigger risk, I'd have thought.'

'Getting belted, sure. It makes you feel good when you just kind of – drop one over the edge. Real sneaky. But you could get hit over the fence.'

'So it's not really running scared.'

'No, I don't s'pose so. Thanks, Mrs Sangster, that's real good. I would've got real mad if she'd cut them.'

'Don't forget those fingernails.'

'I won't. They're good colours, eh? Don't you reckon?'

'Very nice. Good for out of school.'

Hayley stood up. 'I don't suppose I can have my gum back?'

'No Hayley, you can't.'

'OK. Bye, Mrs Sangster. Thanks a lot.'

That skirt is still too short, Norma thought. But that could wait for another day. In fact the skirmishing would never stop, it was part of school life and although it was maddening, and ugly some of the time, you had to learn to live with it. Now and then you worked your way round the edge and came upon another person there – Hayley Birtles. But very likely Hayley would change back to her other self tomorrow. Norma did not expect good times every day.

Driving out at lunch-time, she stopped at the Amnesty cake stall by the oak tree.

'Is there anything left? Oh, those look nice.' She bought three bran muffins, three rolled oats cookies – three of everything not sold: cup-cakes with shocking-pink icing, cup-cakes with green icing and hundreds and thousands, and sticky squares made, it seemed, of puffed rice and icing sugar.

'How much have you made?'

'More than forty dollars, Mrs Sangster.'

'It's a very good cause.'

'They torture people, Mrs Sangster. They cut off their hands and hold their heads under water and drop them out of aeroplanes,' Belinda Round said.

'We're very fortunate we live in New Zealand.'

Sometimes I'm too bland, she thought, driving out the gate. Her heart seemed to fill her breast and throat. Why didn't I just scream? She checked a spurt of vomit in her throat and drove through town and along the valley. There was no connection she could make between those sticky cakes on paper plates, riding beside her in the passenger seat, and torturers and victims and the bleeding stumps of arms. Her girls might be victims one day, it was possible, and did that mean torturers were among them too?

She stopped her car and stood by the roadside, holding her handkerchief to her mouth. Below her the river ran in glossy undulations over tan gravel and variegated stones. Green weed pointed downstream and made a fishy movement at the point. I suppose all this is beautiful, Norma thought; but could not respond. She felt soggy, malodorous, filled with heavy tissues and sticky blood. The air she breathed out seemed wet and bad and left a scum on her mouth.

It's a kind of hysteria, she thought; I don't want this, go away, I'm only me. She tried to call up all the good people she had known but they were shadows. Burning, tearing, gouging, filled her mind.

A car stopped behind hers and Josie Round appeared in front of her. A hand like a coloured insect settled on her arm.

'Are you all right, Norma?'

'Yes . . . I felt a little sick . . . that's all.'

'It's no wonder if you've been eating those.'

'Oh. I bought them. At a stall.'

'You're sure you're all right? You're pale as anything.'

'I don't know, Josie.' She wiped her eyes. 'Sometimes I just can't stand being alive.'

'Man trouble?'

'No, no. Oh Josie.' Norma laughed. 'I'm all right. Really I am.

These things pass. I was just driving up to see Lex Clearwater.'

'With half a ton of cakes it looks like. I seem to recognize some of those.'

'They're from Belinda's Amnesty stall.'

'Yes, I thought so. Puffed rice nothings, that's Belinda. She gets all concerned but five-minute monstrosities are all she can stretch herself to. Are you sure? Sure it's not a man? I'll organize a squad and we'll de-bollock him.'

Norma laughed and closed her yes. De-hand, de-bollock. Josie was a good person, she supposed. 'I'd better get on, Josie. I've got to see Lex.'

A car swept by. 'Someone's beaten you to it. You know all about them, I suppose?'

'Sandra Duff? Lex and Sandra?'

'Oh, you don't. Well, no harm done, they're over sixteen. They play games on the lawn, according to Stella. A wee bit careless, if you ask me. I've got to go, if you're all right. Good grief, it isn't Lex? No, of course not. One thing you've got, Norma, is standards.'

One felt this edge of malice in Josie. It seemed quite undifferenti- ated so the best thing was not to take it personally. Norma was more concerned about Lex and Sandra – and not pleased. Wanted, she understood, to have her staff something less than human in that quarter. They had been discreet though, she admitted. And Stella Round had been discreet. Or was it common knowledge among the girls? Norma felt in less than full control. Her hands, she noticed, putting them on the car door, trembled a little. Now she could not be sure of the cause.

'Life isn't all affairs,' she said to Josie.

'I know that. The best part's got nothing to do with men. Oh Norma, thanks for being nice to Duncan. He came home all lit up the other day. Jesus, Jesus, don't I choose my words. I can't get used to it. I can't get used to seeing him like that.' She beat a tattoo on Norma's car roof. 'You're a teacher, tell me what to do.'

Norma could not find anything to say. 'Treat him the way you treat the girls.'

'Oh how easy. Thank you very much.'

'I enjoyed seeing him the other day. He's a very interesting boy. Do you know – ' She was about to describe his mind but stopped. Duncan unveiled what he chose, to whom he chose, she was sure of it; and Josie might have been shown something else.

'I think he's got a great ability for learning things. I think he should be taught properly.'

'I saw the book you gave him. It's a bit of a funny book to lend a boy.'

'Oh, that was really just to try him out. The accident changed him, I don't have to tell you that. But it didn't, well, put a stop to him.'

'Tom thinks so.'

'Well Tom doesn't get a vote. I told Duncan to come and see me again. Is that all right?'

'Of course. If you can do something . . . anything. You've no idea how grateful . . . Sometimes I think I'm going mad. Sometimes I think there is God and he's having fun with Duncan and me. How's that for an old card-carrying atheist?'

'Considering what happened I think you're doing well.'

'Ta very much. Well, I'd better go and feed him or he'll fill himself up with water biscuits. See you, Norma. Don't let the bastards get you down.' She banged the car roof and ran back to her little brand-new Japanese bug and zipped past, tooting goodbye, before Norma had her car in gear.

Norma drove slowly, feeling the camber of the road. Way ahead the bright metallic lid covering Josie sped like a ground-hopping aeroplane. It flashed blue to silver, butterfly wing, and made a cruel right-angle turn on to the pink-shell road leading up the hill to Tom Round's house on its terraced lawn. It was hard, Norma thought, to imagine Josie and Tom, with their bank accounts, investments, careers, their waterfall house, suffering as other people suffered. Yet without the accumulated worries and defeats that weighed on others – on the Birtleses – how huge and bare their tragedy must seem. One would have expected it to give them dignity. But instead Tom squealed and hid himself and Josie started in a dozen ways and followed none. The only ones with dignity, she thought, were Duncan himself and Belinda.

She crossed the bridge over the tributary creek that gave Tom his private water supply and kept his lawns green in summer droughts, and drove in willow shade, with golfers across the swimming holes on her right – a woman in a red hat putting, and a man in twenties clobber, knickerbockers and pudding-bag cap, holding himself in fractured stance as though for a photograph.

Lex's house came into view. It stood on a narrow ledge on the hillside, with patches of bracken like quilted place-mats all about, and tea-tree, broom, gorse, a froth of green and yellow, tumbling to the road. The plane of the ledge was tipped towards her and she saw Lex's ute standing there; and Sandra's car pull into place beside it. She felt an irritation that this affair, if it was affair, should be taking place in school time; wondered if she would find Lex and Sandra 'playing games'. It did not stop her, made her grim, and she turned into his drive, ground up in low gear with the car rocking in clay ruts and foliage scraping its sides. On one corner a tethered goat watched her go by with a nose-in-air look. It would not have been out of place at a royal garden party. An old bath quarter full of scummy water stood on the next bend, with a plastic duck, lop-sided and green with slime, but jaunty still, sitting in it. It must have belonged to – she could not remember the child's name and was not even sure of its sex.

There was no place for her car on the lawn. She stopped in front of the shed and climbed out and smoothed down her skirt. The house seemed crumbling to its elements, as dry and fractured as the hill above, with bits sliding off and others suffering breakdown or decay. A broken window had a piece of hardboard nailed across it. Knives of glass gleamed in the weeds. She went across and gathered them up and slid them under the porch. Sandra came out of the house and watched.

'Waste of time,' she said.

'Is Lex at home?'

'He's not inside. He's probably up the hill. I only came to see he hadn't broken his neck or something.'

'Has he been sick do you know?'

'Not yesterday. Unless you count sick in the head.' She shook herself, trying to shake her hardness off, and her bells made a sweet tinny tinkle. 'Listen Mrs Sangster, I don't know how much you care about Lex. I guess you're just worried about him doing his job. But I'm not sure he can any more. He's not in touch with real things, that's what I think. You might as well know he's giving notice. But if you ask me he should stop now and see a doctor. Because he needs someone to grab hold. Before he gets too far away.'

'When's he giving notice?'

'At the end of the year.' She saw a movement high on the hill and jumped down from the porch to the lawn. 'Lex,' she yelled; and turned to Norma again. 'Stop worrying about your school. You can get a replacement. I'm trying to tell you about Lex.'

'What do you think's the matter with him?'

'I don't know. He's in some fantasy world with his goats. They're like some kind of lost tribe and he wants to lead them to the promised land.

'Lex, come down,' she shouted. 'We can see you.'

Norma could not see him. She saw goats in the bracken, all with their heads pointing down the hill, but no sign of Lex. Huge white slung-belly clouds sat above the pine-row and the world seemed tilted over and the ground beneath her feet on a slant instead of flat.

'Come on, Lex. We haven't got all day. The boss is here.'

'Where is he?'

Sandra pointed. 'Over by the fence.'

She saw him then, with just his head poking from the bracken. He looked like a grub in a hole. She knew, with certainty, that Sandra was right, Lex was sick, and felt at once she must protect her girls. School was not a world without sin, but large sins, large sicknesses, must be kept out. She realized she had never seen Lex clearly, that a cloud of darkness hung about him and she had tried to dissipate it by laughing at him and pitying him, and lost sight of the damage he might do. She was filled with a retrospective fear and felt her eyes glitter like swords as she prepared to cut him down.

Lex unfolded, stood in the bracken waist deep. He held a small goat in his arms and turned to lay it down out of sight.

Sandra made a hard sound of amusement. 'Enkidu before the harlot got him. Well, I'm off. Tell him I'll come up tonight. Or maybe not. Flesh and blood can only stand so much.'

She got into her car, reversed in an arc, drove swishing through the grass round Norma's car, and set off down the drive with thin dust smoking behind her.

Lex slid and leaped down the hill. He too left a trail, as though he scorched the ground in passing. He braked by grabbing handfuls of tea-tree. She thought he would run through the fence, but he pushed out his sole against a post, making it give a loud crack. His other foot skidded through shale and sent a spray of stones against the stile. 'Gidday,' he said, climbing over.

'Hello, Lex. I thought I might find you sick in bed.'

'I've got a sick goat.'

'What's wrong with it?'

'Pneumonia.'

'Is that serious?' She smelt him as he came close: fresh and stale sweat mixed. There was a smear of something like mucus on his shirt.

'She'll die,' he said, and shrugged.

'Shouldn't you get the vet?'

'Don't like vets. They've got to die of something. Where'd Sandra go?'

'Back to school. She does have classes, Lex. I came up to see why you hadn't telephoned. We managed to get someone to fill in but what we really need is reasonable notice if you're sick – or one of your goats.'

'Yeah. I got stuck up there. I didn't want to leave her.'

'Well Lex, that's as may be, –' Norma frowned, not liking the phrase, ' – but the fact is, teaching can't take second place. We have to know you're where you're meant to be – barring major emergencies of course. And I can't see . . .' A goat dying of pneumonia – how much would that measure on her scale? She had a glimpse of vastly different places in Lex. Margins of familiar ground running into shadow.

'Sorry,' he said, 'I guess I wasn't thinking too clear.' He smiled at her and a slight goofiness, his overlapping front teeth, reassured her.

'Is everything all right, Lex? Are you sure you're well? Sandra's worried.'

'I'm OK. Sometimes I guess I don't eat enough. I forget to go to the shop.'

'Have you got any food in the house now?'

'Probably not.'

'Here then, take these.' She brought the plates of muffins and cakes from her car and put them on the porch steps. 'It's all right. I bought them at a stall. I wasn't sure what to do with them.'

'Hey, that's great.' He took a muffin in each hand. 'Fact is, Norma,' chewing, 'I've quit. I'm not coming back any more. I was going to ring you up but I forgot.'

'You're supposed to give more notice than that.'

He put half a muffin in his mouth. There was nothing goofy in his eyes. 'But you don't care, eh? You're glad to have me out of the place. It's not as if I'm doing a good job.'

'Well, I don't know.' Once she had walked in on a sixth-form class where he was explaining history and legend and myth. King Alfred (Lex said), though he may not have burned the cakes, was historical. Robin Hood was legendary – no large meanings there – and King Arthur a step to the side, between the legendary and the mythical. Something changes in our way of seeing, need comes in and Arthur becomes more than a man. Then there's the myth with religion in it, Orpheus and Persephone, Adam and Eve – attempts to answer questions about why and who. And folk-myth is different again – trolls and green men and leprechauns.

Norma was fascinated. It was, she supposed (she hoped), the standard exposition, but Lex – was it his voice, his manner, his way of seeming, put himself back there? – made it thrilling. 'And what were we like even further back?' he had asked. 'When we had no why or when or until or because? When things just happened? A time when we weren't what we call human, still part ape?' (Norma was alarmed. This could lead to trouble with Mr Stanley.) 'All we had was now. *Now* was it. We didn't speculate on things but were locked up in our self. And what we touched and ate and saw were part of *me*.' He banged his chest (and couldn't help looking a bit like Tarzan). 'Long before *me* was an idea.'

'If it was so long ago?' a girl said.

'Yes?'

'How come you know all this stuff?'

'Well, I don't,' Lex grinned. 'I'm only guessing.' He let them down. 'How and why and when, eh? It can be a disease.'

'You were a good teacher, Lex. At least I thought so. Until you split up with Ros. Not that I've got any right . . . What will you do?' She was anxious not to let him change his mind. She felt that a sore place in her school was suddenly healed.

'Stay here and look after my goats.'

'Can you make a living from that?'

'I've got a bit of money in the bank.' He was vague, and he took a pink cake and looked at it as though he did not understand the

93

colour. Her sense of his vast strangeness returned. How had he moved so far from normal concerns without her hearing signals of danger and setting herself between him and the girls? She looked for signs of sickness in his face, but, though three-day whiskered, it seemed simply thoughtful, a bit neglected. His dirty tartan shirt and dirty jeans were quite usual for a goat farmer, she supposed. As for the house and property, one must not fit everything to that little wheel of hers that went round and round with even clicks. Other people were happy with other things. But the goats; it was the goats, browsing on the hill, unconcerned, primeval, that shifted Lex and made him unacceptable. Goats as partners, goats as friends, who made a kind of sympathetic goatness in him? She wanted to shake him; cry at him that he must not go along that way or he would lose himself. Was this what Sandra felt? Was this why Sandra played woman to him on the lawn?

'Lex –'

He spoke at the same time: 'There's no problem, is there? Getting someone to take my place? Plenty of out-of-work teachers in this town.'

'That's no problem. But Lex –'

'What I want to do is, come and say goodbye to 4Cl. I've got them last period today. That OK? I've got some work to give back.'

'I can take it, Lex. There's no need –'

'They're good kids. I'd like to say goodbye.'

'Are you sure you'll be there?' She did not want him in the school again. 'I'll have to look in. They'll be confused otherwise.'

'Sure, no trouble. Then I'll be gone. You can stop worrying, eh? Get some nice lady to take my place.' He was making easy fun of her, and she smiled: 'Don't eat too many of those cakes, otherwise you will be sick in bed.'

Their conversation wound its way down. Lex climbed the hill to look at his goat, while Norma turned her car on the lawn. She drove slowly down the rutted drive, and stopped by the golf course and looked back. He was coming down again, holding the goat under one arm. That probably meant it was dead. He would dig a grave and bury it and forget. That, she was sure, would be his way. She could not see what else might be added, yet somehow it did not seem enough.

Norma saw Duncan Round on the shell road. She waved at him and sped back to her school.

94

8

When he walked in the class made a hiss, then started to talk all at once.

'Sir, sir, we thought you were sick, sir.'

'We thought you'd got the sack.'

'We thought you'd run away with Miss Duff, sir.'

'How's your goats, sir?'

'Sir, you're not supposed to wear jeans at school.'

Mrs Sangster came in the door as he reached the table. Everyone stood up and after the scraping of chairs it was so quiet, laughter in the next room sounded as if it came from the book cupboard.

'Thank you, girls. Sit down,' Mrs Sangster said. 'I want to apologize for intruding. I'll go away in a moment but I wanted to look in because – you don't mind if I tell them, Mr Clearwater? – Mr Clearwater is leaving us.' She waited until the noise died down. 'This is the last time you'll be seeing him. And as I won't have the chance of saying thank you at assembly and telling him how very much we're all going to miss him I thought I'd take the opportunity now . . .'

Hayley did not believe a word of it. What had happened, Lex had got the sack. It wasn't hard to see why when you looked at him alongside Mrs Sangster. She was like one of the Golden Girls. Lexie looked as if he'd been lost in the bush. Hayley liked his beard, it was kind of blue and made him look like a crim, but the stuff like dried snot on his shirt was real yukky. From where she was sitting by the window she could see a bit of red underpants where the seam of his jeans had come unstuck and his sneakers had holes in them at his big toes. One of his toes went up and down like he couldn't wait for Mrs Sangster to get finished. Real neat. Mrs Sangster was trying hard to look like everything was OK, but you could tell she had ants in her knickers. Hayley felt a bit sorry for her.

'Well, I'll leave you now to say goodbye. I'm not quite sure yet who your new form teacher will be but we'll get that sorted out later on. Thanks, Mr Clearwater. Thank you, girls.' She did not want to go, that stuck out. She probably thought Lexie would start giving sex lessons. Sheryl Thomas said, 'Mrs Sangster, we didn't have time to buy a present.'

'Yes, I'm sorry about that. We only found out this afternoon.'

'We could collect some money now.'

'I've got a dollar,' Michelle Hunter said.

'I've got fifty cents.'

'No, no. Well,' Mrs Sangster said, 'it's up to your form leader to organize. I'm sure Mr Clearwater –'

'I don't want a present. I really just came to say goodbye.'

'What school are you going to, sir?'

'Are you going to keep on farming goats?'

'I'll leave it to you, Mr Clearwater, now. Perhaps you could look in at my office as you go?' Mrs Sangster left, with a hesitation at the door and a nervous blink round the room. She would probably sneak back and listen in the corridor, Hayley thought.

'OK, pipe down,' Lex said.

'Why are you really leaving, sir?'

'Did you get the sack?'

'I would have if I hadn't got in first. You might be in luck and get a real teacher when I'm gone.'

'You were neat, sir.'

'You didn't yell at us anyhow.'

'Or keep on telling us off about our hair. You haven't had a shave today, sir.'

'I mightn't ever have a shave again.'

'Hey, your beard would grow down to your feet.'

'You wouldn't have to wear trousers, sir.'

'Everyone shut up.'

Hayley thought he looked tired, sick of things. He looked as if he might walk out. 'Yeah, shut up,' she said. 'Let Mr Clearwater say something.'

'Thank you, Hayley. There's not much I want to say. Mainly, I'm sorry for wasting your time. I can get out but you're stuck here for a while, most of you. There's nothing for you to do except keep on and learn what you can and not butt your heads against the wall, not too hard. There's some not bad teachers in this school. Mrs Sangster's OK. So's Miss Duff.'

96

'Miss Duff's your girlfriend, sir.'

'So?' He looked out of the window at Stovepipe Hill, and was gone so long questions started flying again and died away. He said, 'You girls are in a machine and it's processing you. That's not good, but it's not all bad. If you keep your eyes open and chuck out the phoney stuff and keep what's real . . .'

He really was tired and he didn't care about this. Part, he was telling lies, and part, just opening his mouth and letting it talk. It scared Hayley, he was so far away. Her mother was like that most of the time. She couldn't see why Lex had come in. The rest of the class felt something wrong too and kept quiet until he stopped. Then Donna Gethin, who would say anything and was so tough some girls said she fucked Korean sailors for money at the port, Donna said a thing no one could believe. 'Sir, what say you were screwing your nanny goats sir, would the babies have people's heads or what?'

Lex turned his eyes round, sad and slow. He swallowed a few times and ran his hand up and down his cheek, making a dry sound on the bristles. 'Donna,' he said, 'don't talk like that. Don't ever say a thing like that again.' He pressed the heel of his palm in his eyes, then wiped his hand dry on his shirt. 'What you're getting at, it isn't true. That sort of thing doesn't happen. All right?'

'It wasn't me that said it.'

'Maybe not.' He was gentle with her, a thing Hayley could not understand. Laughter came from the next room again and squeaky shoes – Pure Muir – moved down the corridor. Lex said, 'I'll give you back your folders. Then maybe we can have a talk. I've got to stay till the end of the period. But no lesson, eh?'

'No, sir.'

'OK. Come and get 'em.' He read out names and girls came one by one and took their folders to their desks. Hayley did not look at him as she took hers. She had written something she was sorry about and did not want him saying anything. Back in her seat she looked at her mark, saw the usual corrections, and six crossed out and seven in its place. It was the best mark she had ever had and she looked at Lex, wondering what he had liked.

'All right, girls. Any comments?'

'You didn't mark these, sir.'

'It's Miss Duff's writing. She does her "ees" like this.'

97

'And she does this cross mark on her sevens.'

'You've found me out.'

'That's cheating, sir.'

'I apologize. But I did read one or two of them. Yours Hayley, liked it very much. Now put 'em away. Let's just have a chat, eh? I didn't come here to play schoolteachers.'

Sir, they said, do you miss your wife? What's it like getting divorced, sir? Do they make you say you hate each other? Do you miss your baby, sir? Were you there when he was born? What was it like? Do you watch Miami Vice? Do you like Pseudo Echo or Culture Club? Is this really a good school? Why can't we wear our hair long? Why does Mrs Muir shout at us like we're not people? Do you and Miss Duff go to bed?

As he answered he seemed to get further away and his words more bare. Hayley was frightened. It was unusual for anything at school to frighten her – but this was not a lesson and what he said came from somewhere teachers were not supposed to go. She wondered if he was sick, she wondered if he would kill himself. He reminded her of the gorilla in the Melbourne zoo, sitting in the back of his cage. His eyes had that hardness and dreaminess. No, he said, I don't miss anything. I was there but I don't remember. All the things she's missed are killing her, that's why she can't see you, that's why she shouts.

When Donna asked about Miss Duff he changed. He came back and turned into a teacher and seemed sad and dirty suddenly. 'Have you heard of the fifth amendment? It's something the Americans have and it lets them refuse to answer questions. So, about that, I take the fifth.'

'Come on, sir.'

'We won't tell.'

'Miss Duff and I are just good friends.'

It was pathetic, a waste of time. Hayley wanted the period to end so she could get down town and look in the shops for the bra her father had given her money for. She wondered if Lex could see that the girls were getting ready to be cruel. Donna would ask about the goats again. Hayley wanted Mrs Sangster to come and take him away.

The bell rang. She zipped her bag and stood up. Girls were rushing at the door. Others clustered about Lex at the table. She went around the back of them.

98

'Just a minute, Hayley.'

'What?'

'I mean it, I like your essay. I think you really got on to something there.'

'Thanks,' she said.

'How'd you like to come up and see my goats?'

'Ooh, Hayley.'

'He fancies you, Hayley.'

'Shut up,' Lex said. 'In fact the lot of you can clear out. Go on, buzz off. Not you, Hayley.'

'Keep your legs crossed, Hayley.'

Lex got them out and closed the door. 'Girls have changed since my day.'

'What do you want, sir? I've got to get down the road and do some shopping.'

'Have you ever looked in a goat's eyes, Hayley?'

'I've never seen a goat. I've seen them tied up at the side of the road.'

'They're interesting creatures. They're a bit like your gorilla.'

'Yeah? He chucked a whole branch of a tree at us. I didn't put that in.'

'Did you really cry like that?'

She had known she should not write it. 'Nah, we laughed. Shelley and me showed him our knickers.'

'Come on, Hayley. We're not on different sides.'

'My sister's boyfriend shot a goat and gave us some meat. Tasted good. Shelley cooked it in a kind of stew.'

Lex leaned back and half sat on his table. He made a little laugh and said, 'I thought you were a stupe, Hayley, but I can see you're fairly bright.'

'Thank you, sir. Can I go now?'

'I'll tell you a thing that happened. A couple of years ago I went around my fences to see if there were any holes and right up the top, place I hadn't looked at for a while, there's gorse growing right up in the corner – I found one of my goats. She was a doe and she'd gone in and reached under the wire for some grass on the other side, and she got her horns caught and couldn't get loose and so she died there. When I found her she was just a skeleton, but her skin was still on, so she was a skeleton in a fur coat. That was pretty horrible, don't you think? But what really got me, while she was stuck there she gave birth. So there was a little skeleton in a fur coat by her side. I suppose it got some milk for a while, and then when the mother died it died too.'

Big deal, Hayley thought. What did he expect, she'd start to cry? He wasn't going to turn her on and off like a tap.

'It's getting late. I've got to buy a bra.'

'Hayley, I'm not asking for anything. I'm just saying if you'd like to come and see me – '

'You're not supposed to see girls out of school.'

He stood up from the table, turned away; looked out of the window. 'You could help me, Hayley.'

She did not know what he meant, but noticed he was contradicting himself – not wanting something, then wanting it. She guessed that 'help' meant he wanted to fuck her. All this because she wrote that stuff about the gorilla.

'You're going to be late for Mrs Sangster.'

'She can wait.'

'I'll have to ask my father if I can come.' She would not ask but wanted to see what Lex would say.

'Fathers have got a way of saying no.'

'Do you mean you want me to come sort of secret?'

'I don't know.'

'What about Miss Duff? She'll get jealous, eh?'

'Hayley,' his eyes blinked fast, kind of sad, 'that isn't what I want you for.'

'What do you want, sir?' She laughed. It was funny calling him sir in the middle of this.

'Just someone to visit me.'

'But I guess we'd still end up – you know.'

Lex leaned his back on the blackboard and put his head against it so words of chalk writing were smudged. He closed his eyes, and said after a moment, 'All this looks like a mistake.' He seemed to be talking to himself. It made her uncertain how to go on.

'I gotta go, sir. I might come, I dunno. I've got a lot of jobs at home and I've got softball practice.'

'Do what you want to, Hayley.'

'Yeah. Bye, sir. I won't tell Mrs Sangster or Miss Duff.'

She went down the corridor and saw Mrs Muir coming towards

her, forward-sloping, skating her shoes along and opening and closing her mouth like a fish.

'Where's Mr Clearwater?'

'In his room.'

'What's he been telling you girls?'

'Nothing. We just been talking.'

'What about? What's he been asking you to do?'

'He gave our essays back, that's all. I gotta go, Mrs Muir, gotta buy a bra.'

'Yes, go. Get out. *Don't run, girl*.'

'I'm walking fast, Mrs Muir. Looks like running but it's not.'

'I know running when I see –'

The end was cut off as Hayley went through the swing doors. She laughed aloud, hoping it would carry to Mrs Muir, and ran down the steps, across the quadrangle, through another wing, to the bike stands.

'What'd he want, Hayley?'

'Ah, nothing. Wanted me to go and look at his goats. I told him I had softball practice.'

She swung her leg over and rode away. (The bike had been Wayne's and she liked riding a man's bike, liked standing in the car park with her leg hooked over the bar, watching all the men perve at her knickers. The old men, the shopkeepers, were the funniest, sly lookers.) Half-way down the hill Lex passed her in his ute and gave a honk. He'd got rid of Muir pretty quick, and hadn't gone to Mrs Sangster's office like she'd told him. Good old Lex.

She tried on half a dozen bras in Boothams and the saleswoman kept on sticking her head in the cubicle, scared she would nick one. She'd nicked a blouse from there once, but it wasn't an easy place – and anyway, since Shelley was busted, she'd given up shop-lifting, even rubbers and biros from Whitcoulls. Her mum and dad wouldn't be able to stand any more trouble. So maybe she'd better not go to Lex's. She'd read in her mother's old diaries that 'a girl should keep herself for one man'. 'Kay told me that when a man does it to you he has to put his thing in and leave it there all night but if he pulls it out there won't be a baby.' Her mother had been sixteen when she wrote that. Totally unbelievable, it wiped Hayley out. But as she got closer to home and her mother – up the side of the creek in its concrete channel, past the car-yards and the wreckers'-yards and the paint factory with the colours on its rainbow faded to different shades of white, great ad – she started to feel the thing come down on her, and feel she was riding out of warm into cold and all her clothes had gone damp and snails were crawling on her chest. Forgetting was a trick she had learned – but turning past the coal-yard on the corner was where it didn't work any more.

Their house was an old house with a hall straight down the middle, from the front veranda to the kitchen. Her father had made a great job of doing it up; put in concrete piles in place of the wood – she remembered that, remembered him sliding under on his back, with only an inch for his face, and coming out covered with grey old webs like dirty lace. She helped him pick them off his hair and face and rolled them into little balls with skeletons of spiders inside. Later on, when she was five or six, he let her and Wayne and Shelley have turns with the paint-brush, painting the walls. He took them up the ladder to the roof one by one and they stood by the chimney and looked along the streets and down the valley to a bit of sea with a yacht race on it – like standing on the top of a dangerous hill. Way down at the end of the garden her mother cried, 'Be careful, Ken.' Her father lifted her and she looked down the chimney. The bricks were warm on her hands, and on her bottom when he sat her there. 'If I do poops will it land in the fireplace?' 'Cheeky,' he said, lifting her down. He put his finger in and got some soot and smudged her nose.

Now she went home to her mother in the kitchen. She put her bike in the shed, carried in her bag, yelled, 'Hi, Ma,' to Mrs Birtles fogged in smoke at the table, went to her bedroom, shucked uniform and threw it on the bed. She put on jeans and hooked her bra on. 'What do you reckon?' standing hands on hips at the kitchen door.

'Put something on dear, you'll catch cold,' her mother said.

'My new bra. What do you think?'

Her mother puffed and let out pale grey smoke. 'Is that new? It looks very nice.' Everything she said was kind of not said. It wasn't *now* but something she remembered from way back. Sometimes it made you want to scream or get a glass of water and tip it on her head. Other times it made you want to cry.

Hayley went back to her room and took off her bra. She put on a

T-shirt, carried her mitt and box of balls out to the yard, made another trip for her Walkman and a tape.

'Hi, Ma. Good day, Ma?'

'Hallo, Hayley. Is that you, dear?'

'Any visitors today? Any burglars? Any rapists?'

'No dear, I've been alone all day. Make sure you're warm enough out there.'

'It's a sunny day, Ma.'

'Is it? I haven't been out the house all day.'

'That's breakfast dishes in the sink. How about washing them?'

'In a minute, dear. I'll just have another cigarette.'

'Do that, Ma.'

She drank a glass of milk from the fridge and took a handful of gingernuts and went out. Half an hour of practice before doing the dishes and tidying the house. Then more practice. She liked to be chucking balls when her father came home.

He had built a stand of netting on the side of the garage with a hole in the middle for the strike zone and a backstop made of hammered tin. If she missed she had to pick the ball out of the net but if she got a strike it rolled in a wooden chute back to her. Real cute. She had four balls and sometimes made it through practice without having to shift from her plate, although she might have only one ball left. If she wasn't doing well she got mad and beaned some imaginary batter a few times – Muir or Stella Round or Neil Chote (what a bastard he was, with his tattoos and his zits and the way he looked at you, trying to make you think he didn't ever have to blink his eyes, a weirdo, a dick), and sometimes Mrs Sangster. You could imagine her head smashing to bits like a glass bowl. Hayley liked Mrs Sangster OK, but sometimes she wanted to *unravel* her and see if she had a bum and tits like everyone else.

She slid her gingernuts into her pocket. They cracked and broke in bits as she pitched and she took pieces out and put them in her mouth and let them get soft and swallowed them – liked the hot taste better than fags, which she did not touch. Three would last her half an hour. She did some stretches, hearing biscuits crack, feeling her muscles and tendons 'organize themselves' as her dad said, then put her Walkman on and started the tape (Midnight Oil). She pulled on her glove and took a ball. She was going to do fast curves and work them down from armpit strikes to knee, but first she put a dozen straight ones in to get her arm loose. She had to go up twice for the ball. Maybe she'd better get Lex out of her head. That was still giving her a buzz, but like her dad said, you had to make like nothing else existed except that ball and strike-zone and bat you had to beat. He'd be real mad if he found her practising with her Walkman on. She took it off. The silence was real good. She took her grip, shielding the ball inside her glove: thumb and little finger curled and middle fingers on the loop. Had her stance; got her eye on target; drove up and back, shifted her weight, moved out in that easy step, with hand coming through by her hip; snapped her wrist, rolled it inside; and the ball was away, curving like a chalk line on a board, and – 'Fuck,' she said – into the net. No bloody good. She wasn't concentrating properly. Stuff Lex Clearwater. Stuff Muir. Water gurgled in the bathroom sump. And stuff her mother!

Hayley kept on. She got her mind in gear, got in a groove. She threw pitch after pitch, sucked triangles of gingernut, watched the ball zip away and clang in the hole and wobble down the chute back to her. Sweat greased her armpit and burned along her elbow crease. She loved the feel of grease made inside her and bits of her sliding on other bits. She grunted as she pitched, and laughed at the fart she made now and then. Some of the best pitchers in the world were always farting on the mound, her father said.

At half past four she went inside and had a quick look round the house but nothing much needed doing. She made her parents' bed and folded her father's pyjamas and straightened the top of the dressing table. When she started the dishes her mother said, 'Leave those, Shelley, I'll do them.'

'I'm Hayley, Ma.'

'I'll come and dry for you in a minute.' Instead she lit another cigarette. Hayley supposed that one day she'd die of lung cancer and wondered if that would happen before she turned yellow all over from nicotine. Her fingers were yellow; the little hairs on her upper lip, her right eyebrow where the smoke went up, a streak in her hair, were yellow white. Her nostrils inside were almost black. But smoking was not her trouble, Wayne was her trouble; Shelley too. Ken Birtles put it differently. 'Life's her trouble.' He had never wanted to blame anyone.

Mrs Birtles left her cigarette burning on the ashtray and fetched her box of curlers from the bedroom, She started rolling them into her hair.

'It's a bit late for that, Ma.'

'I like to make myself nice for Ken.' She forgot about it after getting the front three in. Hayley stood her up by the shoulders and guided her into the lounge and sat her down. 'Television, Ma.' She switched on the set and went back to the kitchen and laid the table. She peeled some potatoes and put them ready on the stove to cook. There were frozen peas in the fridge and her father and Shelley would bring home fish. Hayley hoped it would be flounder. Her father cooked those in the electric pan. He made a kind of party out of flounder.

Back in the yard she threw risers, then moved on to drops to rest her wrist. Her gingernuts all finished, she chewed gum. She did not think she would be able to pitch if she didn't have something in her mouth.

Her father and Shelley drove into the garage at half past five. They stood on the back path and watched her and she sneaked three pitches in a row into the bottom right of the zone.

'She's trying to make like Debbie Mygind,' Shelley said.

'She's doing OK. Got your fingers far enough on the seam?'

'Yep,' Hayley said, and threw another.

'Good stuff. I've got some flounder, Hayley, so I'll cook.'

Shelley had a shower – trying to wash the smell of fish out of her skin. Their father had got her a job on the packing chain and Shelley seemed to be trying hard, but hated the stink. She stood her tape-deck on the window-sill and played an old Bruce Springsteen real loud so she could hear it above the water. Steam rolled out the window. It couldn't be doing the deck much good, Hayley thought. She threw another dozen, and beaned Neil Chote to finish off.

Shelley was drying herself. 'You stink of sweat.'

'You stink of fish.' She put out her arm to block the flick of Shelley's towel. 'Only kidding. Hey, Shell,' stripping off her T-shirt, 'Lexie put the word on me today.'

'What do you mean?'

'Asked me to go and see his goats.' She stood one-legged, getting off her jeans. 'He's screwing Duffie, that's for sure, but I think I might be next on his list.'

'You better not let Dad hear you say that.'

'I'm not dumb.' She stepped into the shower. 'Lex quit today. Pure Muir was sniffing round like he was going to load us all in his ute and take us with him.'

'Don't you go there, Hayley.'

'I might. I can look after myself.'

'Hayley, listen. For Christ's sake listen. Turn that fucking water off and listen. You start sharing it round you'll end up on the meat market, same as me. Are you listening? You stick to guys your own age. And make it one, for God's sake. And the right bloody one or else you're meat. You'll end up with a bastard like Neil who wants all his mates to have a share. You listening, Hayley? Get that bloody dumb look off your face.'

'Neil's in prison.'

'He'll be back. He's coming out.'

'Dad won't let him come here.'

'So what? He just has to let me know where he is.'

'You don't have to go.'

'Don't I? He'll kick shit out of me if I don't do what he wants.'

'You could go away. You could go to Aussie. Auntie Beth's.' But she saw from the way Shelley looked at her and turned away that she could not; she did not want to.

'Lex wouldn't be like Neil.'

'Jesus Christ, Hayley, he's old. He must be forty. What do you think he's after, eh?' – jabbing her finger at Hayley's crotch. 'You said it yourself. And you can't handle that, you're only fourteen. OK, OK. But he won't just screw you, he'll screw you up. Hayley, don't go. Please. OK?' – talking low and hard under Bruce Springsteen. 'Stick to Barry or Gary, whoever it is. And you better be careful too. If you go down the chute like me and Wayne it's the finish of Dad.'

'I don't do much. I don't do much, Shell.'

'You do more than I used to do.'

'Shell, why can't you go? Auntie Beth's OK. There's better jobs in Melbourne.' Tears started rolling down her face. 'He's such a dick.' She tried to laugh to stop herself crying. 'He's even got zits.'

Tears were coming from Shelley's eyes too. She shook her head; shook it hard, with gritted teeth.

'Get a move on, you two,' their father yelled, 'the flounder's on.'

'Coming, Dad.'

106

'Last one gets the midget.'

'You don't really smell of fish, Shell.'

'Yes I do. And you stink of sweat. So get washed. And remember, eh, 'cause I probably won't say all that again.'

Hayley got back into her jeans and put a clean T-shirt on. She dried her hair for five minutes with Shelley's blow drier and got to the table as her father served the meal.

'The late Miss Birtles. Where's your leathers?'

'Took 'em off. Me and Mrs Sangster made a deal. I can wear them at matches.'

'That lady should be in parliament. Eat up, Joanie. I'll get the bones out.' He stripped the flesh off his wife's flounder and dropped the skeleton in the waste. 'Eat a bit of spud with it. Make you nice and fat.'

'Yes, Ken.' Mrs Birtles ate several mouthfuls of mashed potato; then some fish, then her peas, to please him. She drank a glass of beer and said, 'Not too much,' as he poured a glass for the girls. Her show of awareness was unusual. They tried to say and do things that might keep it alive. Shelley gave her more peas from the pot. Ken said Mrs Ward, a woman she had played tennis with, had asked after her and was looking forward to seeing her back at the club. But Mrs Birtles drifted far away and ate no more; spoke again only when he pushed away his plate, 'Thank you, Joanie.' She smiled with pleasure: 'I think we'll have a tin of fruit, don't you?'

Shelley opened peaches and they ate them with ice-cream and chocolate hail. Then Hayley and Shelley washed the dishes, while their father watched the TV news and their mother sat by his side and opened her third pack of cigarettes for the day. (Her cigarettes cost forty dollars a week.) He held her hand, said, 'Look Joanie, that's quite interesting. Unbelievable what people do.' He had to be alert and switch channels fast. There was a lot of fire and people burning on the news.

The Birtleses sat watching until late. Hayley skipped her homework and Shelley decided not to go to her girlfriend's place. At the end of the evening Ken Birtles took his wife's curlers out and took her to bed. He came back to his daughters while she had her cry. There was something about the end of the day that brought Wayne back.

Shelley said, 'She can't go on like this. Nor can you.'

Hayley leaned her head on his shoulder.

He held their hands and said, 'It's a great life, kids, if you don't weaken.'

9

The distance between the Birtles's house in Spargo Street, Duck-ham Square, and the 'toasty warm' Round house above the river and golf course in Coppermine Valley can be measured socially. I won't attempt it; will drive you through Saxton instead. First though, a bit of history.

Saxton was a Wakefield town. A vertical slice of old England was meant to take root there. When the settlers came ashore in 1841 they marked out sites for a jail and a courthouse, a magistrate's house, a church and a school. Agriculture and commerce did not need marking out.

The town had bad times but good times followed, social distinctions became blurred, Saxton grew into an egalitarian New Zealand town. There are people here descended from first-ship settlers and, in the minds of some, a Saxton aristocracy, but most of our citizens are not impressed by such things. Climate, topography, hard work and ambition and greed and commercial chance determined the town's shape more than social theory and distinctions.

The gap between rich and poor is widening again but that isn't peculiar to Saxton.

Geography has been a determining factor. Hills and sea cut us off from other places. We're not on a direct route except to smaller towns. The nearest city is forty minutes by air but if you go by car and ferry you must travel all day. Some people like this. A visiting Classics professor said that Saxton reminded him of a Greek city-state. He said, jokingly, that it should secede from New Zealand and was kind enough to suggest Athens not Sparta as a model.

Fishing, timber, horticulture, pip-fruit sustain us. One mustn't forget tourism. American and continental English are heard in the streets. Japanese honeymooners ask locals to photograph them on the cathedral steps – focus and timing pre-set. Dutch and Swedish travellers pick apples in the season. Saxton is remote, but the world passes through.

Things you may be shown or come across: the cathedral, which gave us the status of city when in fact we were still a town (we still are a town); the art gallery, founded by a bishop and bearing his name (it is funded, not too willingly, by the city council, and has recently been enlarged in a style most people, though not Tom Round, find very tasteful); Queens Gardens (Victoria was the queen) and the duckpond, lying just away from the town's main street (beautiful roses, filthy pond where ducks wait out the shooting season, squabbling for bits of bread lunching shop-assistants throw); Founders Park, where a pioneer town has been set up, using old buildings saved from demolition; the waterfront drive, named for, opened by, the present queen. The list could go on but there's no need. There's nothing here that simply must be seen, though one or two things are unique: a plaque marking the field where the first rugby match in New Zealand was played; a hill known as the Centre of New Zealand; a boulder bank enclosing mudflats and the port. It's a geological phenomenon found nowhere else in the world. (That, at least, is what we are told.) And there are three or four lovely wooden churches.

Saxton is comfortable for the visitor. There's a Quality Inn and plenty of hotels and motels and boarding houses, and three camping grounds, one at the beach, and a youth hostel and several private hostels. The sunshine hours are the highest in New Zealand. You can swim at the beach or in the rivers (the rivers now, those out of town, can make you feel in a world new-born), or go north into the maritime park and find yellow beaches, clean blue sea, tramping tracks through unspoiled bush (the world new-born again), or south to the lakes and ski-fields. You can fish for trout. You can visit the potters and weavers and print-makers and silversmiths and glass-blowers (Saxton attracts them), and set off round the vineyards on the wine trail and pick your own tree-ripened apples and peaches. You might easily decide Saxton is a place free from troubles.

Look harder.

Stay around a while and keep your eyes open. Walk in the back streets. Go up river if you prefer. Only a hundred yards past the Arts Society ladies sketching willows and toi-toi by the footbridge you'll find a concrete bridge with 'Donovan Sux' spray-painted on a pier – Donovan is our mayor. In a dark cave underneath, kids are sniffing solvents from plastic bags. There are street-kids squatting in an empty corner-dairy by Duckham Square. That house-truck at the swimming hole – rather picturesque, with the young woman sitting on the step breast-feeding her baby and the man with the carburettor spread out on a sack, and shirts and towels and underpants drying on the grass – is there because there's nowhere else to go. Police will move it on before long. And while we're up the river, and speaking of police, that helicopter rattling your teeth is making a marijuana sweep. Back in town school's out and schoolboys and girls are smoking the stuff while their older siblings, unemployed, are drinking in the pubs.

Let's not worry about time of day. That drunk fellow who falls over by the streetlamp and takes five minutes climbing to his feet is a Russian sailor from a tuna boat. He's lost his liquor-store bag of whisky and gin and his two pairs of jeans and his Lada parts. He won't make it back to his ship. Local goons (one of them's a mate of Neil Chote) roll him in an alley and kick him senseless. He'll be three months in hospital and then will be flown home and will never really understand what happened to him in Saxton.

Go down to the courthouse on a Tuesday. Sit in the waiting room with the butt-scorched floor, with young fellows in boots and broken sneakers and jeans and bush singlets and leather jackets, listen to them speak, listen to the girls, with their nicotine-stained fingers and red-rimmed eyes. It's not the same language used by those lawyers who go by – young fellows, young women too. See how they dress. You can illustrate a two nations argument here. What are the charges when the accused, those in here, those brought in from the cells, face the judge? Cultivating cannabis. Possession for supply. Driving with excess breath alcohol, blood alcohol. They've pissed in a doorway, punched the neighbour or the *de facto*, kicked in the window of a menswear store. They've stolen from a container lorry parked up for the night. Threatened a constable with *numchukkas*. Threatened a chemist with a knife and got away with a pocketful of prescription drugs. They've kicked a Russian sailor half to death. They're mill-hands, knife-hands, labourers, bushmen, fish-splitters, sickness beneficiaries, solo mothers, unemployed. The judge sentences them to prison or periodic detention, puts them under supervision, orders reparation. He fines them and disqualifies them (the shop manager too, the estate agent, the retired shoe salesman). Every Tuesday there's a new batch. Shelley Birtles has passed through (theft of a chequebook and a credit card). Shelley is under six months' supervision.

Meanwhile, in plush offices – no, that won't do. But Saxton does have what John Toft calls its 'little millionaires and clever bankrupts'. No, he says, New Zealand doesn't belong to the big foreign boys, not yet. It's the little guy who's got it, inflation millionaires, there are more than a dozen in this town, mostly land agents. They buy and sell, buy and sell, and produce nothing along the way. (John gets angry.) They take the money and other people take the debt. You try and buy a bit of land at the edge of town, for a fair price, you can't do it. They own it all, these fat fellows, these little boys. You don't believe me? Look at the registration of properties. They sit there waiting for the value – ah, not the value, the price – to rise. (But the spirit goes out of John, he seems to die one of his little deaths. Says to Norma, 'Don't ask me, ask your friend Tom Round. He plays their little game with them.')

We've moved away from history and seem to be back with the Rounds, so let's do without that drive I mentioned and stay with them. It's half past seven. They have their dinner later than the Birtleses.

Josie and Belinda and Stella and Duncan are eating millet and tofu patties and vegetables marinaded in lemon juice, honey and ginger and stir-fried in oil. Belinda had her last meat meal on Saturday night and is a vegetarian now. Josie sees no reason not to go along with this. She has several recipe books from her own vegetarian days, and makes a tasty meal as a gesture of support but is irritated by the time it takes to prepare and makes sure Belinda knows about it. Tom Round has a steak. Tom is not playing.

'You'll grow slant eyes on that stuff,' he says.

'That thing you're eating was cut off the body of a dead animal,' Belinda retorts.

'It would hardly be a live one.' Stella.

'In some recipes,' Tom, 'they boil geese alive to improve the flavour.'

'Da-ad!'

'They boil crayfish that way. You're not cutting crayfish out of your diet, I'll bet.'

'This conversation has gone far enough,' Josie says. She is not certain where Belinda's soft places are or how far her publicized toughness extends, but believes there's an unease in the child, expressing itself in an attachment to causes – loud attachment – while leaving its true object unrevealed. Josie has found it difficult to know her daughters – oh, knows all the technical and theoretical stuff, doctrinal too, but can't compress it into a Mandy, Stella, Belinda shape. Is Belinda troubled by an awareness of pain and death (when does that come? Josie must look in Gesell and Ilg), or is it something more mundane and personal? What, apart from Duncan, could worry her to such an extent that cracks and flaws begin to appear in the (Josie hunts for an adjective) splendid persona the girl has created – a work of art – and lead one to these speculations? Apart from Duncan? Josie seizes on that. The attachment between Belinda and him, two-way traffic, is lovely to see, but doesn't he, doesn't his accident, and Wayne Birtles's death, take one beyond the personal to those universals, pain and death? So . . . Josie is confused. She's not quite sure where she has arrived. Does any of this have a connection with Bel, wolfing millet patties, here and now?

She looks at her daughter with an admiring but cold eye. Not pretty. Definitely not. Mandy and Stell are the pretty ones – Mandy with her heart-shaped face (true, though it's straight out of Barbara Cartland) and Stella with a longer more thoroughbred countenance and a pink and white porcelain skin. Belinda has a square-built face that has a lived-in look. (Josie likes that phrase – cliché or not it's from a better class of fiction.) Her cheek-bones have the Tom Round corbel structure and her eyes the Round Mongolian slant, but her mouth and chin are Josie, pure Josie, built to signal defiance of others' will. She eats her vegetarian meal in defiance of her father – but in his blood-savouring way.

'It better not be vegetarian pudding,' Tom jokes.

'Feeble, Dad,' Belinda says.

'There's no pudding.' Josie enjoys the squirt of anger in his eyes. She likes to put him out of control.

'Elementary. Look at the cutlery,' Stella says.

'Why not?'

'Because the meal took so long to prepare. I've got other things to do with my time.'

'Sure, sit on a flax mat saying *Om Mani Padme Hum*, Down from heaven and up my bum.'

'It's not humm it's hoom.'

'Fair enough, up my boom.'

'I'll open a tin of fruit,' Stella says.

'And ice-cream,' Tom shouts as she goes to the pantry. Then, being angry, can look at Duncan. 'And how do you like leeks and lentils?'

'There's no leeks and lentils. It's millet and tofu,' Josie says.

'It won't put lead in his pencil, that's for sure.'

'I like it,' Duncan says. 'It tastes like nuts.'

Tom makes some monkey jabber and scratches his armpits.

'You're no good, Dad.' Belinda shows him how and he appreciates the tightening of her T-shirt on her breasts. He has often said that daughters are a floor show. He's also said (only to Josie, in the bedroom) that having Duncan round is like a long-running horror movie. Josie is ashamed of having agreed, although it was a bit of post-coital easy deception, spoken in a time of mellowness. Now, when the whole of their marriage is post-coital, she wants to cry, 'How dare you speak of him like that! How dare you con me into saying yes!'

Stella brings lichees to the table and Tom says, 'Sheep's eyes. Monkey balls.'

'Shut up, Tom.'

'Do we have to have this Chinkee stuff? What happened to good old honest Wattie peaches?' Suddenly he gives her a mock leer and Josie blushes; it has been part of their sexual play for Tom, feeling her ready, to say 'Wattie peaches'. She's annoyed at the interest it rouses in her now. 'Food doesn't have nationality,' she says sharply. 'And there's nothing very honest about sugared fruit. Bring some ice-cream, Stella. We can't eat it alone.'

In spite of his manufactured disapproval Tom eats the lichees with pleasure. He likes shape and texture in his mouth, and resistance that suddenly goes soft, and there's a pleasing tartness in the taste. He says to Belinda, 'How did your Amnesty stall go?'

'We made forty dollars.'

'Good girl.'

'Mrs Sangster bought some cakes.'

'The android lady. Does she eat?'

'I ran into Norma today,' Josie says. 'She was going up to see Lex Clearwater. Is he sick?'

'He was at school,' Belinda says. 'You could see his grundies through a hole in his jeans.'

'I meant to tell you,' Stella says, 'he's quit. Or left or whatever. At least I think so. I heard Pure Muir say, Good riddance to bad rubbish. Not the most original thing to say.'

'Who are we going to have for Social Studies?'

'Who's the Duff lady going to have as her playmate, that's more to the point?'

'Does it mean that's got to stop?' Josie asks, and Tom looks interested: 'You mean there's two schoolteachers having it off? I'll have to talk to my friend on the board.'

'They do it on his lawn.' Stella grins. (She would claim she never grins.) 'I saw them one day.'

'Just as long as you're getting an education.' He winks at her and wonders why she suddenly switches off. Daughters though are an aphrodisiac. He takes another lichee and pulps it on his tongue; and thinks that he might need to visit Stephanie tonight. (Stephanie owns a boutique in town but lives twenty kilometres out in the hills, which makes her less available than he'd like. She is 'the mistress'. Josie is 'the wife'. The captions are meant to be a joke but somehow they're not funny all the time.)

Tom pushes back his plate and goes into the lounge. 'Get lost,' he says to the cat in his chair. Dribble 1 is his name for her. The dog – asleep in his basket – is Dribble 2.

'Come here, Heloise,' Josie says, 'there's room for you,' wedging the animal between her thigh and the arm of her chair. The old cat purrs, is musical, contented again, and lives up to Tom's name for her. (Once there had been a companion, Abelard – 'Josie likes to show her credentials,' – but he had kept his male ways in spite of his doctoring, and failed to settle down in the new house. Went over the wall, became a bush cat, competed with hedgehogs in the night for his saucer of milk. He had a fatal encounter with a van taking a load of children to the Baptist camp. The weeping and wailing on that day. 'He's in cats' heaven. They prayed for him.')

Stella brings her parents a brandy. Belinda and Duncan, kneeling on a mat far away in the room, start a game of *Trivial Pursuits*. Tom reads the paper and Josie reads a novel half a sentence at a time – comes across the words 'naked hideous male gratification'. Goes back and reads with more care. Killing gratifies in this case, but the phrase, she decides, is a beauty, and she looks at Tom's face to see what she can discover there. She regards herself as a connoisseur of male expressions, and is of course world expert on Tom Round's. His face is like a spring, she tells her friends, and new things come bubbling up all the time. There's no way he can put a cover on, he's too self-centred. 'It's a pretty muddy spring too.' Sexual thoughts make his mouth swell and his eyes bulge. Power thoughts, gaining thoughts, pleasure in praise, anger, disappointment, kindness, love – she'll allow those last two, although they're nastily adulterated – aesthetic imaginings, mathematical intuitions, balancing calculations, all show in their various ways on his face. She's reconciled to him, in a small way, by what she calls his architectural thoughts. She believes, and has warned him, that they're starting to grow weak, but there's a lack of evidence and she's forced to admit there's no reason why a selfish man, nasty person, inadequate individual, utter bastard, poor weak sod, people-eater, should not design beautiful houses. Josie finds his houses beautiful and knows from experience they're marvellous to live in. Her marriage is over, she understands, but she's not leaving this house for Tom Round or anyone. It's like a child, she thinks, and God knows I'm better at loving things than he is.

She is not, in fact, better at loving the house. Tom loves it too, in all the obvious ways, but also in a way that lifts him and makes him soar. He goes beyond possessiveness and pleasure and reaches a condition of knowing. He describes himself – it's a form of self-praise – as 'a pretty basic individual, no crap', but claims to be, in his craft or art, 'a one-off job'. 'I tell you man, when I do *this* not *that* it's because I bloody *know*.' Nobody else knows, not in the territory he works, and he won't be interfered with. Oh, he'll take advice, even take instruction, in practical matters – durability, stress and strain, etc. – but if someone gives a sideways look and says, 'Well, I don't know', over a matter of design Tom will stamp on him like a bug. He isn't good with clients, wants them to keep out of his way; has lost a number of jobs because of it, but doesn't care. 'They want a bloody cave, they can hire Alley Oop.' There's a time when he soars away from cares of this sort, and the hard engineering of his job (though he likes that too). It doesn't happen every time, and he's savage then (punched a builder's foreman down a flight of steps), but when it does, Tom loses bodily sensation and lives in mind in a state of bliss. Time vanishes. Nothing holds sway over him; he is, in his own phrase 'a free spirit', engaged in 'the pure creative act'. He only talks about it when he's drunk; and makes no sense; but opens the experience, 'memory box', when he's in his solitary mood, feeling the pressures of mortality, oppressed by betrayals of the body, sorry for himself – but only a little – needing to pick up what's special to him. Then, after he has restored himself, gets basic again; flings himself about, makes a lot of noise, and, Josie says, 'crunches a few people up'. (She was looking at a book of Blake's etchings one day and came across Kronos devouring his sons. 'That's Tom,' she said.)

But he loves. He loves his houses; and this one above all the rest. Believes he reached a perfect marriage with himself when he designed it, and says (drunk again), 'That's my baby. Who needs kids?'

Now he puts his paper down and weighs the pleasures of sitting here against the pleasures of Stephanie. He spent the whole of yesterday with her in his boat, trying the motor out on a long run up the coast, and he scarcely laid a hand on her. Self control of that sort deserves a reward. But who needs a twenty-kilometre drive after dinner? Why doesn't she get a flat in town instead of playing little Miss Self-Sufficiency in the hills? Why can't she live right here with him, in his house – and Josie could be cook in the kitchen and bring them breakfast in bed.

Tom finds his wife watching him.

'You should get a new face, Tom. That one's a traitor to the cause.'

'I hope you two aren't going to fight,' Stella says. She has been watching her father too, but doesn't have Josie's skill in reading him, and makes her comment sharp because she's annoyed at not understanding. Her mother has told her about Stephanie (hasn't told Duncan and Belinda). Stella is pleased – thinks the affair a safety-valve; but wants more information, wants everything, for reasons only she and Mandy know. Quarrels are unproductive though, quarrels are a pain.

117

'I don't mind, but the pair of you are so unoriginal.'

'I deny that,' Josie says, laughing.

'The best insults improve with age.' Tom.

'Pipe down,' Belinda calls. 'We can't concentrate.'

'Sorry, love.' Josie picks up her novel, but doesn't read. Listens to their questions and is surprised by how much they don't know. Don't they know the Friendly Ghost is Caspar? Has so much time gone by? Caspar is the friend of the middle-aged now. She feels the loose skin at the angle of her jaw, then bunches it and wonders how much a surgeon would take off to make her young.

It is Tom's turn to watch. 'Don't do it, Jose. I like you the way you are.'

Her annoyance is increased because it's true. Tom has a taste for women passing out of their prime (see Stephanie, see Norma), and likes especially faces that had once been beautiful. He claims to be a face fetishist; bum and boobs, he says, can't compete with mouth and eye; and nothing brings him on more than skin loosening its hold or muscle just beginning to lose tone. The hint of ruin makes him sad and cruel. He likes his women short of time and desperate. Either that or starting out, eager, untried. But it's still the face he likes, even when the bodies are sensational. He likes to see fear and surprise.

Josie knows all this, and knows why Tom still wants her now and then. She decides to rise above him, for the children's sake, and goes into the kitchen and stacks the dishwasher, thinking about their mental growth; tries to penetrate the mystery of where they are going. Mandy will be a doctor, and a gynaecologist too if she has her way, and Stella a lawyer, specializing where property and power hand each other upwards step by step. They're both quite precise about what they want – but the women they will be remain obscure. Will they be happy? Will they hurt and be hurt? Their bodies will come to that inevitable sag and decline – not important – but what will happen to their minds, and who will be in there, behind the face, and will that person survive? None of her children has the openness she wished for; none of them is *sunny*; they are, she thinks, a slithery lot. Then takes the judgement back about Belinda – leaving Duncan aside, a special case. Belinda has a sunny side to her. Josie hears her laughing in the big room, with a bell-bird lilt, and a caw and squawk of ruthlessness. She has beaten Duncan.

Josie hears him laugh. It has no effect on her for a moment, then makes her skin prickle and contract. She has not heard Duncan laugh since before his accident.

She goes to the door and watches them. Belinda is packing up the game and Duncan lies on the rug (fiery orange!) and grins at her. 'How did you know that one about the cubit?'

'I didn't. I read your mind.'

'If I play this game a few more times I'll know all the answers.'

'Skite. I'll still beat you.'

'The Egyptian cubit was 20.64 inches. The Roman was 17.4. The English was 18.'

'That wasn't on the card.'

'I read it somewhere.'

Tom says, 'The Egyptians used the cubit when they built the pyramids.' Josie sees he's jealous of Duncan's knowledge. 'I'll take you to see the pyramids one day, Bel. They'll blow your mind.'

The girl looks at him with a tightening of her face, as though she's shrinking him and taking measure, then fits the board in the box and clamps the lid on. The hole in what he's said, where Duncan should be, appals Josie; she can't measure him, he's large and horrible.

'Come here you two,' she says to Duncan and Belinda. 'I haven't done your heights since . . . when was it, Bel? Ages ago.' She must be quick and get Duncan back in the family. She goes to the kitchen, takes pencil and ruler from a drawer, waits by the door into the laundry. 'Get a wriggle on.' Belinda comes in with Duncan in tow. A glance at her face: she understands.

'You first, Dunc. Look, look at this,' – a little screech, she woodpeckers her fingernail on the jamb – 'I haven't done you since,' reads the pencilled date, 'my God, September 1984.' She takes his shoulders, bossy, rough, cancelling significance from the pre-burn date. She lays the ruler on his head and levels it with her eye. 'Heels in. Against the wall.'

'You've got the ruler sloping downwards, Mum,' Belinda says.

'How's that? Right?' She marks the wood and Duncan steps away. He has grown two inches, more than two, and she wonders if his burned skin grows at the normal rate – grows at all? His scarring, which she has seen so close a moment ago, strikes at her and almost makes her cry out. She takes an exact measurement. 'Two and a quarter inches. That's . . .'

'Six centimetres,' Duncan says.

'And it makes you – five feet eight and a half.'

'Sure,' he says. He knows what she is up to. He's aware of Tom watching from the door.

'You'll end up a six-footer,' Josie says.

They all know he won't grow that tall. Tom gives a muted, 'Poof!' Now that it's Belinda's turn he walks across the kitchen.

'I'll never grow tall,' Belinda wails.

'There's nothing wrong with five foot four. You've got years of growing anyway.'

'I won't be as tall as Stell and Mandy.'

Duncan goes away, unseen. Tom says, 'Short girls are the best. Nice strong waists and round behinds. I can't stand these praying-mantis women.' He extends angle-jointed arms, grabs and munches.

'Oh, Dad.'

'At least you won't end up with a boyfriend shorter than you. Hey, did I tell you what I saw in the car-park today? This girl and bloke came out of the health food shop and she was six feet tall, no kidding, she could have been an All-American basketball guard, and he was five foot three, he came up about as high as her shoulder. They had their arms around each other and every couple of minutes they'd stop and have a kiss.'

'What's wrong with that?' Josie says.

'He had to put his face up.' Tom is filled with glee. 'And she had to bend down. Can you imagine, for God's sake, a man putting his face up to be kissed? Hee hee hee.'

He makes her feel a little sick: the rancour, the ill-wishing, the glee. Surely, somewhere along the way, he learned them, but now they seem as natural as crying and laughing in other people. There's a rage in him to hold Tom Round intact. Other men especially seem to threaten him by simply existing. She looks at his grinning teeth and is glad those two front choppers are acrylic. (The builder's foreman came running back and gave Tom the Liverpool kiss.)

'I won't measure you Tom, you're shrinking.'

'Ha bloody ha.'

'I'm going to have a swim before my homework.' Belinda.

'It's too soon after dinner.'

'No it's not. By the time I get my togs on it'll be half an hour.'

'I'll come in with you,' Tom says.

'I thought you had your water-sports yesterday.' It has no effect, he takes attacks of this sort as a sexual compliment.

She half-reads her novel again, listening to them splash in the pool. First Belinda rescues a bee, which Tom tells her she might as well squash because it won't get back to its hive in the dark; and if it lasts till morning and goes back it will have lost its swarm scent and the guards will treat it as an intruder and sting it to death. Belinda finds that cruel. She puts the bee on a leaf – 'Give it a last meal of honey' – and when they're in the pool Josie sees, through the green corridor of the conservatory, Duncan come from somewhere in the dark and sit in the shadows watching them.

The old dachshund, Sos, drags himself from his basket and waddles through the room with his belly brushing the floor and stands by the pool making half-hearted yaps.

'He wants to come in,' Belinda says.

'Not with me in here,' Tom says. 'I'm fussy who I swim with.'

'Just for a minute. He needs a bath.'

'No way.' He climbs out and brings his dive gear from the garage. 'I'll give you a lesson.'

Josie shifts to a cane chair in the conservatory, where she can get a better view. Ferns and flowers keep her company – she believes, currently, in personality, fear, desire, in plants – and Duncan too is company in a way. He has shifted into the rock garden, two levels up by the brick wall, and is sitting on a stone, which probably has some warmth left from the sun. She can see his body but not his face – and that, she thinks, is a bit of luck. Tom straps a diving-tank on Belinda and helps her with the mask, making her monstrously embryonic; and when she's in the pool and out of sight, Josie imagines her curled up and kicking in that womb. Little moths dance in the green light of the garden. It's more pleasant to watch them, she thinks, and push back imaginings and keep family out. Nice to be here all alone, wouldn't that be nice, oh wouldn't that be loverly, flitting with the moths and finding some corner to sleep in, high up in a corner in the dark.

Belinda floats weightless in dim water. She feels that rules have been changed and is frightened and elated equally. Duncan, looking down from his cooling seat, sees her elongated, sees her as oily convexities and yellow lozenges of light, yet knows it's her; faces a huge perceptual gap and wonders how he can measure it.

Tom porpoises around her, butts and lifts her, and can't understand why his energy seems frustrated, why his happiness runs backwards, breaks inside him and is gone. After a while he pulls her out and unstraps the tank, puts it in the garage. He comes back and dives into the pool and swims alone. Up and down, up and down, twenty-five lengths. He grabs his towel and leaps sure-footed up the rock garden (sees Duncan slip away) and sits on the brick wall drying head and torso. Along the valley a light burns in Clearwater's house. Westward the city glows and pricking lights stand on the port hills. Clearwater cannot see the city but can see the caretaker's house at the Baptist camp. We're like a row of warning fires, Tom thinks. Maybe the Vikings are coming. Maybe Te Rauparaha is on his way down. A good massacre, a bit of blood-spilling, wouldn't do Saxton any harm. Burn the place, he wishes, knock it down, then I can build a town worth looking at.

Belinda turns her light on and closes her curtains. Josie strokes her throat as she reads. Tom wants his house washed clean of them – Stella, wherever she is, Duncan lurking in the dark. He feels the house, he floats his mind into each space and level and feels himself co-extensive with it. It's as though he had flung a lump of house-stuff at the hill, then moulded it and squeezed it and hollowed out the rooms, and breathed his furnace breath and baked it hard. The people in there dirty it somehow, they're an infestation. He'd like to spray them out with a giant aerosol, a people-poison; or let off a small neutron bomb, get rid of them and keep his house intact.

He stands up and towels his body. The rubbing of the cloth brings a hunger leaping in his mind, and he runs again, down the rocks and through the house; like a boy, he thinks. He dresses, grabs a bottle, roars nastily with his car, sprays the lawn with sea shells, and is gone.

Thank God it's her not me, Josie thinks. Naked, hideous, male . . . She feels the gratifications of stillness and possession of herself. The smells of soil and dampness surround her. Far away Belinda practises her guitar. Duncan closes his bedroom door. Like Tom, she lets her mind flow out and fill the house. She would argue that living inside it makes it hers.

*

We've lost Stella somewhere. Let's say she's in her room studying. Her scholarship exam is getting close.

Before beginning her French she writes to her sister:

Dear Mandy,

It's starting to happen so we'd better get ready. He can't help himself but that's not the point. And she's so innocent I can't believe it. What's worse, she's so soft . . .

TWO

Dry Times

10

On her way to visit John, Norma stopped at her parents' house. The boy wanted to wait in the car. 'Come on, Duncan, they won't bite, try and face up to people.' That was a little unfair as he still had John ahead of him. He climbed out and went inside and let Mrs Schwass pat his face. 'Poor boy, I do hope it doesn't hurt too much.' She gave him a plate of peanut brownies.

Mr Schwass, with a white towel round his head and his stick held rifle-like across his knees, looked like a mad old desert sheikh resting from the sun. 'One of the few, eh laddie? Spitfire pilot?'

'No Dad, he wasn't even born.'

'No time to bale out, eh? Bad luck.'

'Has he got Alzheimer's disease?' Duncan asked as they drove away.

'Yes, he has. Where did you find out about that?'

'My grandma's got it. Last time Dad went to see her he said, "I suppose you'll say you don't know who I am," and she said, "No, who are you?"'

Norma laughed. 'Once Dad said to me, "Are you my mother?" He thinks Mum's his nurse or one of his girlfriends or a cow. "Get a move on, Gert."'

'Was he a farmer?'

'All his life. He never went to the war, though you wouldn't think so. Now he wants to drop atom bombs everywhere. We're still fighting the Germans and Japanese. Every time he hears a German name he goes "Oink, oink".'

'Schwass is German.'

'He doesn't think so.'

'The ridges on the brain shrink and you get fluid in the space between the membranes, that's the reason. Is the man we're going to visit old?'

'He will be to you, not to me.'

She was following an intuition in taking Duncan to John. In the three Saturday visits he had paid her she had not so much built up a picture of him as reduced him to a manageable size. In one way it had been like unwrapping a joke parcel and finding a bent penny or a chicken bone inside. He had a huge amount in his head but nothing in his mind. She left aside the memory feat, which was, she thought, no more than a kind of magnetic adhesion, pins and paper-clips, no credit to him, and had not looked at yet (was afraid of looking) the psychology of it, the flash of agony and flash of sight, and what she sensed must be the dangers of accumulation and not being able to forget. She kept her attention on mental uses and had not found him teachable so far. It was, she believed, a matter of getting him interested. Then perhaps he would differentiate and select, and learn instead of remember, and use instead of store up, and throw out all the things he did not need. But was he, she asked, when all was done, when you got past the victim with his sickness, this weird mechanical ability, and came to the ordinary boy, was he equipped for learning, was he able? She had not answered that question yet.

For the rest of it, she found him likeable. She enjoyed his jokes, admired qualities of silence and abruptness he possessed and found his physical over-emphasis – in turning not just half away but turning his back, in squatting suddenly when he wanted privacy, in swinging his arm (the left, unburned) faster and faster, in a wider arc, when he was angry – found it amusing, and sometimes alarming. She worried about the corresponding emphasis in his head, did it hurt? She wanted to touch his little, melted, yellow-rose ear and the horny spike (surely it could have been removed) on the angle of his jaw, try with her fingers if it was sharp. At times she felt like a tourist, like a voyeur, and felt she was indulging herself. She had always hated saints who kissed sores.

It was time to move the boy out of sole care and introduce him to a second teacher. She hummed with anticipation as she drove along; and was pleased with Duncan. He had fitted one of the bits of information in his head – Alzheimer's disease – to someone he had come across. He'd made the connection. She wanted to reward him but could only think of childish ways.

'Would you like an ice-cream, Duncan?'

'No thanks.'

'Eat one of those peanut brownies then.'

'I'm allergic to peanuts.'

128

'Really?' She saw that he had made a joke.

'I'm getting sick of nuts, Mum puts them in everything. Belinda's turned vegetarian.'

'And that means the rest of you have to be?'

'Not Dad. He keeps on talking about things like tripe and liver just to try and make her feel sick.'

'Does she? Feel sick?'

'She keeps on eating. I guess it's Mum who feels sick. Dad reckons she's neurotic in her stomach as well as her head.'

'I wouldn't say Josie was neurotic.'

'Everyone is in our house. Except me.'

Was that another joke? It was spoken in a neutral tone. She suspected him of taking cover from her and was disappointed he should think it necessary still.

Duncan had learned that by seeming to shift moods and opinions he could make her resemble a girl. It caused a little flicker in her outline. He enjoyed that not maliciously but because he felt a largeness in himself when it happened.

'You don't have to worry about Dad making passes at you.'

'Oh?'

'He's got a new girlfriend. She sells dresses. They go scuba-diving in his boat.'

'How does Josie take that?'

'She doesn't care. She calls her the mermaid. She tells Dad not to stay down too long.'

Mrs Sangster blinked and the car made a sideways hop. He had thought his mother said it in a double kind of way.

'I practise with Dad's gear when he's at work. I stayed down five minutes yesterday.'

'In the pool?'

'Yeah. Belinda does it too, he's teaching her, so she gets the blame for the tanks not being full.'

'That's not very fair.'

'Bel can take it. She's Dad's favourite.'

'Youngest daughters often are.'

'Did Mum tell you Bel's got a job? At Golden Hills on Sunday mornings.'

'I would have thought she's too young for that.'

'She told them she was sixteen. Anyway, she's only washing dishes and serving tea but all the old ladies think she's a nurse.' He put his hooked forefinger up and said in a quavery voice, '"Nurse, nurse, you forgot to put sugar in my tea." Bel loves it when they call her that. There's one lady there a hundred and three. That means she was born in 1883. And there's a lady who says, "Here you are again. What do you want? I've got nothing for you, go away." She tries to hit Bel with her walking stick.'

The car went past berry farms and kiwi fruit orchards enclosed in black mesh windbreaks. It crossed the river, where a shingle scoop was working, and went through fields of young corn and by two potteries with big brown jugs and blue plates standing in the windows. (One of his mother's friends made little white porcelain jars with red and green and yellow eyes on them and those were the ones Duncan liked, he often turned them round in his head and looked at the eyes looking out.)

'See those birds over in the paddock?'

'Sure. They're plover.'

'They only arrived in New Zealand recently.'

'Yeah, like swallows. I found a swallow's nest under the bridge. They build them out of mud.' He wondered why everyone thought he was loopy about birds. Birds were OK to watch but it seemed you had to get worked up about them and say how beautiful they were. The good thing was how their wings worked and the way their feathers were designed to shift the air and give them lift and momentum. Some of them did up like zip-fasteners. 'With one wing he swept the water.' An eagle could weigh ten kilograms yet fly a line as thin as a piece of string and if you drew its curve – on the water, say – the angle of the arc would never vary. That was the sort of thing that interested him, not what colour they were or how they fed their young or if they had one mate all their lives. It would be better if they didn't have mates and lived alone.

He said, 'That guy Zeno you told me to look up, he was a nutter.'

'Oh, why?'

'All he had to do was look and he'd see Achilles pass the tortoise.'

'Of course. But you do see the paradox? It's possible to prove mathematically that a fast thing can never pass a slow one.'

'A fast car can't pass a slow one on a bendy road.'

'Come on Duncan, you know what I mean.'

'No I don't. It's tricks, that's all. Like that thing with beans under walnut shells.' He knew it was more than that – had seen that Zeno was both right and wrong, and known there must be proof about the wrong, but he couldn't find it and gave up trying after a time. He had drifted off to sleep that night with the paradox in his head. He saw it might drive someone mad but he liked the evenness of it. The weight of the idea pressed on the weight of the real thing, the balance was exact, and back and forth they went like a perpetual motion machine. The same sort of thing had happened when he found a Möbius strip in a book Mrs Sangster had lent him. He made one out of paper and tried to see how it was possible. It wasn't like the paradox, the real thing seemed wrong; but there it was in front of him. He ran his pencil round it, ran his mind: one continuous surface, a band with a single side. It delighted him. He carried a Möbius strip in his head and every now and then zipped through it on a roller coaster ride.

'It was part of an argument for Zeno,' Mrs Sangster said. 'He was trying to prove that Being – that's everything – can't be broken up in little bits. Even Aristotle couldn't prove that he was wrong. You've heard of Aristotle?'

'He was a Greek. He owned some oil-tankers.'

'I sometimes can't tell when you're joking.'

He grinned at her. 'Aristotle. Greek philosopher. BC 384–322. I like it the way dates go backwards before Christ. Makes you think they started old and grew down into babies.'

The idea of gravestones lifting up and wrinkly old people coming out, wrapped in bits of rotten cloth, with earth dropping off them, made him laugh; but babies crawling back into their mothers was gross, it hurt his head. He frowned and got away from it. 'This guy we're going to see, is he a Scot?'

'Scot?'

'You know, Scot no friends. Nobody likes him.'

'I just can't keep up with the language,' Mrs Sangster said.

'I got that one from Bel. She reckons Stella's a Scot. I'm one too because of my face. I can look at people and make them turn into stone, eh? Like Medusa.'

'Med-you-sa, not Medussa.'

'Yeah. I saw her in the pictures. There was this guy Perseus, what

131

a name, he got her by looking in his shield for a mirror. Whacked her head off. I was hoping she'd get him. I liked her best.'

'I didn't know they'd made a movie of it.'

'Then he used her head to kill the sea monster. She was the best thing in it. Her hair was snakes. I'd like to be like her, eh? Pow! Stone.'

There was something benign, though, in his wish. She was almost prepared to say that he looked on humans as a soft species, squashable, a bit like, say, caterpillars, and he handled them with care, put them in a safe place; forgot them. And looked on himself as hard and solitary, free. Non-human or non-caterpillar? that was the question. He must not be allowed to withdraw from the human race.

'John isn't a Scot,' she said as they drove up the valley. 'He's just a man who's happy with his own company.'

'So what does he want to see us for?'

'Oh, he likes to see people. He's not a hermit.'

John was sitting in a canvas chair on his lawn, reading a book and drinking a glass of beer. He wore a sun-visor that gave his face a greenish graveyard tint, made him look ill. When he pulled it off, his long, northern face took a russet hue and his nose gleamed like a misshapen strawberry. Duncan turned half away as though by putting himself side on he might be invisible. 'Yeah,' he said to Norma, 'nice place.'

'Duncan, this is Mr Toft. John.'

The boy gave him a quick look. 'Hi.'

'So you are him, eh, the boy Norma talks to me about? You can learn whole books is what she says.'

'That's not the only thing about him,' Norma protested.

'And you have these bad burns, yes I see. Do they still hurt?'

'They itch a bit. Sometimes they ache.'

'And the doctors, they had you wrapped in tin foil like a loaf of garlic bread?'

'For a while.'

'And they robbed you of some skin from your bottom for your hand. Is that fair to your bottom, do you think?'

'It's a bit sore sometimes·when I sit down.'

'Does it feel like hand skin now or bottom skin? Perhaps it has some memory of where it belongs.'

132

'John, for heaven's sake, you'll give him nightmares,' Norma said.

'And goes crawling in the night, eh, back to its proper place?' Duncan said. 'Hey, that's neat.'

'The pair of you are being quite revolting,' Norma said. She felt some comment of that sort was called for; but, like Duncan, had grown interested. How had John known that the boy would play this game?

'I've got a bit of leg skin on my face.' He touched his cheek-bone. 'I guess it feels OK there. It give me a speedy sort of face, eh?'

'Medical science is mighty clever,' John said. 'They can move the skin around, and change over livers and kidneys, and make rubber hearts, or is it plastic? And soon, no doubt, they will graft fast feet on to slow runners and make them win Olympic gold medals.'

'Stick tails from sharks on swimmers,' Duncan said.

'And maybe eagles' wings on men and women and make them fly. And all this will alter our minds. We will have a great new age.'

'I have dreams where I fly.'

'Too near the sun, like Icarus. You know that story?'

Duncan was still a moment. Norma almost felt his mind go click. 'Yeah, I read it. His old man made him wings but the sun melted the wax. He was dumb.'

'There are other ways of getting close to the sun.'

Norma moved away. They could be left. 'I'm going for my walk, John. I won't be long. Oh, there's peanut brownies in the car.'

'Your car runs on peanut brownies, I think.'

'There's a car that runs on gas from pig manure,' Duncan said.

'We must do away with fuels and aim for telekinesis. Move about with our brains, what do you think?'

She left them talking and climbed the slope through the Gravenstein trees. The apples, green and hard and ready for thinning, made her mind shiver and contract. She pictured it for a moment like a walnut in its shell, unreceptive. She did not care for the sort of fantasizing John and Duncan had fallen into, thought it shallow, possibly damaging, yet liked the ease it created for them. She felt exhausted herself – Duncan had that effect, he kept one alert, but at the end one suffered a collapse from the hard work of it all. Perhaps that was why the springing greens of the orchard failed to refresh her – she was too small and dry, and time rather than place would

133

work a renewal. The long grass swished and tickled round her knees. She bent this way and that like a Balinese dancer, avoiding branches. She splayed her hands, arched her fingers back (wished for long nails), made movements of her forearms on a plane, and slid her head back and forth in the dancer's way; proceeded several yards through the trees in silken gown and head-dress, making ritual flight from a demon; then laughed at herself, caught in her own kind of fantasizing. But was refreshed, in that quick moment. Wonderful, the mind, its powers of renewal. Perhaps telekinesis too was in human possibility. Not now, of course, or for centuries. But Duncan might be a pioneer, one never knew.

She did not, though, want to think of Duncan. She had thought about him too much in the last few weeks. Her time in the orchard was for herself. She thinned an apple cluster, hoping that she left the right ones on. Trade skills, trade knowledge, even at their most simple, demanded respect, and were an aspect of, well, spirit, what other word? She felt she had been guilty of a minor blasphemy, of taking easily what should be treated with reverence, and wished the apples back on the tree, left there for the hand of one who knew. Then laughed at herself, trilled out amusement. Fantasizing again – investing the mundane with, oh, deep significance. Looking for pathways to a hidden meaning. What a disease it could be. One had to deal firmly with these symptoms or find oneself outside the quotidian, and that was the end of being useful.

Really, she thought, I'd better just find some sunshine and lie down.

She reached a fence with rusty wires and posts furred in lichen. Beyond was a paddock left for hay, then the forest began. How pines darkened a landscape. Even in this stillness, how they stilled. One could imagine . . . no, she declared, enough of that. No gnomes or trolls or wood-sprites; and no pantheistic transports. Sensuous things only, please, she asked. Grass stroking her legs, sun on her skin, clean air washing out her lungs. Scent of pines. Brittleness of lichen. Valley, mountains, to delight the eye. More than enough.

She climbed the fence, half afraid the rusty wires would snap, and walked up the paddock to the pines. There would be hay-making soon, and one more apple harvest, then the valley would be turned to another use. No need for John to repair fences. His house would be pulled down. Bulldozers would root out his apple trees – loop a chain around them, give a tug, out they'd come like thistles in a garden, and a new crop, little glossy, green, bristling pines would take their place. Aggressive little trees those, invaders, survivors; but she could not work up the hatred for them some of her conservationist friends felt. One had to look on pines as another crop and see that it was kept in its proper bounds.

She sat on a mat of needles and looked down the paddock, over the orchard, to the house. John and Duncan were setting up one of the telescopes on the lawn. They must be going to do some sun-watching. She hoped John had warned the boy not to look directly, then put that worry out of her mind. Duncan would know. He had brought out John's binoculars and was looking down the valley – perhaps over the plains, over Saxton, at the mountains of the Armitage, lovely clean-limbed Imrie with the gleaming mica face, and jagged Corkie where the aeroplane had crashed in the winter. She wondered if the glitter on a ridge was part of it. One of her girls had died in the crash. When you had nine hundred girls the deaths came all too frequently.

Sheryleen Cato was the child's name, a first year preppy. Norma had not known her well but had studied the class photograph later on, and saw a bright-eyed face with pointed nose, a beetle black-ness, beetle sheen, in her hair, and a happy shyness on her mouth – all smashed to pieces on a mountain-side. Five died in that crash, pilot and family, and Norma tried to see a flashing away of souls, like shards of glass, to some bright home, but could not make the figure, and came back to the thing she knew – child grinning at the camera. Loss and pain, she thought, that's what we're equipped to know, not happy futures or eternal life. She sometimes tried to put the child's few years into a sum, add them to the total of human experience, as though increase made a sort of meaning, no matter how short the life had been. But that left her out, that Sheryleen, and meaning went flashing off to nowhere, like those bright souls she could not see. The only thing to do, she thought, is grieve until you stop, and then go on with what comes next.

She looked back at the house and found Duncan watching her. She was, at once, violently angry. How dare he watch? With those strong glasses he must have seen her thoughts upon her face. She made a chop with her arm, turning him away; and, yes, he had

135

been watching, for he swung the glasses in a new direction.

Rotten boy, with that way of gobbling down whatever he could find. She felt that he had taken Sheryleen. She moved into the pines, climbed a little hump that hid the house from view, and came down to the paddock edge again, into sunlight. She sat, then lay, on pine needles, feeling their elasticity. The tree-heads seemed to rotate and their movements increase. That, she thought, was caused by passing cloud wisps in the sky. There was no promise of rain in those clouds, no rain in sight anywhere. (No rain since those October storms five weeks ago.) The stars would shine for Duncan tonight and he could suck them one by one like sweets and add them to the sum of himself.

She folded her hands under her breasts and closed her eyes and let herself drift to the place Josie Round called the plateau. Edges slipped, events, both imaginary and real, ran into one another, then grew thin and distant, went away, leaving her without any substance, and her consciousness without any weight. She sometimes came back frightened – by what, she could not say – but usually was refreshed and leaped up as though from a plunge in some cool stream. She wondered if, simply, the trivialities of her daily life, all the dust and muck of her feelings, were somehow put off like a skin. But being fresh, shouldn't she remember where she had been? And what caused the fear she sometimes woke with – came back shrinking with, terrified to move in case she might be noticed, in case an eye might slowly turn on her? Did she visit some good part of herself, and then – thank God, less frequently – visit a bad?

On this day, in the pines, Norma drifted a little way, then slept; and was woken by the shadow of John Toft falling on her. She sat up with a cry, not knowing him or the world.

John apologized for frightening her. 'I have never seen you wake, Norma. It is a very naked thing.'

'What did you see?'

He sat beside her. 'How tiny and fragile you are. How thin the margin between sleep and death.'

'It would be nice not to wake. But then . . .'

John laughed. 'Ah, you have your double vision still. One of your eyes sees dark, the other light.' He lay on his back and sighted up a tree at the sky. 'This boy, he is unusual. I don't know if I can work him out.'

'Where is he?'

'Down at the house. He reads some books, then looks at the sun, then reads some more. I think he is like a dog and doesn't know when to stop eating.'

'Have you tried him out to see if he remembers?'

'No, I'll take your word. The problem is, as you say, to turn it into some useful course.'

'He won't go back to school. And he doesn't want a job.'

'Jobs are a long way off, I think. Perhaps he will never have a job.'

'But he must. We can't just let him opt out.'

'You are talking like a teacher.'

'That's what I am. And I'm not going to let a good brain go to waste. Anyway, you said "useful" yourself.'

'I meant useful to himself. So he can turn from, what shall we say, acquisition? Turn to interest. Turn to enjoyment. Otherwise, I think, he will reach an end one day and close his eyes and die.'

'Ah, you've seen it too. All he's doing is filling himself up. Does he like the sun?'

'I think it has a special taste for him. But it's no great thing. "The size will crush you," I said. "And the distance will make you smaller than an atom. You must not try too hard to take possession because you cannot hold even a small piece of it all." He said: "Aw, that's easy. Ninety-three million miles, that's easy."' John laughed. 'And as for size – he turns it in his hand like a tennis ball.'

The image of the sun slides off the screen but the movement is the movement of the earth. Duncan smiles. Easy, easy. And zooming right down from huge to tiny, easy too – thousands of kilometres an hour down to this. A tortoise could go faster. He laughs. There's no need any more to fill huge spaces. All he needs to do is set up lines back to himself. 'Make leaps,' Mrs Sangster has said, 'you don't have to walk heel to toe all the way' – and it looks as if she's right. He can make a kind of web in the world, a web in space, and sit in the middle – he doesn't mind 'like' any more – like a spider.

He puts the lens cap on the telescope and pauses to look at the instrument. The finder-scope is set in the main tube at an angle.

That means mirrors inside, bending rays of light in a new direction. Interference, pressure, influence. His interest in levering and bending is coming back. And light – he blinks at the sun – must have the greatest influence of all. Does it have weight? There must be tons and tons of it pouring out of the sky. If you could concentrate it, bring it all together in one place ... And does it have a sense of its own speed? Is speed a thing that happens to light or a part of it?

Duncan is not ready for that. Hard vibration starts in his mind. He picks up the binoculars and looks at the pines and the stillness and the darkness relieve him. He goes into the apple trees and walks in the shade. A track of bent grass leads to the top of the orchard. He sees where Mr Toft followed Mrs Sangster. They're somewhere in the forest, and maybe they want to be alone. That amuses him. Two old people like fourth formers in love.

He finds a place where he can straddle the wires. The grass is fat, with heavy heads of seed, though farmers are complaining they need a week of rain for a good hay crop. It's great, he thinks, how seasons come and go all because the Earth is tilted on its side. If it was straight there'd be no cycle of things and no life. It all started because of an accident, the way the Earth was lined up with the sun. Millions to one against, that was the odds, which was why people thought there must be God. He cannot see the need for God himself – chance was an OK explanation. And when you thought of the number of galaxies out there, it must have happened thousands of times, so there could be thousands of races with brains as good as ours in the universe. If you believed in God you had to believe human beings were the only ones.

Duncan is happy, he's elated. He walks up the paddock to the pines and goes a little way into the shade and sits with his back against a trunk. Trees go off in every direction, side by side. His mother thinks, or says she does, that plants can be happy or afraid. He doesn't believe it. His mother likes to play games, that is all. But he's fascinated by the identity of each one, the chance of its being here, right here, and its atoms and molecules being *here*, not somewhere else. He looks at his hand and has a strong sense of his good fortune in having it – in being alive, in being himself – and is possessive, jealous of his identity.

Mrs Sangster and Mr Toft walk by in the paddock. She's holding on to him like his wife, though it makes his other arm go kind of stiff. Stella and Bel would love to hear she's got herself a man, and so would Tom, but Duncan won't tell. He hears her voice, which seems too neat and sing-song for the country: 'I've been thinking about a girl who died in a plane crash. One minute she was alive and happy and the next . . . And Duncan's friend, alive, then dead. And Duncan with his burns, all in a moment. For no reason . . .'

Duncan curls his lip. Of course there was a reason, Wayne did something dumb. Mrs Sangster got easily worked up and that made her thick about some things. With all the stuff she knew you'd think she'd be a bit smarter and not worry about what couldn't be changed.

Duncan watches them walk down the paddock. They sink into the slope until their heads are floating like two balls on the sea, and those go down and nothing's there. It seems like a message to Duncan. It seems to say people can be gone and it will make no difference to him. People can be emptied from his life and he won't care. The warm, yellow paddock is left. The sun and sky are left. And he's left here; and he's enough. He can let people move from left to right, or right to left, across his mind and not be touched. He can, of course, touch them if he likes and use them for some fun if he likes – but there's no need. 'Whee!' he says softly to himself. He's a little alarmed. He wonders if there's something he has missed – some bit of danger he can't see. But he puts the binoculars up and looks at the sky and swings across: nothing there. He lowers them and looks at the valley. Most of the orchard is out of sight, but a farm stretches down to the plain. In a paddock by the creek a girl is jumping a pony over a white-painted log on a trestle. She could die too, any minute, fall off and break her neck, but right now she's alive and having fun. He watches her through the binoculars, sees her teeth grin as she goes over, and her helmet jog crooked on her head. It's a school friend of Bel's, Kirsty something – Davidson. She puts up a hand, straightens her helmet, pats her pony on the neck, then spits, a long one, curving, and jerks round to see no one's watching her. I'm watching, Duncan grins. He doesn't mind telling Bel that her friend spits.

He walks away from the orchard, past a fire-break separating the pines from native bush. A bell-bird calls from up the hill but Duncan goes down, throwing his arms round trees to keep his feet. The creek in the gully is almost dry. He crosses it with a leap and climbs to a clearing by the road. A car is parked alongside a picnic table and a woman lies on a rug with a straw hat shading her face. Duncan, standing in the bush, is interested in the way the weight of bone in her legs spreads her muscles out and how her breasts flatten with their weight. If we walked on four legs, he thinks, our muscles would have a different shape and our bones would bend in different ways. He looks at her husband playing with two children further off. It's a game his father and Bel used to play, but this man isn't half as good as Tom. He doesn't show his teeth and hook his fingers and make a meal when he catches a child. 'What's the time, Mr Wolfie?' cries the girl. 'Half past three,' the man drones, pacing along. 'What's the time, Mr Wolfie?' says the boy. 'A quarter to four.' Pathetic. 'It's time I got my file and sharpened my teeth,' Tom would have said. All the same the children are in a state of fright and when the man cries, 'Dinner-time,' and gallops after them they scream more with terror than enjoyment and the boy is almost in tears as he runs into his mother's arms. The boy is the favourite, Duncan sees. His father has chased him twice in a row.

'Yum yum,' the man says, eager now. He pulls the child from its mother and bites it on the stomach.

'Me, Daddy, me,' the girl screams.

'That's enough,' the mother says, and turns half away in disapproval. Sees Duncan. Her eyes dilate and her mouth drops open. She's caught between breaths and can't make her lungs work. Duncan thinks, turned her into stone.

'Dan,' she says, 'Dan,' reaching up and hooking her fingers in her husband's belt.

The man puts the boy down, steps at Duncan, lifts his arm as though chasing off a dog.

Bugger you, Duncan thinks. He comes out of the bush and strolls by. 'Bird-watching,' showing his binoculars. 'There's bell-birds and grey warblers in there.' The boy has a bite-mark and saliva on his stomach. I might have saved his life, Duncan thinks. He winks at the girl, making her squeak.

'Come here, Gail,' the mother cries.

Duncan walks backwards two or three steps. 'Don't let them play with matches,' he smiles. Then he goes on down the dirt road towards the orchard, shading his face from the sun.

Turned her into stone. Bloody good.

11

Shelley walked through the right-of-way. She was on her way to visit Neil Chote but not even Hayley knew that. Hayley rode her bicycle close behind, with her swimming togs and towel on the carrier. She was heading up the river to Freaks' Hole (so named in the sixties when a tribe of hippies camped under tent-flies on the bank and scandalized Saxton by swimming without togs). Hayley hoped to meet her boyfriend Gary Baxter there.

As they entered the turning-bay an old lady ran from her door. 'Girls,' she cried, 'come and help me please. Ken has fallen down the stairs.'

'Who's Ken?' Shelley said.

'My husband. He put his stick on the wrong step.'

'Is he hurt? Do you want a doctor?'

'I just need someone to help me get him up the stairs.'

'OK,' Shelley said.

Hayley leaned her bike on the fence. They followed the woman into the house and saw an old man in a dressing-gown lying on the carpet. He was mooing like a cow and waving a big walking-stick around. A broken vase of flowers lay half-way down the stairs and a scent of freesias filled the hall.

Shelley squatted beside the man. 'Anything bust?'

'Now Ken, don't hit, she's come to help,' the woman said.

Hayley tried to take the stick away but the man held on. 'Too many women.'

'Take it easy,' Shelley said. 'Let's get you up the stairs, eh? Grab his arm, Hayley.'

Although he looked big in his thick gown the man was light. They lifted him and made him take a step.

'Ha, pretty girls. Let's dance a rumba.'

'Behave yourself, Ken,' the woman said. She put her hands on his back and tried to push him up.

'Don't need you, old girl. Damn it,' he dropped his stick, 'the world's going round and round.'

He had the smell of something going off, cabbagy and meaty. One side of his face grew silver whiskers and the other was shaved, making him look broken in half.

'He's got my leg. Ow, shit!' Shelley cried.

The old man had her thigh in one long paw and was digging in. The woman said, 'Be good, Ken,' but Hayley saw he was holding on, not attacking Shell. She tried to help her sister break the grip and got the hand away after a moment. 'I'll have fucking bruises,' Shelley said.

'Oh my dear, you shouldn't swear.'

'It wasn't your bloody leg.' There were tears of pain in Shelley's eyes.

'Let's just get him up, eh?' Hayley said. 'Got him, Shell?'

They levered him into a sitting-room and guided him backwards into a chair. 'Throned,' he cried. 'My stick, wife, bring my stick.' The woman fetched it from the stairs.

'I just about cut my foot on that bloody vase,' Shelley complained.

'You should wear shoes. No Ken, don't hit. Stay out of range, girls. He's very pleased to see you but he gets excited. Oh, it's nice you've called. We don't have enough visitors. Sit down. No, the sofa, Ken did some wets on the chair.' She started for the kitchen. 'I'm going to make a cup of tea for us all.'

'I don't want tea. God, it stinks of piss round here. I'm going,' Shelley said.

'I want to wash my hands.'

'Me too.' They went into the kitchen. The woman was plugging in the kettle. Shelley and Hayley rinsed their hands at the sink.

'One of you girls put some peanut brownies on a plate.' She had thin legs and heavy humped-up shoulders and cushiony breasts. If she fell over, Hayley thought, they'd have to get a crane to hoist her up.

'We've got to go. Can't stay for tea,' Shelley said.

'Oh, what a pity. Ken will be disappointed. You must let me give you some money for an ice-cream. In that tin, dear. No, not that, that's Ken's treasure trove, the other one.'

Shelley closed the first biscuit tin and opened the next. It was half filled with ten and twenty and fifty cent coins.

'Take a handful, we've got far too much. And you must let me give you a bag of peanut brownies.'

They went back through the sitting-room.

'Who the hell let you in?' cried the man.

'Come and see us again,' the woman said. 'And next time you must have a cup of tea. Ken enjoyed your visit.'

At the corner Shelley dropped the paper-bag of cookies over a fence. They counted their handfuls of silver and had more than three dollars each. Shelley laughed. 'Money for an ice-cream, shit!' She did not tell Hayley about the notes in the other tin – five hundred dollars at least, maybe a thousand. There were orange and red notes at the bottom, underneath a fat stack of green. And Hayley had no time, before she and Shelley went different ways, to mention the photograph of Mrs Sangster she'd glimpsed on the dining-room sideboard, and the wrinkled ghost of her in the old lady's face.

Her old man's mad and my mother's mad, Hayley thought. It surprised her that teachers should have troubles of that sort.

She chained her bike to the fence and walked along the shingle bank to Freaks' Hole. No one was there. Most people went to the big holes downriver, where you had to swim with screaming kids and pot-bellied men who perved on you and dogs chasing sticks, even though notices were nailed on the trees: *No Dogs Allowed*. You had to dodge beer cans and broken glass. Here it wasn't deep, not up to your chin, but at least you got it to yourself. If it wasn't for the golfers through the willows and the Rounds' house along the hill you could swim in the nick like those hippies.

She changed into her togs and sat on the sand. The river was low because of the drought and slimy weeds grew on the rocks. You had to ignore that when you swam, or have fights with it, wind it round your neck like a scarf. It only looked dirty, really there was nothing wrong with it. The water was so clear you could see pebbles, brown and green and white, magnified on the bottom.

Hayley had a swim, diving and porpoising and doing back somersaults. She swam the length of Freaks' Hole under water and was in the rapids at the top, letting water run over her, when Gary arrived. 'Bugger him,' she said. He had brought his creepy friends, Tuck and Legs. 'What did you bring them for?' she said when he swam up.

'Why not? They won't look.'

'They won't have nothing to look at.' But in the deeper water they rolled all round each other. She helped him get his fingers in, not that it felt any good, and held his cock and rubbed him till he came. She would have let him put it in if it hadn't been for Tuck and Legs watching from the bank. She kept up-river from his come and watched it curl away like bits of weed.

'Some lucky slag down in Monday Hole is gunner get that,' Gary said.

She swam away from him, not liking him, even though he was so neat to look at. On the bank she took a fag from Tuck and lay on her towel and smoked, listening while they told jokes that got more and more filthy. Some of them made her feel sick. She saw their cocks slew round and stiffen in their togs and wished someone would come so they'd have to roll over and shut up.

Gary took a can of beer from his bag. 'No thanks,' Hayley said. She'd told her father she wouldn't drink or smoke and she threw her cigarette away, deciding she'd keep the whole of the promise. She went into the water and swam around and when Gary joined her she said, 'You brought those two for a gangie.'

'No I didn't. You're all mine, eh?'

'You're a liar. Why do you hang around with creeps like that?'

'They're all right. They buy me booze.' He was feeling between her legs. 'Give old Tuck a hand job, eh? He's never done it.'

'No.' His cunning pretty face made her sick.

'I'm gunner put it in this time.'

'You're not.'

Then Tuck and Legs surfaced beside her. They came up like seals, poking up their heads, and rubbed themselves on her bum and hips. Their arms unrolled and slithered round her neck. She thought they were going to pull her under and was terrified at the thought of drowning. Someone – it was Gary – stuffed weed in her bikini pants. Legs pulled her bra down and made a finger-bite on her breast. 'Lay off,' she screamed; and punched him with ridged knuckles on his throat. She found a hand pressing her mouth and bit as hard as she could and heard Tuck scream. She spun away from Gary, jerking her head through the noose of her bra, and made it to the bank; grabbed her jeans and T-shirt and ran.

'There's people watching you,' she cried, half-seeing a golfer in red through the willow trees; and although she was sobbing her fear was gone, because she knew she was better with her body than any of them, better at fighting and running, quicker and harder at everything. No one like Gary would get her. She stopped and picked up a stone the size of a hockey ball. Legs was on his hands and knees at the edge of the water. Tuck had his bitten hand hugged to his chest. She lined up Gary and threw at him underarm, hard and flat. He spun side-on, with a shout that turned into a scream as the stone hit his forearm. He fell over, rolling on the shingle.

Hayley pulled her T-shirt on. She walked the rest of the way to her bike. Her knickers were at the pool but the bikini pants would do. She took the weed out – it felt nice and cool, better than Gary with his fingers – and pulled on her jeans. At the first bend in the road she found a place where she could see the lower part of Freaks' Hole. The three of them were sitting on the shingle, nursing themselves. She'd wiped out the whole lot of them.

Hayley laughed. 'Jerk each other off,' she yelled, and she turned round and rode back up the valley, past the bridge to the Rounds' house, past the golf course. She wasn't ready to go home yet, she'd find a place and have another swim. She felt this was the best day of her life. She'd got past creeps like Gary Baxter and felt she had travelled a long long way and good things would happen to her now. All the same, as she rode, she sobbed in her elation. They would have raped her, they would have drowned her. She knew that she could easily be dead and felt something dark and horrible close by her shoulder.

She found a pool by the top of the golf course and washed her face and swam up and down, twenty lengths, in her T-shirt and bikini pants. She was not even puffing when she stopped.

'Plee,' a voice said.

She looked up the bank and saw a Japanese man in a neat little cap with a white pom-pom, smiling at her. She had not heard his ball land in the pool but went where he pointed, and dived and brought it up and lobbed it to him. He caught it in one hand, gave a little bow, laid something on the grass, 'Fi' dollar,' and dropped the ball over his shoulder. She watched him play his shot, and scrambled up the bank when he had gone. A five dollar note lay on the grass. She was a little insulted that he'd taken her for a child. He wouldn't have offered money to a woman, probably tried to chat her up instead. She watched him join his friends on the green, and the four, in bright trousers, take their turns at putting. Golf was expensive in Japan, her father said, so the trawlermen brought their clubs to New Zealand. They'd never get near a course at home.

Hayley walked across the pool, holding the note, and put it with the silver in her jeans. Everyone was giving her money today. She felt happy now that something stood between Gary and her and she smiled at the way the Japanese golfer had said please.

Two joggers went by along the bank. Stella Round and her big sister, whose name Hayley could not remember. Their faces were bright red, over-heated, and Hayley was sympathetic, although she usually hated Stella Round. She watched them cross the footbridge single file and go away through the willow arch, flashing on and off like lights, red and blue, red and blue. The big sister was the one who had saved her brother's life. She hadn't tried to save Wayne, of course.

Hayley turned her face away. When she remembered Wayne she felt her chest go empty as though her heart and lungs were taken out. She saw how it could happen to anyone. If Wayne was dead, Wayne who had tried wrestling holds with her on the floor, and smoked fags in his bedroom and used the air freshener before their father came home, and eaten with his mouth open – 'Chew with your mouth closed, Wayne' – if Wayne was dead then she could die as quickly, just as easily, one day soon.

Hayley jumped up and pulled on her jeans. She rode up the valley and saw goats in the bracken by the road. A drive with ruts in it curved steeply in the scrub. She got off her bike and wheeled it up, not sure this was Lex Clearwater's place, and not sure he'd want her if it was. She couldn't remember anything special now in his invitation and felt like a pupil walking up.

A goat was tied to an iron stake where the drive elbowed back. She stopped to feed it grass and was amused by its comic chewing and troubled by the sharpness in the black part of its eye and a kind of blindness in the yellow. It was as if it saw, saw everything, but didn't have any interest. Didn't give a stuff. Only for itself. Nothing could be more greedy than its mouth.

Pellets as black as licorice fell from its bum. It's just a machine for eating, Hayley thought, and was a little disgusted even while the goat's greediness attracted her. It butted her hand for more grass.

She walked on with her bike and found a house at the back of a sun-baked lawn. Dry land stood behind it like a wall, crumbling away, and dried-out bracken grew higher up, and only the pines on the top of the hill seemed alive. The tea-trees and the gorse by the fences seemed made of crinkly wire and broken sticks. As for the house – she couldn't believe Lex would live in such a run-down place – if it was Lex's. She looked about for a sign. No ute. No clothes she might recognize on the line. Goats were the only thing and plenty of people had goats. She thought she had better go away.

'Hey, Lex,' she called; then, small in the silence, 'Mr Clear-water.' Goat heads looked at her from the bracken. She wondered if goats ate people at all. They seemed to eat anything they could find. She did not want to go back down that drive closed in with scrub.

Hayley stood her bike on the lawn. She hoisted herself on to the porch – it was really just a deck made of planks, not even nailed, curling at the ends and making warps. Her father would be disgusted, but she was half frightened, half excited, feeling she'd reached a place where rules were put aside and did not count. She looked in the door. 'Lex?' she said.

A torn envelope lay on the sack used as a doormat. She picked it up and read 'A. G. Clearwater', and felt her stomach give a lurch. She expected to see him come from one of the doors leading into the room. 'Hey, anybody home?' Blowflies, bush-flies, drilled at the window panes over the sink. A bird with sharp claws slid on the iron roof. Hayley wondered if Lex was dead. The stillness in the house was like TV, before you opened doors and found a body in the shower. She crossed the living-room and went down a hall, looked in three doors – junk-room, bathroom, bedroom. The bed sheets were filthy, yellow grey, and the pillow had no case and bits of chip foam-rubber leaked out one end. She curled her lip, then giggled as she thought of Sandra Duff in there with Lex. It stopped her thinking of bodies, though she looked on the floor beyond the bed. A glass of milk with a rubber skin stood on the window sill. A folded dollar note (more money) lay beside it. It looked as if it had been jammed in the frame to stop it rattling. Hayley was tempted to keep it, but she smoothed it and put it on the dressing table, where old half-used bottles and pots, Oil of

Ulan, skin balm, female stuff, stood like a forest of stumps. She blew the dust on them but it was thick and greasy and wouldn't move.

Hayley went back to the kitchen and looked in the fridge but found only butter and cheese and half a tin of herrings. Maybe he ate goat's meat or maybe fish and chips. Men were supposed to stop looking after themselves when their wives walked out. Lex had sure done that. Socks and underpants soaked in a bucket on the sink but the water smelled bad so they'd been there a long time. She could wash them and hang them out; saw herself pegging socks on the line when he came home, but sniffing the water put her off. She sat on the porch and enjoyed the sun and watched the goats. Over the golf course the willows by Freaks' Hole made a patch of green against the foot of the hill. She couldn't see if Gary was still there. She'd better give him a bit more time, she wouldn't put it past him to ambush her as she rode home.

Lex drove up in a Land-Rover. He pulled up on the lawn beside her bike and climbed out and looked at her distantly. 'Yeah, gidday.'

'I thought I'd come and see you like you invited,' Hayley said.

'You should've rung up, eh. I'm busy today.'

'I didn't know I was coming. I'll go if you like.' She did not want to go and found herself trembling from the shock of Gary's attack. It was as if he had waited until now to leap on her. She felt cold and crushed and tears ran on her face. Lex Clearwater brought himself up close. She saw his eyes make a painful cranking on to her, and she thought, He's mad, he's loony; but wanted him to comfort her.

He put his hand on her shoulder. She slipped down from the porch and stood in front of him, leaned on him, arms folded on her chest.

'What is it, Hayley? What's wrong?'

'Nothing. Something happened, that's all.'

'Where? At home?'

'At Freaks' Hole.' She had not meant to tell anyone, but poured it out, that moment in the water when they closed around her. She felt his finger trace a mark on her throat and chest.

'What's this?'

'They scratched me, I guess.'

'They sure did. You want me to go and sort them out?'

'No, I did that.'

'Yeah?'

'I punched Legs in the throat.' She put up her fist with the middle knuckle jutting out. 'I bit Tuck in the hand.' She had a sudden memory of blood in the pool. 'And I chucked a rock at Gary. I think I might have bust his arm.'

'Jesus then, there's no need for me.'

'Gary shouldn't have brought them. He wanted me to take them on as well.'

'This Gary joker's your boyfriend, eh?'

'Not any more.'

'You want to be careful, Hayley. A bunch of blokes like that – plenty of girls have ended up dead.'

'I thought he liked me. I liked him.'

'Did you used to fuck?'

'Sort of. We were careful. I always made him wear a condom.'

'Sounds like more than sort of.'

'What I mean,' she shook her head, did not want to tell him, 'he wasn't much good. He was after what he could get.'

'Who isn't?' He took his hands away from her. 'Want a cup of coffee? I'm having one.'

'I don't like coffee.' She put her arms around him, hugged him hard. He smelled of sweat and goats, and of the sun.

'Cut it out, Hayley. That's not on.' He reached behind him and broke her grip.

'You told me to come.'

'Not for that. How old are you? I'd end up in jail.'

'I won't tell. You want to,' grabbed his fly, 'I can feel.'

'Stop playing hot pants. Shall I tell you something, I could be just as dangerous as those guys in the pool. You better stop putting yourself in situations like this. Anyway, I haven't got time. You want that drink? There's some Ovaltine left if the mice haven't got it.'

'Ovaltine,' Hayley said bitterly.

'Take it or leave it. You can have a glass of water if you like. You want me to put some stuff on that scratch?'

'So I don't catch Aids, eh?'

'Shut up, Hayley. You're not as tough as you like to think.' He went into the house. She followed him across the planks and watched from the door as he put the kettle on.

150

'I'll have coffee.'

'Thought you would. How's school? Work all over?'

'Yeah, we're frigging around, clubs and stuff. Prize-giving practice. Not that I'll get any prizes.'

'None for softball?' He lifted the bucket of soaking clothes to the floor and got two mugs from a cupboard; looked in them, wiped their insides with a baby's napkin worn to rags.

'She doesn't look after you very well.'

'Who?'

'Miss Duff.'

'You're out of date. Sandra doesn't come here any more.'

'Couldn't she stand the gunge? I couldn't stand it.'

Lex laughed. 'Get it off your chest. Here,' went to another cupboard, 'Mercurochrome if it hasn't dried out. Put it on yourself, I'm not touching you.'

'Wouldn't let you.' Hayley grinned at him.

They drank their coffee sitting on the porch. A breeze coming up the valley made a hissing in the scrub. She shook out her hair to dry and pulled her damp T-shirt loose from her breasts. She was glad now that Lex had said no. Sitting with him, talking, wasn't as much fun, she supposed, but it made her relaxed.

'Where's your ute?'

'I sold it.' Gestured at the Land-Rover. 'She'll go more places.' He threw his coffee dregs on the lawn. 'Want to see?'

'Where?'

He hooked with his thumb. 'Up the valley. Won't be back till, maybe after six.'

'Can I ring Dad?'

She told him she was helping Mr Clearwater with his goats.

'That's all right, Hayley. Try and be back before dark, I'll keep some tea. Hayley?'

'What, Dad?'

'Where did Shelley go? Did you notice?'

'Judy's, she said.'

'Yes, all right.'

'What's wrong?'

'I heard Neil Chote is back in town.'

'She wouldn't go with him.'

'No, I hope not. Goats, eh? Be careful of that pitching arm.'

'I will.'

Lex had backed the Land-Rover round behind the sheds. She saw him busy in a pen with three goats. 'Grab that one in the corner. Get his yoke off.'

'What for?'

'They won't need them where they're going.' He stripped a big nanny of her yoke and tossed it into the shed, where it rattled empty bottles. Hayley fought with her goat, a half-grown male, and wrestled the yoke from its head. 'They're strong, eh?'

'You'll find some bits of twine on the bench.'

She fetched them and Lex threw the goats one by one on their sides and tied their legs. He carried them to the Land-Rover and laid them on sacks in the back. They kicked and twisted, trying to get free, and he climbed inside and held them still, 'Take it easy, easy now, everything's all right.' Hayley got in beside him and felt their warm sides and ran her hands on their silky hair. She felt the tender dewlaps of the small billy and looked in his deep blind-seeming eye.

'Put those sacks on them.'

'They're not cold.'

'I don't want anyone to see.'

They covered the goats and climbed out and Lex closed the door.

'Where are we taking them?'

'Up the valley. Up the side of Corkie.'

'Are you setting them free?'

'Yup. There's no feed for them here. I'm only keeping half a dozen.'

'You're not supposed to set goats free, are you?'

'There's lots of things you're not supposed to do.'

She got in the front beside him and he drove down to the road, past the tethered goat, and turned up the valley. He told Hayley he'd released twenty-three goats in the last week, that was why he'd bought the Land-Rover. 'You've got to keep it secret.'

'I will.' She was delighted. 'Where are they all?'

'Some up on Lud Hill. Some over on the coast, back of Salty Bay. I took six way up past Coppermine yesterday and another six last week across by the Heaphy, back of Bainham. Nearly got caught by some trampers there.'

'Won't they just get shot?'

'Some of them will. Some will probably get caught again. I've told them what the score is. They're all willing to take their chance.'

'You don't mean that.'

'Sure I do.'

'You talk to goats? They understand?'

'Better than fourth-formers, I'll tell you that. Those three in the back, they kicked a bit, don't like all that handling and tying up, but that's just something they've got to do. They know where they're going.'

Hayley laughed uneasily. It made her nervous, Lex being loopy, though loopy was not a bad thing when you thought of some of the people who weren't.

They went on to a metalled road by the Baptist camp. It followed the course of the river, switching from side to side over one-way bridges with rails shattered where hoons in cars had hit them. The Saxton water-pipe made a curving leap across the gorge. Before, when she'd seen it, Hayley had wanted to walk across, but felt today she'd left that behind.

'Will you try and catch them when the drought's over?'

'Nope. They're on their own. I'll go back and see them now and then, if I can find them. I mix them bucks and does so they can breed. I guess they'll team up with wild ones though.'

'What will you do when you've got none left?'

'I'm keeping the ones at home. These are the last I'm turning loose.'

'Yeah, but for money, for a job?'

'You sound like Sandra.'

'Is that why she's not your girlfriend now? Cause you've got no money?'

'I've got some. She left,' he grinned at her, 'because she reckoned I was turning myself into a goat. She reckoned I'd start saying baa pretty soon.'

His eyes were like a goat's eyes, Hayley thought. The pupils were OK but the coloured part seemed blind, or saw what people weren't supposed to see.

'I like goats better than people,' Lex said. 'They only know what they've got to know.'

They turned into a track climbing in scrub and came out in a forest of pines. It seemed like a different level of the world. Hayley leaned on him for company. The pines were no taller than the Land-Rover but soon the road ran into a block of older trees that hid the sky. She wanted him to say something friendly.

'Hey, Lex.'

'Yeah? What?'

'You used to teach Shelley, eh?'

'Who's Shelley?'

'My sister. She used to run.'

'What about her?'

'Her boyfriend's back in town. He's been in prison. Dad's scared Shelley's gone back to him.'

'He the one who got her to use that credit card?'

Hayley was pleased. 'That's him. He's, like, got her hypnotized.'

'Who is this bloke?'

'Neil Chote. He acts tough but he's not really tough, he's kind of crazy. He'll do anything. He doesn't care.'

'Sounds like Shelley should steer clear of him.'

'I think she wants to but she can't. He tried to make her take some LSD. One time he burned her with his cigarette.' She wished Lex would offer to sort out Neil Chote.

'Better stay away from him, I reckon. Up here we go. It's pretty rough so hang on tight. Don't lean on me, I can't steer.'

She moved away, offended. Below her door, the land dropped into a gorge where little fans of white water showed between boulders. The front wheel spun and pointed, angling out then back, a tire's width away from the edge. If the clay caved in they'd end up a hundred metres down, smashed on rocks; but she wasn't scared. She did not believe Lex would make mistakes; and she forgot his coldness, yelled, 'Hey, this is great,' and put her arm outside and banged the door.

'Beehives,' Lex said.

They stood, a city, pink and blue and white, in a clearing on his side of the road.

'Bush honey, better than clover.'

Then it was behind and branches thrashed the Land-Rover on his side while empty air pulled them like a magnet on hers. If the track got any steeper, she thought, they'd turn over backwards and roll all the way down to Saxton, end over end.

'How far now?'

154

''Nother twenty minutes. We've got to get round the side of Corkie, where she runs into the mineral belt. The bush opens up there. Goats have got to have a bit of space.'

'Will we meet anyone?'

'Shouldn't do.'

'Can I drive?'

'No fear, you'd have us down the gorge. No more pines eh, real bush. This is the way it used to be.'

She put her head out the window and looked back. A bit of Saxton showed, scraps of grey, like dirty paper, beyond half a dozen folds of hill. The plains, with orchards and gardens indistinct, dull green or navy blue or faded brown, went off to the foothills and the mountains and the sky. The inlet was full, milky blue, with Stoat Island, Jacks Island, lying flat and ragged and half swamped. Long Island, with its pines turned black and a thread of breaking sea on its five-mile beach, closed the inlet. Yachts and trawlers sailed on the bay, making little smudges on the glitter, and a black and yellow tanker lay off the Cut.

'I've never been so high,' Hayley yelled. 'My ears went pop.'

They bumped over a ford where the water was almost dried up, and further on Hayley got out and dragged a fallen branch from the track.

'That means no one's been here. Not for a while.'

'There could be trampers. But they mostly go up the top of Corkie. We turn here. See how the bush is getting stunted? This is the snowline.'

They drove in a dry creek bed, with the Land-Rover crawling on rocks and easing its tyres down the other side. It turned so far over, her way first, then Lex's, it would have capsized if it had been a boat. When she looked back the long view was gone. Tops crowded round and the way they leaned inwards made her shiver.

'What's up?'

'I was wondering if you'd turn into a goat.'

'Not today. You're pretty safe.'

They stopped in scurfy beech trees no higher than her head.

'This'll do. See over there, those brown hills are in the mineral belt. So they'll have the open country and the tops and the bush for shelter lower down. Real goat country. Better than being fenced in, eh? There's too many concentration camps.'

155

'With those oblong pupils in their eyes, do they see things kind of square?'

'Maybe. They see things different, that's all I know.'

They lifted the goats out and Lex untied their legs. At once they scrambled up, almost threw themselves on to their feet, and clattered away ten metres on the stony ground and suddenly stopped.

'Go on. Get lost.'

'Do they want to say goodbye?'

'Goats don't go in for that. They're sizing things up. Piss off, you silly buggers. If you hang around here some bastard with a gun will come and shoot you.'

'Maybe they want to stay with you. Aren't you their friend?'

He moved away from her and she felt as if he'd pushed her out of a room and closed the door. If he did not want people sharing his goats why had he brought her with him then? She leaned on the tail of the Land-Rover and watched. But Lex did nothing more and the goats walked further off, stopping to look at him in their side-headed way as if they expected him to follow. They scrambled up a bank and went around some beech trees and were gone.

Then Hayley felt Lex shift out of himself. She felt him travel off with the goats. It was like a tearing, part from part, in his head. 'Lex.' She went towards him, unsure what to do, and put her arms round him from behind. He made a hard twisting of his shoulders, enough to throw her several steps away.

'Come on, Lex.'

She held him again, pressing her cheek in his shoulder blades. He smelled of goats. She knew she must bring him back from there.

After a while he loosened her hands and turned around. She had thought he might be crying but his eyes were dry and hard, a human look.

'All I had to do was start.'

'Then I would have been left here alone.'

Lex was quiet. He laughed. 'That never crossed my mind.' He put his arms around her and she thought, It's going to happen. She was terrified. 'One day, Hayley, I'm going where they are. And I'm not coming back.'

'What would you eat?'

He smiled, and said, 'I've got to get rid of all this stuff we carry round. So if you and me fuck it's a oncer. You can't hold me to it later on.'

'You'll be a goat, you mean?'

'I don't know what I'll be. You want to do it? I don't mind if you say no.'

'Yes, I want to. Where do we go?'

'In the back.'

'The goats have pooped in there.'

'Drag all those sacks out. Just leave the clean ones on the top.'

'I don't want to do it where the goats were.'

'Sure, OK. I guess it's kind of soft over here.'

She took off her T-shirt and laid it on the ground and knelt beside it. 'Lex.'

He was watching her.

'Don't just open up your fly.'

'Is that what your boyfriend does? Sounds like he's got a lot to learn.'

'If it's just for once it's got to be proper.'

'Don't worry Hayley, it'll be proper.' He knelt in front of her and pulled her close and when she tried to unzip his jeans would not give her room. She quietened down, kept still. He seemed to step them back and make a place for them to start again.

They made a bed of all their clothes on the ground.

'No, cut that out,' holding her face where he could see.

'I thought you'd like it.'

'We don't need any tricks. Nice and simple, that's the way.'

He made her move easily and slow. She had never come properly with Gary, but came soon after Lex was inside her, and he stayed in and talked to her a while, then moved some more and she came again, and was doing it all the time, it went on and on and when she thought it was going to finish another one started. She heard her voice calling out, making sounds not words, and heard herself panting as though a race was over.

'Noisy, aren't you?' Lex said.

'I hope no one heard.'

'I heard.'

'Well, I wanted you to. Are you supposed to stay hard like that?'

'I hardly moved. I let you do all the work.'

'Haven't you come?'

'Not yet. Wasn't easy.'

'I want you to. I want everything.'

'Do you want to get pregnant?'

'Don't go. Stay in, please.'

'You couldn't come again if I stayed all night. No you don't, no mouths. Your hand is fine.'

She did it with her hand and was happy at the shout he made.

'Is it always as good as this, Lex?'

'Depends on who you're with.'

'Can't we do it another time?'

'Nope. A deal's a deal.'

'Where can I find someone as good as you?'

'It ain't easy. But listen Hayley, don't start shopping round.'

'I won't. No more Garys, that's for sure.' She closed her eyes and smiled. She was so pleased with herself she wanted to make purring sounds.

'Come on, time to go.'

'Was I asleep?'

'Yep. On my jeans. I can't get dressed.'

'Do we have to get dressed?'

''Fraid so, Hayley. If I'm going to get you back.'

She pulled on her clothes. 'What are you looking at me like that for?'

'So I'll remember. Give us . . .' He took her hand and moved it between his own, to feel the way her bones ran side by side. He pressed his fingertips on the edge of her nails.

'Oh, Lex.'

'Hey, we're OK. Nothing bad is going to happen.'

'Why don't you be like other people?'

'Come on. In the cab.'

'Why, Lex?'

'Can't, that's all. Thanks, Hayley. I'm glad you came to see me. I guess it was more than I deserve. Hands off. No more.'

They drove down to his house and said goodbye.

Hayley rode home along the valley.

And Shelley, who went to visit Neil Chote, where is she? As Hayley rides by the river and through town Shelley is in a car by the soccer ground. She sits in the back, where girlfriends sit, and every now and then she puts the back of her hand to her mouth and brings it away smeared with blood.

The sun goes down and the sky above the mountains turns red. Around the soccer ground and over the water by the marina street-lights go on. She leans on the car door, her cheek on the window, and waits. She waits for nothing. She does not care what happens to her now. The pain in her swollen wrist, which she holds in front of her as though her forearm is suspended on a hook, scarcely seems to be part of her.

She hears feet running far away and shouts like seagull cries and squeals like a dog. Then they stop.

Slowly the evening turns to night. The lights harden up and make a field of yellow round themselves. Voices are talking in the right-of-way. A policeman comes out and looks around and crosses the road. He opens the front door of the car and shines a torch on her. His smile gleams in the dark.

'Shelley Birtles, eh? We thought we might find you in on this.'

12

The dog snored in his basket by the sofa, the TV set laughed in another room, Stella and Miranda competed in knowledge of the world, in the clever word, and Norma wished herself at home. She had not come to listen to these girls. She'd had enough half-bakedness, articulate or not, in her year, and wanted to relax and chat with Josie, who had phoned and asked her round for a pot-luck meal (salad and quiche, nothing pot-luck about it, vegetarian cordon bleu). Tom was on the tiles so the pair of them could have a couple of drinks and a good old natter, Josie said. Norma had supposed Mandy and Stella would be out.

'It's not a drought, it's simply a dry spell,' Miranda said.

'Abnormally dry.' Stella.

'Oh but it's hardly summer yet. To talk of drought when all we've had is six weeks without rain –'

'And spring's scarcely over –'

'And the rivers are full of water –'

'It shows how much the farming mentality rules in this country. If the grass doesn't grow we're in mortal danger one would think.'

Belinda put her head in from the TV room. 'Ever Decreasing Circles,' she shouted, and was gone.

'I think some of those redneck farmers would sacrifice virgins for an inch or two of rain.' Miranda.

'They'd keep the virgins,' Stella, 'and sacrifice their dried-up wives instead.'

'Ever Decreasing Circles,' Belinda cried.

'You should try to wean her off TV, Mum. God knows what the inside of her mind is getting like.'

'Oh, I watch that.' Miranda stood up. 'It's one of the more literate sitcoms.'

Stella blinked. Remade herself. 'That main character has got a very interesting psychosis.'

'And there's a dishy neighbour,' Miranda said. 'I fancy him.'

Miranda was growing up, Norma thought, almost liking her.

Stella's confusion was likable too. Would she follow Mandy? Yes, she would, though awkwardly. 'It's nearly holidays, I guess I can slum.' It took a Round to wrong-foot a Round.

'Let's sit by the pool,' Josie said. 'You can swim if you like. I'll lend you some togs.'

'I don't think I will. Chlorine makes me sneeze.' She settled in a canvas chair and looked at the luminescent surface. 'There'll be water restrictions soon. You'll have to close it.'

'Oh, Tom pumps from the river. There's nothing in nature Tom can't overcome. Droughts, floods, you name it. He just pops into a phone booth and changes costume.'

Norma laughed. She hoped they were not going to talk about Tom.

'What he can't handle is other people's feelings. Other people's feelings,' Josie puffed her cigarette, hunting for something shrewd, 'trespass on his space.'

They were going to talk about Tom.

'He'd like us all in neutral,' Josie said.

'This Stephanie,' Norma hoped she had the licence, 'doesn't she take the pressure off?'

'Increases it. He comes home and seems to think he's got to re-establish himself here.'

'With you?'

'It's the idea he likes. Running two women.'

'Let's not talk about Tom,' Norma said.

'Why not? He makes for pretty good conversation. I think I climbed Tom because he was there. He's just something I stuck my flag on top of. Mount Tom. Nice when the sunset catches him. I wish the bastard wouldn't keep coming home.'

'Climb another mountain.' She was not sure flippancy was called for. Wasn't Josie asking for help?

Josie laughed. She turned up her face and blew smoke into the air. 'I have no desire,' – with a nasal pitch; delivery comic, content hard.

'For another man?'

'For anyone.' Josie smiled. 'Tom still gets me twitchy but that's habit. What I've found out in the last few weeks, I don't need sex. Correction. Sexual partners. I just need me. It's wonderful. I'm going to write a book and start a revolution.'

Norma took a cigarette. She did not often smoke.

'You're shocked,' Josie said.

'I guess I'm shocked at solitariness. I don't think that's the way to go.'

'I'm not solitary, I'm talking to you.'

Norma took a puff and stabbed the cigarette out. What a foul taste. 'Are you sure you haven't rationalized it, Josie? Other men are no good after Tom and women won't do?'

'No. I'm talking about – God, what? Norma, something marvellous is happening to me, with work and friendships and my kids, and being by myself and not needing anyone else. I've always had people chipping at me, running away with bits I need. Jesus, Tom got off with a barrow load. But now it doesn't happen any more. When I said revolution just now, it's a sort of no-sex I'm talking about. I mean, when it gets so I need something – hell Norma, it's like a cup of Milo before bed.'

'Don't you get lonely?'

'No, I don't.'

'Don't you want someone there with you?'

'There's nothing wrong with a bit of fantasy.'

'So you do want someone.'

'You're talking about yourself. Loosen up. Sex isn't in it really, you know. Being enough for yourself in every way is what it's called. I'll tell you what, I'll come along and give the prize-giving speech. I'd love to get the message to those girls.' She grinned fiercely.

'What do your own girls think about it?'

'Oh, families are different. I can't tell them.'

Norma laughed. Suddenly it shrank to nothing at all. Another Josie fad, bee in her bonnet. What Josie could find arguments for Josie would do. Some things worked for a while, no doubt. She sat and looked at the night and the stars glittering emptily over the hill, and thought about the difficulties of living alone. One learned a set of stratagems and put all those other ones of daily connection by. Forgot whole areas of play and desperation and all those cunning thrusts, discoveries of the mind and the affections. What had Josie done? – made a move because of pressures on her. Free move? Oh the pressure was inescapable, but the move was free.

I should stand up and cheer. She's on an ascending curve; and

Norma wondered where she was herself. Starting to descend perhaps? On her way down from a place where she had known contentment? Discontents were making their bat-squeak now.

'You know what I miss most?' Josie said. 'Loving my kids. No, I mean physically, of course I love them still. But touching them and hugging them, they don't want it any more. Even Bel is getting past it now.'

No child, no lover. But isn't it my corner-stone that I'm not troubled by regrets for things I chose not to have? How would an adman put it – regret-free? And look now, my career. See how it sparkles and shines. Norma laughed.

'It isn't funny.'

'I'm sorry, Josie. Just some nonsense in my head. There must be other satisfactions. Seeing them grow up into women.'

'That's when the pain really starts. I wish I could,' made a lifting movement with her hands, 'pick them up and shift them where I am.'

'No you don't.'

'Don't be so bloody pious, yes I do. You think there's some virtue in that stuff with men? Love and trust and kicks in the teeth? You kept clear, I notice.'

I won't get angry, Norma thought. But really, does she have to be so crass? She shouldn't be so *careless* as that.

'Duncan is a man. Or he soon will be.'

'Don't kid yourself. Duncan is a nothing. No, no, sorry, I mustn't say that. Duncan is – what? – evidence?'

'He's got some life, you know, outside your mind.'

'Yes, he has. But I keep on thinking someone said, "That'll bloody teach you." Duncan as a lesson to me. Isn't that what God's supposed to do? Cut us down when we get uppity. Jesus, if I thought the prick had used Duncan on me . . .'

'Oh shut up, Josie.' Said it pleasantly. But self-indulgence of this sort really was disgusting. 'Tell me about his telescope.'

'He just went out and bought it. Four hundred bucks' worth. Drew the money from his own account. The day after he met your friend.'

'Well, isn't that good?'

'Is it? Do you think it makes a jot of difference how he'll end up? Why in hell did you bring up Duncan? I'd managed to forget him for a while.'

You managed to forget the way you feel. Duncan isn't something in your head. 'Don't have another drink. You've had enough.'

'Who are you to tell me what to do? Oh Norma, I'm sorry. You're my friend. You're right, I won't have another. Booze just screws me up, I can't think straight. Duncan is improving, isn't he?'

'I think so.'

'He took me up,' she waved at the top of the section, 'and showed me a globular cluster last night. It was beautiful. I had no idea. And he knows all the names. In a week.'

'I'd like to get him back to school some time. At least into classes of some sort.'

'Yes, please do.'

But how? And where? And to what end Duncan might choose? There was a long way to go and Norma had the sense of being excluded. It seemed she might have played her part, and John Toft his, and Duncan be moving on his own. She felt robbed of possibilities for love, astonished at her sudden nakedness. She had not thought him much more than a job, an exercise in – caring? – the fashionable term? The boy had not looked at her or spoken at the table, had gone without a word at the end of the meal, and later she had glimpsed him climbing through the rock garden, dropping over the wall, with a squat black box in his arm.

'A telescope,' Josie had explained.

'It's one of those short ones,' Belinda. 'You can see the moons of Jupiter.'

'Ah,' Norma said. She had felt elated; and depressed.

He sits in his possie in the firebreak and finds M7 in Scorpius. Viewing low in the west isn't good because of the city-glow over the hills. But there's no single light anywhere. Duncan has chosen his place. The house is hidden by the curve of the hill, and Clearwater's and the clubhouse at the golf course are blocked by trees. There's only one small stretch of road where car lights show.

Saturn is gone. He is too late for Saturn. In all that time he wasted it was there, passing over from east to west. Now it's in the city-glow and it won't rise again until next June. Venus is nearly gone too, but Venus doesn't interest him. He wants to see rings and satellites. He does not want ordinary, unmarked, perfect things. Soon he will shift to Jupiter, high in the north. At half past nine Io

164

will disappear into eclipse. East to west is the movement after opposition. Duncan means to time the event. In the meantime he practises finding the Messier objects in Scorpius, then uses Venus to find Neptune and Uranus. The distance of those two makes him smile. He spans it between his finger and thumb.

His stand for the telescope works fine, there's not the slightest bit of wobble now. Hard work lugging up that length of tanalized post and the four half-buckets of concrete, and tricky getting the level right and screwing on the chipboard plate and vinyl pockets for the tripod legs. On the plate is written in felt-tip: Equipment for Astronomical Observations. Do not Disturb. R. Observatory. The 'R' stands for Round but Duncan hopes forestry workers and trampers will take it for Royal. He is using the stand for the first time tonight. He thinks he might show Belinda soon, and maybe his mother. Not Mandy or Stell. And what about Mrs Sangster? He feels a little guilty about her; the sudden way he found he didn't need her any more. He's embarrassed by the kind of crush he had, but knows it isn't fair to act as though they haven't been friends. Next time she comes he'll talk to her.

Now, though, he doesn't want anyone. He looks up to the north and finds Jupiter with his eye, just like a star among the stars. The ancients were pretty bright to notice that it moved. You couldn't blame them, he supposed, for working out their crazy stuff as an explanation.

He gets Jupiter in the spotter-scope, then shifts to the big scope and makes the planet jump towards him, millions of miles, with its raft of Galilean moons; and there is Io on the eastern side.

Duncan bares his teeth. 'Beaudy,' he says.

'I think I'll have a swim after all.'
'What about your sneezes?'
'I'll just have to try mind over matter. Will you come in?'
They went to Josie's bedroom and Josie found a one-piece suit for Norma and bikinis for herself. 'Why use these things? Tom's not here and Duncan's gone.'
'Don't let me stop you.' Belinda might be sensible but could any child resist such a tale – Mrs Sangster swimming in the nick? She put on the togs, wishing these little freedoms were not denied her. They made her buttocks feel as though set in cement. Josie put on

hers: perfect fit, body all ship-shape. That must be the aerobics she did.

They were at the water, dipping their toes, when Belinda cried, 'Phone for you, Mrs Sangster.'

'Nobody knows I'm here, who is it?'

'It's a man,' Belinda grinned.

'Hallo, Norma Sangster.'

'For God's sake Norma, where have you been? I've been phoning all over town.'

'What's the matter, Clive?'

'It's Mum and Dad.'

She turned from Josie in the conservatory door. She put her hand on the wall to touch something firm. Clive's nittery voice went on and on.

'Yes,' Norma said, 'tell her I'm coming.' She put down the phone. 'Josie, I'm sorry, I've got to go.'

'Is it something bad?'

'Mum and Dad. Dad's in hospital.'

'Oh, Norma.'

'Someone broke in and tried to rob them.'

'Hurt them? Attacked them?'

'I don't know.' She went to the bedroom and took the swimsuit off. It had cut deep marks in her thighs. 'Don't tell the girls. I'd prefer not to have it round the school.'

'Is your father all right?'

'Clive thinks he's dying. I'm sorry Josie, bad news makes me rude.' She went out to her car and drove away. How absurd, she thought, to find out a thing like this wearing someone else's tight bathing suit. She could not, yet, think of what had happened.

Clive was in the ward foyer, leaning on the window sill. He ground out his cigarette. 'They stick me out here because I smoke. Non-smokers get a waiting-room.'

'How is he, Clive? Can I see him?'

He led her along the ward, put his head in the sister's office, 'I'm taking Mrs Sangster to see Mr Schwass,' and showed her into a small sideroom. The empty bed by the window made her gasp, then a curtain squeaked back round a second bed and a woman came out. Plain woman with one off-centre eye. Her white coat meant she was a doctor.

'This is my sister, Mrs Sangster,' Clive said.

Norma saw her father through a gap in the curtain. He was sleeping with the stern look she remembered from her childhood.

'He's deeply unconscious, Mrs Sangster,' the doctor said. 'He's not in any pain. I want you to be certain of that.'

'Is there any chance that he'll recover?' She was pleased that she could speak right out and not waste words. She watched the doctor weigh her.

'I don't think so. A massive stroke. I don't think recovery – we shouldn't wish for it.'

'You can't say that,' Clive began, but Norma stopped him.

'And he won't hear anything we say?'

'I think perhaps I'd sit and talk to him and hold his hand. But really he's deep down and far away.'

Norma had a flash of admiration for the woman – to say these ordinary words and yet avoid cliché . . . 'Thank you,' she said, and went behind the curtain and sat in a chair by her father's side. 'Hallo, Dad,' she whispered, putting her hand on his. The skin was papery and moved on the hand-shape underneath. 'Can you hear me? I love you, Dad.' She managed that before Clive came in. He stood at her side and seemed to be waiting for some act she might perform.

'Did they hurt him?' she asked.

'He's got some bruises here, on his shoulder,' he touched his own. 'No, he's not hurt. They held him down. God knows, his mind just kind of, I don't know, went bang.'

'Did they hurt Mum?'

'One of them got a handful –' Clive turned away and swallowed, ' – he got a handful of her stomach and twisted it –'

'God.'

' – trying to make her say if there was any more money.'

'Is she –'

'Mum's all right. Mum's pretty tough.'

'Who were they, Clive?'

'I don't know. Two of them. Not Maoris, both of them white. There was a girl in it too.'

'What girl?'

'I don't know any names. She waited outside in a car. Don't talk about it, eh Norma? Not in front of him.'

Norma sat and held her father's hand. She lifted it and was surprised by its weight. One did not feel that weight when lifting one's own. With this thought she felt him go from her; and though he lived she gained a sense of ending, of something done and brought to its close. Tears ran on her face. She kissed his brow.

It seemed this was what Clive waited for.

'I think you should go and see Mum now. I'll stay here. If you want to come back when she's asleep we'll work it in shifts with the old man.'

'Yes, I'll do that.'

'Bring me a packet of smokes when you come.'

She drove out to the berry farm and found her mother drinking tea.

'I can't get her to go to bed,' Daphne said.

'I'll have to take one of those knockout pills when I go to bed so my stomach won't keep hurting where that silly boy twisted me. How's poor Ken?'

Norma kissed her. 'No change, Mum. He's still unconscious.' She knelt by her chair and held her tight.

'Ouch, dear,' Mrs Schwass said. 'I think he loved his adventure today. He was always talking about fights.'

'He's had a stroke, Mum. Don't you understand?' Daphne said. She had red eyes and a swollen nose.

'He was marvellous trying to hit them with his stick.'

'Do you want to tell me?'

'You shouldn't make her remember it,' Daphne cried.

'I certainly don't intend to forget,' Mrs Schwass said. Norma had not known her so sharp in years.

'I'd love a cup of tea, Daphne. Did you know them, Mum? Had you ever seen them?'

'They had stockings on their heads so they looked all squashed up like plasticine. When I opened the door I thought they wanted pennies for the guy. "It's too late for Guy Fawkes, boys," I said. Then they just pushed in, absolutely rude, and one of them – the fair one because he had some hair sticking up through a hole in his stocking – he caught me round the jaw and squeezed my mouth . . .'

'No squeals, grandma, or I'll break your fucking neck.' He spun her round so fast her head went dizzy and ran her at the stairs, with one arm round her throat and one round her middle. His knee butted under her behind and lifted her up at each step. The other man ran ahead. She heard Ken shout and saw him swing his stick and catch his attacker on the arm. 'Good one, Ken,' she tried to say. Then her captor threw her on the sofa and the other man lifted Ken and clapped him in a chair. He hooked the handle of Ken's stick under his chin and pulled his head back.

'How do you like that, you old fucker?'

'It was like a butcher's hook,' she says, 'as though they were going to hang poor Ken on a rail.'

Her man pulled her up. 'OK grandma, let's see what you got. Money first.' He put his arm over her shoulder in a way that might have been friendly if the forearm had not angled back and forced up her chin. She wasn't afraid and tried to tell him so. She wasn't afraid for Ken. It would satisfy him if his life ended in this way. She did not care for the cruelty of the men and their language was so nasty she wished they would give her time to say what she thought of it.

'Where's this money in the biscuit-tin?'

The queen was on the lid, smiling away. A fat lot she knew. Men like these would never come within cooee of her. He pushed her into the corner between the sink and stove, made her sit, put his foot on her to hold her down. That was degrading but she did not struggle. His face, flat and fat and ugly in the stocking, made him somehow – what was the word – incommunicado? He must like such unhumanness. The sprig of hair poking out the hole would annoy him – so boyish, she thought.

He ripped off the lid, grunted at the money. 'How much?'

'It's Ken's nest-egg. He'll be angry if you take it.'

He stuffed the notes into a plastic bag from his pocket. Looked in the coin tin. 'You can keep this for ice-creams. What else have you got?'

'Peanut brownies if you're hungry.'

He pushed his foot into her. 'You're a cheeky old bitch. Jewels and watches, eh? Where do you keep it?'

'No, you're mistaken, we're not rich.'

He opened crocks and tins. Felt in them. He emptied sugar on her, flour, tea, and she spluttered and coughed. 'That's a dreadful waste.'

He pulled her up. His misshapen face was alarming, but she was not going to be scared. 'I'm going to call the police in a minute.'

'Try that and you'll get your tongue ripped out.'

That was too absurd to frighten her. She guessed though that he would hit or squeeze her, choke her maybe until she died. His judgement would be poor on a thing like that. She wanted to see what the other one was doing to Ken.

'There's a few things in the bedroom but they're not worth very much.'

'Where's the bedroom?'

He marched her back, arm under her chin. Ken was sitting upright in the chair, his face purple and his eyes closed. The man had put the stick down and was holding him by the shoulders, but she thought that wasn't necessary. 'This old fucker's passed out.' It was more likely that he'd had a heart attack. 'Oh, Ken,' she said.

'He shat his pants.'

That would have been from rage not fear. She wanted to explain that much at least. But the man, the boss, kneed her into the bedroom and pushed her face-down on a bed. He rummaged through the dressing-table drawers and stuffed her rings and brooches into the plastic bag on top of the banknotes. In the bottom drawer he found Ken's Kruger rands.

'What are these, grandma? Are they gold?'

'They're Kruger rands. Yes, they're gold.'

'What else is around here?'

'There's nothing else.'

He pulled her up. He took the slack of her stomach through her dress and gave a twist and she cried out, but the pain was too much for her to cry loudly. He let her go and took her head in two hands. 'A little twist and it might come right off, eh?'

'There's no more. No more money or anything.'

He let her go. His hands were white with flour from her cheeks. She could see from his open mouth and his teeth wet through the stocking that the gold had excited him.

'It's a pity you're so ugly or I'd bend you over a table and screw a tail on you.'

*

She does not tell Norma this; will tell no one. There's no reason to spread ugliness and cruelty.

'The police came then. It was Mrs Butler. She's really quite fanatical with this Neighbourhood Support. They sneaked in from the right-of-way but she saw. The fighting downstairs, so much got broken. Ken would have loved it. It took both policemen to hold the big one so the bossman got away and ran up the road but they caught him later. And they were just boys, like I thought. Only nineteen and twenty.'

'What were their names?'

'Neil Chote was one. He was the one who held me. Stephen Cater-Phillips was the other. Just think of that, a hyphenated name. I imagine they'll both go to prison for quite a long time, and I think they deserve it. They could have had our money, there was no need to be cruel.'

'Clive said there was a girl in it?'

'Yes. Ken fell down the steps in the morning so I called in two girls who were passing. One of them used such bad language too. It was her, I think. She saw the money.'

'What was her name?'

'A pretty name. Shelley Birtles. I hope she didn't go to your school, dear.'

Norma drove to Saxton to sit with her father. It was after midnight – Monday, a new week. I need someone to touch me, Norma thought. I need someone to love. John Toft would dole out his spoonful of warmth and then withdraw. Someone else.

I can't be happy alone, I want to know someone. Oh that ambiguous 'know', what a word.

She was ashamed to have needs so complete, with her father dying. She tried for – felt in surges, most unpleasant – hatred for those boys; but ended up with sadness, Shelley Birtles. Where are you from, Shelley, where will you go?

I need someone to love. Being alone doesn't work any more.

She had forgotten cigarettes for Clive. He drove back to the berry farm to fetch some. Norma sat by her father and held his hand. She was alone with him when he died.

13

The publisher made her speech – moderately lively – and the girls started up in bands of five to get their prizes. There were the usual things: German dictionaries, *Pride and Prejudice*, popular science; but *Asterix*, marginal; and was that *Hollywood Wives*? Not the best idea to let third-formers choose for themselves. The publisher looked startled, handing it over.

That's right Tania, hold it so everyone can see.

Now the big guns, top echelon. Each year they pranced up, fat or tall or thin; pretty and plain; blonde and brown; but what did anyone know of their minds?

'Three cheers for the head girl,' the deputy head girl cried.

'Three cheers for the dux,' cried the head girl.

Wasn't it time to get rid of élitism? (Were some of those fourth-formers crying 'Quack'?) Get rid of prize-giving, in fact. In its place a big picnic, everyone in mufti. We can eat and drink and laugh and cry and swim in the sea (and Phyllis can stop fizzing and spitting at girls who wear scarves in their hair). Tonight, at the end of it, the prize mums and dads will sip their tea and shine with pride and half a dozen fourth-formers will jump in the pool in their uniforms.

Hayley Birtles isn't with her form.

How nice that Stella Round isn't dux.

She looked at the seventh-formers; girls no more, young women. Their only worry now was being free. Oh you'll find out, she wanted to cry, good luck to you; and covered her confusion with a smile.

How brave she is. Her father doesn't get buried till tomorrow.

There are men in stocking masks at everyone's door. There are men in stocking masks hiding in your minds – hear me, girls – and one day, no matter where you turn, they'll come leaping at you, absolutely rude. How many of you will survive the attack? Pink and happy, blue-eyed, brown-eyed, fair. You've had some luck tonight that Ms Johnson didn't confuse you with advice. Don't be advised by us sitting here, but don't ignore us. The men in stocking masks come for us too.

Tea and sticky biscuits. Make-believe coffee.

'Norma, I was so sorry to hear.'

'Norma, so brave of you to come.'

'Gidday Norma, that's bad luck about your old man.'

'Thank you, Tom. My word, your girls carried off the prizes.'

'Yeah. Stella's going to be mad. Mandy was dux in her year and anything Mandy can do . . .'

'It's the science side that gets it, usually. She did well.' What greedy eyes he has, greedy for everything, money, fame, sex, and the whole lot a second time, vicariously. His daughters are a three-course meal for him. And I'm a meal, with added flavour, sauced with grieving. He wants me before Dad's in his grave.

'Anything I can do, Norma, just sing out. Is anyone seeing you home? It must be lonely in that house, time like this.'

Can he see that I need someone? Does he think he's someone? At least he lets you know, and it's bad luck he won't do.

It's bad luck anyone won't do.

But good luck, great good luck, this heightened clarity in her moral sense. It makes startling pictures in her mind. Rutting stag! Beast in a wallow, urinating, defecating. The coat of ordure makes it large and dark and makes it smell . . . Tom with raised head and swelling throat . . . She moves away.

'Oh, there's the usual silly girls, been in the pool. I didn't think Belinda would do that.'

Drenched and lovely. Plump and clean. A vision too. And Norma sees Tom get the sight of her and get the scent. Blood rises higher. Blood beats in him and swells him up.

Misshapen face. Face at the door.

Then he shrinks and smiles and turns away.

But it's too late. Too late for Norma. She knows. And tries to turn and shake it off. But knowledge clings; it's fixed in her and won't let go. She could more easily shake off one of her arms.

Run, run, run. She takes a step at Belinda Round. Her man in a stocking mask will be her dad.

'Are you all right, Mrs Sangster?'

'Perhaps I'd better sit down for a moment.'

'Do you feel faint? You've gone very pale.'

173

Where was evidence? And sanity?

'Oh Mrs Sangster, I've just been told about your father. It's really most extraordinarily brave of you to come. You know, we've got a little book on our list about coping with grief. You must let me send you a copy.'

'That's very kind –'

'One mustn't bottle up. One must let go. Scream if you like.'

Shall I scream? Run, run, Belinda. Get away.

'Josie, I want to talk to you.'

'I want to meet Ms Johnson. Ms Johnson, Josie Round from Wimmins Werk.'

'Ah yes, I've heard of you.'

'I wanted to know – a book about our co-operative, not a weaving book or a craft book you know, but women working together, would it go?'

'That's a very interesting idea . . .'

On Sunday it was a book about not needing anyone . . . Josie, I need to talk to you.

'I thought if each of us did a chapter, there's weavers and potters and jewellers and leather-workers, we'd get the feminists and the crafts people too.'

'What a splendid idea.'

'Emphasizing how we all work in and help each other – practically and ideologically as well.'

'Absolutely splendid.'

Stella Round is standing alone.

Stella, Stella.

'Congratulations, Stella.'

'Oh, thanks.'

'You don't feel too badly about the dux thing?'

'I would have liked it. But I don't think she's going anywhere.'

Old-fashioned malice, just as pure as water from a spring. Stella would make a marvellous wicked queen. But in one version wasn't she made to dance in red-hot shoes until she died, while Snow White watched? Stella was in her red-hot shoes already.

'You don't need childish things any more. A name on the honours board doesn't mean a thing.'

'That isn't what you've told us for five years.'

Oh little girl, poor child, don't try so hard, relax, enjoy. Could one give that advice? The stocking-man had his way in far too bloody a fashion. And this girl looks down her bony nose at my confusion. This woman on her way, going somewhere. She's putting by her last bit of childish disappointment and clearing her systems. Poor child is wrong.

Poor child, nevertheless.

'Your father . . . Oh Belinda, there you are. I don't approve of jumping in the pool.'

'It's kind of traditional, Mrs Sangster. Mandy and Stell both did, in the fourth form. I wasn't going to be left out.'

'Where's Mandy? Didn't she come?'

'Home with Duncan. Watching the stars.'

'Pure escapism, looking out there,' Stella says.

What caused her glass-sharpness, iron-hardness, her minimizing of herself? This falling back to a position she can hold, or believes she can. There must have been some other, larger person growing there. Now – an iron lady; or corrugated iron, for Stella will not endure. He will come for her. Or – that shock! – had come already? Had Stella seen her father's face?

'Belinda, you'd better dry yourself. Stella, if you've got a moment, there's a book I'd like you to have.'

What can she say? What possible approach? That dreadful acuity, that knowledge, is gone. There he is, all innocence and desire, predatory and naked, and no damned good at it, moving in, trying to, on Sandra Duff, who gives sharp answers from the look of it. Yet a force. He is a force. Because he believes in himself. *There* is ground for evil to take root.

'I never thought I'd come in here again. Do you mind, can I sit behind the desk?'

'Oh, help yourself.'

'Feels good. What's it like, being in charge?'

'Not much fun.'

'I can believe it. Can I give you a warning, Mrs Sangster?'

'Please do.'

'Miss Duff read us a poem yesterday. And Julie Stanley went all, you know, white around her nose. I think you'll get Mr Stanley calling on you.'

'What sort of poem?'

'One she probably shouldn't have. I thought it was a bit juvenile.

Quite funny though. Anyway, I'm not complaining, just warning you.'

And enjoying yourself. Advantage is a wonderful thing, but Stella, you like the taste too much.

'How are things at home, Stella?'

'With Mum and Dad you mean? Is this going to be a little talk?'

'With everyone. Stella – families . . .' The worst things happen there, the very worst, in that hothouse fug. 'There are lines that get tangled in families. And yours doesn't seem, well, happy any more. There's Duncan of course. And your mother and father becoming – not good friends . . .' How arch, how prissy. I know she knows tough language, real words, but how can I say them? 'I think he's a fairly complex man. But childish too, in a way. And possessive. I mean, things in his family are his. A kind of dominion. And who knows how it gets tangled up? Proximity and ownership – and a confused sense of right – '

'If you're saying what I think, there's no need.'

'I don't really know what I'm saying.'

'It's not a new thing, Mrs Sangster, it's happened before. Or, just to set your mind at rest, it hasn't happened.'

'What hasn't?'

'He has to be drunk to try it on. And drunk makes him sentimental and he gets lost in, oh, the philosophy of it all. Our little Round fortress in a hostile world. And our special sense of right. Nothing happens. He goes all soggy before it can. There's just a nasty smell around, that's all. And of course, he forgets. He thinks he's world champion at fathers.'

'Mandy too?'

'Oh yes, Mandy. Except I'm not so sure nothing happened there. She won't say. But look, we don't need you. Belinda is all right. Mandy and me are watching things.'

She's not so collected as she makes out or she wouldn't get her grammar wrong. And that bad smell has poisoned her – and made her too. She's terrifying and magnificent, and oh so sad.

'How did you find out, Mrs Sangster?'

'I didn't find out. I don't know. It's just, I've got a nose for things like this. Stella, there's a book, *I Couldn't Cry* – '

' – *When Daddy Died*. I've read it. So has Mandy. Is that what you were going to give me? I thought you were just getting me here.'

'Yes, I was. Does Josie know?'

'She's too dumb. Mum hasn't got a clue.'

She'll pat my shoulder now and humour me and comfort me. Because I'm dumb like Josie, haven't got a clue. I'll promise to do nothing and tell no one. I believe, believe in her, in Stella Round. I'm going to leave the future to her. World to her.

'You look as if you need some sleep. Why don't you sneak out, Mrs Sangster. No one'll notice.'

No one notice if the principal goes? Of if they do, she's got her father's funeral tomorrow, it was very brave of her to come.

Stella pats and kisses, bending down. A kiss from Stella! The door gives a click. She is gone. Beautiful and damaged and hard. Her limbs should be all broken and set wrong to signal the breaking and resetting in her mind.

I can't tell whether she is more or less.

Norma finds a side-door and goes, leaving her school vibrating, brightly lit. She drives home and meets her cat in the garage. She sits on her chair, drinks a glass of sherry, with music insubstantial in the room.

I want the dreadful danger. I don't want to be alone any more.

After the service Norma and Clive and Clive's two daughters drove to the cemetery and watched the coffin lowered into the grave. They touched it before it went down and one granddaughter, Francine, placed a yellow rose on the lid. Deborah, the nurse, was the only one who cried. She had seen death many times but that lowering, putting away, was a thing she had not understood.

Norma felt her own breathing stop and wanted to shriek. The hole, with shaven sides, was so far down; and earth and clay so solid, so close-packed. She could not breathe until she turned away.

The jollity at Clive's house made her uneasy. Was there some good thing she'd not been told? Not many of her own friends had come. Clive's, eating sausage-rolls, seemed to draw away as she approached – too dark, too down-turning in the mouth? As for old-timers from the valley – she had to look ten seconds in their faces before they settled into shapes she knew; then exclamation seemed the only way to advance. Her mother sat in Clive's big chair in the glassed-in porch and had them brought to her one by one.

177

'I think your mother is enjoying this.'

'Why shouldn't she?'

'Sorry, I guess I put it badly . . .'

She had always made Tony Hillman dither. Sharpness had been her part, and apology, redefinition, his.

'What I meant – '

'It's all right, Tony, I know. I don't mean to be rude.'

'You've every right to be, on an occasion like this.'

Did he want her still (or was it again)? She had not bothered lately to check on him. But his condition now – yes, no mistake, that soft pushing out of admiration and desire. She was grateful and amused and, as usual, unexcited. But perhaps this was a time for second-bests.

'Norma, what I'm going to suggest, I'll understand if you say no – '

She laughed. Still he prefaced his attempts with an escape clause for her. Would a man so decent do?

'What's the matter?'

'Oh nothing, Tony. Just a release of tension, I suppose.' And that was true. She was a long way now from her near-shriek at the grave. Yes was the way to move in answer to whatever he might ask.

'Some little place that's quiet, so you can relax. And maybe start to put it all behind you. A thing as horrible as this . . .'

'Yes, Tony, all right.'

'Unless you want to spend the evening with your family.'

'I said yes.'

'Oh. That's good. That's great. You understand, I want nothing for myself. I know that once . . .'

Oh no no no, he'll never do. Why should I go backwards to this man, he's a wet. Did I ever like him? A neat and tidy partner, that was all. Presentable. And once or twice we went to bed for the fun of it. But it wasn't more than adequate as fun. Afterwards, my God, he always said, 'Was that all right?'

She wouldn't, couldn't, go through it again, not even for the hope of being in close company a while.

Dinner though, dinner would be all right. He was a face.

'I asked for a window table so we could see the sea.'

'That's nice.'

'And the alcove so . . .'

'Dining out, you mean, when my father's scarcely in his grave?'

'They love to pass judgement in this town.'

'That isn't confined to Saxton, Tony.'

'No, of course. Is the sun going to be in your eyes?'

It was but she wouldn't admit it. The thought of changing seats made her impatient, though the sun still shining in the sky would interfere with her appetite. Daylight-saving stepped away from nature. It caused a lag or misstep in the day. She disliked and disapproved of it. But all those yachties coming in, those windsurfers with plastic peep-holes in their sails, those families in rented dinghies and rowers in their shell and fishermen reeling up spotties from the piles, and fizz-boat drivers making feathers of spray, and skiers walking water – it was plainly just the thing for them, enlarged their lives. She must not be selfish and complain; must shield her eyes and eat her dinner.

'I don't think the sunset will be anything special.'

He meant there were no burning towers or bloody scimitars. She smiled at his wish to provide the best for her. Gratitude wasn't in her tonight, or generosity, neutrality even, but for her own comfort she made responses designed to keep him from trying too hard.

The food was very good. She found her appetite. And the sun, when it finally went down, made nice pink blushes, apricot washes, in the sky, and then a teal-blue colour of startling purity.

'That's good,' he said as though he had ordered it.

'What have you been up to, Tony? Interesting cases?'

'Well, I don't have cases actually. Property business.'

'Making people's money multiply?'

'Well, yes . . .'

'Solemnizing the marriage between greed and legality?'

'I don't mind if you make fun of me.'

'You're in with Tom Round, aren't you? I suppose Tom is busy stuffing himself?'

'I can't really talk – '

'It's all right, Tony, I don't want you to. Weren't criminal cases more fun?'

'They were instructive. One gets past them.'

'Property is more grown-up than people, you mean?'

'I'm sorry if it seems like that. Actually, dealing with violence and cruelty – I found it was making me uncertain of myself.'

She found that interesting. It was the first interesting thing he had said.

'Do you mean you saw the possibility of those things in yourself?'

'Oh no, good God. I mean I felt surrounded by threat – and civilized behaviour was a little island in a sea. With a kind of beastliness lapping round. This isn't the conversation I wanted to have.'

And less interesting than she had hoped. He really had no questions about himself.

'You seem to believe in an elect.'

'Not at all. There's nothing about my position I haven't made for myself.'

'And the criminals, the failures, they're self-constructed too?'

'Yes, I think so. Don't you?'

'Is Tom Round one of your elect?'

'That's not my word, Norma.'

'Is he on your island? And that girl, the one who sent her boyfriend to rob my parents, is she part of your sea of beastliness?'

'I don't know about her. The men are, certainly.'

'Did you go to court? Did you see them?'

'Norma, do we need to talk about this?'

'I'd like to, Tony. Why were they charged the way they were? I thought there'd be manslaughter at least.'

'No, your father – the medical position – '

'They pleaded guilty right from the start.'

'If they'd been my clients that's what I would have advised.'

'So it will be straight back to prison for them. I can understand that as punishment. But what about when they come out? Are they better? Worse? The same?'

'Who knows?'

'Perhaps we should shoot them or lobotomize them. Why didn't Shelley Birtles plead?'

'There's a dozen reasons. Come on, I'll take you home.'

'I'd like some brandy, Tony. Tony, I knew her, she could run like the wind. She was beautiful and clean and innocent.'

'No one's that. We're Fallen.'

'Ah, so you get on to your island by being a Christian. And I thought it was just hard work. And learning how to hold your knife and fork. Tony, you don't believe in Original Sin?'

'It explains a lot.'

'And God?'

'Oh yes. We're in a hopeless case without Him.'

'So it's need?' She lost interest in the argument. The blue light over the mountains drew her sight into immensities of distance. She saw Shelley Birtles running there, with her limbs shining and eyes bright. How could this girl become that one? Had she always been that one, and innocence and beauty a bit of wishing? That was almost certainly the case: a Shelley Birtles for our need, like Tony's God.

'I think I'd like to go home now.'

'Are you feeling all right?'

'A little drunk. You can probably take advantage of me tonight.'

Did his fingers tremble while his expression cried no, no? Would man or gentleman come out on top? He was suddenly so rudimentary that she could not care. Does Tony in her bed cure loneliness? There's a morality in it, of what she owes herself that she must pay. Nevertheless she sinks into a kind of sullenness. Sees herself as snobbish, cowardly. Another drink will cure her doubts. A hand or mouth touching here and here. Wants the man, but wants Tony Hillman out of it. After their coupling he'll be there, naked and careful and – wrong. Self-dismay comes after that.

'Tony, I'm sorry, I won't ask you in.'

He kisses her cheek and goes away, wrapped in his moist penumbra of desire. Coughs his car, drives into the night.

Norma has her cat on her knee again but drinks plain water instead of sherry. If Tom Round had brought her home she would have gone to bed with him, and been deeply sunk in self-dismay. She thinks of Tom a moment and turns her face from him. She thinks of John Toft; sees a falling in him towards an end. There are no others. She puts all men aside and considers living alone and knows she can carry on with it – not easily, but carry on. A large time exists for private life no matter how one fills the day with business, and she looks at the attractions of self-improvement, mental stretching, of travel, friendship, music, etc; of placidity; of self-indulgence. Doesn't care for the Norma Sangster that she finds. Sees an evenness in her life brought about by a kind of settling.

Father dead. Mother with her brother – where she'll stay? Death closed in its pearl – but other bits of grit that lacerate. Shelley Birtles. Neil Chote. The family Round. Settling still has a way to go.

She sips her water, strokes her cat. Regrets, for a moment, Tony Hillman, anodyne. Then is pleased to be rid of him. He'll eat no more dinners where reasonable expectation makes a side dish. She's sorry for Tony but not inclined at all to charity. Stroking will be reserved for cats. Norma laughs and shivers. How many cats will she outlive?

It's nearly midnight when she goes to the telephone. It burrs for a long while, then a voice, sleep-thickened, says, 'Hallo . . . Anyone there? . . . Hallo, who's there?' She puts down the phone. That was a crazy idea. 'Mr Birtles, I rang to ask . . . did she really . . . was it her . . . did she really send those men after my parents?'

I should ring and say I'm sorry for waking him.

And who is Shelley, Mr Birtles? What sort of world does she think she's in?

Dear Mrs Sangster,

My wife and me express our sympathy at the death of your father.

I'm sorry for what Shelley did. She was stupid but she didn't mean to be bad and she didn't mean for things to turn out the way they did. She didn't even mean for it to happen at all. But this is all on the side. We're sorry that's all.

Hayley had nothing to do with it. That's one thing you've got to believe.

Yours sincerely,
K. Birtles.

It was a curious note, and touching in its ill-concealed pain. As for the peremptory tone of its final sentence, that must hide – what? – desperation? One daughter down, only one to go. K. Birtles was right to feel desperate. Hayley had nothing to do with it because she had been somewhere else.

Am I justified in believing that? Norma thought. She's coarse-grained and sudden and physical, but people of that sort are often kind. They cry easily and kiss and stroke. But Norma had to admit she knew very little about Hayley Birtles, and nothing at all about

Shelley. As strange to her, after half a lifetime spent with girls, as creatures from the deep parts of the sea.

She worked in her office that afternoon and there had a visit from Mr Stanley. Norma had forgotten Stella's warning. She liked to be calm when he called and well-prepared with disarming phrases. She was unready when he laid the poem on her desk.

'That's a photocopy. I've got copies for the Board of Governors too and I'm sending one to the Minister.'

'You're well prepared as usual, Mr Stanley.'

'It wasn't easy to track that down. I had to phone a friend in Wellington, a librarian. It's lucky Julie made a note of the title.'

'You've trained her well.'

'Read before you sneer at us, Mrs Sangster. Go on, read it.'

'These parts in highlighter –'

'They're the worst.' He squashed words with his finger. 'That. And that.'

He had ringed as well as coloured them – 'fart' and 'sodomy'. Norma thought, Oh you silly girl, you really are determined to get fired. 'I'd like to read it all before we talk.' And found it, for a while, pedestrian; then gave a start of pleasure. 'I know this poem. I must have read it twenty years ago.'

'It should have been banned then.'

'Shsh, let me read.' And there it was: Old ghosts and bags of wind, gourds of the Judas tree. She could not help grinning at Mr Stanley.

'It didn't make me laugh, Mrs Sangster.'

'I'm sorry. Well. It's a fairly tough poem, but for girls of seventeen ... If you take these bits you've marked in context, and remember that the man is dying of a heart attack –'

'Sodomy.' He squashed it again. Then seized the paper. '"Happy I could be at the end of a black journey / If one of you, or two, even by borstal, larceny, sodomy, destruction and revolt –" In black and white.'

It was, she agreed, inescapable. She wished the poet had left sodomy out.

'There's one or two quite beautiful lines. "Be reconciled to terror: the night is terrible / In which we move and live and find our being."'

'You find that beautiful?'

183

'Our teaching could do with a bit of contrariness. And Miss Duff is gifted, no mistake. The girls respond –'

'Sodomy. You think they should be taught about perversions?'

Norma had no energy for the fight.

'What do you want me to do, Mr Stanley?'

'Plain and simple. Fire the teacher who read that to the girls.'

'I can't fire teachers.'

'The Board of Governors can, with your support.'

'I've had one girl already who liked the poem.'

'Ah, so you do know about it.'

'She found it amusing.' And heard moral laxity in the word. So there was nothing for it but to let him talk some more. He had dry, well-brushed hair and a beautifully shaven face and a nose with twin white pressure points at the tip. Hotness in the eye, not unattractive. Like Tony Hillman, presentable, but scoring lower on her ten-point scale – she couldn't give him more than five – because of the over-neat way his ears hugged his head. She had always been put off by ears of that sort – and was interested to find (again) that when she disliked someone strongly enough there was always a physical thing she could get them with. But this was more than just dislike. She realized she detested the man: his dryness, his neatness, his deadly cramped-up mind. If he did not go away she would throw her biro and spear his cheek. Then she would be accused of being a woman. A man could lift him by the collar (would his legs curl up?) and put him out the door and gain by it.

'Mr Stanley, would you mind? I've heard enough.'

'What?'

'I'll consider it. But I can't give you any more time.' She went to the door and held it open. That was a way of putting out, though it seemed for a moment it might not work. Then he set his mouth and walked by her; and Norma sat trembling in her chair. Sudden tempers, sudden tiredness, sudden elation; strange desire. Was it, she wondered, a part of grief – part of something she could not feel in the normal way? (Was there a normal way for grief?) Or were there simply too many actors in her life? – though none with the closeness she would like. Too much importuning; too many supplicating hands?

She laid her palms on her desk. Waited. Heard. She was all alone in her school but was connected, still it purred. There would not be any change in that.

184

And out there, in the world, who would ask her next to act or care? And would she step up close or step away?

Neil Chote. His leather jacket slid on him like hide on a starved animal. He looked light enough to pick up and carry. The blond hair Mrs Schwass had seen standing through a hole in his stocking was combed flat, bringing out the egg shape of his head and making it look breakable.

It's a well-shaped head, if you believe in heads, Norma thought. She did not. Appearances almost always cheated. The advantage, the yard start, given by good looks was something she had learned to take away in the final assessment, and she did sums for the ill-favoured too. The acne scars on Neil Chote's neck were not evidence (any more than Mr Stanley's ears).

The other man, Cater-Phillips, had needed no scaling up or down. He had ordinary looks of the manly sort. The snake-entwined broadsword tattooed on his forearm was pleasing or deplorable, according to taste. He had left the dock grinning at his sentence. That was prescribed, Norma thought. But the way his eyes blinked was all his own. She wondered if he would cry back in his cell. She could picture him doing that more easily than half-throttling her father with his stick.

Neil Chote would not cry. The policemen were quick to his side, but she had no sense of danger, not of the usual sort. He was like, she thought, searching for something outlandish enough, a piece of anti-matter, burning what it touched by a natural law. There's nothing in him that can change because there's nothing in him. Ordinary questions – where had he come from? where was he going? – did not apply. And punishment, correction? She blinked like Cater-Phillips. Neil Chote would do his time as easily as other people walked across a room, and nothing would change. He was – she turned the word over, knew it right – incorruptible.

Norma went out as the next case was called. A man walked down the steps ahead of her. 'Mr Birtles,' she said; and when he turned, 'Thank you for your letter.'

'That's all right. Least I could do.'

'It was good of you all the same.'

'I wasn't trying to be good.'

'No. I realize.'

'If Shelley had kept her mouth shut they wouldn't have gone there, that's all I mean. We did it, so we're sorry.'

'"We" seems going a bit too far.'

'Well lady, you haven't got any kids.'

'No, I haven't. But I don't hold you responsible. Or Shelley either, beyond a certain point.'

'Thanks.' A bitter edge to that.

She tried to explain what she meant. 'After seeing that boy, Neil Chote . . .'

'Yeah, he's something.'

'I don't think that Shelley . . . When does her case come up?'

'Tomorrow. Do us a favour, eh?'

'Of course.'

'Don't come. Yeah,' he stopped her, 'I know your father's dead. I know all that. But this is . . .' She saw his struggle. 'It's different now.'

It had to do, he meant, with his love for Shelley and her survival and Norma Sangster had no part in that.

'Yes, all right. Mr Birtles, what you said about Hayley, I accept that.'

'Yeah. Good.'

'How is she taking it?'

'She's OK. Hayley's got her head screwed on.'

'And – Shelley? How is she?'

He turned away, looked across the car park. After a moment said, 'She's a job. I don't know if Shelley's going to make it.' He walked across the asphalt and got into his car. It came by her as she unlocked her own. She saw the care he drove with, as though each move were something he must practise or forget.

She closed her car again and walked by the river. Water, willows, salt-smell from the harbour, toi-toi flags shifting in a breeze: that loveliness should be medicinal if taken in sufficient quantity.

She walked along the path from bridge to bridge. She set herself to notice actively: the breeze, the flow. But all the way Shelley and Mr Birtles followed behind. Whenever she stopped trying, there they were.

'Oh please,' she whispered.

She would hate them if they did not go away.

14

Women like that made him angry, they could never let their minds be still but always had to shift to some new place; sliding out of the way all the time, using words like bloody roller-skates. They hid behind their good looks and saw things from one step further back where they were safe. He didn't believe they had the same feelings as everyone else or lived the same way; sat fagging at a table with curlers in their hair. You'd almost think they didn't piss or shit. She reminded him of Maggie Thatcher; covered in vinyl. Stand her in a corner at night and wipe her down with an oily rag.

My girls are real, Ken Birtles thought.

As he drove beside the drainage ditch he saw Hayley riding towards him. She had her arms folded and was pedalling easily, with the bike running a line so straight she could have been on top of a brick wall and not fallen off. He honked his horn and stopped and she put her hands on the handlebars, made a sweeping turn, and drew up by his window.

'I thought I asked you to stay home, Hayley.'

'I got sick of it. They're OK. Shell's got Mum doing exercises.'

'No kidding?'

'Sure. Jazzercise or something. On TV. I'm going down the park with Jen and Vicky.'

'Well don't be late. Be back for lunch.'

'What did he get?'

'Two years.'

'Is that all?'

'Two years is pretty long.'

'He's going to be out before Shell's twenty-one. If he comes back here I'll buy a gun and shoot him.'

'How would you feel,' he swallowed, 'if we got out of here ourselves?'

'Out of Saxton?'

'Australia say? Started again? You and me and Shell and Mum?'

'I don't want to leave Saxton.'

'It's just an idea. You think about it, eh?' He saw her glove in the tomato-box latched on her bike. 'You could be an Aussie rep. Bigger than New Zealand.'

'Not as good. We can beat them any time.'

'Think about it. We'll probably stay.'

He watched her ride, arms folded again, in his rear-vision mirror; thought of a new country, Shelley winning races, Hayley pitching no-hit games, Joanie well again, everyone happy. That still left Wayne dead, but Wayne was dead. All the rest was possible. Jobs weren't hard to get there, not as hard, the money was better, houses weren't too dear. Beth had told him all this, selling Melbourne, wanting her sister. The weather was good, though it couldn't be any better than Saxton. And it needn't be a city, a smaller place, some country town with beaches and farms, would be the thing. He saw Hayley and Shelley running down the yellow sand and diving into waves as tall as houses and coming up on the other side, sparkling and streaming and alive. 'And no bloody sharks,' he said, fear jolting him.

Fear lived with him all the time. It followed after every hope he had. There was a biting in his chest, he felt as if an animal was there, with teeth hooked in, and tearing it away would leave a hole filled up with blood.

As he came into the kitchen he heard that soft, sexy American voice, 'Come on, you can do it, one more time, don't forget to breathe. That's good, hands on hips –' and the music that wouldn't leave you alone. The girls with impossible legs and haunches like elongated hams were prancing and folding on the screen; exercises that should split their sinews; beautiful timing though, he had to admit. Shelley, barefooted on the carpet, was just as good. She could do anything those girls could. He watched her – shorts and T-shirt, bandaged wrist, hair that bounced like in the TV ads, even though she had it shaved at the sides in the ugly way girls went for now. He felt the fear come up and choke him.

'Mum?' he asked when she saw him. Without losing rhythm she pointed at the bedroom and he went in and found Joanie lying on the bed.

'Hayley said you were doing exercises.'

She put a hand over her eyes. It was as if people glowed and the light hurt her. 'I stopped.'

'Like a cup of tea?'

'I'll make it, Ken. I'll just have a little rest.'

He went to the kitchen and put the kettle on. 'Tea, Shell?'

'Thanks.' Then she darted at the set and switched it off. 'Jesus, I forgot him. What did he get?'

'Two years.' He went back and laid out mugs and sugar and milk. She sat at the table.

'It won't make any difference to Neil. Two years is nothing.'

'Two years ago you were at school, winning races.'

It was a dangerous thing to say but instead of flaring up she slumped at the table, drooping her head. He could not bear the naked bending of her neck. 'Shell, he's out of the way. You can get him out of your system. You've got time.'

'How long did Steve get?'

'Two. The same.'

'I'll go to prison as well.'

'Not if the lawyer handles it right.'

'I told Neil where the money was. I waited in the car while they went in.'

'Only because he beat you up.'

'He beat me up because that's what he likes. I went to see him, Dad, I didn't have to, that's what they'll say.'

'Why did you, Shell?'

'To see – I don't know – to see if I could get away. But I couldn't. I started telling about the money to make him notice me. And I got scared, so I stopped. Then he made me tell.'

'Can you this time? Get away?'

'I don't know. I think – dunno. I've got to go to prison, Dad. Maybe that'll be the end of it.' A careless note had come into her voice. She was not facing it any more. He gave her a mug of tea and took one to Joanie; propped her up with pillows, put the mug in her hand.

'My cigarettes, Ken?'

He brought them from the sitting-room and put an ashtray on the bed beside her.

'What time is it?'

'Half past eleven.'

'I'll make you some lunch soon. I hope I remembered to buy eggs.'

'There's plenty of everything, Joanie. I want you to have a shower after lunch. Shelley will help. You've got your clinic this afternoon.'

'I don't think I'll go today.'

'You've got to go. We can't go to Australia if you don't get well.'

'Australia?'

'See Beth. Drink your tea, love.'

Shelley had left hers half-drunk and gone to the bathroom. He heard the pipes come alive as the shower went on and took it as a good sign that she didn't sit around. She'd quit her job on the fish-chain, though she could have taken sick-leave with her wrist. It troubled him less than it might have because he wanted better than packing fish for Shell. She had wanted to be a physical education teacher once, before Neil Chote. She could never be a teacher now, with a conviction, but there had to be work somewhere that would make her happy with herself. After prison. The pain he felt made him cry out. Two years ago their lives were right. He remembered being happy. Now it had come apart, everything was broken and he did not know what to do.

In the afternoon Hayley rode into town and looked for clothes she'd like to buy. She didn't need new gear but it was something to do. A couple of times it would have been easy to walk out with stuff, but that was all they needed, two Birtleses up in court. The power other people had to put Shelley in a van and drive her away and lock her up made a sort of ringing in her head. Her mouth kept turning dry and she had to swallow.

In Calamity Jane, Miss Duff came out of a fitting-room holding a pair of jeans and making a face. 'I swim in them. Hallo, Hayley. Everything's baggy on me.'

'Those are supposed to be baggy, Miss Duff.'

'Are they? Well I don't like it. You're lucky having a figure that fills things out.' She picked up a blouse.

'You've got the best figure. Models are supposed to be thin.' It made Hayley excited knowing they'd both been in bed with Lex. She wondered which one he had liked best and grinned when she thought of comparing notes. She didn't mind Duffie having him too.

Miss Duff frowned at her. 'Yes, I would look stupid.'

190

'I wasn't laughing at that.' She took the blouse and held it up to Miss Duff's shoulders. 'That colour's good on you.'

'You think so?'

'Makes you look kinda, I don't know, like you slink around at night. Kinda sexy.'

'That's exactly the impression I like to give.'

Why were teachers scared of coming straight out with stuff? Miss Duff knew all about sex so why get sarky? 'I gotta go. Got some shopping to do.'

'You think I should try this on?'

'Sure, Miss Duff. I bet Mr Clearwater would like it.'

She rode across the car park and looked at videos in Video World. Teachers were everywhere today. There was Mrs Sangster in the section where the foreign films were kept. She'd do better getting out something like *The Rocky Horror Show*, she looked as if she could do with a laugh. Hayley kept behind the shelves and slipped out the door.

Saxton was too small. Everywhere you went there were people you knew. It might be good living in a place as big as Melbourne.

Space World was full of third formers, and no chance of getting a game. Anyway, she was sick of games, they just went on and on, the same thing repeating itself. In softball every batter was new, you had to figure her out and pitch a different sort of ball. She decided to go home and practise; but stopped on her way to the door and stood in the crowd watching Duncan Round on '1942'. The lights on his face made him look like something from Elm Street. There was nothing wrong with the way he played though. Planes were coming at him from every direction but he picked them off like dabbing up breadcrumbs from a table. Suddenly he said, 'I'm finished, who wants it?' and a kid quicker than the rest was at the controls; and was done for straight away, explosions zapping his planes off everywhere. Hayley laughed. She followed Duncan outside.

'Why didn't you finish?'

'Gets boring. That's Wayne's bike.'

'So?' She felt as if he'd said something insulting.

'Is that his safety chain?'

'What if it is?'

'Six three one.' He grinned – she supposed the showing of his teeth was a grin – and walked away.

191

She unlocked the bike (631) and wheeled it up the footpath, keeping behind him. So he had a good memory, what did that prove? And who gave him permission to talk about Wayne? She speeded up and got beside him.

'You shut up about Wayne.'

'Why?'

'He was my brother, that's why.'

'What harm does it do, talking about him?'

Donna Gethin and two of her friends went by.

'Who's your boyfriend, Hayley?'

'He's real neat-looking, Hayley.'

'Dumb bitches,' Hayley said.

'You don't have to walk with me, I don't care,' Duncan said.

'I wasn't walking with you. But I will if I want to. Anyway, I've got to go. Just shut up about Wayne.'

'OK, if that's what you want.'

'My family's got enough trouble.'

Riding home, she saw Gary Baxter outside the dairy. He had his arm in plaster. She did a loop in the road and went by him a second time. 'Did you hurt your arm, Ga-ary?

'Did you do it combing your pretty hair, Ga-ary?'

She went round a corner and rode on, feeling good. His Escort came up behind her but she turned on to the footpath, gave him the fingers, turned down a right-of-way and crossed the footbridge over the drainage ditch. Shelley was walking back from the super- market with a bag of groceries. Hayley got off and walked beside her.

'Put them in my carrier, Shell.'

'They're not heavy.'

'I just saw Gary Baxter. I bust his arm.'

'What? When?'

'That day he tried to get me to take on his friends. I chucked a rock at him. He's in plaster. I didn't know.'

Shelley turned her face away.

'What's the matter, Shell?'

'Jesus,' Shelley said. She was crying.

'Hey Shell, I didn't mean to upset you.'

Shelley kept on crying silently. Hayley tried going round to see her face from the other side, but Shelley turned her head. Tears made her cheeks shine and she wiped them with the bandage on her wrist.

'Shell? Is it going to court?'

'It's everything. You and Mum and Dad. Everything.'

'Why me? I'm all right.'

'You're doing the same I did. With Gary Baxter.'

'No I'm not. I bust his arm.'

'You know what I mean. Going with creeps. Are you still pinching from shops?'

'I haven't done that for ages.'

Shelley put down the bag of groceries. She took out her handkerchief and blew her nose. Hayley picked up the bag and fitted it into her carrier box. 'You want to ride the bike, Shell?'

'I'm all right.'

'Has Dad told you about Aussie? That would be real neat, eh?'

'It doesn't make any difference where we are. Mum's not going to get better, she'll get worse.'

'Being with Auntie Beth could make her better.'

'Maybe.'

'And Neil Chote couldn't find you there.'

'There's other blokes like Neil. Neil's sort of blokes are everywhere.'

'You don't have to go with them.' She tried a joke. 'You have to bust their arms like I bust Gary's.'

Shelley gave a laugh. After a while she said, 'That old man with the stick is dead.'

'He was real old though. He had to die some time. It's funny him being Singsong's father. Hey Shell, you didn't do it, it's not your fault.'

'Neil tipped sugar and flour and stuff all over the old lady.'

That seemed horrible to Hayley too. 'Neil's round the twist. But you're not, Shell. We're not, eh? If Neil comes after you I'm going to shoot him.'

'Great, then we'll both be in prison. I'm going to cook a real good feed tonight, get ready for bread and water, eh?'

'You won't get long, Shell. Maybe just a fine.'

'I don't want a fine. I want prison.'

Their father's car was at the gate and he came down the path with a hold-all.

'Where's Mum?'

'They've admitted her, girls. I'm just taking round some stuff for her.'

'Why'd they admit her? Because of me?'

'No, Shell.'

'Yes it is. Jesus, I wish – '

'They've got some drugs they want to try on her. That's all it is.'

'What sort of drugs?'

'I don't know. Something that kind of – maybe gives her a shock. Anyway . . .'

'They wouldn't admit her just before Christmas.'

'Well – ' He looked away. 'I got her in a private place.'

'You can't afford that,' Shelley cried.

'Yes I can. It's only a month.'

'Because of me.' She went up the path and into the house.

'Go and talk to her, Hayley. I've got to take this stuff.'

'It is because of Shell, isn't it?'

'They thought your Mum should be out of the way. Don't say that though. She's got enough things to worry about.'

Shelley was lying on her bed. 'Go away.'

'Shell – '

'I'm all right.'

'Can I make a cup of tea?'

'I don't want one. Close the door. Leave me alone.'

Hayley went into the yard and threw some fast balls, rattling the tin. Then she cooked the big meal Shelley had joked about.

Her father rang Melbourne that night and Hayley heard herself being shifted around. Auntie Beth would pay her fare, but why did her father want her in Melbourne? He would be alone, and wouldn't he need her?

'I'm not going.'

'Yes you are. Beth's making the bookings and they'll telegraph them through.'

'Why can't I stay and help you?'

'I don't need help. I'll be working all day, and nights I'll have to visit your mother.'

'When do I go?'

'On Friday. You'll be back in time for the tournament.'

'Stuff the tournament.'

'Take your mitt with you. Do some practice.'

She started to say no, but saw his eyes. The look in them was like the gorilla in the cage.

She went into her bedroom and turned off the light and lay face down on her bed, trying not to cry.

In the morning Shelley said, 'I don't want you there.'

Hayley understood that. She did not want to see Shelley getting told off and taken away; she felt that she would stand up and shout things at the judge.

'And don't come in the cells. Dad's not coming either.'

'Shelley,' her father began.

'No one's coming in the cells. Say goodbye, Hayley.'

They kissed and hugged.

'When you and Mum come out it's Aussie, eh?'

'Sure.'

'Don't get any tattoos, Shell. They're dumb.'

She put her togs and towel on the bike and rode towards town. Her father and Shelley passed in the car, tooted the Birtles goodbye, long and two short, and went round the corner out of sight. She speeded up, but they were gone round the next corner too. She felt lonely riding down the road and wondered where to go. There was no one she wanted to see. Then she thought of Lex and decided there was no harm in riding that way. She would see if the Land-Rover was there but not go in. It would have been good though to talk about Shelley even if Lex had nothing to say.

It was cooler in the valley than in town. Already cars and bikes were at Monday Hole and kids were swinging on the swings. Someone had a canoe on the water and a ghetto blaster was going at full bore, 'Funky Town'. She rode by Freaks' Hole – no one there. Women had the golf course today and she pedalled slowly, watching them swing, and knew she could do better than them if she played. But golf was too slow and stuck-up and what Pure Muir would call ladylike. Even the men who played seemed ladylike.

She stopped at the bend by Lex's hill. Some goats, the last six left, were crossing the face. It was so steep they looked like cutouts pinned on a board. She wheeled her bike behind a willow tree and looked for Lex. In a moment she saw him come out of a

195

shed and climb the hill behind the house. Up and up he went towards the pines.

'Hey, Lex,' she said. Then louder, 'Hey, Lex.' He was wearing the red shirt he'd worn on that day with her. Once he stopped and hacked at something with his heel. Puffs of dust went up. 'Lex,' she yelled, behind her tree. She saw him turn and look out over her, and she said quietly, 'My Mum's in the loony bin, Lex. And Shelley's going to prison today.' He turned away and climbed again and went into the pines. Hayley got on her bike and rode down the valley. She felt happier. She couldn't visit Lex again, that was the deal. She'd felt things with him she would never forget – fucking, sure, but more than that; going with him up into the hills. It seemed to prove that things would end and other things start up and the bad luck in their family wouldn't be for ever.

She hid her bike off the road in case of Gary Baxter and had a swim in Freaks' Hole by herself. Soon Belinda Round came along the path on the other side. She dived in and came up alongside Hayley.

'Gidday.'

'I thought you had a swimming pool up there.'

'We do. Mum's friends are using it. Anyway, I like the river better.'

They swam a while, paying no attention to each other, then sat on the shingle side by side.

'Haven't got a fag, have you?'

'No,' Belinda said.

'What's your Mum and them doing, drinking fancy drinks?'

'They're supposed to be planning a book. But what they're doing is lying in the sun and swimming nuddy. There's too many white boobs for me.'

Hayley snickered. 'What sort of book?' She didn't know you had to plan for books.

'About weaving and feminism. Stuff like that.'

'It sounds dead boring.'

'Probably will be. If you have to be fit for softball why do you smoke?'

'I thought you'd say that and you did.' She grinned at Belinda, thinking she was OK all the same. 'I saw your brother yesterday.'

'Where?'

'In Space World. He's neat on those games. He got the highest score in "1942" I've ever seen.'

'Mum told him not to go there.'

'Why?'

'The kids pick on him. They call him Yuk.'

'He should belt them.'

'The intermediates are the worst. One of them stuck a notice on his back. *Walking Wounded*.'

'If I was there I'd sort them out.'

'Me too.'

'I've got a sister – ' Hayley stopped. She had meant to say that Shelley, like Duncan Round, was a sort of cripple and had to be helped, but that wasn't true, and it seemed like giving in. 'You remember Shelley?'

'She used to run. She broke all the school records when I was in the preps.'

'She's in court today. She's going to prison.'

'Is that about Mrs Sangster's father?'

'It wasn't her fault,' Hayley said. 'She's got a boyfriend called Neil Chote.' She told Belinda about Neil; then how she'd broken Gary Baxter's arm.

'I saw him,' Belinda cried. 'I was riding home. They were helping him over the fence and he was crying.' She looked at Hayley with awe. Later, after another swim, she talked about Golden Hills.

'One lunch-time Mrs Kirby was fighting Mrs Satchell, whacking her on the side with her walking-stick, and when I got them apart the sister told me why. I'd put Mrs Kirby's feeder on Mrs Satchell. They all have their own feeders and you can't get them mixed up. Miss Freed cries when she doesn't get hers.'

'Do you have to feed them?'

'Yes. Like babies. Open wider, Miss Freed.'

'Jesus, I couldn't do that.'

'I didn't think I could at first. But now I love them. I have to take Miss Freed for walks and one of her legs won't work. So I tie a stocking round her foot and hold the other end and lift it up each step. We go right round the lawn. She likes to put her hand on my cheek so she can feel what young skin feels like.'

'How did you get that job?'

'I just went in and asked.'

'If I tried they'd say no.' Because, she thought, of how I look and talk, 'anythink' and 'youse', just to get up the teachers' noses most of the time. Who wants to feed old ladies anyway? She turned her head the other way because tears had come into her eyes. Belinda Round was stuck up without knowing it. If her own friends or Belinda's were here today they'd never talk; they'd probably never talk to each other again.

She looked at her watch. 'I gotta see Dad.'

'I hope your sister will be all right.'

'Yeah. Thanks.' She pulled on her jeans and T-shirt over her togs. 'See ya.'

Along the bank she stopped and called, 'Hey, Belinda. I told your brother not to talk about Wayne. But tell him it's OK. He can if he wants to.'

Ken Birtles sat in the front row of chairs and watched her bare neck and the white scar on her elbow where she'd skinned it to the bone falling off her trike. He wished he could see her face but guessed she had set it in a mask. Only her feet, shifting weight, showed that she was more than just a dummy set up to give the appearance of listening.

That's my daughter, he wanted to cry. Don't you talk to her like that.

He wanted to get up and lift his chair over the rail and put in in the box. The judge was sitting, everyone was sitting now the lawyer had had his say. For God's sake, she's a woman, let her sit.

The reporter was writing in her pad; a girl not much older than Shelley. All this would be in the paper.

Her long legs in their jeans were beautiful. Her ankles were thin and beautiful. How can they talk about her as though she's just a thing? He felt they were trying to strip her down – take away the times that were past, the time she'd spent growing, the things they'd done, all the days and years, the arguments and good times and the love they felt, take it all away, say it meant nothing, and make her just a dummy in a dock for half an hour, with nothing more to her than they could see, nothing more than they had written on their sheets of paper.

Plenty of paper, hundreds of sheets, but Shelley was more than that. Why didn't they ask *him* who she was?

Birtles, the judge was calling her; as though what she'd done had cut her down to a single name? He wouldn't talk to other women that way. He was saying, what was he saying? – judge with sandy hair and jug ears and raw face – he accepted that she was sorry now, accepted too that she had been subjected to physical abuse and hadn't meant . . . But it was all something he'd said before, thousands of times, and Shell was Shell and could only be spoken to in words for her. And no one could say them, not even him. A turning point . . . chance to pull herself together . . . Her feet shifted weight. If she really had a chance now, it was not because of what they said to her, but what went on inside her head.

He made himself calm. You can do it, Shell. And when the judge's weighing was all done and she would go for six weeks' corrective training, he thought, Yes, that's all right, she can do it; and felt she was back from the place they'd put her in, and this court the worst that was going to happen, and prison would be bad but she was Shelley still at the end of it.

She turned and came out of the three-sided box and he stood and hugged her over the rail, and she went away out of court.

He turned when she was through the door – policeman's hand an inch behind her back – and side-stepped past knees all turning as though a wind had hit them. The exit door whack-whacked. He crossed a room of second-class young, down-staring, elbows on knees. Green tree-heads stood at window height. They looked as if you could walk on them like little hills. He went down the stairs into open air, then ran to the side of the building to see her taken over the lawn to the station cells. But either they had got her out fast or were keeping her in a courthouse room until a batch was ready to ferry across.

Waiting broke his promise not to see her. He went to his car and drove away. Town was overflowing with shoppers and schoolchildren. Touring cycles with foreign flags on their panniers moved in the streets. There wouldn't be an end to them, and the campervans and back-packers and tour-buses, for three months now. Shelley would miss them. The tourists were the best thing about Saxton, she said, they reminded you there was a world out there. He did not like the tourists himself. They made holes in Saxton his daughters might fall through.

He drove towards home but the empty house turned him away and he went up the port hills and the long hill to the lookout and sat in his car looking at the bay. Miles of pale blue sea with currents running through it, silver white. The land around the edges looked dried out and used up. The two huge yellow cliffs across by Darwood were a kind of sliding away and giving up. It seemed as if strength had failed and part of the land been lost. It all fitted in with Shelley and Wayne.

He got out and looked at the sighting plaque; identified the mountains one by one. Imrie. Corkie. Mt Misery. He supposed some early settler had been miserable there – got lost in a blizzard, died in the snow. And Cannonball, named because it was round and smooth. The knobby one was Devil's Toe. New Zealand was full of toes and thumbs and elbows, boots and forks and dining-tables, the devil's. Anything crooked or unusual got his name. That seemed a tiredness in people new to a land.

I'm new and I'm tired, he thought. Go somewhere else. A flat land would be better. He'd been climbing up and down ever since he came here. No smooth places. No straight lines except the edge of the sea. He looked out there and wanted to round his family up and go.

I don't belong any place, he thought. So it doesn't matter where I am, any place will do.

He went home and found Hayley putting out plates for lunch. She had baked beans heating in a pot and she dropped an egg on top the way he liked. He told her about Shelley and said six weeks wasn't long. Joanie would be back in six weeks too.

'I want you to suss things out in Melbourne. You can post me the house-for-sale ads. And the situations vacant as well. And go and look at some suburbs you'd like to live. Get Beth to take you. Ask her about small places too. Towns on the coast, with beaches, eh? But there's got to be a place where I can work.'

'Sure. OK.'

'Cheer up, love. There's places as good as Saxton.'

'I know.'

'Go and look at some softball matches. See if they come up to our standard.'

Hayley had been in Saxton all her life. He knew it would be hard for her to leave.

15

Norma telephoned the Round house and asked for Duncan. 'I just wondered how you were getting on.'

'Good. Everything's good.' She heard him crackle like a voice from space.

'You haven't been to see me for a while.'

'No. I've been busy.'

'Your mother told me you've bought a telescope.'

'Yeah.'

'And do you like looking at the stars?'

'Yeah. It's fun.'

She could keep going for a long time with girls, wear them down, but had no energy for it with Duncan.

'All right, Duncan. I rang because I'm going out to see Mr Toft today. I wondered if you'd like to come.'

'Can't, I'm sorry. There's lots of things I've got to do.'

She thought of asking what, but gave it up.

'Well, as long as you're busy. Goodbye, Duncan.'

'Bye. Hey, Mrs Sangster.'

'Yes? What?'

'Next time you come round to see Mum, if it's night, you can have a look in my telescope. If you like.'

'Yes. I'd like. Very much. Thank you, Duncan.'

Tears of gratitude sprang in her eyes. She wiped them away. What a state I'm in, weeping because a boy of sixteen drops me a crumb. She put through a wash and hung it out, cut the used-up flea collar off the cat, walked around the house and straightened the pictures (had there been an earthquake in the night?), read two pages of *The Blind Watchmaker* and thought, old arguments, how they keep on. There was beauty, though, in cellular splitting and she was calmed. Time and chance murder and save. Two billion years as saviour and judge, a lovely idea, though it did not let one off the hook of individual being.

She drove out to the berry farm for lunch. The glassed-in porch had become her mother's retreat and Daphne was nervous of going there. Norma felt sorry for her, robbed of part of her house, but admired the way her mother had found strength and cleverness with her husband gone.

'She's such a fusser,' Mrs Schwass said. 'I can't bear her pulling and straightening things. She even counts the flowers in the vase for even numbers. And she nearly choked me with a scarf this morning. Who needs a scarf with weather like this? I'm going back to my house after Christmas.'

'Yes Mum, I think you should.' For Clive and Daphne's sake. Daphne would need nursing if this went on.

'And when I can't look after myself I'll go into a home. You're not to think of looking after me.'

'No Mum, I won't.'

'When I die I want to be cremated, not buried like Ken. You can throw the ashes over the hedge to annoy the neighbours.' She had taken her husband's aggressiveness. Perhaps it was loyalty or sympathetic saving. There would be no peanut brownies from now on.

'I see the girl got six weeks.'

'Yes.'

'They should have given her six weeks with Daphne, that would straighten her out. Do you think she'll go back to that fellow?'

'He got two years.'

'What was his face like, Norma?'

'Oh, empty. Like – nothing.'

'Don't be silly, dear. He's under the same rules as you and me.'

'Well, he's, I don't know, spoiled.'

'His mother's fault, is that what you mean?'

'Not that sort of spoiled. Pushed on an angle. Not facing the same way as everyone else.'

Her mother lost interest. 'I'm going to write to that girl, Shelley whatever, and tell her she's not to blame for Ken. She's not, you know. But I'll tell her what I think of her choice of boyfriends.'

'That's a good idea.'

'Can you find her address for me? I don't mean prison. I suppose someone can send it on?'

Norma walked with Clive in the boysenberries after lunch. They talked about their mother. Her change was contrariness to Clive. 'You're going to have to take a share of her. She's too much for

Daphne. After Christmas she can come to you.'

'She's going home,' Norma said. 'That's the proper place for her.'

'I've got tenants for that house. She can get three hundred a week in the holiday season. Three fifty.'

'She doesn't need three fifty, she needs to be in her own place by herself. I'll be close, I'll keep an eye on her.' And if she has an accident and dies that's in the natural course of things. But she did not say that to Clive. She let him sputter on, then heard his complaint about his pickers – slowness, absenteeism, bad language, berry fights, short shorts, no bras, picking green, dropped trays. Most were college girls and Norma was to blame.

'I'm on holiday,' she answered, 'I'm keeping out of it.'

She turned away before the packing tent and went by irrigation ponds into a strawberry field. Picking was finished there, but small berries lay hidden in the leaves. She walked along, eating the smallest – they were sweetest too – and dropping the rest into her basin. The plants were mulched on black polythene instead of straw and the berries were robbed of part of their name – and their flavour too? Every now and then one left a tinny taste.

She filled her basin, made a hill on top, some for John, and walked back, sweating lightly, through the boysenberries.

'Norma,' a voice called.

For a moment she did not recognize the woman: zinc on her nose, baseball cap shading her eyes.

'Sandra? Yes, it is.'

'I didn't know you either in your garden-party hat.'

'Are you working here?'

'Yes, I pick every year. It's my holiday. I'm one of those people who can't sit still. Worms in my head.'

'Do you like it?'

'This place? I came because it's closest to town. Never again.'

'Why?'

'He's a mean bastard. It wouldn't surprise me if he's born again.'

'He's my brother,' Norma said.

'Jesus, put my foot in it.'

'From what I hear he's got cause for complaint with some of our girls.'

'They're on holiday. You can't blame them.'

'But they're taking money.'

'They still get plenty done. The sun heats them up.' She grinned. 'So do the boys. I look the other way.'

'You've been eating his boysenberries.'

'Yeah, purple-stainèd mouth. It's legitimate perks.'

'Have a strawberry.'

'Thanks.' She took a handful. 'I'm sorry for what I said about your brother.'

'That's all right. He wouldn't approve of life if it wasn't a battle. Sandra – ' she looked at the girl (wasn't she a woman though, thirty-five at least?), pretty, hard, confident, quick-eyed, and did not think what she had to say would spoil her day – 'there's a poem called "Prize-giving Speech".'

'I was waiting for this.'

'Was it only seventh formers you read it to?'

'Yes. We had some spare time. I thought of sending Julie Stanley out, but what the hell! It was her, I suppose?'

'Yes, it was. Her father's sent copies to the Board. There's one word in particular that he doesn't like.'

'Sodomy, I can guess.'

'I think it was rather poor judgement, Sandra –'

'Look,' she flared up, 'I didn't give it to them as a programme for revolt. Just an alternative view. It's a kind of dramatic monologue, a bit like Browning. I wanted them to consider it as literature.'

'And an alternative view.'

'Yeah, sure. Why not? They're hardly going to go out and rob banks.'

Norma ate a strawberry. The position was difficult. She did not know what to do and was angry with Sandra for making trouble; did not like her, liked her very much.

'They're going to want to get rid of you.'

'That's nothing new.'

'I don't want to get rid of you.'

'Tha-anks. Gre-eat.'

'Though I wonder why.'

Sandra looked savage, then suddenly grinned. 'Stroppy bitches make the best schoolteachers.'

'That's debatable.'

'Well, I'm one. And I'm the best English teacher you've got.'

Grinned again. 'If you fire me you've struck a blow for mediocrity.'

'It won't be me who does the firing. Sandra, all I can do is – put your case.'

'In words like that? You really make the language stand up and sing.'

'And you are a nasty piece of work. What's the matter, Sandra? Is it your nature or did something go wrong?'

Sandra laughed. 'OK, good. You can bite. One thing, I'm not apologizing. And I'm not giving them hosts of daffodils either.'

'Do you want to stay?'

'Yes, I do. I like Saxton and I like the school. Although more and more I wonder why.' She grinned, Norma could not tell whether to soften or emphasize. She looked a little joky with her Nell Gwyn tray of berries at her waist, and her thin zinc-whitened nose and starved-clown cheeks. She's starved for kindness too, Norma thought. Sandra was confusing, contradictory.

'I'd better pick some boysenberries or I'll get the sack from here.' She turned away, then back. 'Hey, you're friends with Tom Round, aren't you?'

'I'm a friend of his wife.'

'Is anything still going on with them?'

'Why?'

'He's trying to move in on me. Sure, you turned him down. That shows good taste. I'm a kind of specialist in bad taste.'

'He's got a friend already, you know that?'

'Friend meaning girlfriend? No, I didn't. The cunning sod.'

'It sounds as if he might be succeeding.'

'It's – fluid. Anyway, thanks. His wife is OK, is she? And the girls?'

'I think,' she had a sudden inrush of loathing for Tom Round, 'I think you'd be doing them all a favour. You mightn't be doing yourself one, though. He's not a man I'd recommend.'

'Well, with me, that's a recommendation.'

Norma did not want to talk about Tom – that bad taste, bad smell in the air. 'Are you still seeing something of Lex?'

'Seeing something of. I love your language.'

For a moment Norma thought she was going to cry. I'm tired, that's all. I need a bit of kindness from someone. Sandra Duff had the mouth of a snapping turtle. Sandra Duff had shark teeth, pick-axe chin. Her sinewy stained hands tore things apart. But I like her, Norma thought, and I want a kind word.

'I mean,' she said carefully, 'do you still visit him?'

Sandra gave a mocking caw; then peered hard at Norma. 'Now and then. If visit's the word. Are you all right?'

'The sun's so hot.'

'Do you really want to know about Lex?'

'I liked him. But it's mainly curiosity.'

'Did you ever see that picture where the scientist turned into a fly? Lex is turning into a goat.'

Norma gave a laugh, just a single note. She was not sure Sandra meant to joke. This sun is going to make me faint, she thought.

'I don't mean growing horns and hooves, or getting goatish in the usual way,' Sandra grinned. 'In fact, I think he's putting that behind him, which is just as well, he could hurt someone. I mean he's trying to see the world the way a goat would and it's got to the point where it's not voluntary any more.'

'I'm not sure I understand.'

'He thinks – God, what does he think? Thinking's out, you see, because goats don't. But in the beginning – which is appropriate – he must have decided that goats were, well, Adam and Eve before the apple, taking all that as a metaphor. The apple was self consciousness, am I right? And goats don't have it, they live in a light perpetual and they don't cast any shadows either. I think Lex is getting rid of knowledge. And he thinks of it as being a goat. Which is what he's turning into, the poor sod.'

'Shouldn't something be done for him?'

'Like what? Put him in a strait-jacket and pump him full of drugs? No, what I hope is he'll get where he's going and then remember the apple and take himself a bite and start coming back. Not that he's going to find me waiting, after last night.'

'What happened?'

'I went up to see him – and God, Norma, he's filthy, he stinks. Don't goats get dipped or drenched or something? Anyway, I went, and I tried to talk him into having a shower, eating some decent food, anything. I told him to change and come into town and we'd get a meal in a restaurant. We were outside in the yard and you know what he did? He just dropped his pants and started having a shit, there on the lawn. You don't believe me, do you? It's true.

206

Goats shit just wherever they shit. The anal sphincter's not under conscious control, so why not Lex?'

'What did you do?'

'Went home. What else?'

'Are you sure' – she felt sick, but wildly amused – 'it wasn't just a clever way of getting rid of you?'

'If it was he should patent it. No, he's loopy-de-loop. But he's a pretty smart fellow too, in some things anyway. I think he's got a good chance of coming back.'

'I hope you're right.'

'I think, you know, he should be walled off and left alone. It's an interesting experiment, after all. Maybe he'll write a book about it one day. God, there's your brother glaring, I'd better pick some berries.'

'He's glaring at me. Do you think it would help if I talked to Lex?'

'No, stay away. Everyone should leave him alone. I'll see you, Norma. Don't let buggerlugs Stanley spoil your Christmas. Oh, I was sorry about your old man.'

She walked down her row and started picking. Norma went to the house and said goodbye. Driving out to the valley, she found a flaw in Sandra's reasoning. Lex might squat and defecate whenever the urge took him but he remembered to drop his trousers. And if he was a goat now, shouldn't he run naked on his hill? Human consciousness was operating, it could not be put off by design. Still, she conceded, he was up to something unusual. She hoped that when he wanted he would turn round and come back. It might be a question of finding the way. He might by then have had too much practice in going too far.

She hoped very much he would not be lost.

John had been reserved; was always Norwegian on the phone. She half expected him to say 'Mrs Sangster'. In his letter he had managed a degree or two more warmth, but one thing he had written made her shrink – 'these dread events that use up all our hope'. It wasn't so. Her hope was not used up by a vicious boy; or any number of vicious boys. She must not let John get away with that. She had almost fallen into the trap of taking her wisdom from him; wisdom from a man who could not love. He had the wise appearance of a crocodile on a mud-bank, and really, she thought, he doesn't know any more about love than a crocodile does. He did though have knowledge of himself, she must be fair; he knew that he had lost his life. John had made not a regressive journey like Lex Clearwater's but a sideways one along a path that turned out to be a cul-de-sac – and it suited him well, there he remained. It had taken her father's death to show that she must not spend her time with John. She drove up his valley without her usual sense of arriving home; yet felt her usual affection for John Toft.

She did not walk in his apple trees. They sat in canvas chairs on his porch and sipped cold beer while she told him about Neil Chote and Shelley Birtles.

'You are a little bit ruined by ethicality,' John said.

Normally she would have turned that over, worried it. Today she thought, He's too easy with his ideas about me.

She told him Duncan Round had bought a telescope and did not seem to need her any more.

'That makes you sad?'

'No. A little bit for me, not for him. There are things going on in that family that would "use up hope" far more quickly than Neil Chote.'

'They are not things I will want to hear.'

No, she thought, you wouldn't.

'You judge me, Norma. You weigh me in your scale and find that I am made of fluff and feathers.'

'I just feel people can't step away all the time. You were very good with Duncan, John. Thank you for that.'

'You brought him with you and I made the effort. But I do not want you to bring him again.' John smiled. 'I am like Lop Nor. You know Lop Nor, the wandering lake? It shifts about, so when the explorers go back it isn't where the last one marked it on the map. I too shift about so you cannot find me again.'

'This way of talking John, it's an evasion. You use it to hold me at arm's length.'

'I must do it this way or we stop.' He looked away from her and gave a little sigh or laugh. 'You are a lonely woman and you look for company. You must understand, I cannot . . .'

'Why, John?'

'You see me move, so I am alive, and you come and stand alongside, and I breathe – yes, he's alive. So you start feeling in with your fingertips, eh? In we go, a little bit, nice and warm, but not far enough, a wee bit more – and what do you find, Norma? Where you would discover John Toft, nothing is there.'

'Because of a woman, is it, John?'

'Aach!'

'I'm sorry. So it's not?'

'You want this story, Norma? I do not need to tell.'

'Tell me, John.'

'Well, two things. Two little parts it has. Then you must go away.'

'I'll decide that.'

'Oh, you will?' He smiled at her. 'Listen then. It is the war. The Germans try to build the atom bomb and what they need is heavy water. And Norway has it, did you know that? They made it at the Norsk Hydro factory at Rjukan. So down it comes to Mael on Lake Tinn, on its way to Germany, and they load it on the ferry there.'

'I know about this.'

'You do? You know about the bomb Norwegian agents put in the ferry?'

'It's a famous story. It helped stop Germany getting the atom bomb.'

'That is true. The little bomb stops the bigger bomb. So – they put it there, clever, in the night. And out goes the ferry, and the bomb goes off boom! Just a little bang, but enough. It blows the bow off the ferry and down all that heavy water goes, in thirteen hundred feet of cold lake water. And twenty Norwegian passengers were drowned.'

Norma did not know what to say. It was another story from the war.

'I knew a man who drowned on the ferry,' John said.

'Yes?'

'And the men who planted the bomb. For a short while I trained with them.'

'I see.'

'Perhaps you do.' Men he knew had killed a man he knew. He could no longer find the principle of order which he had been taught to look for in his work. Humans especially came to seem random in their behaviour and he came to look on them as a failed species.

'John, I do see. After the Lofotens – '

'Ah, the Lofotens. That was prologue. And Tinnsjö part one. You want part two?'

'If you want to tell.'

'It was at the war's end. I was up in Finnmark. You do not know about this campaign?'

'No.'

'We followed the Germans down from the Russian border, and they burn and run and blow up and run, all the way down to Lyngenfjord.'

At Tromsø he saw the *Tirpitz* lying keel up in the shallow fiord – the warship that saw scarcely any war, whose usefulness lay in the fear she caused. The bombers had come from inland on that day six months before. The *Tirpitz* had had no time for a smokescreen. Bombs smashed through the seven-inch plates of the deck and exploded in the innards of the ship. She had been built to withstand the bombs of 1939 but not these twelve thousand pounders with noses of hardened steel – Tall Boys, they were called. (Fat Boy came later.) The *Tirpitz* rolled over and sank and nine hundred crewmen drowned inside.

John looked at her shape in the waters of the fiord – a long roundness, like a resting whale. But he drew back from that natural likeness. He felt the terror of nine hundred men as they suffocated or drowned inside the hull. Men and women and children had been dying in that way – and ways more horrible, with their killers closer at hand – for many years, which he had known, but had not *known*. Now he saw *Tirpitz* and he knew. He looked beyond her at the hills and coast, which had been his; and took his further step. We do not belong, we do not belong in the world.

'So, I – withdrew. There is no step along a human path for me to take. Do not try to lead me that way.'

Others faced with things as bad, or worse, did not shrivel up and die, as John Toft died on that summer day. He knows. John is a man who knows many things; has thought his way time and again out of the dark place he is in, but cannot make spirit follow thought and so falls back and will not come out, although he is able to look out; see others there, happy there, whom he cannot think of as failed. If one is not, if he or she . . . if Norma is not . . . So he thinks;

but cannot come out of his dark and cold and join her.

Norma sat silent. She grew angry with John; looked down the valley so she would not burst out. The waste of it!

John said, 'It is a little bit sad, this story, eh? One wipes the eye, but curls the lip.'

'Yes. I suppose so.'

'I think perhaps you should not waste your time with me.'

'It hasn't been a waste of time. I like you more than anyone I know.'

'But you can't go on liking me. Otherwise you will stand in one spot. That will not be good for you.'

'You do know more than a crocodile.'

'Eh? What's this?'

'Nothing, John. Where will you go when you sell the orchard?'

'Oh, it is sold. This week. The papers are all signed. This season we will pick and then I must go.'

'Where to?'

'That is decided too. I have bought some land. It is on the Coast, you know, it is south from Westport. There is three hectares and a tin house on a hill and the sea all in front of me, down a track with a thousand steps. I have been reading Axel Munthe again. Do you know it, *The Story of San Michele*?'

'I couldn't read it. It was sentimental.'

'You did not read far enough. You did not reach the rats in Naples eating the dead bodies. He is a strange man, this Munthe. It is as if he wears spectacles and one lens magnifies and shows all that is horrible and cruel and the other makes things fuzzy and pink – all butterflies and angel babies, eh? But, I will sit above the sea, like Munthe. I will build my house. There will be no villa of Tiberius to dig up, no broken heads of Nero eh, and no red Sphinx to stand before my door, or monks with crossed hands to re-inter. I will go down my thousand steps to an empty beach, not to Capri. That will suit me well, to be alone and have no past. I would say come and visit me, up my steps, but you will not.'

'I might. Who knows?'

'No, you will not.'

She tried to imagine him building a new house round an old tin one, putting in fruit trees, digging a vegetable garden, planting vines; and in the evening walking on the beach, and trudging up his hillside path with driftwood tied in a bundle on his back. It was not real, it was sentimental, but perhaps that was the only way to keep a hold on him, through unreality. I can't do it, she thought, I can't lie about him. But unless I do he becomes something I can't bear to face. She was terrified that she would come to loathe him.

'I don't think I'll come John, I'll just imagine you.'

'Better, I think, if you forget.'

'Will you forget me?'

He looked at her. 'Yes, yes, no trouble. You see, I am truthful. *Skol*, Norma.'

'*Skol*.'

She hoped she would forget him. If she did not she might drive to the coast one day and sneak in through the bush and tumble him head over heels down his thousand steps.

Norma is having a bad time. She is not getting anywhere. But after leaving John's place she has a lucky meeting. She drives away from the valley for the last time and instead of turning right on the highway to town, turns left instead and drives to Long Island where, in pre-Toft days, she used to go for solitary walks; long Saturday afternoon walks on the five-mile beach.

She avoids the picnic ground and parks her car at the end of the public road. A forestry road runs beyond the gate and she walks in the pines for a moment, then follows a winding track through dunes and comes out on the beach. The tide is out as far as it can go, the sea is a quarter mile away. She takes off her sandals and rolls her linen slacks half-way up her shins and walks through the dry sand and over the hard wet sand, stopping to let a sand yacht roll by – not enough wind for sand yachts today. Along in front of the picnic ground people are swimming and floating on lilos, playing beach-cricket, sunbathing, throwing frisbees, trying to fly kites – not enough wind for kites either. Walkers are scattered for miles and at the eastern end half a dozen horses are wading in the sea. But where she is going, along at the western end, there is no one. She paddles a while, moving away from town, but turns and walks backwards and looks at Saxton now and then. It really is very tiny, just a blot or smudge – or brightly shining waterfly, on another angle. The coast runs away north-east, headland beyond headland, mountain rising at the back of mountain. There is Imrie, there is

Corkie, and the big ones of the Armitage further back. A light flashes from Corkie, from the top – some tramper signalling his achievement home. It seems brave and foolish, the sort of thing John Toft would not do.

She comes out of the water and starts to stride out, passing groups of strollers, smiling at those she knows – what a lot of people she knows. Soon there is no one in front of her. She sees a man and woman sunbathing naked in the dunes. She is passed by, circled round by, two joggers. They have used her as a mark. 'It's nice to be useful,' she says. She starts to be happy and has the feeling, I can make it, I can get by, that she has learned to enjoy for itself.

The beach is cut and broken at the western end, with sloping banks of shell-strewn sand running down from the marram grass and white tangles of driftwood and logs stripped of their bark. There are wide lagoons, shallow at the edge and deep in the centre, and fields of corrugated sand making a huge diamond shape where water from the estuary has rushed out. Norma walks the edge of the lagoons and plods on the soft corrugations out to the point of the diamond, making oyster-catchers and shags lift off. There she stands, wide-legged, with her face pointing at the sun and her arms flung out. Her straw hat hangs like a Viking shield on her back.

Ken Birtles sits on a log by the estuary and watches her. Some loony dame, he thinks.

It is Ken Birtles she will meet.

As she comes back by the waterline she sees him. They recognize each other and neither is pleased. He too has been thinking, I can make it.

She can walk by – wants to walk by – but thinks he will take it for stand-offishness, so half raises her hand and changes direction.

'Hallo, Mr Birtles.'

'Gidday.'

'I thought I was alone here.'

'Me too.' He stands up. That is polite. She turns and looks across the sand, where the oyster-catchers have settled again. 'Isn't this a lovely place?'

'Yeah, it's good. That's not blood, is it? You OK?'

'Oh.' She looks at the sleeve of her blouse where she has leaned on a vine row, talking to Sandra. 'It's boysenberry juice. I got it at my brother's place.'

'Looks like blood.'

'Doesn't it? Gruesome.' She cannot interpret the twist that comes on his mouth but suspects she has lost ground with the word – if she had any ground to lose. 'Well, I'd better get on. I usually go right round the back and come up through the middle to the beach.' But she can't go yet, there's something she must say.

'I'm sorry Shelley went to prison.'

He hoods his eyes. It means he doesn't want to talk about it.

'Yeah,' he grunts.

'I was talking to my mother this morning. She wants to write to Shelley.'

'What for?'

'She wants to tell her she's not to blame for my father's death. I can stop her if you like.'

Ken Birtles picks up a branch of driftwood. He's going to hit me, Norma thinks, but knows it is impossible. He drags it in the sand, makes a trench, wipes it level with his foot; then whacks a shell sitting on a sand tee like a ball. It whirrs away and hits a log. She's reminded of the whirring of the softball he picked out of the air in front of her face.

'She means well. She really doesn't blame Shelley at all.'

Ken Birtles throws the stick away. 'OK. Tell her to go ahead. It's Arohata. Corrective training.'

'Oh, she'd address it your place. You can send it on. If you want to read it – '

'I wouldn't do that.'

'If you think there's anything that might upset her . . . My mother thinks she should be put straight about the Chote boy.'

Ken Birtles sits down on his log. He wipes his hand over his face. It's as if he takes a skin off and Norma flinches for him.

'Hayley wants to shoot him,' he says.

'Who? Neil Chote?'

'But Shelley can't get out of it by putting it all on him.'

'Does she want to?'

'No, she doesn't. Shelley knows,' he shrugs, 'she's mucked things up herself. Still, if she hadn't met him . . .'

Norma waits. 'I'm going this way, if you want to walk.'

His jandals go smack-smack on the soles of his feet.

'How is Hayley taking it? Apart from shooting him?'

'She's in Australia. I sent her to her auntie.'

'And your wife?'

'She's in hospital.'

'I'm sorry. I hope it's nothing . . .'

'It's in here.' He taps his head. 'She's never got over Wayne. I feel a bit like Job in the Bible.' He laughs.

'I saw in last night's paper where you lost your job coaching the softball team.'

'Ha, that's nothing. That's chicken-feed.'

'But you must have enjoyed it?'

'Yeah, I did. There's other teams. They got some tough new sheilas at Deepsea and they didn't want a man for a coach. Suits me. They'll lose from now on.'

'I hope they do.'

'I hope they don't. They used to be a good team.'

She finds his accent hard to place. It doesn't seem Midlands after all. 'What part of England did you come from, Mr Birtles?'

'A town you've never heard of. Hartlepool. Fourth Division.'

'That's on the coast south of Newcastle.'

'Yeah,' he says, surprised. 'You're the first New Zealander who's ever known that.'

'I've got the sort of mind that retains trivial facts.'

'Hartlepool is trivial all right.'

'I didn't mean that. Oh dear.' She sees he doesn't like her 'oh dear', but this time he looks at her and says, 'Where do you come from?'

'Here. Saxton. South of it actually. I was brought up on a farm in the Stebbing Valley.'

'Where they have the floods. I guess you're used to rain, like me. In Hartlepool it never seemed to stop.'

He wants to talk but hasn't got the words and she wonders how to help him without his knowing it. Carefully she says, 'Do you find Saxton very strange?'

'I like Saxton. It's a good place.' They have walked along the side of the island. Across the inlet orchards bend and dip in the hills. Mudflats shine in the sun and the little Darwood wharf sags on its mussel-crusted piles. 'I like things like that.'

'It's beautiful, isn't it?'

'It's OK. It's a long way from the beach at Hartlepool, I'll tell you that.'

He went into the ironworks, he tells her, but after a year of that knew there had to be something better, so he quit; and worked as a labourer for a while, then, almost too late, got apprenticed to a plumber, learned a trade. Now he's a maintenance man at Deepsea.

'There's going to be redundancies next year. I'll be gone.'

She does not know what to say. 'You are like Job.'

'I'm not religious. I got a fair dose of the Bible from my mum. She was pretty strong on Revelations. St John, you know? But heaven seemed so damn noisy to me. All those trumpets and choirs and beasts roaring and so on. You wouldn't go there for some peace and quiet.'

Norma laughs, though not sure he means it to be funny. Perhaps he means it to be sad.

'I usually go inland here and walk in the trees. We can get back on the beach if we take one of the roads further along.'

'Yeah, OK. I could do with some shade.'

'Softball seems unusual for an Englishman. I thought all Englishmen played was cricket.'

'I used to bowl.' He picks up a pine-cone and bowls it at a tree. 'But I don't know, I got here and I went along to a softball match with a mate of mine and it was right. Lots of noise, lots of things happening all quick, and the whole thing over in an hour, it was right. Like I really was in a new country. No three-day games and everyone taking their time. Anyhow, I was good at it. I was a Saxton rep before I got married.'

'Now Hayley will be.'

'Yeah, she will.' He seems uncertain. 'She'll be good.' He under-arms a pine-cone at a tree and hits it square. He is, she thinks, a man who needs to put his body at things, with skill or force, and line things up and calculate and do. She sees him squint and knows he's getting trees in a row. Then he gives a nudge and makes them knock each other down like dominoes. Yet he's not a violent man. He just needs to put himself in touch, and if not with his body, then his mind, in a practical way. He is, in fact, quite a gentle man. See the way he sets a toadstool upright.

'Seven of them, for the seven dwarfs.'

They come to a block recently milled. It looks as if a tank battle has been fought. Norma is shocked. 'There used to be a clearing over there. It was a nesting place for black-backed gulls.'

'Not any more. There's a rabbit, eh.' He sights an imaginary rifle but does not shoot. Leads her through the wasteland, climbs a log, gives her his hand to help her down. 'Pines grow quick. In a couple of years there'll be a new crop as high as your head.'

We touched, she thinks. Is he as unaware of it as he seems?

They come to a pond with most of the water gone. Fat black tadpoles rise and sink in an amber soup. A decoy duck with flaking paint rests in a bay of rushes. Ken Birtles leans out and floats it with a stick. It makes a lop-sided voyage to the centre, watching them with its faded eye. He twists a cone off a cut branch and lobs it like a hand grenade at the duck, which bobs on the ripples and noses back into the reeds.

'Seems bloody cruel doesn't it, luring them down with wooden ducks then blasting the tripes out of them?'

But all right playing hand grenades, she thinks. Men need reconstructing. His cone very likely killed a tadpole, but he wouldn't think of that. All the same she does not like him less. The print of his hand is still on hers and she does not know whether it is pleasant or not. And he's made a print, more delicate than large, on her mind. Am I so hard up any man will do? But she's found him gentle, found him active in a strange way in his mind, and found him hurt. That makes him more than just any man.

In the trees again, he walks in front. These are big old trees, due for milling, and five finger and whitey wood have grown underneath. Ferns lean down and touch the path. He goes more slowly, bends his head. He has forgotten her, and dare she say, is it too intimate, 'What are you thinking about?'

'Me? Nothing. I was just . . .'

Remembering my kids. A day in the waterworks reserve, and trees as big as this, natives though, black beech and matai and rimu, and a path with ferns bending down from a bank and touching the ground. The Birtleses have been up to the forks and paddled in the river, and eaten boiled eggs and sausage-rolls, have drunk Coca-Cola and river-water; and Joanie and Wayne and Shelley walk

217

ahead, and he comes on slowly, droning a song to Hayley, two years old, in his arms. The others go round a corner, out of sight. He walks with the ferns brushing his legs. The river flashes white through the trees and lies in glass-green pools under the bank. Hayley sleeps.

That was the happiest I've been, Ken Birtles thinks. He sees Joanie walking ahead. He sees Wayne and Shelley hiding underneath the curve of the ferns. The gleam of Shelley's glasses and Wayne's white fists are four little giveaways in the foliage. He goes by humming Hayley's tune, with his face turned to the river, and hears them rustle out and pad behind him, whisper, squeak.

'Where's Wayne and Shell?' he asks his wife.

'I don't know, they must have gone ahead,' looking at them.

'I hope they don't get lost.' So they walk along, until Wayne and Shelley burst with glee, and Hayley wakes . . .

'Do you remember Shelley when she ran?'

'Yes, I do. She was marvellous.'

'The thing I remember most is the way she put her head back at the tape and her glasses went all different colours in the sun.'

That's what I was missing, Norma thinks. She sees the girl running down the straight, miles ahead. Her glasses flash and gleam and make blind ovals on her face. I saw her all clean and innocent, but I left her glasses out.

'We didn't know her eyes were crook until she was three. Then one day she said to her mum, "Why have I got two plates of porridge?" '

'Double vision?'

He nods. 'We took her to a doc and she had one of those operations, you know, where they turn the eyeball over and cut the muscles at the back. It still makes me sick when I think about it.'

'It's just as well they can though. You don't see cross-eyed children any more.'

'She had to wear specs after that. Sometimes she had to have one of the lenses covered up.'

'It didn't stop her being a champion runner.' He is not looking for comfort, he's remembering aloud.

'She got contact lenses last year. She didn't seem the same any more.'

'Girls like to try themselves without spectacles. They're very conscious of how they look at seventeen . . . Shall we go down on the beach again?'

'Neil Chote knocked one of her contact lenses out when he punched her.'

That's terrible? That's sad? She does not know what to say. That's the way it turns out, you take a step, follow an inclination, or you just make a mistake, and find you've crossed into a place where civilized rules don't apply, and things like contact lenses get punched out of your eye. And how do you find your way back, if you want to come? The easy step can't just be reversed. There are labyrinths to find your way through.

They follow a track in spiky grass and walk in sand above the high water mark. He kicks a beer can. 'Japanese beer, you get all sorts of stuff.'

'I found a message in a bottle once. But it was a class of children from Darwood School. They'd only written it the day before.'

He laughs. He kicks the can again and sends it arcing over a log. She finds his need to use himself all the time alarming. But the skill of it, the fine calculation. He'd managed a cushion of sand between his foot and the can so he would not hurt his toe.

'Crab shell,' he says, picking it up. 'Nice one, eh?' He gives it to her.

'Do you think you'll be able to get Shelley running again?' She hears the ambiguity, regrets it; but he does not seem to hear.

'I'll give it a try. She reckons she wants to.' He looks along the beach, sees people there, and does not want to talk about Shelley any more. 'Dead fish.' Pointing at a group of gulls by the water. They walk down.

'Barracuda.'

'Wicked teeth.' He's back to not liking the way she speaks – doesn't like 'wicked'. I'll talk the way I want to, she thinks. 'He's really not much more than a machine for killing.'

'He just does what he's got to do.' He lifts the barracuda by its tail and swings it round his head and hurls it into the sea. Wipes his hand on his shorts. He's used to the smell of fish, she supposes. Walkers, passing, look back over their shoulders. Yes, here I am, headmistress of the college, paddling at the beach with the main-tenance man from the fish factory. Take a good look.

'Once,' she says, 'there were millions of krill washed up here. This whole end of the beach was pink with them. Tiny little things like baby lobsters. It's funny to think of them being the food for some of the biggest creatures in the sea.'

'Must have looked funny,' he says.

'And there's a season, if you come out here, when you can see millions of tiny shellfish. They wash up with each wave. They're no bigger than your little fingernail. The water leaves them stranded and then they start to burrow in like mad. Before the next wave comes they're gone.'

'It's easy to see you're a teacher.'

Norma is hurt by that.

Norma is angry.

'I'm just conversing with you, not giving lessons. But if it offends you, I'll stop.'

He's startled, but manages a grin and won't back down. He dabs his forefinger in the air. 'You got a way of talking from up here.'

'From on high?'

'Yeah, just like that.'

'Well I'm not aware of it. Words are just words. I try to make them say what they mean.'

He seems to lose interest suddenly. His troubles have come back. Well, she thinks, I'm not a doctor, I can't cure him. 'Yeah,' he says. They walk a hundred yards while small waves wash their feet. Wish-wash, they say; but Norma thinks she'd better not repeat it. In spite of their argument she feels easy.

'My car's up here,' pointing at the pines.

'Mine's along there.'

'I'm glad we had a walk. And talk.'

'Sure. OK.'

'Even if I talk like a schoolteacher.'

'It must be a tough job.' Lifts his arm, goodbye. And he enjoys, she notices, even that; exact movement, just the way it should be.

'Oh, Mr Birtles,' going back to him a step or two, 'I've got some strawberries in my car. Far too many for me.'

'No. It's all right.'

'Perhaps you could take some to your wife.' She asserts herself. It's punishment, a little, and he deserves it. Takes him through the dunes and along the path. The berries she had meant for John Toft are in a plastic ice-cream carton on the back seat of her car.

'There.'

'That's too much.'

'Take them. I can't eat them. Goodbye.'

She starts the engine, reverses out from the pines. I enjoyed that, she thinks. What a nice, awkward man. Yes, I enjoyed that.

She toots her horn as she drives away.

16

New Year's Eve and still it does not rain. The pine forests are closed to picnickers and the hand on the fire danger clock points at Extreme. Hosing restrictions are in force and back-yard fires are banned. None of this affects the Rounds' New Year's Eve party. Tom sprinkles his lawn and freshens his pool with water pumped through holding tanks from the river. (There's a notice for busybodies on the gate – *Private Water Supply*.) And no one expects a barbecue. 'How bloody bourgeois can you get?' As for his sauna-house, built against the brick garden wall and furnished not with an electric heater but a wood-burning stove and real stones, it isn't quite finished yet, so no one feels short-changed on New Year's Eve.

Professional caterers have done the food. 'If you think I'm cooking for a hundred people, think again,' Josie says. It's laid out on tables by the pool – hot and cold, sweet and savoury – and looks ready to be photographed for an up-market magazine. 'Gastronomical porn,' Sandra says. The drinks – better quality booze than she's used to – stand on trestle tables on the lawn so if any bottles fall they won't break. The caterers have sent a barman too and Sandra agrees with Josie, he's the best-looking guy at the party.

Sandra and Josie are alike and Norma finds it surprising that they get on. Sandra has made it clear why Tom invited her. 'I'll go away if you like but I'll have something to eat and drink first. He promised me food.' There's something hectic in her manner tonight. Sandra is a little feverish. She looks beautiful in a vulturish way. She still wears her Indian cottons though. Tonight's dress has tiny pieces of mirror sewn into it but still has a grubby appearance. Sandra declares that she won't pretend or even try. Take me or leave me, Sandra says. She looks, in spite of her gauzy dress, more than ready to bite and tear, and Norma wonders if Tom Round likes the threat of being hurt.

Josie laughs at Sandra's sharp remarks. Perhaps she wants Tom to be hurt.

*

Tom has admiring acquaintances but no friends. His friends, he believes, live in other towns. He names to himself a number of men, successful, gifted, practical, with whom he would live on close terms, of shared interest and ability, of special knowledge, if he chose to shift to Wellington or Auckland. He meets them when he goes there, and comes away dissatisfied: lack of time stops him from getting the friendship he deserves. Tom believes he has a gift for friendship and cannot see his need to be first. He looks around his Saxton acquaintances at the party and feels himself exiled among little men.

Make no mistake though, they are useful to him. He understands that very well.

Tony Hillman has come along. 'Get your tie off, Tony. It's not the Royal Garden Party, mate.' The lawyer is only half a man, Tom believes. His Christ's College accent, summer suit, pained smile, are symptoms of an inability to grab hold and hang on and gobble up. Tom has little time for pickers and choosers. 'I don't think Tony's balls have ever dropped.' It would shock him to be told that Tony has 'scored' with a woman who turned him down.

Deputy Mayor Don Compton is there, in clothes that really lower the tone: black shoes and baggy suit. He has his jacket and waistcoat off and – it's unbelievable – his trousers are held up with braces. 'Jesus Don, where'd you get those, they're off the Ark.' Tom snaps them against the deputy's lardy tum. 'The smart thing – the name of the game – ' Don Compton converses, lifting and kneading huge invisible breasts as he makes his point.

There are half a dozen of John Toft's 'little millionaires and clever bankrupts'. There's Rock Edison, who got his name because of his resemblance to the actor. He enjoyed it for many years, promoted it, but would like to get rid of it now. Tom Round has started making pansy jokes. There's Morris Martin, who owns a BMW but drives a clapped-out Cortina when he goes to visit the hard-up farmers he arranges loans for. His wife drives the BMW in town. It's Tom's feeble joke to call Morris Aston. There are . . . but they don't matter, they fill the lawns and rooms, and fill the night with their opinions. Their wives are more interesting because, on the whole, they've had to work more on themselves and make finer adjustments. But they don't come into our story either. They walk by the pool, eat, drink, watch their husbands, talk about the things that make them the same as and different from each other (golf, gardens, fashion, travel, the beach-house, grandchildren, World Vision). One drinks too much and cries because her life seems empty. One walks into the dark and lies down in the dry grass and listens to the party and wishes she could go further away, deep into the earth, or up into the sky and glitter there with the Southern Cross.

Tom Round thinks there's no one here who can understand him. They can't have even a glimmering of his other dimension. How can they know about the thing that happens in his mind, in his *being*, when all the preliminaries are done and creative functions take over; and the struggle begins, his to control them and stay aware, and theirs to run away with him; and out of this, this pain, this joy, out of this, by God, out of this Passion, there comes . . .

Tom, alone by his garden wall, knows he is a great man and no one understands. The house, how it glows there, glows with him, and no one sees. His wife and daughters there, Stephanie and Sandra, Norma Sangster, each one his – yet none of them even starts to see. If he just turns and goes away and never comes back their lives will collapse. They'll snuff out and have no existence any more. He sees himself as put upon, and groans under his burden, but grins in fierce enjoyment of himself. If I close my eyes they're dead, if I turn my back . . . He puts his glass on the wall, looks into the forest, blocks his ears; he's wiped them out. And now I'll let them live again – and they glitter, screech, perambulate, with the moment's being he allows.

Tom laughs. His daughters at the pool edge arrange their limbs to suit him. Wet and brown, they make arcs and cones of gleaming light. Josie, in flowered silk, levitates and crackles at his command, Stephanie splits with ripeness her red bipartite blouse, Sandra tinkles, floats, has sugared points and edges under her eastern dress, and Norma Sangster now, all smoothed-down, Norma will do for another day, Norma will keep.

The fat and skinny rich men, they are his, and their wives, though if he decides it he'll do without the lot. He can live in his house all alone if he wants, and be enough, be rich with all the things they can never have. There's a splendour in that he finds overwhelming. He dreams a blaze of cleansing radiation, a washing through of light that empties his house, de-bugs his house, and

224

leaves him pure and solitary. 'Ha!' He throws his glass into the trees and hears it tinkle . . .

'Hey!' His son is climbing in the grass with his black box in his arms. 'You nearly hit me.'

'Where do you think you're going?'

'Up the forest. There's a couple of hours before the moon comes up.'

'If you spot any flying saucers – ' but the boy has gone. By God, Tom thinks, I might just find someone to talk to there, men from Arcturus eh? But he can't sustain the fantasy and he climbs down the rock garden and crosses the lawn for another drink. Not long ago he read a novel where an Indian boy was blinded by measles and his father, the chief, picked him up by the ankles and knocked his brains out on a rock. He loved his son but the boy was no good any more.

Tom understands. He overlooks the fact that he has never felt any love for Duncan.

'The worst thing about working in a shearing gang,' Josie says, 'is you get all these tiny hairs stuck in your nipples. You've got to pick them out every night or they itch like mad.'

She's proud of her days in the shearing gang and often tells her daughters and friends about them. ('Yes Mum, mutton for breakfast, mutton for lunch, mutton for dinner, we know.')

'Your hands get beautiful with all the natural lanolin in the wool. I've never had hands that soft again.' She means to put her shearing stories in her chapter on weaving but isn't sure her friends will approve. Perhaps I'll write my own book, she thinks. Decides on the spot that's what she'll do. Betrays them without a second thought. All they've done so far is talk and some of them can't put two words together anyhow. It hasn't been the friendliest time, these last two weeks.

She feels warm towards them all the same. They've had so many problems of the sort she's had, and battled through them, battled out. They talk about meditation, breathing, rebirthing. They talk about Mums.

'I took her overseas with me, staying in Youth Hostels and carrying a pack and hitching rides. When we came back she was wearing jeans and a T-shirt and no bra. Dad just looked at her at the airport and turned round and walked away. But it took him only a couple of weeks, you know. She's back in permed hair and high heels again. She doesn't come and see me any more.'

'Mine doesn't come either. My old Tom Sergei, you know, with his eye torn out, he ate her chihuahua. All we found was his head on the doormat. Well, they're so much like rats, chihuahuas, aren't they? I don't think Mum's ever coming back.'

Josie laughs. She has a taste for gruesome stories. Perhaps we can write a book about mothers. She was such good friends with hers though, until she died, that she would have nothing to contribute. You can't put good things in that sort of book. New Year, she thinks, and is disconcerted to find her eyes filling with tears for her mother. Goes across to fill her glass from the dishy barman she feels no desire for at all. He's just a pretty object and she wouldn't mind hanging him on the wall.

'Norma, how's your mother getting on?'

'Oh, adjusting. It takes time.'

'Will our daughters have to worry about us the way we worry about our mothers, do you think?'

'I don't have daughters.'

'Well don't make a long face, you're lucky. Look at them there. The potential for trouble in that lot. If you were a man could you keep your hands off?'

'Probably not.' There's something false in Norma's laugh. Norma looks tired and as if she wants to go home.

'Well, I'm glad to be out of it. Out of that – ' Josie thinks – 'sticky hormonal web. I know you thought I was joking, but I'm still alone, all alone oh. And loving it. It's like getting washed in cold water. God, you feel clean and fresh and ready for yourself.'

'I'm glad.'

'Look at poor dumb Stephanie. She thinks she's won first prize. And your little Sandra waiting for left-overs.'

'I don't think Sandra waits for anything.'

'They're welcome to him, you know. I just don't care.' She walks across to Tom and Stephanie. 'If I was Solomon,' she includes Sandra, sitting elbows on knees in a chair nearby, 'I'd say chop him down the middle. But I think, Tom dear, they'd both say go ahead.'

'Shut up, Josie.'

'His left side is better than his right.'

'Shut up, I said.'

'You could clone him.'

'What's that you're wearing, Josie?' Tom sniffs elaborately. 'It smells like dunny freshener.'

Josie laughs. 'You didn't know he was a wit as well.' She ambles back to her friends. Being free is marvellous, she thinks.

'Happy families,' Sandra says. 'I think I'll go home.'

'There are probably one or two of them quite happy. Josie is happy, I think.'

'That boy with all the scars, was that the son?'

'Yes. Oddly enough he's happy too.'

'The girls are not. Stella's not anyway.'

'Stella is ambitious.' And other things as well.

'The oldest one is giving the barman the eye.'

'That's Miranda. She's in med. school. She wants to be a gynae-cologist.'

'I'd sooner be a horse-doctor. Looking at all these,' looks and sneers, 'sisters.'

'Well, in the mass we're not very lovely. But each one of us . . . ' Leaves it unsaid. Why bother?

All the same Sandra says, 'I suppose that's why you're a head-mistress, eh? You always know the right little cheesy thing to say.'

'Oh don't, Sandra, please don't, not tonight. I'm not up to it.'

'OK, OK, sorry. I'm a bitch.'

'Don't run yourself down. You've got so much going for you.'

Sandra grins. 'Jeez, Norma, I like you. You're consistent.' She steps back to let a couple by and a fern-leaf fingers her neck. 'Let's get out of here before we get strangled.'

They go out of the conservatory and stand by the rock garden. Tom Round yells, 'Belinda, get that dog out of the pool. I told you before.'

'Aw, Dad –'

'Now.'

The girl puts her arms on the pool edge and heaves herself out. She sits with her feet dangling, reaches in the water, takes the dog high on its forelegs, grunts with effort. Lifts the old huge-bellied thing and wraps it in her towel.

'Pooh to you, Dad.'

227

'He's not really the swimming companion I'd choose,' Tony Hillman murmurs.

'Oh Tony, you gave me a fright. Do you know Sandra Duff? Tony Hillman.' Maybe I can do them a favour. But though he smiles his even smile she sees him recoil. Sandra, bright and clever, in her bazaar clothes, will not do. Not even for slumming; though really it is Sandra who would slum.

'Let me guess, you're a lawyer.'

'Does it show?'

'You've got a way of floating an inch or two off the ground.'

'Indeed?'

'And saying indeed.'

'If you'll excuse me,' Norma says. Sandra is too bloody-minded. And Tony too bloodless. She wants to sit quietly in the dark, and goes into the house, misdirecting Tony, who will get rid of Sandra and look for her; goes through Josie's workroom, where the loom stands arms akimbo, and down the steps into the garage, skirts the cars in the yard, slips through an archway and along by a wall and finds a stone seat – astonishing, still warm from the sun. Sits smiling with pleasure at her successful flight, watching them, Sandra, Tony, Tom, Stephanie, the guests and girls, all of them, and thinks, yes Sandra's right but I'm right too, we're light and dark, and sweet and sour, this and that; all those things. As her father used to say – looking in the innards of a tractor – 'It ain't nonsense but it don't make any sense.'

Her gin and tonic runs out and she puts the glass in the angle where the seat meets the wall. Tom Round's lovely house – walls of Mediterranean white, earth-coloured tiles, conservatory like a ferny cave; and pool with inward-looking eye, lawns with shaven cheeks, chunky rocks and pricking rock plants and white little flowers like stars – lovely house, lovely place. Tom is a very clever man, and more than clever perhaps; but a man who is horrible as well. She does not know any word, or combination of them, any idea that will contain him. Watches him eye Sandra, who wanders by the pool, while cupping Stephanie's bottom in his palm. Desire, lust, whatever it may be, isn't horrible; but that lust to own, possess, to gorge, increase . . . people as food, as nourishment . . . it makes her shrink and shiver and angle her head and turn her eyes. Does he eye Belinda as well? She cannot look.

Soon she hears a rustling in the grass over the wall, a thud and hiss and snorting, and thinks, There's sheep out there. The wall makes a tiny tremor where something bangs it. Hooves scratch.

'Mrs Sangster.'

'Oh Duncan, it's you. I thought . . .' She looks at his face looking down; smiles at his horror-movie face.

'Do you want to have a look through my telescope?'

'Yes, I'd love to.'

'Go round by the gate. I'll meet you there.'

She does as she is told; walks a short way down the crackling drive and finds a picket-gate in the fence. Duncan holds it open for her.

'There's a lady lying in the grass over there.'

'Is she all right?'

'Drunk, I guess. She keeps on saying, "Lovely, this is lovely." I think she wants to be left alone.'

'Where's your telescope?'

'Up in the fire-break. In the pines.'

'Are we allowed there?'

'No one knows. As long as you don't smoke it's OK.'

He turns on his torch and lights her up the hill. Her soles slip and she has to take handfuls of grass to hold herself.

'It's easier in the pines. I've got a track.'

She looks back from among the trees and finds the house and lawns and party shrunken: toy figures on a table, like a war game. The women's coloured clothes look beautiful and what a slithery motion on the water. She is suddenly afraid of the dark trees and the boy. His torch, as he angles it through the trunks, makes ridges, oily planes, on his face.

'How far is it?'

'Not far.'

The trunks move by like men, bracken crackles at her waist and she's thankful for her linen slacks.

'Gorse here,' Duncan says, lighting it. Half-way through she slips and grabs; cries out as prickles stab her.

'Are you all right?'

'I got a handful. I'm all right.' Sucks that sweet-sour taste, that living her.

I should be home. Oh damn New Year.

Duncan climbs in clay steps with the torch angled back. She remembers that clay is a missing link. Clay was there when the spark of life made its primal flash. It seems unlikely, feeling the stuff slide and crumble under her feet. She is not keen on the spark of life. Would almost as soon it had never flashed.

The party is gone: an isolated cry, a bodiless laugh. The sky rolls open on the other side of the ridge. 'Here,' Duncan says. He shows his telescope on its stand. 'I've got some sacks on the ground. You can sit.'

She does so, gratefully. He flicks off the torch – and Norma cries out at the splendour of the sky.

'Duncan, look at it.'

'Yeah,' he says, as though it's his.

'I've never seen so many stars.'

'Not all of them are stars. There's planets and galaxies and nebulae and globular clusters. Most of them are stars though, in our galaxy.'

'There's a shooting star.'

'I see a couple every night.'

'I'll make a wish.' No reply, he disapproves, but she makes it all the same: a happy encounter for herself.

Duncan is busy at the telescope. 'I've got Jupiter if you want to see.'

'Yes, I'd love to . . . I can't see.' That black hood is her eyelid – but when she tries again the planet is there, a yellow ball, but weightier; and huge and perfect; huge. She feels all her breath go sucking out.

'See the moons? There's Europa and Io and Ganymede.'

'Yes, I see them.'

'There won't be any eclipses tonight. Callisto is the one way out. I don't think you'll see it. See the red spot?'

'Yes.'

'You could drop two Earths in there. I like the red spot.'

'I'll have to stop. It's making me shaky.'

'Yeah. It did that to me a bit. Do you want to see a binary?'

'Yes, all right.' She knows about binaries from her evenings with John.

'See the Southern Cross, way down low. Now find the big star in the pointer. That's Alpha Centauri. You think that's just a single star, don't you?'

Squatting, she looks through his telescope at the two stars holding hands.

'It's three stars really. There's Proxima Centauri too but you don't see that. It's a red dwarf. Those two you can see go round each other every eight years. Proxima takes millions of years.'

There's nothing glib or easy in it. He holds this stuff as natural. His scale is different from ours, Norma thinks. These times and distances are things he can reach out to and take in. The band he can work in is stretched, it's widened out. Millions of years? – it seems to have a meaning for him. Would he understand a pico second? And all those dreadful chances and improbabilities . . .? Norma wants to back away from him, and hug him too. Is it alcohol, loneliness, possessive desire barely in control? She does not simply want to admire.

He says, 'The moon will be coming up in a minute.' She looks along the spiny back of the hills to Imrie and Corkie and sees a white radiance over their twin hump.

'Can we look at it?'

'We'd have to get binoculars. This is not a moon telescope.' He starts to dismount it from its legs. 'Hey, Mrs Sangster, I was wondering, are there courses I could do in, you know, physics and maths and astronomy?'

'I'm sure there are.'

'I can, like, read all the books and remember them, but most of the time I don't know what it means. I never got to physics at school.'

'You could go back.'

'No. Are there correspondence courses? I'd ask Mum but I thought you'd know.'

'I'm sure we could get you correspondence courses. Would you like me to find out?'

'That'd be great.'

'I think you'll learn like a fizz-bomb, Duncan.' She is elated. He wants to know meanings and she sees her part in it. She believes that he is out of danger now and will be a great man one day.

He puts his gear in the box and snaps it shut. 'See.' Imrie has a molten tip. 'Up she comes.'

They watch the moon take shape and break free, and it's too heavy, Norma thinks, to stay in the sky, it should crash down and burn through the Earth like a cannon-ball. Except of course – but she knows all that. Openness, susceptibility – that is the better way tonight; although the boy beside her is a fact.

'The moon's too close. I don't want to go there,' Duncan says.

'Well, you never will.' He'll work in little rooms, with instruments and figures – but travel out of course, travel far.

They walk down through the trees, climb and slide, and hear and see the party again. The house gleams like mother of pearl and the golf course spreads out from the foot of the hill, smooth pale slopes and pits of shadow. The cars on the drive are vertebrae – are rounded slickly shining butter-pats.

Duncan puts his case down by the gate. He darts away and comes back grinning. 'She's gone. All there is is a flat place in the grass.'

'I don't think I'll come back to the party. Duncan, there's my bag in your mother's room. It's a cloth one with a red silk scarf tied round the handle.'

'Sure,' he says, and runs up the drive and through the garage. She leans on the gate and waits for him. Like waiting for your boyfriend, she remembers, but not with any sadness or longing. The night has made a gift and she's satisfied.

He brings her bag. She knots her scarf round her neck. 'Goodnight Duncan. Thanks for showing me.' She kisses him on his undamaged cheek and walks down the drive.

'Hey, Mrs Sangster. Happy New Year.'

'Happy New Year, Duncan. Same to you.'

Her car is parked by the bridge. She gets in and sits a while with the window open, listening to the water and the far-off chirp and chatter and the crack of gum leaves in the night. Here, she thinks, here or anywhere is good enough. I don't really have to want too hard.

People are serving themselves at the bar. The barman has stripped to his grundies and is horsing with Miranda in the pool.

'He's a student too, surprise, surprise,' Belinda says.

'Hey Duncan, come on in,' Miranda yells.

He sees the barman discover him and the guy is pretty good, just a flicker.

'You do anything bad to my sister, I'll come and get you one foggy night.' He shows his teeth.

'Duncan,' Mandy screeches, 'you little bastard, I'll get you for that.'

Miranda is pleased with him. Mandy likes me, I never knew.

A woman with rings on her fingers, big fat rings, solo-waltzes by, humming 'Greensleeves', and takes off her shoes and dress and tights and climbs into the pool in her knickers and bra. She swims like a learner to the middle and stands bouncing gently on her toes. 'Come on, sausage, come on out,' pleads a man in a Hawaiian shirt, but she turns from him, dog-paddles away, still humming her tune. Duncan thinks it won't be long before more people go in, with no togs on probably. It would only take a push with his little finger to tip the man; who's so anxious about his wife he doesn't notice half his drink slop in, though the ice goes plop. How long will it take before it melts? Duncan goes to the bar and gets some cubes and drops them in the pool one by one.

'Give me, Dunc,' Miranda cries. She grabs one and tries to stuff it in the barman's grundies. Duncan has never seen her like this. She must have had too much to drink. Someone should get her out of the pool. He looks for his mother, but sees her trooping with her friends into the weaving-room. That's the end of her for a couple of hours.

A men's platoon led by his father comes out of the garage. Tom has his golf-clubs on his shoulder – it looks crazy in the middle of the night – and Rock Edison is carrying the bucket of balls. They go past the pool and round the side of the house and through the door in the brick wall to the flat bit of paddock Tom keeps mown – his Scotchman's tee. Some mornings before breakfast he spends half an hour out there shooting at the seventh green in the bend of the river. The whack of his club wakes everyone up; and when he's finished Belinda goes down with the bucket to find the balls. Five dollars if she comes back with every one, which she usually does. Tom doesn't often miss the green. One morning he scored a hole in one and made Josie drink a glass of whisky to celebrate.

Duncan hoists himself on the wall. The barman is out of the pool pulling on his black trousers and white shirt. Mandy has scratched him under the jaw. None of her boyfriends get very far with her, she won't be touched. The teacher in the Trade Aid dress is wrapping a towel round her, so that's all right. The men look like burglars in the moonlight; or murderers, with their golf-clubs flashing in their hands.

'What do you use here, Tom?' Morris Martin asks.

'Me? A four iron. Some of you jokers are going to need the driver.' Tom laughs.

'I think you should be handicapped for local knowledge, Tom,' Rock Edison says.

'I think you should start from further back.' Don Compton.

Duncan knows who most of them are. They come out in twos and threes, talking business. They're in a deal – Tom is a partner and the architect as well – to build a retirement village out by Darwood. It's going to cost hundreds of thousands of dollars to get in, but it's value for money, Tom says: croquet greens and bowling greens and a cinema and shops and a hairdresser and health club and an indoor swimming-pool, all private. There'll be a security fence round it all. It's a concentration camp for the afflu-old, Josie says.

'Who's holding kitty?'

'Me.' Tony Hillman.

'I'll put an extra hundred in. That's my handicap.'

'Fair enough.'

'How much in kitty?'

'Nine hundred now.'

'Everybody choose a different ball. Tony, how about making a note of them?'

'Hot Dot, that's no good, I want a Dunlop.'

All of them are rich, but Duncan sees how eager they are to win.

'Do we putt as well?'

'No. It's the closest to the pin.'

'There isn't a pin.'

'Yes there is. See that piece of stick with a cloth tied on. You can just see it. I put it in as soon as it got dark.'

'You planned this, you cunning bugger.'

They've got no hope. His father will win.

'Do we draw for positions?'

'Nah, let's do it alphabetically.' That will make Tom at the end.

Duncan climbs down and runs along the inside of the wall. At the front of the house he climbs again and drops into the paddock. The dry grass is up to his hips and makes a hissing noise as he slides into a grove of silver dollar gums. Dead leaves snap under his feet but they're arguing so loudly on the tee no one can hear. He climbs a barbed-wire fence and ducks along a row of young macrocarpas, tree to tree. The house lights edge out from behind the gums. Women stand with their backs to the windows in the lounge. As he runs on rough inside the macrocarpas the men on the tee come into view. He keeps the trees as a barrier and gets to the willows on the river bank. The course stretches away, so white in the moonlight it seems coated with frost. Over the road and river the south-facing hills are dark. There's no light in Lex Clearwater's house (the reason: Lex has not paid his bill and his electricity is cut off. It doesn't bother him. Lex doesn't need electricity any more) and no lights in the clubhouse. The men up the hill are like hunchbacks and cripples. They seem to slide leftwards all the time, pushed by the moon. All except Tom. He stands up straight and bounces the light off his face.

Someone hits. Duncan doesn't see the ball but hears it crash in the gum trees. That was Mr Compton and he's done his hundred dollars. The next one, Rock Edison, takes a long time and the others start heckling him in a way that would be cheating in a proper match. Sound comes clearly in the night, as though things that block it in the daytime are removed. Each bit is round and smooth and seems to chime in a hollow place inside itself. Something ragged though begins to sound from the other way. It's like a yard-broom sweeping; then it turns to water. Ducks, he thinks.

Rock Edison's ball lands between the pine trees and the green. Duncan hears him swear, as clear as a morepork. More splashing comes and he eases into the willows and sees a woman walking in the river, holding her skirt bunched in front of her. He thinks at first it's the crazy woman, then recognizes Stella from her throat and jaw. He lets her come up close enough to touch.

'Gidday, Stell.'

'Jesus.' She drops her sandals in the water. He hooks them with his foot and picks them up.

'Didn't mean to frighten you.'

'What are you doing here?'

'Watching.' A ball hits the willow trees beyond them. 'That was Mr Geldard.'

Stella climbs out and crouches on the mat of willow-hair. 'I'll kill you if you scare me like that again.'

'Sorry, Stell.'

She's quiet for a moment, peering up the hill. 'Are you sure they can't see you?'

'Not if we stay in the trees. Mr Hillman's next.'

'I'll bet you've got the same idea as me.'

'What's that, Stell?'

'Don't play dumb. You're going to shift Dad's ball.'

'No I'm not.'

'Liar.'

'I'm going to put someone else's closer to the hole.'

'Whose?'

'Anyone's. As long as I can find one.'

They hear the whack of the club from up the hill and wait for a time that seems too long. Then they hear a thud. A ball jumps half-way across the green and runs over the lip on the other side.

'That one will do. I like Mr Hillman,' Stella says.

'I thought you'd want Dad to win.'

He hears a little sound in her stomach, some liquid squeaking through a place that's bent because she's squatting. It surprises Duncan that Stella should make a noise like that. Her insides should be clean as clean and work like a Rolls-Royce engine.

'You like him don't you, Stell?' Mandy can do his operations and Stella can bail him out is just about Tom's favourite joke.

She doesn't answer. Wipes her nose on the back of her hand – another thing he's never seen her do. 'Can they see balls on the green from up there?'

'No.'

'I just don't think he should always win.'

'He won't tonight.' Another ball lands short of the green. 'That was Mr Martin. Munday comes next. Then Pelham. Then Dad. Why don't you like him, Stell?'

'It's none of your business.'

'I thought you all did except Mum and me.'

'I'll be away from here next year. Thank God for that.'

'Next year's in,' peers at his watch, 'sixteen minutes. If we weren't on daylight saving we'd have an hour to go.' He thinks about that and sees how clock-time doesn't mean a thing.

Mr Munday's ball lands in the river.

Mr Pelham's ball takes a very long time and hits the front of the green and backspins out of sight.

'I'll be sorry when you go, Stell.'

'You shouldn't be. I treat you like dirt.'

'No you don't. Like dog shit.'

'I don't know how you can joke about it.'

'Here comes Dad.'

They see him waggle his club. They see his forearms shine.

'All the rest of them are second rate,' Stella says. Her voice sounds as if she's got bits of glass in her mouth. Duncan wants to put his finger in and find out. He's alarmed at the way his mind is working tonight. It brings him and other people close. It presses them together so he can feel their lungs and hearts inside. He slides his finger between his cheek and gums. Warm and slippery; and that's how Stella is. With hard bits inside her that can break. He touches his teeth. It's like touching his father.

'Eee,' he says.

'What?'

'Do you like Mum?'

'Mum's all right.'

'Yeah, she's not bad.'

'She's doing the best she can for herself. Don't you worry, Dunc. Mandy and I are going to look after you.'

'I can look after myself. I'm going to do some correspondence courses next year. Twelve minutes.'

He feels sorry for Stella. She's like one of those dolls with a joint in their necks. She can only do eyes front and when you want to make her look at something else you've got to twist her head, you hear the click. He looks at her profile in the moonlight and sees how pretty she is and wonders why she doesn't have any boyfriends.

Tom Round swings his club. There's a delay in the sound reaching them. Duncan thinks if he could measure it he could work out the distance between his father and him, down to centimetres. Tom stands with his arms wrapped round his neck, hugging himself. He's like an illustration in a golf book, the Golden Bear or the White Shark, and his club-head at his shoulder glitters like an eye inspecting him.

Thud goes the ball and they find it by hearing first, then sight. It bounces past the hole, not very far, and stops as though the green is magnetized. It must have a lot of backspin on. Duncan admires his father for being able to do that. The men up the hill are talking

237

in loud voices. They troop off the tee with a gloss of moonlight on their foreheads.

'When they're in the gums,' Duncan says. He hears them crashing and laughing. Tom Round does his Tarzan yell.

'Now,' Stella whispers, and gives him a push on his behind.

Duncan runs round the edge of the green. Mr Hillman's ball should lie on the fairway, but it's not there. He tracks this way and that. 'I can't find it.' It must have rolled and rolled and gone into the rushes in the dry patch of swamp. The men are out of the gums, the first ones are climbing the fence.

'Why didn't someone tell me it's barbed wire?' Don Compton yells.

Duncan finds the ball and grabs it. Sees Stella running on the green. She's stealing their father's ball and she's just in time. He rolls Mr Hillman's and it vanishes over the lip. There's enough speed to take it near the hole. He retreats into the river, not bothering to take his sneakers off, and wades in the shadows to their hiding place. Stella has climbed down from the willow mat. She stands in water up to her knees. They look past the roots at eye level and see the men in a herd between the macrocarpas and the green. Tom is leading.

'Only one on the green. You're a bunch of no-hopers.'

Stella squats. The back of her skirt dips in the water. 'Stell?' She rests her forehead on the spongy mat.

'Are you scared of him, Stell?'

'Yes.' She hisses the word. He can't tell whether she's angry or frightened. 'Get down. The moon's on your face.'

He squats beside her, feeling water cold on his bum.

'Here's one at the front. Pro-Flite. Who's that?'

'Me.'

'Hard cheese, Jeff.'

Their feet go scuff and thud. One of them belches. One of them laughs.

'Ten feet. I'd hole that putt. Not bad for night-time, eh?'

Duncan risks a look. Their shadows angle on the green, making even stripes as though they're ruled. The ball makes a foot-long shadow too. Tom stands with legs apart and hips stuck out – the way he stands, Duncan thinks, peeing in a hedge. He likes the ball and doesn't pick it up. Rock Edison, creaking, bends and scoops.

He holds the ball close against his eye. 'Top-Flite?' he says, looking at Tom.

'That's me.' Tony Hillman.

'Let me see.' Tom grabs it, reads. 'Jesus then, mine must be in the hole.' He's at the flag in three strides and pulls it out. Looks inside. Squats and puts his hand in. Geldard laughs. He thinks Tom is joking. The others don't laugh.

'I should have put a mousetrap in,' Duncan whispers. He feels Stella trembling and bends his head down and looks at her face. Her eyes are tightly closed. She looks as if she's going to be sick. He pulls her hand out of the willow-hair and she holds him with a tightness that makes his finger bones roll on each other.

'Hard cheese, Tom,' Morris Martin says.

'Some of you bastards have done a switch.'

'Aw, come on!'

'We'll have another.'

'No way.'

'Not for me.'

'I'm not climbing down that paddock again for anyone.'

They walk off the green, leaving Tom alone. He looks around. He turns in a circle. He knows his ball was on. Tom Round *knows*.

'Is he coming?' Her eyes are closed.

'No. It's all right.'

Tom tries to break his home-made pin but the hard tea-tree resists. He turns and seems to look at Duncan and Stella; takes a step and throws the pin like a spear. It hisses through the willow tops and flies across the river, where its sharpened end fixes in the bank and its flag torn off a shirt dangles in the water. He shakes his head, making his hair flick round his eyes, then smooths it and turns, a baffled circle; gives a yell. He walks off the green after his friends. They go into the macrocarpa trees and climb the fence. A shrieking wire makes Stella jerk.

'He's gone, Stell. It was just the wire.'

Duncan unclenches her fingers and takes the golf ball from her hand. He puts it in the water and lets it sink. 'In case he looks tomorrow. Listen Stell, that's New Year.'

The men in the gum-trees are yodelling and whistling. People on the lawns call out and bang things together and car horns toot from behind the house. Someone puts a loud record on.

'Come on, we'll walk to the bridge.'

She straightens up. Releases his hand, then grabs it again to steady herself.

'That's one time he didn't win,' Duncan says.

Half-way to the bridge she stops and kisses his cheek. 'Happy New Year, Duncan.'

He smiles.

That makes two times tonight I've been kissed.

17

Norma was happy when she left the party but happiness subtracted in quanta as she put her car in the garage, walked up the path, let herself in, turned on the lights, saw kitchen and living-room and bedroom. 'Here I am again.' That chair, that bed, that dressing-table, that familiar *House and Garden* emptiness. It was tidy and comfortable, but had a squalor of insufficiency. The cat had followed her from the garage. It rubbed about her calves to be picked up, so she picked it up; then held it under its middle and dropped it on four feet; pushed with her toe. She was not going to have her closest touching with a cat.

How, she asked, did I get into this state? Was it the party? It had been successful as parties go. Lots of shiny good-fellowship; rather like a polished apple in fact, but little spots of black, little spots of nastiness here and there. She had enjoyed Duncan; but Duncan was insufficient too. He wanted only small things from her now, which she could give. Her main function was to watch him as a spectacle. Duncan's life would fill him to the limits of his mind and with any luck there'd be an overflow into his feelings – she must hope – and possibly exteriors, face and body, would not count. But watching was not a role that could satisfy. Duncan passed like a jogger, gave a shout and wave, and loped away; not of her kind.

She washed her hands. She took a needle from her sewing box and tried to dig a gorse prickle from her palm. It would not come. Blood filled the hole she made and swamped the speck, so she put Vaseline on a bandaid and covered it. Thinking all the time, what is K. for?

'Thanks. K.B.': the note in the ice-cream container in her milk box. Fancy someone going to that trouble, returning a disposable container, the very next day. It was ludicrous. She was, though, excited by his B. instead of Birtles. She read in it a kind of ease their walk on the island had made grounds for; but had not been able to decide that a next move must come from her.

Next move, she thought. Good God, is it like that? I'm forty-five and I'm damned if I'll play teenagers again. If I want a man to go to bed with me I'll ask, that's all.

Norma smiled. Now she'd had a triumph over herself; had brought it from its hiding place – go to bed. Appropriate phrase, for she wanted more than just sex; but less of course than a lasting relationship. Not perhaps even ongoing – dreadful word. Going on for a little while though – a week or two of close-touching would suit her fine. But no, no, definitely not just sex. She smiled in recollection of a friend – another town, another age – a nursing-sister who had made do with not very frequent one night stands: 'There's nothing like a good fuck to set a girl up for the winter.' Norma had been shocked, but she understood now. Wanted, though, something more than just a four-letter act for herself.

I could have brought Tony home, she thought. Tony Hillman, known quantity, very safe. K. Birtles was a mystery. K. Birtles might be dangerous. He might even be the kind of man who would get into a fit of puritan rage. She did not think so. Knowledge of him might be discovered; it was only a matter of friendly invitation. He might say no to a New Year's drink; or she could send him home after it; or anything.

Norma looked up his number and telephoned. He was probably at a party of his own.

'Oh, Mr Birtles, it's Norma Sangster. How are you?'

'Hello. OK.' She wanted to laugh at his surprise.

'Thank you for returning my ice-cream carton.'

'No trouble. I wasn't sure you'd want it.'

'No, I didn't. Still, it's the thought. Mr Birtles, I know it's late, but I was wondering if you'd like to come over for a New Year's drink.'

Now there's a silence, Norma thought as it went on and on.

'Are you still there?'

'I'd never make it. It's ten to twelve.'

'Oh well, time doesn't matter. What's a few minutes either way?'

'Have you got a party on?'

'No, I'm all alone. Are you alone?' She had not thought of that. Perhaps his wife was out of hospital.

'Yeah, I am.'

'Will you come then?'

Silence again. It wasn't that her brain was quicker than his, just that she knew what was going on.

242

'OK, I'll come. I'll bring a bottle, eh?'

'No, I've got plenty. I'll see you soon. Goodbye.' Norma hung up. She was full of confidence, so why was she trembling? The thoughtful woman had a quick shower; but evidence of that might alarm him, and really she was clean enough. I want to give him signs I'm just like him, because I am, I'm nothing special, and we can surely have the odd bit of sweat from the day. In the bathroom she cleaned her make-up off, guessing he'd like her more that way. Then she checked that beer was in the fridge, though hoping he'd choose a more interesting drink. She spread a few crackers with pâté and blue vein cheese. Put out olives? Yes, why not? Olives for me. If he doesn't like them that's too bad. Wondered if entertaining, feeding him, would turn out to be all she would want.

He took longer to arrive than she had expected. Cars went by but none stopped. Horns and hooters sounded in the town. It was New Year. He's got cold feet, he's chickened out. She ate an olive and poured herself a drink. All the while she knew that he would come.

'Hallo, you made it. I didn't hear a car.'

'I rode Hayley's bike. It hasn't got a light so I had to hold a torch.' Held it in his hand. 'Those things are not easy to ride with one hand.'

'I'm sure they're not.' He had not wanted to leave his car at her gate. There's delicacy for you, she thought; but tried then to put that smart way of responding off. He did not thrill or even interest her. She admired the plainness of him, body, mind, and knew her instinct had been right, they would manage joining of an undemanding sort. Pleasant and plain. Oh do stop it Norma, she told herself.

'I brought the bike in, round the back.'

'It's very thoughtful of you.' Stop it, stop it.

'Ten-speed bikes get pinched.' He was hostile.

'Come in here. Put your torch down. What will you drink?'

'What have you got?' He held his peaked cap – baseball cap? – in one hand and when he sat wore it on his knee. 'Rum, eh? Rum and coke. You got any coke?'

'No, I'm sorry.'

'Whisky and ginger ale then, that'll do.'

When she handed it to him he pointed at her blouse. 'That's not boysenberry juice.'

She looked and found the spot. 'No, it's blood. I pricked my hand on a gorse bush.' She showed him the bandaid. 'I can't get the prickle out.'

'If there's a prickle in there it's not gorse.' Such dogmatism. 'Gorse doesn't snap off. I know. I was always digging prickles out of the kids.'

'Well, it might be a barberry. I think there was some barberry up there.'

'Yeah, barberry's a cow. I don't know why you people let it in.'

'Oh, we made hundreds of mistakes of that sort. Rabbits and possums and blackberry and old man's beard. And gorse of course.' Repeated it for the rhyme. Why are we talking like this? 'Here's to a Happy New Year.'

'It's got to be better than the last.'

They drank and looked at each other. She liked what she saw up to the point of finding him original. Beyond that were none of the things she looked for in a man. To put it simply, mind in a face. Mind, of course, was not always trustworthy and sometimes in the end had little weight – see Tony Hillman. But K. Birtles – Norma looked and saw – had his hard experience marked there, and that was something. Men usually managed to cover that sort of nakedness.

He had come in sneakers and jeans and windcheater. And baseball cap. Original, for this sort of assignation. Norma liked it.

'What does K. stand for?'

'Ken.'

'That was my father's name. I'm Norma, Ken.'

'Gidday.'

First names were somehow a step back – deleting that bit of – what? – elemental strangeness from the situation. We're in danger of getting social, we're going to get embarrassed, and then he'll go away.

'I asked you round because I thought that we –'

He stopped her by opening his hand. 'I know, I'm not dumb.'

'I never thought you were. The last man I went to bed with, he was dumb. But not you.' There, it's out. He sat and watched her with an expression between – was it more of interest or distaste? 'On the island, I liked you, and I thought that you liked me. And we're both grown up. We can say what we like.'

'I've got a wife, you know.'

244

'I know. And I suppose that makes me a temptress.' Wrong word. She hurried past it. 'Please don't do anything you can't do. If it's a betrayal, don't do it then. If it hurts her, or hurts you.'

He looked away and took a big swallow of his drink. 'As long as it's not any big deal, eh?'

'I don't understand.'

'Some big experience. Something we've got to get,' fluttered his hand in the air, 'way up here about.'

'Sex has never been that way for me. But it's not nothing either.' Too much talk. 'Ken.' She went to him, knelt by his chair. 'I think I'm only asking for one night.' She took his hand. It made a jerk, involuntary, then closed hard on her own. 'Jesus,' he said. Began to shake. He lowered his head and let his forehead rest on hers. 'Jesus, Norma.'

'It's all right.' She kissed him softly, quickly, on the mouth.

'I been working all day. I need a shower.'

She could smell him but it seemed new sweat, not old. 'I don't mind if you're dirty.'

'No. I need a shower. Where do I go?'

She led him to the bathroom and gave him a towel. He sat on the edge of the bath and undid his sneakers and seemed to want Norma to go away. She went to the bedroom and turned down the bed covers – that bed that was three-quarter, generous and discreet. Is it better to stay dressed or get undressed? She chose undressed, and wiped her damp armpits with a Snowtex. Took the clips out of her hair and let it down. Then turned off the light – did not like love-making in hard light, but wanted a shaded low-watt bulb somewhere near the bed. Tonight though, moonlight, what could be better? She pulled the curtains back and let in the glow; silver but buttery and dulcifying too. I'd better not use words like that with him – and gave a snicker; then felt she had betrayed him and herself.

Norma sat on the edge of the bed. She heard the shower running. She felt girlish, inexperienced in here, though it was a cool thing to strip off and wait on the bed. I'm not alone, she thought, I've got someone, and the thought of company, more than sex, made her heart jolt hard, it really thumped her.

He'll get out of the shower and wonder what in God's name he's doing, he'll want to go. She saw it would alarm him to find himself

245

naked in her house, he'd wonder if he had made an awful mistake, the cops were coming; so she had better be there when he turned off the water and came out.

She went to the bathroom and saw him blurred behind the plastic curtain. He seemed to be washing his hair, and that was weird – was ominous: washing temptation, Norma Sangster, out?

He turned the water off and stepped on to the mat. She handed him his towel and he covered himself. 'Sorry,' he said, starting to blush.

'How did you get like that, in the shower?'

'Thinking, I guess.'

'Stop thinking. Ken?' She put her arms around him, his wet back, felt her breasts slide on his chest, and lower down the abrasive towel, and his hard penis denting her.

'Come on, not here.'

They lay on the bed and his hair dripped on her.

'Oh, that cat.' She slipped away, grabbed the willing thing, and dropped it out of the window into the night. 'No one can see. Don't you like the moon?'

'Yes,' he said. 'Norma. I don't know any fancy stuff.'

How foolish; how sad to have to say a thing like that. 'I'm just a plain girl. Ken, I do like kissing.'

They made love. He was very plain, delighting her and making her feel she was with someone; as she had not in bed with Tony Hillman – despite his willingness and care – and other men. Some of those acts might as well have been solo for all the interchange in them. But Ken was present, oh he was present, working there like a man with a pick and shovel, involved in his job, practical, unfussy, strong and neat. He forgot his lack of fancy knowledge; had no need for anything like that. And Norma went with him, open wide and wrapped around, her hands clapped on his hard resistant back.

Remembering that night, it was not love-making she brought back but things he said that made her smile, whether they were funny or not. For example: 'Since I got married I've never slept with anyone but my wife.' And: 'I guess I should have told you it's safe, you know, for you. I had a vasectomy when Joanie got sick. Not that I needed to because we stopped doing anything.' Twice he mentioned his wife, then not again.

She woke to hear him leaving the bed, finding the toilet, peeing, flushing it. When he came back he seemed hesitant, ashamed perhaps of that natural act, so she went too, though she had no need; and back in bed pulled him round to face her and found that he had been thinking again. She bossed him, speeded him then slowed him down, and would have got on top, except he might find that too fancy – another time – and it was less energetic, less of a lovely gallop than the first, but more pleasurable, and Ken Birtles somehow more full of being than before. His hands were abrasive, ridged and hard. All her life the hands of her bed-mates had been soft. This was the first time she had felt palm and fingerpad that had worked. She felt he would be making marks on her and liked the idea. She had made marks on his shoulder with her teeth.

Another thing she remembered: in the dawn he sat on the bed in his underpants and pulled the bandaid off her palm and tried to squeeze the prickle out. It would not come so she fetched a needle and he put the point on the embedded prickle and waggled it – that hurt a bit – and eased it out and laid it on her palm. 'Barberry. I told you.'

'Thank you, Ken. I'd never have got it out with my left hand.'

'You people are bloody lazy. Look at this.' He picked up one of his sneakers and unlaced it, then laced it again at, oh, high speed, using only his left hand. 'Anyone can do it. All you got to do is practise. When I played cricket I used to bowl right-handed but I did a left-hand googly now and then. That really screwed them.'

He rode away in the dawn.

'Will you come back.'

'If you want me.'

'Yes, I do. Listen to what you're making me say.'

'Hey, it's equal. I want to come.'

Forgot his torch. He rode round in the twilight the second night.

She cooked for him once, thinking (grinning) of the vegetarian lover who eats roots and leaves. She cooked fillet steak seasoned with garlic and a lemon pudding, one of her mother's, that she liked as much for its behaviour in the oven – the sauce and sponge changed places – as its taste. He told her Shelley's letters from prison were OK, she was getting through it OK; said she might start running again when she came out.

'It'll be touch and go. It'll be a kind of balance, I reckon.' He was afraid.

247

'A new country might make all the difference.'

'Yeah, I hope.'

'When does Hayley get back?'

'On Saturday.'

'I like Hayley.'

'Yeah, Hayley's good. She goes at things. I just hope she doesn't go too hard.' Afraid for both his daughters. She wanted not to pity or comfort him but stand by him and be his contact. That night, in bed, she showed him one or two fancy things, not too much – did not, after all, know much herself. Fancy wrapped round plain. She got on top, which, for a while, offended him. Then he enjoyed it.

'You must have been around a bit.'

'Oh, not that much.' He did not mean to insult her. 'It's a matter of what feels good. And it was a nice change, wasn't it?'

'Yeah, it was.'

'No one's boss.'

'I guess not.' But his man's role seemed to stay in his mind for a moment later he said, 'I'd like to take you out somewhere.'

'Where?'

'I don't know. The pictures. Dinner somewhere.'

'We don't need to do that, Ken.'

'I just come here and . . .'

'Go to bed?'

'Yeah. I know we can't risk it, being seen. But I don't know, it seems – ' Was this his version of a puritan rage? She saw that it might be dangerous.

'Well, get dressed. Take me for a walk in the park.'

'What?'

'I'd sooner have that than the pictures, Ken.'

'It's' – he looked at the clock – 'half past one.'

'What does that matter? I'd like you to take me for a walk.'

They dressed and went across the clover slope and through the graves. She showed him her grandmother's grave, traced the name 'Anne' with her finger. 'It's nice to have an ancestor close.'

'I don't know where mine are.'

'You could find out.'

'I don't want to. I reckon, what we've got is here and now.' He shone the torch on headstones. 'Cremation's best. That's what I want.'

248

'Where will your ashes go?'

'Anywhere.' He was, she thought, trying to get back on top. She took his hand and led him among the trees and he grew more easy out of the graves. They stood still and listened to a branch creaking in the wind. On the tennis court two cats faced each other in the moonlight, until one turned and crept away. Ken shone his torch at the other and the luminescent eyes stared back, not giving way.

'Thank God we're bigger than they are.'

They sat on a bench deep in shadow and looked out at the moonlit town.

'I found Saxton by accident,' he said. 'I was just wandering round, having a look, and some joker on the ferry asked me if I could drive, he was feeling crook. So I said yes, and drove him here. It's the only time I've ever driven a Jag. I was really heading down to Christchurch.'

'And you stayed?'

'I liked the look of it. It's been a good place. Until Wayne.'

'Will it always mean that to you? Wayne?'

'What do you think?' He took her hand. 'Sorry. It will though. Wayne and Shell. And,' a shrug, 'the rest.' His wife. 'I'm glad I met you though, at the end.'

'I'm glad too. It was hard, ringing you up.'

'I should've done that, rung up.'

'It doesn't matter who, as long as it happened.'

'Yeah.' He shone the torch around. 'It's good out here.'

'Better than the pictures?'

'I dunno. I could do with a packet of Jaffas.'

He joked so rarely that she laughed aloud. 'Oh Ken, have me instead. Any way you want. On top or underneath or back to front.'

'Nice girls don't talk like that.'

But back in bed he said, 'What's this back to front?'

'Shall we see?'

He made love to her from behind. After that, for the rest of their time, they had three ways, and no one chose.

'I never knew I could do it as often as this. Or get so hard. It's like I was sixteen again.' (That was another thing that made her smile.)

Every night they walked in the park.

*

On Friday the 8th they said goodbye. 'I guess this is the right time, eh? I guess it would have ended anyway.'

She knew him fairly well, knew lots of things about him. She knew the ironworks in Hartlepool, and the windy beach at Seaton Carew, the weekend trips to Saltburn and Whitby, and with his yobbo mates to Middlesbrough; and Saturday afternoon on the terraces, grey squalls sweeping over as United, in its blue and white strip, lost again. And Mum and Dad in the little house, worrying. She knew the shock summer heat gave him in Saxton, amazing all day sun, day after day. She knew him well enough to know, yes it would have ended anyway. She had not reached the end of it herself and was never less than pleased by his talk and his behaviour and all the things he knew and could work out; and by his ignorance and narrowness. They were a part of his spoor, a mark of his passing left on her. She found his limits all the time and did not want to teach or change him.

'When will your wife be coming home?'

'They're not sure. Sometime next week.'

'And is she really better, do you think?'

'It's hard to tell.' He looked at her suspiciously.

'I hope so, Ken.' Felt she'd had to ask, and finished it.

He went into the living-room, where this time he had left his torch, and she followed him. He turned around slowly, said, 'All this,' meaning her books and paintings and records and bits of china. He looked puzzled and ready to be angry, and she saw no need for it, they could say goodbye without widening a gap. She felt a yearning for him, and their touching; a wrenching from the base of her throat to her abdomen.

'I don't know –'

'Ssh, Ken. Don't.'

In the porch he made it all right: looked back at her and put his torch and baseball cap down. He came back to her in the doorway and worked his fingers under her dressing gown cord, pulled it undone. He opened her dressing gown out and looked at her and put his arms inside, round her back. He stepped in close and held her for a moment. Did not kiss her. She felt his prickly skin scratch her cheek. Then he left; sweeping up his cap and torch with one hand, jumping down two steps, grabbing his bike, getting away.

Norma went inside and closed the door.

'Oh wonderful,' she said.

She tied her gown and hugged herself. 'Wonderful, K.B.'

She was not so chirpy by Sunday night. Not so very chipper at all –
was chipper a pommie word he would have used? She had not
loved him, love had had no time, but liked him more than any man
she'd known. That did not mean she had never been in love but
meant perhaps that liking was a better thing to have. Liking was far
better in middle age.

Norma laughed. She would not feel that way if she was in love,
was sensible enough to recognize that; but did not want it ever
again, with all its exaggerated joys and dreadful pains. What she
wanted was Ken Birtles back, for comfort and pleasure.

'Well,' she told herself, 'you can't have him.' Their week together
had a margin on its near side, it was defined; or would be if she
examined it. Which she should do, and see it whole, and make an
artefact of it perhaps, of great value, and put it away in her deposit
box of memories. 'Huh,' Norma said. 'Arty-farty. Ken had missing
teeth and smelled of fish.'

She thought of him a quarter-hour bike ride away. If I had a bike I
could ride round and see . . . It was then she decided to get out of
Saxton for a while. So, on Monday morning, she took the cat to the
cattery, and called at the berry farm to see her mother – 'When I
come back, Mum, I'll help you shift' – asked Clive to check her
house and pick the mail up now and then – 'It's still my busy
season,' he complained – and drove over the zigzag ribbon road to
Sutherland Bay, where her old teachers' college friend Audrey
Scanlan was married to a mussel farmer. A downturn in that
industry had the Scanlans worried but good years had left them
with no shortage of good things and Norma was comfortable in her
airy room in the big new house – not a Tom Round house but just as
good, it sprawled so warm and natural in its paddock up from the
beach. She lazed in a swing-couch, drinking long non-alcoholic
drinks, and swam in the sea and washed off the salt in a rock basin
in the creek behind the house. She did not bother trying to forget K.
Birtles. Thought of him often in fact. 'I'm getting a man out of my
system,' she told Audrey. Audrey wanted to know, was nosey in
an almost prurient way, and was disapproving as well. What a
matron she had become. Chastity was the rule for unmarried

high-school principals. Norma laughed and turned her aside. 'You need a man now and then,' she said.

'It sets you up for the winter,' she said.

She walked in the bush to the waterfall, she watched the tame eels being fed, and she took a launch trip round the point into the maritime park and ate her lunch of drumsticks and pitta bread on the beach at Pear Tree Bay. A red and yellow fizz-boat came in, crunched its nose into the sand, and Tom Round and Sandra Duff jumped out.

'The Mona Lisa of Pear Tree Bay,' Tom said.

'What are you two doing here?'

'Exploring the coast,' Sandra said. 'I've never been up this far. It's beautiful. Isn't this the most beautiful beach you've ever seen?'

That was a very naked comment for Sandra. I didn't know she had that level on her mind, Norma thought. Or was geared for simple happiness. Could Sandra be in love?

'Stephanie's got the boot,' Sandra said while Tom went to the boat for the chilli-bin. 'Poor old Steph's the past, I'm the future. But it ain't a future that's got any future. Not that he knows it, poor old Tom. Every girl,' she grinned, 'should have a rich man once in a while. Expensive things are so enjoyable.'

'Are you on this launch, Norma? Where are you staying?' Tom asked.

'Round the point at Sutherland Bay.'

'Don't go back on that old tub. We'll take you in the boat, only take ten minutes.'

'No thanks, I like to putter along.' Still he hankered after her, and maybe dreamed of threesomes. Sandra winked. Half an hour later, up at the point, they made figure of eights by the launch, with Tom one-handed at the wheel, a long-stemmed wine glass in his other hand, and Sandra in dark glasses and captain's hat and skimpy togs.

The launch captain gave Tom the fingers.

Thank God, Norma thought, mine wasn't like that. Thank God for Ken Birtles with his baseball cap and missing premolars and lumpy hands.

After that she seemed to have everything in place and thought of him less frequently.

The house in the cul-de-sac was spick and span. Daphne had been in to dust and scrub. Daphne had washed the curtains. Clive had repainted the front door for a new beginning and kept the lawn green with a watering-can and hoed and weeded the garden, making sure the flowers stayed alive.

Mr Schwass's big chair was gone but there, in its place, was a la-z-boy, a present from Norma. Mrs Schwass sat in it and tried the controls and showed off to neighbours who popped in to welcome her back. Norma stayed for dinner. This first night they had Dial-a-dinner, another present, and Mrs Schwass said, 'What a wonderful idea. I might do this every night.'

'Why not?'

'Though I must say these' (spare ribs) 'are what we fed the dogs with on the farm.'

They washed the dishes and watched television and Mrs Schwass said she wouldn't get ready for bed till Norma had gone, she wasn't going to be supervised through a crack in the door. Norma kissed her goodnight and left. There was going to be a time of frequent attendance that would need to be disguised as dropping in.

She put her car in the garage and turned to come out, and found Ken Birtles in the door.

'Don't do that, Ken. You gave me a fright.'

'I've got to see you.'

'Was that your car out there?' Her tone was light but she was angry. 'I don't think I like you parking at my gate.'

'Why not? You're the headmistress.' He made a placatory gesture with his hands. 'It's OK, Norma, I'm not coming back so don't get jumpy. I've got to see you about something else.'

'Oh? What's that? Come in, Ken. We can't stand here.'

In the house he said, 'Shelley's records. I heard about what you're going to do.'

'Records?' She thought he meant enrolment, examination results. 'What am I going to do?'

'Wipe them out. That's what I heard. You're the boss there, you must know.'

'Well, I don't. Her running records? Is that what you mean?'

'Yeah, they're going to wipe them out. I work with this bloke whose wife does cleaning at the Maules's house. Mrs Maule told her. This guy Maule is chairman of the board or something like that.'

'Chairman of our Board of Governors. What did Mrs Maule say, Ken? Tell me exactly.'

'Just, cross off her records from the books. Make it like she was never there. Jesus Norma, you can't do that.'

'No, we can't.' She was astonished, then pleased, to find herself trembling.

'You know what it'll do to her? Just when she's got a chance of coming right?'

'Yes, I know.'

'It's like, I don't know, hosing down the yard, and Shelley's some bit of shit in the corner, something like that.'

'Ken.' He was trembling too. He had to wipe his eyes. 'Ken. It's not going to happen. Not while I'm running the school. Ken,' she made him look at her, 'I had nothing to do with it. Believe me?'

'I guess I do.'

'Now, listen.' She went to the phone and rang the Maules's number, got Mrs Maule, asked for her husband. 'Yes Mrs Maule, it is important. I'd like to speak to him right now please.'

She heard his elevated talking-down voice, knew he was angry, but his anger was no match for hers. 'I've got a parent here and I've just heard a story that I hope isn't true. Perhaps you can tell me. You plan to wipe out Shelley Birtles's running records?'

'I don't think I'm prepared to discuss – '

'Is it true or isn't it, Mr Maule?'

'Well some of us – ' she had him rattled – 'some of us had an informal discussion. This will come up in the normal course of business, Mrs Sangster.'

'No it won't. It will come up tomorrow. And stop tomorrow. I'd like to see you, and whichever "some of us" are in it with you. I'll be in my office at nine o'clock, Mr Maule, and if we can't sort it out and finish with it then I'll take some action that you will be most unhappy with, I promise you.'

'I see.'

'Goodnight, Mr Maule.'

She hung up. She had never spoken to him like that before – had differed and demurred, had smiled, agreed. There had been in her a muted click and whirr, almost sub-aural, and perfect motion, as in a watch; but now something was broken. She felt jagged ugly bits in her.

254

'Ken, does your wife know about this?'

'No, she doesn't.'

'Is she home?'

'Yeah, since Friday.'

'Well, don't tell her. It'll all be over by tomorrow. Does Hayley know?'

'I told her. She's hopping mad. I had to talk about it with someone, Norma.'

'Make sure she keeps quiet. The important thing is not to let Shelley hear. It's only a few people doing it. A few stuffed shirts. Are you still going to Australia?'

'I hope so. Hayley and Shell are going the week after next. She's out next week. Joanie and me are staying until we sell the house.'

'Ken.' She wanted to touch him and kiss his cheek, and send him away. 'Are you all right? Is everything going all right with you?'

He stood in the middle of the room and looked about as though he had not been there before. 'It's – I don't know – it kind of got away from me a bit. I didn't think it was going to. I thought, Why not? It's a bit of fun. But it got so it was . . . What I've got to do, I've got to cut it down to size, I guess, and make it so it wasn't so important.'

'It's like that too, for me.' She would not tell him she had managed it, and was going on now, easily.

'I'll get there. God knows, there's enough other things to keep me busy.'

She smiled, relieved, and not the slightest bit hurt, that he was not concerned for her. 'Shelley's records will stay, Ken. Don't you worry. But of course some other girl will come along and beat them soon.'

'That's OK. I don't mind that. As long as you don't make out she didn't exist. Jesus, that's . . .'

'I agree.' She got him to the back door and he stood on the step with one foot lower down on the mat and his cap, his eternal cap, turning in his hands, and she thought, There may have been only one week, one week in both our lives, that were able to match so perfectly and run together, and what a marvellous piece of luck, a marvellous fluke, we found them. But it's over now, no more weeks. Even if we had no other troubles, no more weeks. She smiled and touched him lightly on the shoulder.

'Goodnight, Ken. Don't worry, I'll fix it. I'll telephone you.'

255

She closed the door.

I don't suppose I'll ever see Ken Birtles again.

'Well, Mr Maule?' Norma said – but Angus Maule of Sanders, Maule, Perfect and Denton would not be treated in that way.

'I'm not too happy to be summoned here. I can let you have five minutes of my time. You won't mind being brief, I hope?'

'I think five minutes is all I'll need.'

The other two were those she had expected, Mrs Alexander and Mr Whiting – Humpty and Dumpty, she thought of them. Whiting though, a wheezer and face-mopper, had never been a joke. Whiting was Moral Right's hotline to the board.

'Can I ask you first, is what Mr Birtles told me true? You plan to cancel Shelley Birtles' records.'

Maule took his moment to consider and made his answer in his tight-lipped way – mouth like the shutter in a camera, contracting to a tiny hole. 'The idea is afloat, and has, I think, general acceptance.' He frowned. 'We thought we'd have your support, bearing in mind recent events.'

'My father is my business, Mr Maule. I don't need anyone taking revenge for me, so leave that out if you don't mind.'

'Very well.'

'You don't have my support. It's only in Russia, isn't it, that history gets rewritten by the state?'

'What does that mean?' Whiting complained.

Maule knew. Delicate and quick, with the middle finger of each hand, he picked dampness from the corners of his mouth. It was exhilarating, Norma thought, to discover you could dislike a person so much.

'It means that a girl came to our school and turned out to be a champion runner. She broke all the school records and no one has come near to them since. Then she left and got into bad company and committed crimes and went to prison. But we fix that up by pretending she never was. We turn her into a non-person. They do that in Russia and other countries all the time. Change history by decree. It's a marvellous way of telling lies.'

'Lies?' Whiting.

'Yes, Mr Whiting. She ran those times. You are getting ready to say that she did not.'

'But Norma dear, she's been a very bad girl,' Frances Alexander said. 'She's no credit to us. This is more like cleaning up after someone makes a mess. It's a bit like housekeeping you could say.'

'You mean she's dirt?' Why not use Ken? 'So you hose her out of the yard like something the dog left? Frances, have you thought of the harm you might do? To her? The girl?'

'Well, the girl, surely she's forfeited –'

'The girl has put herself on the other side,' Whiting said.

'I didn't know there were sides, Mr Whiting. I thought we just had pupils and we did our best for them.'

'It's a two-way thing. If they choose not to obey the rules –'

'Oh Mr Whiting, do be quiet.' How she enjoyed saying that. And look at him now, purpling up and getting ready to Jehovah her. Finding oneself so much disliked, that was exhilarating too. 'I'm talking about our conduct now.'

'Did you say – did you tell me –'

'Yes, I did.'

'Norma, I think you ought to know,' Frances Alexander said, 'you won't have all your staff on your side, dear. I'm not saying we went behind your back, but you were away and Mrs Muir was here.'

'Ah, Mrs Muir.'

'She agrees.'

'Yes, she would.'

'You've nothing against Mrs Muir?'

'The time for Phyllis to have her say is twenty years past. She's still in the hat and gloves era, Frances.'

Maule clicked his teeth. 'We're getting off the subject. When you telephoned last night you said you'd take some action I wouldn't like. What was that?'

They had come to it, and Norma found it hard to say. She did not want to put it out there, where it might be turned into a fact.

'If the Board votes to go ahead with this I'll resign. And I'll do it with maximum publicity.'

'Meaning?'

'Oh the papers and the radio. I'll say what I've just said about telling lies – yes, Mr Whiting – and rewriting history. And what we owe the girls we teach. I will not continue in a school that thinks it can flush someone away down the drain.'

257

She heard them breathing, Whiting wheezing. Frances Alexander creaked her chair.

At last Maule said, 'We wouldn't want to lose you, Mrs Sangster.'

'No?'

'But I don't appreciate the threat.'

'I want you to know what I'll do. It's no threat. It simply follows.'

He kept his unblinking gaze on her – and was there some pity coming in? He sighed at last and dabbed with middle fingers, one, two, fresh dampness from the corners of his mouth.

Why pity? And why – yes, it was – complacency? Had something happened she had failed to see?

'Mrs Alexander?' he said.

'Well, Norma puts it far too strongly, I feel. But I see her point. I don't want to lose her, certainly.'

'Mr Whiting?'

'I'd let her go. If it was left to me I'd show her the door.'

'You're outvoted, Claude. Though I don't have to tell you – ' a smile at Norma – 'there isn't any voting going on. This is just a gathering of interested parties. The Birtles girl. We can be persuaded, I think.'

Does he know about me and Ken?

But if he knew he'd want her out today, with none of this manœuvring. Shelley's crime would shrink to nothing at all.

'I think we should call it a day,' Frances Alexander said. 'I think this little kerfuffle – ' she grinned at Norma – 'can be hosed away.'

'No,' Whiting cried.

Maule controlled him with a finger-dab. 'It's all done, Mr Whiting. It's decided. Although the proposal had some merit, I believe. Now – there was that other matter you wanted to raise?'

'Yes,' Whiting said. 'But it's linked, you see. The whole thing starts in her attitude.'

'Come on, speeches another time. Norma isn't on trial,' Frances Alexander said.

'She is with me.'

'Mr Whiting,' Maule said, 'I haven't much time.'

'All right, all right.' Whiting mopped his face. 'Immoral poems in the school. How about that?'

Maule looked at Norma with a small lift of his brows. 'You know about this, Mrs Sangster? You don't mind discussing it now?' Then, too much the ascetic for triumphs, he looked out the window and dabbed his lips.

He's let me put myself in a corner. Now comes the trade-off, now the deal. He doesn't want Shelley Birtles, he wants Sandra Duff.

'Ken, can we talk?'

'Yes, they're watching TV. It's OK.'

'I talked with Mr Maule and some of the others. They're not going ahead. You can stop worrying.'

'Are you sure? What'd they say?'

'Oh, they were going to do it all right. But I stopped them. It's all over.'

'How? How'd you stop them?'

'Does it matter? I did, that's all.'

'Come on, Norma.'

'I told them I'd resign.'

'Would you have? Resigned? Over Shelley?'

'Yes, I would.' But you can't make the same threat twice in a day. And anyway I wouldn't have done it for Sandra. But I would have made a fuss. So Maule's got rid of her without all that; and he's kept me, oh he still wants me, because I'm good. And Shelley he never cared about.

She felt sick that he had known her and used her so well.

'So, it's all over. Goodbye, Ken.'

'Hey, wait a minute Norma. Norma, thanks.'

'That's all right.'

'I think it would have flipped her, that's all.'

'Yes, it would. I hope it will be all right now. For all of you.'

'Yeah, it will. Hey Norma, I meant to say, Shelley got your mother's letter OK. But she's, I don't know, she's not up to writing back right now. She will one day. But she says thanks. Will you tell your mother?'

'Yes.' She wished he would stop putting things on her. 'I'll pass it on.'

'OK, thanks. For everything. I mean it.'

'Thank you too.' She put down the phone. Repeated thank you too for the rhyme. So that was that. She was very tired, a wearing day, wearing fortnight, already it was an exhausting year. She really hadn't been set up by her nice affair. Well, reconsider that –

she knew she would dispute that later on. And find some meaning in it if meaning was in it to find. And store away a memory or two. Not now. Not today. Today she had been knocked down and trampled on.

She put a record on and found herself a drink and sat down in her chair and stroked her cat.

Nice cat. Nice little devil, you are.

18

The Rounds have been on holiday. Tom and Josie own a share in a little house in Oyster Bay. It's a time-share arrangement and they own two prime weeks in January. Josie and Duncan travel up by launch and Tom brings the girls in his boat, with food and drink, books and clothing, for two weeks. Tom does not stay over. He has things to do in town.

Oyster Bay is private land surrounded by the park. There are twenty or thirty baches and cottages, with bottled gas fridges and battery TV sets. Some have generators and are just like home. The Rounds' little house has everything.

The coastal track, a three-day walk, goes through Oyster Bay. Huts for the walkers are south over the inlet behind the bay and north at Pear Tree Bay. In summer-time the backpackers come, Danes and Swedes and Germans and Australians and North Americans and a few British and one or two French. Most of them are young. They're girls and boys in fairly equal numbers. From Oyster Bay you can see them approaching on the track round the inlet or waiting on the south side for the tide to drop so they can walk across and save two kilometres. The daring ones come at half-tide, with their packs resting on their heads. They look like a line of coolies approaching but turn into blond Europeans, sun-burned Aussies. They sit on the grass in their shorts to dry out. Some of the girls don't bother with tops.

Belinda tries her German. 'Guten morgen.' She learns 'God dag' and 'Hej' and 'Tack så mycket.' Stella and Mandy ask them in for a can of beer, and ask the ones they like to stay for a meal. Some nights two or three climb into their sleeping bags on the living-room floor or put up pup-tents on the lawn. The Round girls enjoy their holidays at Oyster Bay.

There are things to complain about, of course. The cruising yachts anchor in Boulder Bay, around from the entrance to the inlet. At night the sound of parties comes across the sea. 'It's like living in the suburbs,' Stella complains. And the speedboats from

Saxton make the air hideous with their racket all day long. Apart from that they're pleased with Oyster Bay.

Josie likes it in small doses. Sun and sea she likes but mosquitoes and cramped rooms and cooking in what she calls 'primitive conditions', and sand in the food, and having to be mingy with the water, and no air conditioning in the night, sleeping in your sweat, and the stink of the chemical toilet, and thump of the generator driving her mad – 'Well, I'm past all that, I'm somewhere else.' Danes snoring on the living-room floor. 'That's for Mandy and Stell. I'm in my civilized forties now.' She wants to be in Saxton, in her studio, at her work.

Duncan wants to go home too. He's read all his books. He has walked north and south, half a day each, and met uneasy grins on the track with a grin of his own; has swum in the evening and sat on the hill behind the bay, looking at the stars, and now he wants his telescope again and lots more books.

'If you do go, Mum, can I go too?'

They stay for ten days, then Tom speeds them back to Saxton in his boat. Mandy and Stella and Belinda stay on at Oyster Bay.

The first thing Duncan does is telephone Mrs Sangster. He wants to make sure she hasn't forgotten his correspondence courses. There's no reply and Duncan worries. 'She's probably on holiday. She won't forget. Norma's very good with things like that,' Josie says.

The following night Tom is home before they go to bed. 'I saw Norma on the beach at Pear Tree Bay. All on her lonesome, munching her sammies. That lady really needs a man.'

'You see,' Josie tells Duncan.

So Duncan reads and sits up late in the fire-break. But he's standing still, he feels, and he wants to start moving again. Filling himself up with stuff is OK, but there's a different sort of knowing and he has to find out what it is.

On Sunday Josie says, 'Try to get them back early, Tom. Belinda's got Golden Hills tomorrow.'

'I don't know why she needs to wipe old ladies' bums. You'd think my kids could do better than that.'

'She doesn't wipe, whatever. And it's good for her anyway. Will you please get them back in time for tea.'

She cooks for the whole family; corn patties for Belinda, the only vegetarian left, and chicken for everyone else. At six o'clock, and seven, and eight, they have not come. Josie fumes. 'That bastard,' she says, under her breath.

At ten past eight the phone rings.

'We're at Big Shelley, Mum. Can you pick us up?'

'What's wrong?'

'We came by launch. I'll tell you later. Hurry, eh?'

Josie drives out across the plains and round through Darwood to Big Shelley, saying, 'This is the end, Tom, you bastard,' at the start, but being fairly calm by the time she gets there. Par for the course, she might have known.

They pack most of their gear in the boot and Mandy and Belinda take the rest on their knees. Stella gets in the front with Josie.

'I'm starving.'

'Don't they have pies in the shop?'

'I don't eat pies.'

'They weren't bad,' Mandy says.

Josie drives. 'What happened to your father?'

'Later, Mum.'

'Don't later Mum me. Tell me what happened.'

'He was drunk. So we came by launch.'

Mandy and Belinda are quiet in the back. Too quiet, Josie thinks.

'How drunk was he, Mandy?'

'Drunk enough. We just thought it would be better.'

'Stella thought.' Drunk in charge of a boat was no crime. She'd kill Tom if he took the children in the car that way, but you couldn't get into much trouble in a boat. 'And here I am driving thirty miles. And dinner ruined.'

'Poor you.'

'Now listen, Stella – ' But Stella turns away and puts her hands over her ears and leans on the door.

'Oh shut up, Mum,' Mandy says; and taps her shoulder kindly, shut up.

There's more to this, Josie thinks. Something else happened.

This is what happened – and best to stand a good way off from it.

Tom drove away early with his scuba gear in the boat. Today he was teaching Sandra to dive. There was no need to pick the girls up before mid-afternoon. He stopped at Sandra's flat and put his head in at the door. 'Ready?' he yelled. She came into the room in her dressing-gown.

'Jesus, Sandra.'

'Sorry. Can't come.'

'Why not?'

'I've got my period. So bugger off.' (Tom likes her directness and bad language, he takes it as a kind of sexual play.)

'That won't stop you diving. Why the hell can't you take the pill?'

'I'm not screwing up my chemistry for you or any man. Now clear out Tom, I'm in a bad temper.' Her period always makes her like this. She likes it because it's something men can never have, but hates the inconvenience.

Tom clears out. He goes out through the Cut, across the bow of a Russian trawler, and sets off up the bay towards the point, where the best scuba-diving grounds lie. He doesn't mind diving on his own – likes turning and nosing in that element, and likes the sense of wholeness in his body, has knowledge of himself, skin and bone and blood and fingertips, and comes upon fantastic shapes and marvellous architectures . . . but cannot find his way to that today. He wonders where Norma Sangster is in Sutherland Bay. If he knew he'd go and get her. He's sorry now he let Stephanie go. Sandra is a scruffy little bitch and needs a good belt on the ear. He sits in his boat and lets it drift and sips whisky from his leather flask. Inshore from him two boys in a yellow boat, same model as his, are getting their gear on, helped by a girl with long blond hair.

Tom closes his eyes. 'Long blond hair.' It's a ceremonial phrase. He says it again – an incantation. He feels close to some vision of beauty. When he opens his eyes the diving flag is up and the boys are gone. She's sitting on the side with her feet in the water. She's topless now, with her bikini pants tied on her hip in a neat little bow. Tom thinks he's never seen anything more lovely. He feels uplifted and inclines his head, saluting her.

'Stop perving, you old prick,' she yells at him.

He feels as if she's clawed him on the face. He feels as if she's tipped some filthy bucket over him. There are tears in his eyes as he drives away. But Tom believes in himself and Tom's a doer, and half a kilometre up the coast he sweeps around and runs at her with his throttle wide. He waits for the moment she will see him; makes

264

her fall into the cockpit, open-mouthed. He shows his teeth and drives his bow at her like a knife. There's a chance he'll hit one of the divers surfacing, but they've only been down a minute or two. He takes the chance and sweeps by a boat-length away, turning sharp and throwing a wave that has her tumbling back again and clawing at the rail.

'Take that, you bitch,' Tom says, and keeps his throttle open, roars away.

He speeds down the coast, bay after bay, yellow bites, and goes through the opening in the bar at Kirby Creek and up the river a little way, and up a side-creek. He has another drink, and is hungry now, but Sandra was bringing the lunch. He gets the snorkel and face mask, kid's gear really, from under the seat, and does a bit of crabbing along the sand, in and out of tree roots, looking at the little silver fish. He won't admit he's hiding. Tom Round does not hide.

Later on he putters down the coast, leaning back in his seat and steering with his foot. He's a little drunk and feels very big and very wise, he knows there's no one like him anywhere. He sips again from his flask and looks at the coast and thinks, My place. He's seen a lot of beaches but these are the most beautiful in the world, with sand so yellow it hurts, and the sea swelling up and swamping them – fucking them, he thinks, the sea fucks the beaches, and that he thinks is beautiful; and the bush green and solid at the back, climbing up and up, ledge after ledge. I'd like to build houses here, Tom thinks, one house in each bay, in the bush, and nothing else. Each one mine. I'd come and live in them one by one.

Oyster Bay is ugly, it insults him: crappy shacks and lean-tos and fatties on the beach. I'd get rid of people, Tom declares. Then he sees Belinda walking there; and God, she's beautiful. I made that, he thinks.

He'll get her out of here. He'll take her in his boat to the beaches up the coast.

Tom noses the boat on to the sand and jumps out and gives it a heave to hold it safe. He runs after Belinda, who has gone into the track through the lupins.

'Belinda.'

She turns and grins at him. 'Hey Dad, you're early. We're not ready yet.'

'Come in the boat. I'll teach you to dive.'

'Now?'

'Sure, why not? Get a bit of food from the house. I haven't had lunch.'

'Can Stell and Mandy come?'

'Who needs them? Just you and me.' God, he thinks, she's lovely, look at her. He wants to pick her up and carry her to the boat and drive away.

'Will yukky meat sausages do? And bread? It's stale.'

'Whatever you've got. Hurry love, before the others come.'

She grins and runs – flashing calves, white soles of her feet – and he turns and stretches at the sky, feels all his joints click and muscles enlarge. When he turns Mandy and Stella stand with shoulders touching in the lupins. Their eyes are pointing at him, sticking in, and it hurts.

'She's not going, Dad.'

'What?'

'You're drunk, Dad.'

'What?'

'You're not going to do it to her too.'

'Mandy? What's she talking about, Mandy?'

'Go and look after Belinda. I'll do this,' Stella says.

Mandy looks at him. She opens her mouth to speak but cannot speak. She runs away.

Mandy knows Stella is right. She has seen him like this once before, with his eyes bulging and his throat mottled pink and red. She stops herself running and tries to walk, but bangs into things as she goes through the house. Belinda is at the fridge. She looks round guiltily.

'Put them back, Belinda. You're not going.'

'I wasn't sneaking, Mandy. I'll ask him to let you come.'

'No one's going.'

'Why not?'

'Because he's drunk.'

'Not very much. I can –'

'No you can't.'

'He was going to teach me how to dive.'

'Well he's not. Scuba-diving's dangerous, you can't do it while you're drunk. He'd have drowned you, Bel.'

'I would've –'

'It's too late. Stella's sent him away.'

'It's not fair.' She bangs the sausages on the table.

'No, it isn't. Nothing's fair.'

They hear the boat start and it screams like a bird and goes straight out, with its wake in a ridge as high as the stern. They see Stella's head coming though the lupins. She walks on the lawn. Her face is white. Stella does not see them. She turns aside and goes into a corner of the hedge, where bushes hide her.

Mandy goes out and stands on the lawn. In a moment she hears Stella being sick.

She said, 'If we see you even looking at Belinda again we're going to tell Mum. We'll tell her what you did to us. You watch out then.'

He points his boat straight out to sea.

Tom does not remember what he did. He can't, he can't remember. He knows he did something with them both.

She said, 'You tried it with me, Dad, and you tried it with her. And I've got it written down and so has she. And if you do one thing, one thing more, we'll give the whole lot to the police. And everyone else. Every one of your friends. Even if you don't go to jail you'll be ruined.'

I'll go to jail, he thinks, I'll be ruined. He sees himself in a dirty room, behind a door, hiding there.

She said, 'I don't know what you did to Mandy, she won't say. But I know what you did to me, and it screwed me up, and I'm still screwed up. But by God I'm not staying that way, not for you. I'll be all right.'

'All I wanted was to love them properly.' He can't believe he's done anything wrong. He can't believe she spoke to him like that; and Mandy, whom he loves most, next to Bel. What are the bitches telling Bel?

Tom turns his boat and aims it at the beach, but there's a fog he runs into there, it grows thicker and thicker, forcing him back. He can't come close to them, Stella and Mandy, and Belinda.

He sends his boat darting here and there. Tom Round does not know where to go. In the afternoon he's in a little bay by Kirby Creek. The boat drifts. His whisky is all gone and his mouth craves water. He looks down twenty feet through sea as clear as tap water and sees white shells on the sand and little fish with stippled backs swimming in a school.

'Fish are bloody lucky. I wish I was a fish.'

Then a shriek, a chisel stab, goes through his head. His boat jumps and throws him on his knees and water sprays on him and his captain's hat falls into the sea. Round and round the yellow boat goes, throwing sheets of water and knocking him down when he stands up, and two men whoop and laugh and a girl bites at him with her white teeth. Tom does not know who they are.

They speed away like a plane from a strafing run.

Tom sits in his swamped cockpit and cries.

'He wanted to take her diving and he was drunk. So we said no. At least Stella did. And he lost his temper and cleared out. And that's all.'

'I still say it would have been all right,' Belinda complains.

'No it wouldn't.'

'It certainly wouldn't. I'll skin Tom alive. You wait and see.'

'I'll never go diving now.'

'Stella probably saved your life. So stop whingeing, Bel.'

'I'll skin Tom alive,' Josie says. She goes to Stella's bedroom and looks in at the door. 'Are you all right?'

'Yes.'

'I'm sorry I snapped at you. You did the right thing.'

Stella, in the dark, says, 'I think you should get a divorce, Mum. And get Bel and Duncan away from him.'

'Oh, you do?'

'Yes, I do.'

'Well, we'll see.' She tries to sound snooty but is thrilled that Stella should say this. She loves it when her daughters speak out and has wanted one of them to say divorce.

'The problem is I want to keep the house.'

'Forget the house, Mum. There are other houses.'

Josie is not so pleased with that.

The sound of his car wakes her. She looks at her clock and sees it's a quarter to three so she doesn't get up. There'll be time for what she wants to say in the morning. Josie turns over and goes back to sleep.

268

All the girls start jobs that Monday morning. Belinda is going to Golden Hills and Stella to the court-house where she's sitting in for the librarian. Josie has arranged a job for Mandy at Wimmins Werk. Only Duncan will be left at home but Josie doesn't worry about him, he seems so contented with his astronomy.

Stella and Belinda drive away in Stella's car. Belinda in her kitchen-hand's smock looks like any shopgirl or skivvy and Josie is relieved they let her do more than kitchen work – feed the old ladies and walk them in the garden. She wants Belinda to be a doctor.

She puts aside five minutes for seeing Tom. He's spread out on his back on the giant bed as though staked out to feed the ants, and with that half erection men get when they need to pee but can't wake up. Josie twitches the duvet across his lower half. He's got a good body for nearly fifty, no fat, and segmented on his chest like one of those line drawings of Greek heroes. His workouts at the gym are paying off. He's nice and brown; and his face is brown but not very nice. Sleep makes it slack and fat and you can see the self in it. Josie can remember loving Tom; remembers now. It's a possession she's pleased to have and is proof to her that she was all right then and is all right now. She flicks his mussed hair off his brow and taps her finger on the bridge of his nose.

'Tom.'

His eyes come open at once, red and dry, with orbs concave. He pulls up the duvet and lifts his knees. 'What do you want?'

'I'm off to work. But there's two things I want to say. If you ever try that with Belinda again I'll make you really sorry, Tom.'

'Try what?' His eyes go away and come back fast.

'You know very well. Trying to take her diving while you're drunk. I thought you knew better than that, Tom.'

He looks away from her and licks his lips. 'Jesus, I'm dry. Get us a drink of water, Jose.'

'Get it yourself. You could have killed her.'

'Balls. It was perfectly safe.'

'No it wasn't and you know it. I'm warning you, don't do it again.'

'Sure. OK. What's the second thing?' He tries to make it sharp and hard but there's something sloppy in it, his mind is somewhere else.

'The second thing's quite easy. I want a divorce. And I want the house in my settlement.'

'Like bloody hell you're getting my house.'

'We'll see, Tom. I thought it was fair to give you warning. I'm going to see a lawyer today.'

'No court would give you the house. I built it. It's mine.'

'And it's also a joint family home. And the girls and Duncan stay with me. Sorry, Tom. Now you can go back to sleep.'

He hears her car start in the garage and hears it crackle down the drive. He jumps off the bed and watches it vanish in the gums and come out on the road and speed away. She changes gears like a Grand Prix driver. That's her way of trying to rub it in.

He goes to the bathroom and has a piss and drinks water from his cupped hands, then goes back and sits on the bed. What she has said about the house puts everything else out of his mind. There's an unease, a coiling and twisting, at the back of things but he doesn't know what causes it and doesn't care. He knows Josie will never get his house. Joint family home! That's nothing against the sort of owning he knows.

His head aches and he lies down again and tries to sleep but can only doze and jerk awake and doze again. Walls and floors and doors slide in and out of his dream. Everything is space and plane and angle, and level set in harmony with and tension against. He's set to break through these shifts into perfect form – but he can't, he *can't*, dark countervailing formless liquid things are stopping him.

He wakes with a cry and stares about. Looks at the clock. Only quarter to ten. But he'll start to fester and stink if he lies here. He goes to the bathroom, showers hard, hot then cold, and shaves with a blade; then dresses in clean clothes, blue cotton shirt and white jeans and espadrilles.

He goes to the kitchen and puts his porridge on. Every morning of his life Tom starts with porridge. Josie calls it his mash but he doesn't care. Porridge, Tom would say, connects him with his roots, and the mixing of it works as a mnemonic and brings back, every morning, that kitchen in the house behind the brickworks in New Lynn, where he grew up. Never fails. He could not stop it if he wanted to. Then it was Creamoata, and that is pigswill, Tom agrees, but he has his own recipe now – two parts of rolled oats, one of bran, one of millet meal, one of kibbled wheat. It's for the taste not for his health but all the same it keeps him regular.

A little bit of sugar, lots of milk. Tom eats at the kitchen table. A shuffle and breathing jerks him round and he sees Duncan's face slide across the doorway like a bead on an abacus. Tom hears the boy go out of the house and click the door. He is pleased to have him gone. Now he's alone; and that's the way he wants it. Tom Round in his house.

He makes coffee and eats an apple – early season Gravenstein, and that too takes him back. He's there with a grin of pleasure, in the kitchen – kitchen with curling lino and match-lined walls (lovely stuff, tongue and groove, perfect fit and function) varnished to an amber glow, and the newly silvered stove with brass tap and moulded door – as his father walks in with a sack of apples from Henderson.

I wish Dad could have seen my house.

A good part of what's essential he gets from his old man, Tom believes. Bill Round was a brickie and by God – Tom to botching tradesmen on his jobs – he'd pick up a brick in his left hand, flip it twice to find the better face, never dropped a single one in his life; spread the mortar on with a wipe of his trowel, spread it like butter, always the right amount, never had to get more or take any off; and if he had to cut a brick he'd do the bloody measurement with his eye, then one tap with his trowel and clean as a whistle a half or a quarter would drop off, and it was right, down to the last millimetre it was right. A tradesman. You don't see them now. He could make you a fireplace like a cathedral porch and get the curve absolutely right with his eye.

Tom gets his gift for putting things together from his old man. And that extra thing from his mother, whatever it is – synthesizing skill, that working towards a whole that exists as ideal form before you get there. Yeah, Tom says. And thinks of her, working-class girl, drain-layer's daughter, reading, explaining, thinking, laughing, in the little kitchen, and a light shining out of her, love and ambition for *him*. And now her mind is all in bits. There's no whole past but bits of past, and no coherent world inside or out, and sometimes when he visits her on his trips to Auckland she doesn't even know who he is. It's cruel, he thinks. And no one here gives him a word of sympathy.

Well that's all right, I'll have them out, I'll have the bloody lot of them out of my house. I can get by on my own. I'm best on my own, Tom Round thinks. There's nothing I want from anyone.

271

He goes outside and hoses down his boat and pulls it into place in the garage. He starts the pump and waters his lawns and checks the water temperature in the solar panels. It's almost too hot to put your hand in. Then he walks down to the gate for the *Dominion* and reads it under a sun umbrella by the pool. Last night, he remembers, I went to see Sandra. She let him sleep on the couch for a couple of hours. He does not like that, sleeping on the couch when there's a bed in the next room with a woman in it. But he'll dump Sandra, she really is a dirty little bitch, some of the things she likes to do. He'll get by without a woman for a while and live alone in his house. It seems to him empty already – he walks through it – and cool and clean and spacious, uncontaminated, whole.

Family home? Family seems dirty to Tom.

Stops at Belinda's room. I wasn't going to touch Bel. What do they think I am? I never did anything to Mandy and Stell. Just a bit of . . . Can't remember what, but nothing bad, a bit of horseplay. Women get neurotic. I wish I'd had three sons instead.

He goes down half a level and looks through the white vista, space folding on space, to the lawn and pool. (The dog walks by with its paws clicking on the tiles.) He sits in a chair and smiles at sunlight burning down but not touching him and the wind belting in the pines. No, he thinks, no sons either. He's the point his parents worked towards, the final product, where it all came into shape. He's shape and he's shape-maker. He's the last in a male line. And who needs daughters even, Mandy, Stell and Bel, whose futures are only points in time directing attention back at him? He needs no attention but his own.

Tom smiles and spreads his legs and puts his arms on the fat, cold arms of the chair. He yawns and scratches his chest and thinks he'll have an hour's sleep; and then, by God, he'll go into town and see Tony Hillman and show Josie Duncan where she gets off.

He starts to drift into that easy sleep preceded by floating images of pillar, cornice, lintel, spire; but again the formless swallows shape. He wakes with a twist of his buttocks. Something sharp is digging into him. He feels for it and drags it out and thinks at first it's a paperback novel of Josie's; then turns it over and reads the back: 'Beautiful, wealthy, and spoiled, Laurie Bennington is used to having things her way. So when Lars Olsen tells her their romance is finished . . .' Belinda's muck. He drops it on the floor.

But Tom is too late. Belinda's there. He has no place to run to. Tom can't put knowledge off any more.

He knows what he meant to do with Belinda. He sees Mandy and Stella on the beach (that lovely round of shoulder, superb articulation of bone and joint) – and Stella alone (blade and edge and point, and the hilt and handle of her mouth). He hears every sharp, cold word again, cutting him. There's no place where he can turn and hide.

He draws up his legs. He tries to be tiny in the chair.

Duncan's morning has not satisfied him. When his mother and Mandy leave he telephones Mrs Sangster. She should be back from her holiday, most people are back. The phone rings on and on. (Norma is in her office at school, getting ready for Maule and Whiting and Mrs Alexander.) He goes to his room and reads but cannot understand the ideas:

Bohm's starting point is the notion of 'unbroken wholeness', and his aim is to explore the order he believes to be inherent in the cosmic web of relations at a deeper 'non manifest' level. He calls this order 'implicate', or 'enfolded' . . .

The words hide things Duncan wants to know. He looks in his dictionary but it doesn't help. Most of the meaning gets away. He feels the excitement of it move out of his reach. There, there, is where he wants to be. Will the correspondence courses help? He knows that for a long time they won't. He'll have to go right to the beginning and fill things in bit by bit – start where the fourth-formers start. He feels better when he understands that. The idea of work makes him happy. The trouble is he wants to start now.

At ten o'clock he decides to telephone Mrs Sangster again. 'Damn,' he says, when he opens his door. The noise of distant water means his father is in the shower. He might come out and pick up another phone and overhear. Duncan reads a page more of his book then puts it aside and opens Belinda's maths book. He can understand that. Later, when his father is eating breakfast – some breakfast, half past ten – he goes for a walk along the edge of the golf course. He watches from a clump of silver birch trees as a woman gets ready to hit a ball on a plastic tee. He knows about the swing from the golf books Tom brings home (and decides he

273

doesn't need to read). It depends on balance and timing and movements joined together in a whole, and he breaks the woman's swing into its parts – sees her like a series of still photographs, right through to the time when the ball goes popping up in a spray of dirt and lands twenty metres away. Duncan knows what she did wrong.

'You brought your right shoulder down too hard,' he yells.

She looks for him and the women in her foursome fan out and peer into the trees, but he scrambles up the needle slope and all they see is the flash of legs. Duncan sits and pants. The phantom golf pro, he exults.

At the end of the course he crosses the river and climbs a track to the top of the hill over Clearwater's house. The iron roof makes a chequered pattern, red and silver and rusty-brown, and the Land-Rover on the lawn is jacked up on one side and has a wheel off but it looks as if it's been that way for weeks. He's not sure, but he thinks he can see grass growing through the tyre on the lawn. Clearwater is sitting on his porch. All he's wearing – Duncan's not sure again – is underpants. The goats are by the road fence, in the bracken, except for one tied to a peg at the far side of the house by the tea-tree patch.

Duncan walks along the track towards home. When he looks back Clearwater has come to the tank behind the house and is letting water from the tap run into his mouth. When he walks away he forgets to turn it off. Duncan watches the water. It falls in a silver line but light reverses it and makes it come out of the ground and flow into the tap. It's a kind of magic, a turning round of laws. He watches for a moment until it becomes just interesting – scientific. He supposes he should call out and tell Clearwater he's wasting water. But the man is hunkered down on the lawn with his arms wrapped round his knees and he looks as if he's set to stay for hours. So Duncan does nothing.

He feels sorry for Clearwater. It's probably true what people say, living with goats has sent him mad.

Tom remembers. With Mandy in her bedroom, no one home. And Stella in the bush at Oyster Bay. *Nothing much*. But it's no use. He can't deny. 'Jesus, no.' His degradation almost knocks him out of the chair. He slides out and sits on the floor, and pushes, pushes, tries to empty knowledge from himself. It won't go. And there's the dreadful thing that follows it. Tom's work is making order and order is something he will never find again. There's a flying about of fragments and he'll never draw them in and make a shape. He does not have the fitness any more and there will be no way to get it back.

Out in the conservatory the dog is licking water from a leaf. It stops and rolls an eye at Tom and its blunt teeth grin. Tom sees: belly like a sack, dribbled line of urine on the tiles. He makes a growl. Tom howls. He stands up and runs across the room to the ferny tunnel. The dog cannot move fast enough. His kick strikes the soft full part of its underside and turns it somersaulting through the door. Tom follows and kicks again, striking the animal's rib cage. It skids on its back across the tiles and tips over, rear end first, into the swimming pool.

Tom has hurt his foot. It stabs him as he walks to the pool. He sees a pointed nose leaking blood and paws sliding, squeaking, on the tiles. Blood threads in the water. He limps on to the lawn and picks up the leaf scoop.

Duncan walks up the drive from the road. His father's car is still in the garage so he skirts the yard and goes round the outside of the wall. He sits in the grass with his back to the bricks, which are cool from the night although the sun's been on them for an hour. As soon as the car goes he'll telephone Mrs Sangster.

He hears his father call out angrily and hears Sos yelp. Belted him, he thinks. Lucky Bel's not home. There's another yell and a kind of thud. Something heavy splashes in the pool. It makes him angry. His father's gone in, probably testing his scuba gear. Now it will be hours before he leaves. Duncan feels the house belongs to him in the daytime. Other people should keep out of it.

He stands up, puts his hands on the wall and pulls himself up. He hangs on crooked arms, looking over. Then he grins. Sos has fallen in and his father is fishing him out. Wait till Bel hears about this.

Tom brings the leaf scoop down. Duncan feels his mind turn on an angle. Parts that lay together shift apart. It's water flowing up from the ground again.

Sos is under the mesh. Tom pushes with his forearms, submerging him.

Duncan falls back. He lies against the foot of the wall. The yellow

275

grass climbs up to the pines and the pines climb into the sky. Is that what Duncan sees? He speeds across vast plains, he bends and climbs and dips vertiginously. Huge emptiness, huge fields of light. And there, at the end, the wall is growing. There is his black wall again.

He comes to the foot of it and his movement stops. He lies down and feels himself contract . . .

THREE

Fire

19

The Saxton forest fire. It has a special meaning for us. Remember though, it's not an exclusive event. Half of Saxton saw the tower of smoke rise in the hills and the flames come dipping at the suburbs. 'Be ready to evacuate your houses,' the Civil Defence spokesman said on the radio. He ran through a list of things people should take. Personal photographs and documents. That really seemed to underline the danger.

Whole families stood on the streets and watched the fire burn into the forest all night long. They did not, in the end, have to leave their houses. (Only two houses were burned, Tom and Josie Round's house and Lex Clearwater's house, and only one person was killed.) They were frightened though, for an hour, and after that upset, awed, excited; felt important. This was the worst and biggest thing that had ever happened in Saxton.

No one knows how it started. Conditions that day were extreme and 'the forest was a bomb just waiting to go off'. (Dennis Kennedy, assistant conservator.) The trees had been baked by months of sun and were full of combustible resin. In gullies nearer town, bracken, gorse and tea-tree made a crackling and dry hissing through the morning and afternoon. The wind, at gale force, from the north-west, was hot and dry and swept across the hills like a broom.

Some say a Ministry of Works team tried to boil a billy and the flame got away; some that the high tension power lines across Lunar Gully arced in the wind; some that a trail bike rider in a fire-break . . . that a broken bottle in the sun . . .

The fire began at ten to three. In the hills on the eastern side of town smoke reared up. It grew into the sky like a huge round-headed tree.

'I'm sliding down a slope and it's rather frightening. Where am I, by the way?'
'Lift your foot, Miss Freed. That's right. You're doing very well.'
'What a small bosom you've got. I had a small bosom too.'

'Yes, Miss Freed.'

'Men attach so much importance . . .'

'Lift your foot.' Belinda works the stocking stirrup and round the lawn they go at Golden Hills.

'Who's that big man standing over there?'

'That's not a man, that's smoke, Miss Freed. There must be a fire in the hills. Shall we go round the front where we can see?'

'Is it smoke? It looks like a man to me. Why is he angry?'

The fire goes down the gullies at the speed of a running horse and up the hills and, with a greater roar, leaves the scrub and enters the pines. It runs down to the river and jumps the road, closing the valley by Monday Hole. All the people at the hole are safely away. The golfers on the course are safe. Most of them sit in the river but half a dozen stand outside the clubhouse drinking beer and watching the show, and one phlegmatic fellow keeps on playing.

East again, the fire jumps Leppers Creek, climbs the ridge, runs into the young pines, no taller than Christmas trees, on Stovepipe Hill, and shoots a fireball four hundred metres across the valley into the mature trees, ready for milling, on the hills east of Lex Clearwater's goat farm. They explode – whoomp, you can hear it in town – and there's no hope any more of stopping the fire. The forestry teams must give away hundreds of hectares, and hold it, if they can, on the next line of hills above Copper Creek.

The children in the Baptist camp are safe. The gully there is in native bush and the fire goes across the hill behind it and down the other side, neat and clean.

Josie, at the road block, cries, 'Duncan is in there. My son's in there. And the Birtles girl.'

'Sorry lady, no one can go in.'

Three people from our story are in Coppermine valley that afternoon: Duncan Round, Hayley Birtles, Lex Clearwater. It's time to go back and take a narrow focus. We'll start with Hayley.

The softball tournament is over and Hayley is having trouble filling her days. She feels cut off from her friends and when she's with them everything that happens seems a part of some bigger thing she cannot see. It doesn't go anywhere for her and there's a kind of sadness and emptiness all round. That's because of Melbourne, she supposes. Melbourne is somehow where she is and she seems to look at Saxton through a window.

The house is going on the market soon. Her father is back at work but has given notice. Her mother is home, and talks more now, but there's a pause in front of what she says as though she has to work out the words. It's good to have her though, cooking the meals and washing the dishes and saying things like, 'Don't be late home.'

Shelley is back, but Shelley is like someone getting over being sick. She's at half-speed most of the time and says only half what you expect. It drives Hayley wild. She goes out jogging with their father though, round and round the park in the dusk, and once when he couldn't go Hayley went instead, and found it hard keeping up with Shell.

Shelley won't talk about Arohata. Hayley thinks her sister is up herself with this suffering stuff.

After lunch on the day of the fire she tells her mother she's going for a swim at the beach. But at the bottom of the street she turns right instead of left and rides past the Post Office and the swimming-pool and up the riverside path into the valley. She wants to tell Lex Clearwater she's leaving for Melbourne next week. She's not going to visit him for anything but goodbye.

The wind makes the poplar trees by Monday Hole whip back and forth. It pushes her up the valley like a hand on her back.

The gate at the bottom of Lex's drive is locked. Hayley has left her safety chain at home so she lifts her bike over and hides it in the scrub. The gorse and broom lunge at her as she walks up. A car would have a hard job getting through and Lex's Land-Rover must have to break its way. It makes her nervous. She remembers every bit of what she did with Lex but it doesn't seem to work in properly with other things – as though you kept on pitching and pitching but all the balls kept bending away from the plate. She's not sure she should come here again, it's dangerous.

She stops where the drive comes out of the scrub and curves round the lawn to the house and sheds. It's so dry the ground is like pumice and white as chalk. That puts colour in everything else. Brown things seem red and grey things blue. The house has a shimmer in the heat and the Land-Rover, tipped half-way on its side as though someone hidden is lifting it, looks hot as a stove. Hayley goes round and sees a jack holding it up and a wheel on the hard-baked lawn with bits of spiky grass through the axle-hole. She nearly puts her foot in a turd. 'Ooh, yuk.' Hops aside. Goats don't do turds like that, it's a human one. It makes her feel sick, and more nervous still, and she looks at the house and calls out, 'Lex.'

A goat coughs by the road. She turns but cannot see it, and shades her eyes and looks up the hill but can't see any goats up there. The pines send waves of shimmer into the sky and have a loud humming like insects inside them.

Hayley goes on to the porch and looks inside. At first she thinks someone has wrecked the house, then sees that nothing is broken or overturned, things have just been dropped and left – cutlery and plastic bags and bits of food and dishrags and socks and shirts. Hayley goes in two or three steps. Blowflies and house-flies are everywhere. The stink is horrible and seems to come from the fridge. She goes across and gives the door a push but it swings back open. She can't see what is bad – maybe some meat in the freezer underneath. But what's the matter with Lex, can't he smell it? She looks at the table. There's a packet of cut bread with the slices growing mould. One slice is torn in half and a bite taken out. There's a pumpkin split in half and going bad. A tomahawk lies beside it with dry seeds where the handle meets the blade. There's a tea towel stained with brown that looks like blood. Hayley lifts it with a finger and thumb and finds a can of baked beans underneath. Someone has tried to chop it open. Jagged bits of tin poke out. There's more blood on the table.

Hayley tries to call Lex's name but it won't come. She wants to get away from the house and back on the road but thinks perhaps he's lying hurt somewhere and bleeding to death. He might be dead already because the blood is old. Hayley does not want to find his body.

She looks down the hall, then walks quickly down and looks in the bedroom. The mattress on the double bed is bare. Bedclothes lie tangled on the floor. There's a bad smell in this room too, as though someone has pissed, and she doesn't want to go in, but gets down on her knees and looks under the bed to see if he's lying in the space by the wall. She looks in the bathroom and sees blood in the basin, where it has congealed and turned black.

She goes outside and runs across the lawn and looks in the sheds, expecting to find him in a corner, crumpled up. She stands on the drive and calls, 'Lex, are you up there? Are you all right?' but her voice gets lost on the hill. If he's in the pines he will not hear.

Hayley decides that Lex has gone for help, or bandaged up himself and gone to town – or gone away perhaps, gone for good. He could have walked out and left his house, that would explain why everything's a mess and going bad. It's the crazy sort of thing Lex would do. He's not here anyway. And Hayley does not like being alone. It's spooky, like a movie. Something seems just out of sight all the time. There's a feeling of something turned the wrong way round, and everything, even the grass and trees, being dangerous.

Hayley runs down the drive. She lifts her bike over the gate and rides away.

Lex Clearwater watches her go. Is it Lex? He doesn't have a name any more.

He squats in his nest in the bracken up the hill and rocks back and forth and makes a singing moan in time with the pain in his hand. There's a ball of rag in his palm, damp on the bottom but dry on top. His fingers are closed on it and he can't open them.

Lex has gone to ground in the bracken. There's nothing down the hill, in the house. The girl moves, makes sounds, goes away, and when she's gone does not exist any more. He lifts his hand to his mouth and licks the cut where it extends across the base of his thumb, but it has a taste he does not like, and it hurts. He puts the hand back in his lap and rocks and moans.

He has a blanket in his nest. He brought it up the hill with him before he forgot what blankets were. He has a plastic sack of potatoes. After a while he needs to eat and he takes a potato and bites a piece off and chews and swallows. He eats the potato, then eats another. A longer while. He needs to drink. The water is in a trough by the fence at the back of the house. He has not drunk since early in the morning. (But Lex does not see things aligned in time, while space extends no further than the distance between his eye and the thing he must have to satisfy himself. Lex lives in his goat mind now.)

He steps down the hill. He must not fall. The water is low in the trough. He leans in, stretching his neck, but his hand knocks the edge of the trough and he cries out. He squats and moans.

After a while Lex tries another way. He reaches into the trough with his good hand and makes a cup and lifts it to his mouth.

Is Lex Clearwater starting to come back?

He is drinking when the fire starts.

The wind is against her riding down the valley. She puts the bike in a lower gear, although she feels silly pedalling fast but going slow. Dust devils race across the golf course. The river shivers as they cross. Lolly papers, pie bags, jump and twist and drop in the car-park. Hayley narrows her eyes against the grit and pedals hard, wishing she'd gone to the beach. The waves out there would be great for body surfing. She does not think of Lex any more.

The gums in front of the Rounds' house rattle like tinfoil. The wind seems to come in lumps and knee her. She scarcely hears the car until it's by her side. Tuck and Legs stick their long arms out. She feels their fingernails scrape her arm. Gary Baxter is braking hard but the Escort runs twenty metres and Hayley has time to turn and pedal back the way she came. Tuck and Legs jump out but she's away, the wind behind her, and they lose time scrambling back in. Gary has to do a three-point turn on the narrow road. He grates his gears and Hayley laughs. She knows where she will go and she has time, and she does not give them the satisfaction of making her pedal hard. She hears the car coming with a whine and she grins back and makes a left hand signal, exaggerated, cheeky, and turns into the Rounds' drive, crosses the one way bridge, rides half-way up the shell drive and dismounts. The car pulls up across the entrance. Gary Baxter gets out and stands looking over the roof.

'We'll get you, Hayley. Wait and see.'

'How's your arm, Gary? Did you get your plaster off? You should have asked me to autograph it.'

'Are you going up to screw the loony?' Tuck yells.

She makes the fingers at them and turns away. She doesn't have to bother with Tuck and Legs and Gary any more. They won't follow up the drive. Neil Chote maybe would have but not Gary. She looks at the house and it makes her nervous, it's so big. But she can say she came to see Belinda. At least she knows Belinda after swimming at Freaks' Hole. She pushes her bike up the drive and goes around the back, where brick walls fold in and lead to gardens and a yard big enough for a netball court. A woman in white trousers and a purple smock stands in the garage doorway, looking at her.

'What do you want?'

'I came to see Belinda.'

'She's not home. Haven't I seen you?'

'I'm Hayley Birtles, Mrs Round.' She supposes it's Mrs Round, she looks like Stella Round and talks the same.

'Wayne's sister?' Mrs Round goes pink when she says the name. Hayley is pleased to see it, it makes her feel less like a trespasser.

'Well,' Mrs Round says. She puts down the potted fern she's holding and wipes her hands on her smock. 'Who was shouting down there?'

'Just some guys who were hassling me. That's why I came up.'

'Hassling?'

'It's a guy I used to go round with. He tried to knock me off my bike.'

Mrs Round strides past her. She goes along the drive between the walls and looks down at the road. Hayley leans her bike on a wall and follows her. Gary's car is still parked across the entrance and the boys are sitting inside.

'You get out of here,' Mrs Round shrieks. It's a real shriek, it hurts Hayley's ears. Gary gets out of the car and puts his hands on the bonnet.

'We can park where we like.' His voice is almost lost in the crackle of gum trees.

'Not in my drive. Get out.'

'You send her down, eh? We've got to talk to her,' Gary yells forlornly. Hayley is almost sorry for him, little dumb Gary down there, and doesn't like Mrs Round, yelling like someone English from her fancy house.

'I know what you did to her, she told me. If you're not gone in two minutes I'll call the police. In fact,' she cries, 'I'm calling them now.' She marches back along the drive. Hayley blows Gary a kiss. She runs after Mrs Round.

'Don't call the police, eh.'

'I'm not going to. That was to scare them.'

'I broke Gary's arm. That's why he's mad.'

'Well, good for you Hayley Birtles. I didn't know you and Belinda were friends.'

'We're not. I know her though.' She hears a car. 'That's them going. Thanks, eh.'

'My pleasure.' And she does look pleased. 'Do you want to wait here a while, Hayley? You can have a swim if you like. Duncan's in there, by the pool.'

Hayley might solve a problem for Josie Round. She feels she should not leave Duncan alone but if the girl can stay for an hour, not watch him but, well, be with him, Josie can get things organized at the shop and then come back and take him to the doctor. Is Hayley the sort of girl she can trust? She's Shelley Birtles' sister, after all. Josie has a sidelong look at her. Big and sturdy – strapping would be the word if kinky sex hadn't taken it over. And pretty enough in a bovine way. There was – wasn't there? – some intelligence in her eye: the quickness of cunning, but a slower movement too, of knowledge was it? Knowledge of what? The girl gave the impression of having had experience of life; of, probably, the seamy side. That was not a disadvantage, necessarily. But did it mean she would rob the house? And would she even see poor scarred Duncan, see him as a fellow human being, as a young man?

Josie runs all this past herself in a second or two; decides yes, she will take the risk, the Rounds and the Birtleses are connected, after all.

'Hayley, you could do me a favour.'

'Yeah, what's that?'

'Duncan isn't well and I'd like someone here, just for an hour. I've got to go to the shop you see . . .'

'Sure,' Hayley says.

'All you need to do is just – amuse yourself, have a swim – you've got your togs? – be around.'

'Sure.'

'He's no trouble. You can go into the house and make a drink.'

'That's OK.'

Josie goes through the archway to the pool and Hayley follows, wheeling her bike. Duncan is sitting in the rock garden.

286

'Duncan, here's Hayley Birtles. She's come to have a swim.'

Better, Josie thinks, if someone from outside the family is the first one back in the pool. That will lift the tapu, so to speak. She isn't keen to be first one herself.

Tears start in her eyes as she looks at the water, that innocent blue, and thinks of poor Sos floating there, with only his shoulders above the surface and the rest of him heavier than was natural somehow; hindquarters down; head down as though searching for something on the bottom. And his little legs – like a thalidomide baby. And Duncan in his room, in the dark, curtains closed. Sitting on his bed with his knees drawn up; and not a word from him ever since. And Tom gone, note on the table – 'Business in Wellington. Will be in touch.' That was better than she had hoped, though disturbing when she thought of it – too much on the neutral side, if neutral could be said to have a side. All in all a bloody twenty-four hours. (The girls though had been marvellous. No tears from Belinda. She helped dig the grave and bury Sos; practical and bravely held in. Stella and Mandy had done the lifting out.)

'I'm going, Duncan. Hayley will be staying for a while.'

'Hallo, Duncan,' Hayley says.

He turns his head and looks at the girl. It's his first sign of interest since yesterday afternoon, and Josie does not like it somehow. Perhaps the question should be, Is Hayley safe with Duncan? rather than the other way round. And there's the question too, Did the dog fall in or was he pushed? And who was home to do it except . . .?

Josie says, No. It's his face that makes her think like that, and it's unfair. Duncan is gentle, she knows.

Whispers to the girl, 'He'll be all right. He just sits. I'll try to be back by – half past three?'

'No sweat, Mrs Round.'

'Remember to get a drink. And there's a cake in the tin. Duncan will show you, won't you Duncan?'

Does he nod? Josie waits a moment to make sure. Then she smiles at Hayley and taps her arm: Thank you.

The car sprays shell chips. She's away. Thinks of the shop . . .

Hayley props the bike up on the lawn. The stand might scratch the tiles and she's watching everything she does, awed by the house.

Through the glasshouse stuck on the back and full of ferns and flowers and plants with big fat leaves, you can see the rooms going on and on and down and down. It's like being in the pictures or on TV, *Dallas* or *The Love Boat* or *Falconcrest*. How do people get that much money? She thought it was just in America.

Duncan is still sitting in the rocks. He's wearing shorts and a T-shirt with something printed on it. Hayley moves further round the pool so she can read: 'Hump your ass off.' The way the Yanks spell arse makes it feeble. But what a laugh – except she doesn't laugh – someone who looks like Duncan wearing it.

'What's the matter? You got the bot or something?'

He shakes his head, moving it just once.

'What's wrong then?'

'Nothing. I don't feel well.'

'Well try smiling, eh. Your teeth want to see what the weather's like.' It's one of her father's jokes and it makes her smile every time. 'Did Belinda give you my message?' That same shake of the head. 'You can talk about Wayne. I don't care.' Now he looks at her, and after flicking her eyes away once she looks straight back, and sees – thinks she can see – he wouldn't have been bad looking if it hadn't been for his accident. The left side of his face shows you that.

'Wayne's dead.'

'Well I know that, dumby.' She feels herself blushing. A lot of people think he's a loony. 'We're going to live in Aussie. In Melbourne.'

'Yeah? Good.' He turns his head away, not interested.

'You going to have a swim?'

'No.'

'Well, I am.' She goes back to her bike and gets her togs from the carrier. 'Where can I change, eh?'

'Anywhere.'

'Thanks a lot.' She goes into the glasshouse but the ferns have spooky places in behind them so she goes into the house and finds herself in a room as big as three or four rooms at home, all white and grey. There are red and orange mats on the floor, big round pools of colour that make her grin they're so bright, and the pictures on the walls ... 'Jeez,' she says. There's one of a huge wood-pigeon flying very high over little hills and patches of bush and a beach and the sea. It looks fat and happy up there and the

288

land is like jewels. And one of smooth white rocks and blue pools you can see right through and a floating string of seaweed like a string of yellow beads. And one, the biggest one, of an empty room, wooden floor, and a staircase and a window of coloured glass. The light comes through making different parts of the room shine with different colours, but there's an open clear pane reflecting a tiny bit of the world outside – a tree with a child's swing hanging from a branch. The child's dead, you know that straight away. Hayley is delighted with the pictures, though they frighten her too. She takes off her clothes and puts them in a chair – what a chair! – and pulls on her togs. Then, with her towel round her neck, explores the house. Bedrooms and, Jeez! a water-bed. She looks back at the door and hops on quickly, tries it out. The waves are like someone rubbing her and it's made for fucking, but how would you get on if all you wanted was to go to sleep?

She does not look in any more bedrooms but goes back to the room where she changed, then down half a level into another lounge and sees a wall of glass in front of her with the golf course out there, people walking on it like little dolls, and the river curving round two sides. The whole thing is laid out as if the Rounds own it. She looks far along the course and sees Lex's house on the same level. The difference is more than Hayley can understand. She goes up two steps to the dining-room, where the table is bare wood without any paint and as big as a snooker table in *Pot Black*. The kitchen is joined on but not joined on. She has seen places like it in the model homes show, but this is bigger and has more things and looks as if it should be full of butlers and maids. Hayley is beginning to be angry. It's all too much.

She crosses the lounge with the pictures again and goes up half a level into an open room beyond the bedrooms. A weaving loom with a rug half-finished stands in the middle with a couple of smaller looms and a spinning wheel. A bed with the duvet half slipped off is under the window. There are dirty clothes on the floor and a coffee cup with dregs in it, a crust on a plate, an apple core going brown, on the bedside table. That's better, Hayley thinks. She feels the Rounds are people after all.

She opens the door on the other side of the room and finds herself on a landing with half a dozen steps down to the garage. It's empty except for a speedboat on a trailer. A speedboat is what you'd expect. It's the flashest one she's ever seen. She goes down for a look but stops at a mark on the concrete floor. It's almost round, about the size of the orange mats in the house, and has the nicotine colour of her mother's skin.

Hayley touches it with her toe. She goes outside, walks through the archway, and thinks Duncan must have gone away. Then she sees him sitting further back in the shade.

'That mark in the garage, is that where Wayne got burned?'

He finds her with his eyes. 'Yes,' he says.

'Why didn't you scrub it off or something?'

'Dad tried. It won't come off.'

'You could have put a mat over it, anyhow.' She takes off her towel and stands on the edge of the pool. There are pine needles and gum leaves and dead insects on the water. A few live insects too. She sees a pool scoop lying on the lawn and fetches it and rescues them, then scoops out the dead ones and the leaves.

'Are you coming in?'

'No.'

'Suit yourself.' She goes to the deep end and stands there hands on hips, posing a bit. She knows how good she looks in her new Melbourne togs and feels that she fits in here all right. Then she dives in and swims underwater as far as the wall in the shallow end. She comes up and stands wiping her face.

'It's a bit too warm for me.'

Duncan walks to the pool and looks in. He squats and feels the water with his finger. She swims along and holds on to the gutter.

'Why don't you put a mat on it?'

'What's the use?'

She swims away and does half a dozen lengths of the pool. He's sitting with his legs dangling in when she stops, and she rests by him, with her arms on the rim. She touches one of the scars on his leg and is startled at the hardness of the ridge where it joins the skin that isn't burned. 'Do these still hurt?'

'No.'

'Will they ever look any better? The ones on your face?'

He shakes his head. 'I can have some more plastic surgery. But I'm not going to.'

'Why not?'

'I don't want to.'

290

'You could get a girlfriend if you did.' She touches his leg again. 'Do these go right up under your clothes?'

'Yes. Round my back.' He touches himself in the crotch. 'It burned me here. I can't have kids or anything.'

'Who says?'

'No one. I just know.'

Hayley feels herself starting to cry. 'Duncan.' She puts her cheek against his thigh.

Duncan says, 'I think I'm supposed to be dead.'

And Lex, on his side of the valley? Lex knows *danger*. He stands to see where the smoke is coming from but the house blocks his view. He scrambles up the hill, using his good hand, and stops at the edge of the bracken and looks back. Flames as high as trees are moving across the scrub on the saddle between Stovepipe Hill and Beacon Hill. They bend and leap, bend and leap, and throw smoke in the air. The smoke is as high as he can see and streaming towards him, flattened out and bending down. Lex coughs. There's a shifting in his mind; a part of him leaps into human mode.

Where has Lex been? Me, here, now. Hallucinating on the single point. But Stovepipe Hill and Beacon Hill: he knows the names. He knows what the wind and fire will do; will jump the road. The safe place is the golf course, the safe place is the river. Lex and his goats will go there. But he does not know how fast the fire will move. No one knows. No one has seen a fire like this. He watches the flames climb Stovepipe Hill. Their licking up and plunging up become a liquid rush. It's as though Lex is tilted on his side.

He whimpers. He slides down the hill and falls on his hand. He screams with pain and sits hunched up on a tiny ledge. The ball of rag is loosened in his palm and he twitches it, then jerks it free and looks with bewilderment at the festering cut running from the base of his index finger across his palm. He remembers tin and axe and twisting the lid to get it free . . . Thinks, Get the doctor; but looks up and sees the smoke and flames.

He slides and jumps, comes to the broken fence and scrambles through. Wire scrapes his leg and blood wells on his thigh. He goes past his house, running hunched to protect his hand. He runs down the drive and feels hot wind pouring in the funnel of the scrub. He reaches the gate; and it's locked. He grabs the padlock, jerks and jerks, then lifts the gate, trying to spring it from its hinges. The goats are bleating further along the fence. He leaves the gate and breaks into the gorse, worming and leaping. He does not remember his cut hand. The booming in the sky flattens him. He has to keep gulping air and pulling it, hot, into his lungs.

The goats are in the corner. They can see the river and they butt and heave and throw themselves against the hurricane wire. He grabs the nearest one and throws it over. It lands on its side and falls down a bank and runs free. He throws another, untangles horns from the wire, throws again. He chases a billy up the fence and heaves it free. Then back to the corner for the last one. It makes a twisting arc over the wire and leaps out of sight down the bank.

Lex can climb the fence now and get to the river in time. But he turns and goes the other way. There's still the goat chained by the tea-tree patch beyond the house.

He can't breathe. There's no air. He reaches the goat, strangling in its collar, and kneels on it and works at the buckle with both hands.

The fireball comes across the valley. It flies in an arc and ignites the hill. As Lex looks into the blinding whiteness, looks and falls on his side, with his hair burning, the house explodes, the tea-tree clump explodes.

Lex Clearwater dies. If he had survived he might have stayed back from being a goat and made some sense of his time there. He narrowed down by sympathetic and intellectual choice and was in control of his movement for a while. Then it got away and Lex went rushing to that minimal I. He felt his mind come folding back at him, like a blanket folding – GOOD, good, good – into the fact, Me, Here, Now. He rested in that stillness. Nothing disturbed him but his needs. Perhaps there's no safe way back from there. Perhaps the fire was his only way.

Goat or man, Lex dies on the hill.

Along the valley, Duncan and Hayley survive.

Hayley lifts her cheek from his thigh. She cannot find anything to say but his name.

He leans back on his arms. He lies down with his legs dangling in

292

the pool. For a moment it seems he's lying down to die. His feet, under the water, are white and dead.

She pushes herself away from the wall and swims to the deep end. When she looks back he hasn't moved – and Hayley begins to be impatient. He's making too much of it; like Shelley does. But when she thinks of being burned down there – touches her own genitals – how can you make too much of that? It does make you dead in a sort of way.

'What's the time, Duncan?' Her watch is in the house with her clothes. 'Hey, did you hear me, what's the time?'

He lifts his arm to show her he doesn't wear a watch. Hayley climbs out of the pool. She wishes Mrs Round would come back. She doesn't like the way her heart thumps with this feeling of sorrow. Yet it's so posh at the Rounds' house she wants to stay. He spoils it, like a body, over there.

She dries some of the water off her legs and goes into the house to find a drink. There's Just Juice in the fridge along with all sorts of cheese and bottles of wine. She pours a glass and goes to the window to ask Duncan if he'd like some too. Smoke stands like a wall beyond the hill, with big puffy lumps on top of it. Hayley can't believe it, there's so much.

'Hey Dunc, look at that.'

She leaves her drink and runs outside. 'Look at the smoke.' She can hear the fire coming up the hill on the other side. It makes a sound like rapids in a creek.

'There's a fire, Duncan.'

He lifts himself on his elbow and looks at the sky. 'Yeah,' he says.

'Is it coming this way?'

He stands up and brushes dust off his shorts. 'I suppose so. The wind's blowing this way.'

'Listen to it.'

'Yeah.'

'We better get out.'

'No, we're all right.'

'It's a bush fire, Duncan. It's a big one.'

'It won't come here.'

Hayley runs back into the house and climbs half a level to the sundeck. Smoke covers the sun. A red-gold colour comes on her skin and the valley goes darker. She sees Duncan walking on the lawn. He sits in a canvas chair and looks at the long wall of smoke on the hill.

'I'm getting out,' Hayley says. Then she sees flames – one, two, three places at once. They come down the valley on the town side of the house, bouncing along the scrub like a ball and sending puffs of smoke up where they touch. They reach over the hill, holding on like fingers, above the house. And up the valley they slide on Stovepipe Hill. A ball of fire with a long red tail shoots from behind another hill and hits the hillside by Lex Clearwater's house. She sees the house and sheds burst into flames.

Hayley runs along the deck and looks down river towards town. Fire is down there too, by Monday Hole. The gully scrub boils up red like liquid in a pot.

Hayley runs back through the house.

'Duncan, we've got to get down to the river.'

Duncan has climbed into the garden to see better. He turns with his hands on his hips and smiles at her.

'It's too late. We're trapped.'

'When it gets in those gum trees it'll be like a bomb.' The slope will be a chimney and will suck flames down the hill. They'll leap from the gum trees to the pines, right over the house and roof it in. It's like a sun-flare, Duncan thinks, picturing that huge leap and curve. Everything underneath will shrivel up and turn to ashes. He doesn't mind.

The girl, Hayley Birtles, runs to the archway and runs back. He sees her mouth with white teeth and red tongue and a black hole going down her throat. He smiles at her. Heat is on his skin, starting to hurt.

'We'll get in the pool,' Hayley yells.

'No good. There'll be no air.' They'll come up and pull hot gas into their lungs. Already he can feel the membranes baking in his mouth.

'Duncan,' Hayley screams. She jumps in.

Then Duncan understands several things. Burning is all right, he doesn't mind, but suffocating isn't what he wants. Yesterday, seeing Sos get drowned, he had contracted, beat after beat. No counter-movement came to make him large. Soon he was tiny, lying like a balled-up hedgehog at the foot of the wall. He could uncurl and wriggle through. He knew there were cracks he could find. On the other side he would be dead.

He stayed where he was. Dying should just happen. He should not have to be the one to choose.

Now the counter-movement comes. He can go over and not die. There's a voice calling 'Gidday, Dunc.' It sounds like him. Does that mean he's already there, waiting for himself? He can put his hand on top and vault across and meet it. Him. Meet me.

There's the wall. There's the voice, 'Come on.'

Over there he can do anything. Can he throw himself away from the fire? Can he be safe by saying, Go? He sees himself arcing across the river and bouncing on the green and taking one step back and sitting on the grass to watch the fire.

So why is he standing here and just thinking about it? He'll never get a second chance.

He's standing here because of Hayley Birtles.

He sees her come up in the pool and feel the heat and grab a breath through her open mouth and go back under. In a moment she will come up again; and find him gone. He sees her swing her head round in the water, screaming his name. He knows the pain and terror she will feel as she dies. 'OK,' he says; and steps back warily. The wall might punish him for saying no.

'Sorry, can't come.'

It seems to blink. The voice on the other side makes a wail. Suddenly both of them are gone.

'So long,' Duncan says. Then 'Garage,' he says; and he runs there. He grabs the scuba tanks from the boat and lugs them back, hearing the fire come pouring down, seeing tree crowns burst on the hill. He throws the tanks in; thinks, Why not? – grabs Hayley's bike, runs it riderless at the pool and sees it tip in like an accident. Then he dives in and when the bubbles rattle away sees Hayley Birtles grabbing a tank. He swims to her, frog-kicking, pushes her away, turns a tap, making air bubble from the mouthpiece. He gets his arm round Hayley, holds her down, pushes the mouthpiece in her mouth, makes her sit and pulls the tank into her lap to anchor her. He turns on his air and anchors himself.

They sit in the pool with arms locked and watch flames streaming over and the surface freckle with debris. Further along Hayley's bike lies on its side.

Duncan is forgetting. He looks up and sees the pool moving like the sky.

I should have saved my telescope, he thinks.